/// Flashmob

Also by Christopher Farnsworth

Killfile
The Eternal World
The Burning Men
Red, White, and Blood
The President's Vampire
Blood Oath

/// Flashmob

Christopher
Farnsworth

WILLIAM MORROW
An Imprint of HarperCollins*Publishers*

This is a work of fiction. Names, characters, places, and incidents are products of the author's imagination or are used fictitiously and are not to be construed as real. Any resemblance to actual events, locales, organizations, or persons, living or dead, is entirely coincidental.

HarperCollins books may be purchased for educational, business, or sales promotional use. For information, please email the Special Markets Department at SPsales@harpercollins.com.

A hardcover edition of this book was published in 2017 by William Morrow, an imprint of HarperCollins Publishers.

FIRST WILLIAM MORROW PAPERBACK EDITION PUBLISHED 2018.

Designed by Bonni Leon-Berman

Library of Congress Cataloging-in-Publication Data has been applied for.

ISBN 978-0-06-283571-0

18 19 20 21 22 LSC 10 9 8 7 6 5 4 3 2 1

For Bryon

/// Flashmob

/// 1

Blunt Knuckles and Shaved Heads

It's not easy to find a nice, quiet spot to torture someone in L.A.

Most of the apartments are cheaply built, with thin walls and neighbors stacked right on top of each other, so the noise carries and there are always plenty of people around to complain. Same goes for the hotels, and even the worst rent-by-the-hour dives have security cameras and require credit cards, which leaves a nice trail for the police when the bodies turn up. Storage units have thick concrete walls and 24-7 access, but random witnesses could show up at any moment.

But L.A. does have a regular supply of people falling off the treadmill of the California dream, failing to make it big and make their payments. This means a lot of foreclosures and vacant homes. A smart psychopath will keep a list of ones out in the canyons, or way off the main roads in the Valley, where the neighbors are likely to think that the screams are just a funny echo from someone's TV.

This is why I'm on my knees in the bottom of an empty pool somewhere up in the hills while a Russian carefully unpacks a red toolbox.

He takes out a cordless power drill and tests the trigger. He frowns at the noise it makes and slaps in a fresh battery. Then he tries it again and smiles, and begins laying out a selection of drill bits, starting with one that looks like it's meant to carve a hole in concrete.

I don't know for sure. I'm not much of a DIY guy.

My client is next to me. Nik. Short for Nikolai. Like me, he's on his knees, hands tied behind his back.

His dad is a Russian billionaire, with interests in oil and gas and commodities and finance. His youngest child, Nikolai, however, wants to be in the movies. So his father tucked a couple million for milk money into Nik's black leather jacket and sent him to Los Angeles. And then he got on the phone and hired me to look after him.

You could argue I'm not doing a great job.

Before tonight, I escorted Nik to a few meetings, mostly with a few indie producers who look at him and see dollar signs dancing around him. (Seriously. It's like in a cartoon.) But Nik has spent more time chasing women than making deals. During a peek inside his head, I saw that he's actually got a list of famous targets in a file on his laptop, with pictures of his favorites. We spent most of his time and his father's money in clubs, looking for Scarlett Johansson. He never met her, but he was able to find plenty of acceptable replacements. Most of the time, I just stood nearby as he sat at a VIP table, dry-humping the leg of any actress/model/whatever willing to put up with him.

He liked to play the hard man. He thickened his accent whenever anyone asked about the Russian *Mafiya*. In reality, Nik had never actually seen a gangster outside of a movie.

Until tonight, that is.

To be honest, babysitting Nik is beneath my skill set. But I'm just back from an extended vacation, and I need to remind the One Percent that they can depend on me to clean up after them again. I thought Nik would be an easy job, unchallenging and uneventful.

Maybe that's why I made a rookie mistake and left him alone in the back room of a strip club with the two dancers earlier. They were both Russian as well, talking a mile a minute in their native tongue, and Nik seemed happy. He told me to fuck off, and I was all too happy to comply. I scanned both of the women and they had nothing but indecent intentions toward him. Visions of a threesome were dancing in his brain. Seemed safe enough if he wore a condom.

I stood outside for a good long while, listening to the thumping bass of the strip club and the thoughts of the people nearby—dull lust from the patrons, mostly boredom from the dancers. Nik and the women were out of my range. I thought I was giving him his privacy. I also didn't really want the image of a strip-club hand job in my head.

After about thirty minutes, Nik hadn't emerged from the VIP area. Neither had the dancers. That was much longer than Nik had lasted in the past.

I went looking for them, but it was already too late. The bouncer stationed at the back door told me they'd left almost immediately.

Little bastard had ditched me. He probably felt pretty smart, getting away from his nanny. But I was fine with calling it an early night. I planned to get some sleep and then find him again in the morning.

I was halfway back to my hotel when my phone rang.

It was a voice with a Russian accent, but it wasn't Nik.

I got an address and instructions to bring a substantial amount of cash in a duffel bag.

I didn't have the cash, and I wasn't about to call Nik's dad and tell him I lost his son. I went to the address anyway.

A bunch of men with blunt knuckles and shaved heads grabbed me as soon as I pulled up in my car. They looked me up and down, checked out my suit and my shoes. They searched me for weapons. Found none. One called me a *suka*, and they all laughed. I smiled and pretended not to know what it meant.

They asked for the money. I told them I didn't have it. So they tied me up and put me in the empty pool with Nik.

I picked up the events of the last couple of hours from his memory easily. One of the strippers suggested they meet up with friends at a bar. Her friends turned out to be these guys. Nik thought they were cool. He finally got to meet real gangsters. He paid for their drinks, listened to their stories of murder and dismemberment with wide eyes, and talked about making a movie about them.

Then they walked out to the parking lot, where Nik's new friends clubbed him with pistols and threw him into the back of a black Range Rover.

I can see the mistake like neon, blazing in the front of Nik's head.

He mentioned his father's name.

His dad is an authentic Russian tyrant: Sergei Denisovich crawled out of the KGB at the end of the Cold War and grabbed whatever he could when Russia collapsed. He moves oil and commodities and currency around the globe now, but there is murder and blood behind him. These guys are fresh enough from the old country to know his story, and stupid enough to figure that he'll pay big money for Nik.

Now every time the goon takes something new from the toolbox, Nik makes a little noise like a dog's squeaky toy. *<ohGodohGodohGodohGodohGodohGod>* is all that goes through his mind, over and over.

Then the alpha male of this little pack shows up.

He walks down the steps into the empty pool slowly, glaring at both of us the entire time. He's milking the moment for all the drama it's worth. It seems to take him an hour.

I read him in a split second. His name is Vasily. He got called out from his cheap rental above West Hollywood by his thugs. At first he was annoyed, but then he heard the name of Nik's dad, and he got excited. He decided he had to be here in person.

Vasily stands in front of us for a long time before he speaks. He's covered in muscle and tattoos, but he's got a weak chin. It looks like he's swallowed half his neck. Unlike the other thugs, he's wearing an almost-new Hugo Boss. He's been watching a lot of TV lately, and he thinks this makes him look like a real gangster. But he didn't bother to get it tailored after he took it off the rack, so the sleeves come down past his fingers and he's got the pants hiked up almost to his sternum.

All of this makes it difficult to take him seriously, despite the gun in his hand.

"Where's the money?" he asks quietly.

He tries to come across with an air of indifferent menace—he's thinking of De Niro and Pacino in *Heat*—but I can tell that he's dancing inside. Nik's dad should be good for at least 500K. That would be enough to get him out of his crappy apartment. Maybe even someplace on the Westside.

He's so far out of his league here, I can't resist messing with him. "Left it in my other pants," I say.

Vasily doesn't take that well. He scowls. That's enough to set Nik babbling in Russian and in English. He promises his father will get the money. He barely knows me, I'm just a stupid bodyguard, Nik can get the money, he swears, just don't hurt him.

Vasily doesn't speak. He kneels down so he's face-to-face with both of us. Nik shuts up. Vasily nods at one of his guys, who starts taking a video with his phone. Then he nods at the other guy, the one with the tools.

"I think we take a few chunks off you," he says to Nik, in Russian, ignoring me now. "We'll send the pictures to your father. And then we see how much you are worth to him."

The goon with the tools leans forward. He's got a pair of pliers in his hand.

He'll do it too. I can see it in his brain. These guys have all learned the thug's secret of success: always be willing to go too far.

So I have to be a little careful here. I clear my throat and speak directly to Vasily.

"Look. I know what you've got planned. You think you just found a winning lottery ticket. A soft kid with a lot of cash. But see, here's where we have a problem. I'm being paid to keep him alive and in one piece. So I tell you what. You leave now, quietly, and I'll let you live."

Vasily cracks a smile as he looks at me, tied up and on my knees, surrounded by big guys with guns. He finds it funny. Or at least it scrapes at the part of him where normal people keep their sense of humor.

He turns his snake-eyed glare on me. "Babysitter. Keep sitting. We'll get to you."

I could have ended this long before now. But I figured Nik needed a little lesson: gangsters are cool only on-screen. The truth is, people like this are not actually capable of the kinds of operatic heights of passion and feeling you see on HBO. They muddle around in the midranges, always looking for the shortcut and the easy way out. That's what makes them dangerous. They will take almost any chance because they never think it through all the way to the end.

Nik is ready to leap out of his own skin, he's so scared. I think he's over his crush on the *Mafiya*. And his terror is making my headache even worse. It's time to earn my ridiculous paycheck.

"Excuse me," I say loudly. "Did any of you wonder how much you were going to get from Vasily for this? Or is he going to screw you all like he did on the pot shop?"

It's like a needle drag in the middle of a song. Everyone stops, thrown off the rhythm for a moment.

This is a sore spot. They hit a medical marijuana dispensary a few months ago—those places are full of cash, since no credit-card company or bank will work with them—and it turned into a clusterfuck. They barely got away before the cops arrived, and had to split up. Vasily had the bag with the cash, and he said they managed to steal only a couple thousand.

But I know the truth because I saw it inside Vasily's skull.

"He took home close to twelve grand. What did he tell you?" I say.

Vasily tells me to shut up, but they all start to talk at once. A lot of Russian begins spitting through the air.

Vasily has to turn away from me and Nik to answer his crew. He tells them I'm lying. But the dynamic in the pool has shifted. Vasily is losing control of the situation.

I decide to help it along.

"Hey, which one of you is Alexei?" I ask, shouting to be heard.

The guy named Alexei thinks, *<How's he know my name?>* It's instinctive. He can't help it.

So I look right at him when I say, "Did you know Vasily here fucked your girlfriend?"

I know he doesn't. I knew it when I took the fact out of Vasily's memories.

But the look of surprise on Alexei's face is so pronounced that it almost makes me laugh.

He turns to Vasily, who's too shocked to hide his own expression, and that's all the confirmation he needs. He begins stalking across the pool, murder in his eyes. *"Vy skazali, chto vy byli prosto khoroshimi druz'yami!"*

Vasily raises his gun. Again, operating on instinct. He sees the threat, and he responds.

But he's just pulled a gun on one of his own. The thugs all get quiet then. They watch and they wait. Suddenly it's not us against them. It's every man for himself.

Not that it takes much of a push. There's really no such thing as honor among thieves.

"Don't feel too special, Alexei. You're not the only one," I say.

Vasily turns and looks at me, mouth open wide. He's still baffled, rather than scared. He has no idea how I know this. But he figures that if he shuts me up, he can still salvage a payoff from this mess.

He pivots to bring the gun around at me.

Playtime is over.

I think hard, and I find a memory of a grandfather who dropped dead of a massive coronary right in front of Vasily when he was five. It left an impression. Vasily doesn't even smoke now. He eats lean meats and spends a lot of time doing cardio.

So I push into his head and light up the amygdala region of his brain. That's the part that controls breathing, heart rate, and the fight-or-flight response. He's suddenly drowning in his own adrenaline. His pulse is hammering behind his ears. His chest tightens. He can't breathe.

He immediately thinks he's dying. He drops the gun and clutches at his heart as he falls to his knees.

The others see this and freeze in place. They're already agitated and angry. Terrified is an easy push from there. I hit them, one by one, fast as I can, with pure fear. Their adrenaline spikes, their limbs feel numb, and their guts turn to water.

They're not sure why, but they all feel like they'd be a lot safer many miles away from me. Only stubbornness and inertia keep them from running for their lives.

So I concentrate and hit Vasily again. I take a memory of being stabbed in the arm—what can I say, I've had an interesting career—and transfer it over to him. It's close enough to the pain of a real heart attack that he screams out loud.

Then I look around the pool, and in the most demonic voice I can manage, I say:

"Run."

That does it. Vasily's crew starts sprinting. I'm going to pay for all of this later, but it's almost worth it to watch them struggle over the sides of the pool and across the dead lawn.

Vasily is huddled in a ball, trembling. I roll off my knees and onto my back, then bring my bound hands under my legs to get them in front of me. I pick one of the blades from the toolbox and slice away the ropes on my wrists.

I cut Nik free.

"And this," I tell him. "is what happens when you wander off on your own. I won't tell your father if you don't. Deal?"

He looks almost as scared of me as the guys who just left were.

<holyshitholyshit> *<what just happened?>* *<what was that?>* "Dude," Nik says to me, wide-eyed. "How did you do that?"

"Magic," I tell him. "Come on. Let's go."

We walk past Vasily, who's still in a heap, eyes shut tight, hugging himself like he's afraid something vital will fall out.

I could kick him while he's down, but honestly, there's no point.

He was never really a threat to me. He's barely even the same species.

///2

Not as Much Fun as You'd Think

Being inside a club in Los Angeles is like wading in a pool of toxic waste, even for someone who doesn't have my particular talent. On the surface, the people are all beautiful and bored, doing their best to keep their pretty faces as blank and still as statues because, in this city, showing emotion really does cost money.

But inside, their minds are churning.

<who's that?> <producer swore he'd call and of course he didn't> <holy shit I saw him on HBO last night now look at him> <never should have blown him> <do I know her? am I supposed to remember her?> <hairline's definitely receding> <fucking manager> <I'm so stupid I can't even fuck my way to the middle> <my god I'm so fat> <I'm too skinny> <got to get to the gym more often I am such a pig> <fucker came right in and took my show away from me> <lying bitch> <goddammit how am I supposed to live on 300K a year?> <I'm supposed to open the restaurant in the morning boss will fire my ass if I'm hungover again> <wasn't she on Nickelodeon a few years ago?> <if I can just get an agent> <might as well live in the Valley> <basic cable trash I'd sooner screw the valet> <why is this guy talking to me?> <who's that?>

It gives me a headache. Everything gives me a headache.

But Nik is in heaven. He needed a drink after his ordeal in the pool, and so I let him drag us to this after-hours place. Then he found two actual porn stars near the bar, and immediately invited them to his table.

Now they are all drinking gold-infused vodka as he describes his favorite scenes with them. It should be graphic and tasteless, but the women find his overwhelming enthusiasm and thick accent genuinely charming. Nik is happier than I've ever seen him. He's finally found people whose work he respects.

Something pings my radar, and I look around. It's not another threat to Nikolai. It doesn't feel like anger or hostile intent. Someone in the club recognizes me. Her focus on me raises thoughts out of the background noise.

<holy crap it is him> <should I say something?> <what are you supposed to say in a situation like this?>

I pick her out of the crowd a second later as she makes her way over to me.

Kira Sadeghi.

A little over a year ago, Kira's father, Armin, hired me to rescue her when she was kidnapped by a couple of amateurs. It was a forty-minute job. I got her home unharmed and alive. The kidnappers didn't do as well.

She'd been drugged out of her skull, and her father packed her off to rehab.

In the time since, Kira has joined the cast of *Tehrangeles*, currently the top-rated reality-TV show on basic cable. It follows the lives of a group of young, spoiled children of Iranian immigrants who fled the revolution and came to America. There are about eight hundred thousand of them in Los Angeles now, the largest community of Iranians anywhere in the world outside of Tehran. The show's named for the section between Westwood and Beverly Hills, where a big part of the community lives. They sometimes prefer to be called Persian, since Americans aren't great at nuance, and they still take a lot of abuse from people who think that they must be Arabic Muslim terrorist ragheads.

Tehrangeles, admittedly, doesn't do a lot to clear up these misconceptions. Armin sent out a proud-father email when it premiered, and I set my DVR to record a few episodes. The show opened with a muezzin set against Arabian electronic dance music. I lasted about twenty minutes before it became too aggressively stupid.

But the actual background of the people doesn't matter, really. The show is all about who's sleeping with whom, who got fake tits, who got drunk and went home with a stranger after the clubs. The answer, almost every time: Kira.

It's made her the indisputable star of the show, as well as the lead villain. She manages to shove her way to the center of every scene she's in, and if the camera leaves her for a moment, she's liable to throw a drink or a tantrum to get it back. Even when she's not on-screen, the other cast members can't help but talk about her.

(All right. Maybe I watched more than twenty minutes.)

Now she's hated by millions of people who have never met her, and they've made her rich and famous. She's become This Year's Girl, with her photo in *Us Weekly* and on GoFugYourself.com every week.

She reaches me through the crowd. "Hi," she says. "Remember me?"

<stupid, Kira> <real smooth> <very original>

She's nervous, but you'd never know to look at her. A born actress.

I decide to be professional. I smile. "Of course, Ms. Sadeghi."

"I'm not sure that's a good thing," she says. "I mean, I was a complete mess the last time I saw you."

I feel a jolt of embarrassment from her as the memory hits. I hauled her out of a Skid Row hotel room and loaded her into my car. She lolled around on the seat, barely conscious.

Now her eyes shine and her skin is clear. Her time in rehab took. Which is good. It usually doesn't. People tend to stick to their habits. Just look at me.

"Congratulations on the show," I say. "Your father is very proud."

"Oh, Daddy," she says. "He's just happy I've got a job." She makes a face, but a little burst of pride, like a sudden ray of sunlight, comes through.

A small entourage trails behind her: friends, hangers-on, and a single bodyguard who's mostly there for decoration. Only eight people—not really A-list size, but respectable, all things considered. They're all trying to look bored, but they all want to know why Kira is talking to someone who's clearly hired help.

<who is that guy?> <spooky> <bodyguard> <is he Russian?> <looks like a gangster ohmigod does Kira know a gangster?>

Now she's hesitating. She knows what she wants to say next. She's talked to her father about me. He's said some things to her, and she's asked around. I have a reputation. That's how I get work. So now she wants to know. Everyone who hears about me wants to know.

She moves in closer. "So. I have to know. Is it true?"

Kira makes a good living off being a sideshow, so I don't blame her for asking the question. But there are times when I feel like the geek at the county fair who bites the heads off chickens for a nickel apiece.

At this moment, right now, I don't want to be that guy.

"Is what true?"

She leans back and pouts. It's cuter in person than on TV. "Come on," she says. "You know. If it's true, you already know what I'm asking."

I just look at her.

She immediately remembers some of the other things she's heard her father say. And what happened to the guys who kidnapped her.

<oh god> <he's pissed>

"Oh no, I've offended you," she says, pulling up contrition and sincerity from her library of facial expressions. She's good. She'll be a hell of an actress someday, if she can scramble out of the sink of reality TV.

Then I notice Nik getting up, his arms around both of the women. Having lost him once already tonight, I don't feel like doing it again. I smile at Kira and nod. "Good to see you, Ms. Sadeghi."

She gives me a certain look, half smiling. "Yeah," she says. "You too."

We go back to The Standard on Sunset and I park Nik and his guests in his room. He is fully recovered from his earlier shock, thanks to the vodka. Now he can't stop singing my praises.

"That was off the fucking chain, bro," he says, over and over again, as he grabs me around the shoulders in a big, awkward man-hug. "Whatever we are paying you, it is not enough."

I resist the urge to tell him to pass that along to his dad. Instead I just remind him of the usual protocol. Don't open the door to anyone but me. I'll be around to collect him in the morning.

"Better make it afternoon," he says.

He turns his head and glances at the women, who have already taken off their clothes as they explore the inside of his suite. Looks like he's getting his Christmas wish tonight after all.

"Late afternoon," he says. "I'll call you." He slams the door in my face. I wait and listen to him engage the security bolt.

Then I step across the hall to my own room. This is where I live.

I checked in to The Standard when I came back to L.A. I haven't gotten around to finding anything more permanent yet, and I get a discount for putting clients like Nik in the suite. The couches and chairs all look like something out of the Jetsons' apartment and there's a model who sits all day in a glass box behind the front desk, a piece of living decoration.

It works for me. I never have to do dishes or laundry, and because The Standard caters to the young and rich and beautiful, I never have to deal with too much pain or worry leaking in around the edges from the other guests' thoughts. A hotel actually spends most of its time empty, except when people come back at night for sex or sleep. I can handle that. And if someone is scared or angry or lonely on the other side of the wall, they're never my neighbor for long.

It's as close as I can get to living in the home of the future I saw in comic books when I was a kid, with robots doing all the domestic work, beeping quietly to themselves without complaint.

I open my door and find Kira waiting, sitting in one of the low-slung chairs.

I knew she was there, of course. I could feel her mischievous grin from out in the hall. I saw the plan hatching in her head when I left the club and she sent one of the minions in her entourage to follow me.

"You know, this is the first time I've ever actually used my fame to get into a guy's room," she says by way of greeting. "It was really surprisingly easy. I just told them you're my boyfriend and they gave me a key. You should probably talk to them about it."

Complain about the beautiful twenty-one-year-old delivering herself like room service? Sure. "I'll get right on that," I tell her. "What can I do for you, Ms. Sadeghi?"

She won't let it go, though. "I mean, aren't you in security? Doesn't it bother you on, like, a professional level?"

"If you were a threat, I never would have opened the door."

She nods. "Right," she says. "Because you're psychic."

I'm tired. And she already knows. So what the hell.

"Yeah. I am."

She's surprised I've admitted it. She expected she'd have to wear me down. "You can read minds?"

I nod.

She's not sure if she should believe me now, despite all she's heard and seen. I don't blame her. I wouldn't believe it either if I hadn't been living with other people's monkey-chatter echoing in my brain my entire life.

She leans closer, and asks the question everyone asks, once they get past the initial disbelief: "What's it like?"

I can see it in her head. She thinks it would be cool, knowing everyone's secrets. She thinks it might even be fun.

I never tell anyone the truth. I work in a field where people try to kill me on a semiregular basis, so I don't go around advertising my weak spots.

But if I were honest, I'd say that I get a little of everyone's thoughts, just by being close to them. I get a percentage of their frustration, their anger, their loneliness, their fear, and most of all their pain. I can feel their hangovers, their backaches, their arthritis, their tumors. I pick up a dose of their bad memories, their childhood traumas, their lingering nightmares. I feel their heartbreak and their anxiety and their need.

And I can't turn it off.

Imagine sensing all the vermin in the walls of every building you set foot inside. Hearing every mouse as it scurries along, the rats as they squeeze out their droppings, every cockroach and silverfish filling every crack and crevice, every beetle and ant behind the drywall. Knowing you're surrounded all the time. You can almost feel all those tiny little lives crawling over your skin at every moment. And there's nothing you can do about it.

That's what it's like.

But I never tell people this. Instead I just say, "It's not as much fun as you think."

Kira frowns. Boredom and frustration flit across her mind. But she's not done yet. She asks the second question, the other thing people always want to know. Because I am polite, I let her ask the question out loud before I answer.

"So, can you make people—you know, do stuff?"

"Control minds, you mean?"

"Right."

I call that the Vegas act. Everyone wants to know if I can pull the same cheap stunts as a lounge-room hypnotist. Make someone bark like a dog or cluck like a chicken or talk in a funny voice. Or even—it's almost always the men who ask this one, usually with a creepy smile—make women take off their clothes on command.

"No. I can't."

She's disappointed and relieved at the same time. "Why not?" she asks.

I smile a little at that. God knows my life would be easier if I could.

I give her the short version of the same speech I always give my clients.

"Think of it this way: If your brain is a computer, I can hack into it. I can read your email and your files, even run some of the programs or rewrite some of the basic code. But I can't reprogram the whole thing from the command line up. People do what they want. I can push, I can shove, I can shout my thoughts as loud as possible into their heads—and they will still do what they want. People are stubborn. People are messy. And most of all, people do not change. It took you a whole lifetime to become who you are. I can't rewrite all that in the few moments it takes to peek inside your brain."

"You seemed to do okay with those guys who kidnapped me."

She's a little scared as she says this. I get a flash of some of the things she's overheard from her father. And she saw the news reports. Both of the men who took her ended up dead on the downtown pavement.

"That was different," I tell her.

"How?"

"That's the flip side of my talent. Being able to read someone else's mind also means I can plant some things there too."

That's putting it mildly, but she doesn't need to know the full menu of options. I can trigger painful memories, dodge punches before they're thrown, and hide in the cognitive blind spots that lurk inside everyone's brains.

These are all tricks I picked up after I left high school and went into the army, where a Special Ops unit found me. My instructors helped me turn my talent into a weapon in the War on Terror. Eventually, I walked away from duty and country and went into business for myself, helping the One Percent clean up their messes and protect their secrets. The pay is a lot better than government work. My special skills mean I can charge more than your average security consultant.

I also don't tell Kira what my ability does to me. I get back a percentage of everything I inflict on another person. I will feel a piece of everything I did tonight, on top of the usual headache of all those other people's thoughts in my skull. I can put it off for a while with concentration and focus—and usually pills and whiskey—but it's just a matter of time before the bill comes due.

So I am not at all sure I want Kira here much longer. It sounds idiotic—kicking a ridiculously hot woman out of my hotel room—but I would really like to get into my Scotch and my Vicodin before the pain becomes more than I can choke back.

And, if I am completely honest, there's more to it than that. She makes me feel old. Maybe it's all the time I've spent playing big brother to Nikolai lately, but I've got barely a decade on Kira, and I still feel used up. Most of my life has been spent doing bad things for people who don't deserve their good fortune.

Kira's mind has no shadows, despite her time in rehab and the incident with the kidnappers. She is one of those people whose thoughts are clear and undimmed by any of the usual grime and squalor that I ordinarily see. She's had a good life, on balance. She sees no reason why it won't stay that way. That kind of optimism is a constant mystery to me.

I admit it: I am envious of her peace of mind.

So I stand up and say, "Thank you for stopping by, Ms. Sadeghi."

She makes no move to get up. Instead she smirks at me from the chair. "You can call me Kira, you know."

"Thank you for stopping by, Kira. Please give my regards to your father."

She finally stands, still smirking, and moves closer to me.

"You know," she says, "I never thanked you properly for coming to my rescue."

"Don't worry about it. They don't really make a card for that sort of thing," I say. She is short, even in her heels. She stands right under my chin. I catch the scent of her perfume. It's becoming difficult to focus on the Scotch or the pills.

"I should still say thank you."

"Not necessary."

"I think it is," she says. "Now tell me what else I'm thinking."

Then she imagines something so incredibly detailed and specific it might even make the porn stars blush.

She sees the look on my face, delighted that the trick worked. "So. Still want me to go?"

As an answer, I open my arms to her and lean down, and she places her mouth on mine.

What the hell. Nik won't be up until late afternoon anyway.

Somewhere around 3:00 A.M. it hits. The panic. The feeling like an iron band clamped around my chest, the hammering of my pulse behind my ears. I am instantly drenched in sweat. I think I can actually feel my heart slamming itself against the walls of my rib cage. And each beat I am totally convinced will be its last.

This is the payback. This is what I get—a tiny percentage of the misery I inflicted on Vasily earlier this evening. Everything I do, every one of my little Jedi mind tricks, has a price. This is it.

I feel like I am going to die. I gasp for air and thrash out of the covers.

Kira wakes. I feel the irritation rise off her as she's jolted out of sleep. I prepare to deal with a barrage of curses—she's got them loaded and ready to go—when she notices what's happening to me.

"What is it?" she asks, suddenly frightened.

I can't swallow enough oxygen to speak. I just hold up a hand, trying to tell her that it will pass in a moment.

And it will. I've done this before.

All I have to do is endure a few minutes of absolute certainty that I am going to die.

I concentrate and try to focus. To ride out the storm, as I have done before.

Then I feel something unexpected.

Kira's hand on my back, warm and soft.

"Easy," she says. "Easy. Try to breathe."

She pulls me in close to her, and holds me as tight as she can.

"You're safe," she says. "You're safe."

My pulse stops racing. The pain in my chest subsides, then vanishes completely. I feel light-headed and weak and small.

But she keeps holding me.

"You're all right," she says. "Nothing can hurt you. You're all right now."

And that's how we fall asleep again. Her arms around me, me listening to each beat of my heart, waiting every time it pauses, not entirely sure it will start again.

Nik's phone call wakes me sometime before noon. The porn stars are hungry, so would I please get my ass out of bed and fetch some goddamn breakfast?

Kira is gone. There is not a trace of her in the room.

Two weeks later, I get the invitation to her wedding.

///3

Even TMZ Wouldn't Follow Him Around

The hotel where Kira is getting married looks like a Cape Cod beach house plunked down right at the edge of the beach in Santa Monica.

The wedding is being held by the pool, which perfectly frames the Pacific Ocean in the background. There are a couple hundred people seated on the lower patio, which faces the water. A railing circles the entire space, setting it off from the rest of the pool area. Hotel guests watch from their lounge chairs and the hotel's upper balconies. I didn't think I'd be able to show for this, but Nik got on a plane back to Moscow at LAX a week ago, having spent all of his allowance. He was exhausted, sore, and, overall, happy to be going home. At the airport, I felt nothing but relief from him: *<this place man>* *<fucking insane>*.

Now I am, as the saying goes, between engagements.

Armin greets me warmly at the elevator. A squat little man, bald on top with a fringe of dark hair around his ears. Looking at him, I find it hard to believe that Kira isn't adopted.

He's all smiles on the outside, but this is a massive headache for him. There are three people hovering near his elbow: the director from *Tehrangeles,* who's in charge of getting all the footage for the season finale; Kira's wedding planner, who's been fighting tooth and nail with the TV people at every turn; and an exec from Kira's network, who seems to have the idea that Armin should do something about the valet parking out front.

But he still finds time to shake my hand and ask me a few questions about my life. He even gives me a hard time about showing up without a date, although I can see in his head that it's not terribly surprising to him. *<who would want to be with a man like this?>*

I'm not offended. I ask myself that question all the time.

Then the producer and the planner and the exec all drag Armin away again. He smiles and apologizes and tells me to get myself a drink, cursing them darkly but never showing a twitch on the outside.

Kira is supposed to be the villainess of *Tehrangeles,* but—try to contain your shock—reality TV is not actually all that real. It's scripted and plotted and edited for dramatic effect, just like any other TV show, with the added bonus that everyone gets paid less.

So the people who are supposed to hate Kira the most—her fellow cast members—are all here, wearing their very best.

Alisha, her best friend on the show, is waiting to march up the aisle as Kira's maid of honor—even though Kira supposedly stole the groom away from her, a plot line that took up most of last season. She's more focused on her makeup than her former boyfriend up at the altar. Behind the scenes, they were barely a couple, but the producers decided that the show needed a love triangle. They manufactured one, and the kids went along with it because they're not stupid.

Likewise, the other cast members—who have all declared Kira to be out of their lives for good at one point or another, usually while throwing drinks or punches—are seated and waiting in the front rows. From my surface read of their thoughts, they're all in a pretty good mood and more or less glad for her. They're actors. They play their parts. But in real life, they're rich, young, and beautiful. A couple of their friends are about to have a great big drunken celebration as they crash their lives together. If it doesn't work out—well, it's just a starter marriage. They've got time for at least two more. No matter what else happens, it's going to be a hugely entertaining diversion.

I head to the bar at the back of the patio for a drink. Kira may be sober, but I'll need a buzz to handle this, and Armin made sure they stocked the good stuff.

The only other person aside from the bartender is Kira's bodyguard. The network hired him, because Kira gets a dozen death threats a day on Twitter alone. Goes with the territory of being America's latest witch for burning.

I'm just a guest, but I can't stop a little professional judgment from creeping in around the edges. One look at him, and I know that nobody's taking the threats seriously. He's commandeered a tray of hors d'oeuvres that sits right on the bar in front of him, next to his drink. His gut pushes his jacket open every time he lifts another mini-quiche to his mouth, showing off his shoulder rig.

I scan him quickly. He's an ex-cop. He does a lot of celebrity work, which mainly involves taking cameras away from the paparazzi. He still knows enough guys on the force that when he punches somebody in the face, he never gets charged with assault. He's not expecting any trouble here today. Obviously.

He sees me looking at him. "Something I can help you with?" he asks, with just the right amount of attitude. *<want to start something, prick?>* *<faggoty Armani suit>* *<beat your ass down>* *<don't care who you are>*

I smile as if I didn't hear the tone, and order a drink. He holds eye contact a few more seconds—alpha-male challenge coming off him like body odor—but I keep smiling. There's always at least one guy at any party who comes ready to fight. Who's looking for the excuse, who secretly hopes that someone will say something to justify throwing a punch. Today, it just happens to be the guy hired to keep things safe. He must have been a lot of fun when he was on the force.

I get a glimpse of how he sees himself. Inside his head, he's a good twenty pounds lighter, maybe a couple of inches taller, and looks a lot more like Tom Selleck. That's probably where he gets his overwhelming sense of self-confidence. Even out of shape and scarfing down appetizers, he thinks he can handle anything that might come at him. It's not that unusual. I've been reading people my whole life, and reality rarely ever makes a dent inside their skulls.

By the time my drink arrives, he's facedown in the appetizers again, his back to the crowd. I go find a seat.

Everyone's talking—and thinking about—Jason Davis. C-list actor who's been charged with attempted murder.

"He was just out walking his dog," one woman says.

"It's insane," the guy with her bleats.

"All he was doing was protecting himself," another man in a beautifully cut suit, no tie, says to his companion, who wears a string of diamonds worth more than a house around her neck.

"Ohmigod, I know," she replies, pretending not to notice as he steals a look at her beautifully installed implants. "Can you believe it? It could happen to any of us."

Here's what happened. Davis. Third-string heartthrob in a series on the CW. Something about a kid who comes back home to his town, finds it's changed, something like that. I've never watched it. Almost nobody knew his name. Even TMZ wouldn't follow him around. He still lived in Van Nuys.

So he could walk his dog, just like a normal person. And then, out of nowhere, this kid comes up to him and—Davis says—begins threatening to kill him.

Davis panics. He's been receiving threats online for weeks, which has made him a little paranoid. So he pulls a Glock from a concealed holster under his shirt and plugs the kid five times out of a clip of fifteen. Amazingly, none of the wounds was fatal.

The kid later says he just wanted an autograph. He wasn't even armed. Davis is up for attempted murder. His lawyers are claiming self-defense. The prosecutors probably would have let him plead to assault, but suddenly there was a firestorm of outrage on Twitter—people pissed off that celebrities always get away with everything in Los Angeles. So this is where the D.A.'s office decided to draw the line.

As a result, Davis joined the A-list almost as soon as he made bail. He's got a new agent, a high-dollar lawyer, interviews on every TV show. Behind the scenes, he's become a cause for a certain class of people out here. There's a legal defense fund, and from what I hear, most of the big agencies and studios have donated.

They are rallying around him because they worry it could happen to them. It's like a shadow behind all their other thoughts.

<can you imagine?> <just like that one girl, whatshername, stabbed to death by that freak> <had to move twice once that site posted my address> <creepy guy at the gym followed me out to the parking lot> <if anything happened to my kids> <how the hell did they even get the nanny's cell-phone number is what I want to know> <waiting there for me outside Starbucks> <really should look into buying a gun>

Anyone who's famous—in any way—lives with this fear. That because they put their heads above the crowd, because they're on a screen and people know their names, they will become a target. That something they do will draw the attention of a pissed-off fan or an online mob. They know, better than most people, that once someone pays attention to you, they usually feel you owe them something in return.

That can turn ugly very quickly. I've protected more than a few people from deranged stalkers. The crazy ones didn't disturb me as much as the ones who were nominally sane. A guy who believes his refrigerator is delivering coded messages that must be passed along to Bruce Willis so they can ride off and defeat the Kodan Armada together—that's just a severe malfunction in the pattern-seeking parts of the brain, a chemical imbalance pulling the steering wheel away from the driver and forcing the car off the road. They have trouble getting dressed in the morning. I could see them coming from a mile away.

The ones who really worry me are the ones who are perfectly normal in every other aspect of their lives—who still hold down their jobs, feed their kids, get the car to the shop when the check-engine light goes on—and yet still have a burning hate for someone they've seen only on TV.

Because those are the ones who almost make sense. I look at this wedding—this hotel where the rooms are a grand a night, the crowd of people who are paid more in a week than most people make in a year—and there's still a part of me that sees it all through the eyes of a kid who grew up wearing clothes from a bin at Goodwill. It's easy to envy all of this, to write it off as undeserved. You want to tell me anyone here works harder than the Mexican who mows a hundred lawns a week in ninety-degree heat?

From a distance, it can seem as random as a meteor strike. Everyone knows the world is unfair. We hear it from our first day at elementary school. It doesn't remove the sting. Especially when the world never seems to be unfair in your direction. Some people out there get cancer. Other people get a first-look deal at Fox.

But as always, I get to see underneath the surface. For instance, that guy over there—the financial adviser in the suit that costs even more than mine. I'd probably envy him if I didn't see the anxiety that rides on his shoulder like a cartoon devil. He's dropping $15,000 a month on his mortgage alone, and another 100K every year for tuition for his three daughters. And the IRS just came up with a bill for $250,000 for back taxes from 2010, plus penalties and interest, and his clients are all ready to bolt, because the market is all over the place, and he can't get any more fees out of them without turning them upside down and shaking them. That's why he wakes up sweating at 4:30 A.M. every day. Lately he's been having chest pains too.

I know, I know. Rich people problems. We should all be so lucky.

He looks over at one of the waiters passing drinks through the crowd, and he remembers doing the same thing when he was in college, working summers at a resort. For a few seconds, he's happily lost in memories of days without obligations or deadlines, without kids or a house, just mindless labor, long sunny days followed by drunken nights, instant friends and lovers. *<that girl> <what was her name> <almond eyes> <god her body> <what was her name, dammit, going to bug me all night>*

The waiter, in the meantime, is looking at the people in the crowd and wondering which one of them could help his career. *<just need one break> <got to get ahead> <someday going to be twice as rich as these pricks> <someday>*

I've spent my whole life inside other people's heads, and it's all so depressingly familiar. Poor people think about being rich; rich people think about being poor.

I drag myself out of the crowd's thoughts as the string quartet begins warming up. Almost showtime.

Because this will be the finale of season three, there are cameramen in every corner. They all snap to attention. Kira's fellow cast members put on their game faces. Conversations drop to a whisper.

At least out loud. I'm still getting everything that's not being said.

<got to be pregnant> <never last, the way she gets around> <I hear he's gay anyway> <wonder how long we have to stay at this thing> <weddings are great places to score> <never going to get married> <I'll die alone>

The groom, for his part, practically shines with boredom. I can't tell how he really feels about Kira, but he doesn't seem like a man thrilled to spend the rest of his life with his soul mate. Mainly he seems anxious to get the whole thing over with.

Then the music begins and everyone turns, their heads swiveling as if on cue. I look back, just like they all do, and I see Armin escorting his daughter down the aisle.

For that moment, everything else—all the hype, the spectacle, the cameras—fades away.

It's just Kira. She looks radiant.

And even the most sneering inner voices in the crowd quiet down for a second. <*Wow*> is the only word going through the head of more than one person.

The priest—Armenian Orthodox, from the church where Kira was baptized as a girl, because her mother insisted—gestures to all of us to stand, and we do.

Kira and the groom hold hands as the ceremony begins.

I do my best not to read her thoughts, or anyone else's. No need to spoil the moment with whatever is lurking underneath.

But I still pick up on something.

There's a manic sense of anticipation coming from somewhere close by. Pure adrenaline. A pulse of fear and power, surging through their brains and bodies like electricity.

I recognize the feeling. For an instant, I am back in Iraq. Afghanistan. Standing with the other guys in my unit. About to go out and fire our weapons at live targets for the first time.

It's so out of place that for a brief moment I am utterly lost.

And then I feel them. I feel the guns they have hidden under their jackets, the trembling of their hands, the tension in their limbs.

They rush out of their hiding place by the service entrance that leads down to the beach. I can feel the grit under their shoes as they sprint.

They round the corner, and I see them as they begin crossing the short distance to the pool.

Black ties, white jackets, cheap polyester slacks. Bad wigs on their heads and mirrored sunglasses on their faces. Fake mustaches. Their idea of disguises.

I'd think it was a joke if I didn't know what they're planning.

They lift their guns.

I'm already moving toward them, screaming at people to get down.

Then the shooting starts.

///4

Teach Her a Lesson

Inertia is a powerful force. Nobody ever wants to be the first one to stand up, speak out, or change seats. It's the reason people will not move to a new checkout line at the grocery store, even when the line is shorter. People will stick with a terrible job rather than look for a new one. It's got to be something wired deep within us, some instinct to stay safe by staying in the herd.

It will even keep people frozen in place while guns are going off.

I get a lot of disbelief from the crowd.

<ohmigod> <what> <some kind of stunt> <what's going on?> <not funny> <seen better effects than this>

The cameras do not help. They swivel and turn from the wedding party to the men with guns, so it looks like just another scene from an action movie.

But I know it isn't.

Most of the crowd just stand there, unsure of what to do.

Then the blood appears on Kira's white dress, and people begin to figure it out.

She slumps to the ground and disappears from my view as people finally start to run.

The couple closest to me stands openmouthed, unable to comprehend what they're seeing. I take them down to the ground and then roll back to my feet.

I start to move toward Kira, but I'm caught in the tide of bodies, my mind filled with their shrill panic. People are screaming, but it sounds hollow and weak compared to the echo of the gunshots.

The gunmen are not experienced. They're spraying and praying—firing almost at random, the guns kicking wildly in their hands.

But this is a small space, and the crowd can't get past the gunmen, who stand behind the railing, on the higher level of the pool. We are fish in a barrel. Ducks in a pond. The gunmen are not running away. They are planning to shoot until they run out of bullets.

I get a sensation of disbelief and glee from one of the gunmen. *<so easy never thought it would be so easy>*

He's first, I decide.

I change direction, away from Kira and the wedding party, and cut across the patio toward the shooters.

I don't have a gun. (I considered it. I decided it ruined the line of my jacket. I am an idiot.) A man beside me drops, and I feel the sudden agony in his leg where the bullet hit.

I use the pain for motivation. I put one foot on a folding chair and I leap—and then I'm over the railing, right next to the shooter in his clownish disguise.

He stops shooting, he's so surprised. He cannot believe someone actually ran toward the guns.

While he hesitates I punch him in the throat.

He makes a noise like a chicken bone caught in a garbage disposal, and falls to his knees. I grab for his gun, but he drops it, and it goes under the railing, down among the guests and the scattered chairs.

His friends begin to realize something is wrong as he goes down. They are distracted by all the noise and the panic—*<look at that WILL YOU*

LOOK AT THAT> <doing it holy shit can't believe we're actually doing it> <yeah take THAT you fuckers>—but then they see him drop, and they see me standing there.

The second shooter turns and lifts his gun in my direction. I think hard. I give him the stabbing pain of a bursting appendix.

He shrieks and doubles over as he feels something go horribly wrong in his midsection.

He still manages to squeeze off a shot. I feel something tug at my jacket and a sudden burning in my side. That's going to slow me down, but it could have been my heart or lungs.

The second shooter is on the deck, clutching his gut. Now I'm getting the feedback from his imaginary appendicitis even as my shirt is getting wet with my own blood.

So I swing my foot back and kick his head like it's a soccer ball.

His lights go out, and the feedback ends. Small favors. There's still enough pain and panic here to fry my brain if I don't end this fast.

I step over the second shooter just as the third and final gunman turns.

His gun is off the crowd and pointed right at my face. Point-blank range. No way he can miss.

He pulls the trigger. And nothing happens.

He'd been dry-firing for a while now. So excited that he didn't realize he needed to reload. From inside his mind, I could feel the difference in the weight of the gun in his hands. I knew what it meant, but he didn't.

I grab his wrist and yank him toward me, pulling him into an armlock. I twist and he screams.

I have him. All it will take is a little more pressure, and the arm will break, and this will be over.

Then something soft and heavy hits me in the back.

I lose my grip on the gunman as someone rides me down to the deck. I look over my shoulder, and see an overweight guy in a suit on my back.

The bodyguard. Finally trying to earn his pay.

He slugs me twice in the head, his body covering mine like a beanbag chair.

The gunman takes the opportunity to spring to his feet and start running. From my vantage spot on the ground, I see him grab his gun and jump over the railing, heading for the beach.

"Wrong guy, you fucking moron!" I shout at the bodyguard, but he's not hearing me. His brain is full of triumph.

<gotcha fucker> <show you what happens> <won't get away with this>

He's already envisioning the reward ceremony, the medal from a grateful mayor, maybe even a TV show. He cocks back his fist to land another one on me, and I decide I've had enough. I don't want to waste any mental energy on him. Instead, I twist under his sweaty weight, then bend at the waist and snap my head into his nose. I hear the crunch and he falls back, shrieking and bleeding.

I stagger to my feet and take a quick look around. The other two gunmen are on the ground, barely visible under the weight of a crowd of people who are beating the living shit out of them. One is completely unconscious. The other guy's mind is a song of pain and fear. He can't breathe. A dozen different hands are on him, all of them grabbing and hitting. He's afraid he's going to die.

Good.

I start running after the last shooter.

The fake waiter runs along the beach path as fast as he can, shoving people out of his way and generally making a spectacle of himself. His wig flew off somewhere behind him, and his real hair, damp with sweat, trails out in a long ponytail. He's still got the fake mustache glued on tight, though.

People do not try to stop him. Just part of the ongoing reality show called life in Los Angeles. Everyone assumes it must be TV, even if they don't see the cameras.

But he's not making any friends. He keeps running into people because he keeps looking back, checking over his shoulder.

I'm gaining on him steadily. He's got on high-gloss loafers as part of his disguise, and he's really regretting it right now. His soles nearly slide out from under him with every step he takes. My Eccos grip like racing tires. Even at a wedding, I'm never going to wear shoes that will slow me down.

I'm almost on top of him when he trips over a little girl on a pink tricycle and sends her sprawling on the pavement. The girl's father grabs him before he can get back on his feet.

"What the hell, man?" he shouts.

The gunman doesn't even look at him. Instead he sees me, just a dozen feet away now.

So he pulls the gun.

"Back off!" he screams. The father jumps back, his hands held high. The mother shrieks and hauls their crying daughter away as fast as she can.

I almost want to tell them it's not loaded when I check the feeling from inside the gunman's head.

Shit. The weight in his hand has changed now. My tussle with the security guard must have given him the time to slap another clip inside.

So when he turns to me, I don't stop or slow down. I lower my head and find the perfect nightmare for him.

Part of my job in the War on Terror was to sit inside torture chambers and wait for the prisoners' secrets to come spilling out. It's one of the reasons I went into business for myself.

But I have plenty of memories stored away from those times.

I share one with him.

Before he can pull the trigger, he suddenly knows what it's like to be strapped to the steel bars of a cell, a hood over his head, while someone touches electric wires to his bare skin. Every nerve in his body sings with pain and fear. It works better than a Taser. He freezes in place, suddenly paralyzed.

This is drastic. I rarely order this one from the menu because the bill that comes later is horrific.

But I think of Kira falling, and it seems worth the cost.

He stands there, stupid as a rock, and I crash into him and take him to the ground.

We land hard on the path, me on top of him, adding my weight to his own. I feel something pop in his knee. I get part of the pain.

I can identify it. That was part of my training too. Dislocation of the knee and a torn ACL. That's a bad one. We're talking surgery, traction, and six to nine months of recovery.

Not that I care much right now.

"Why?" I scream at him.

Because there is an answer. This is not just some crazy people with guns. I can feel it. There is intent behind this. There is a motive.

And I am going to know what it is, goddammit.

I get a jumble of images, mostly mixed up with his pain. I stand above him. His leg is bent at an unnatural angle at the knee. He's high on adrenaline and rage.

<bitch had it coming> <thinks she's so hot> <show her> <teach her a lesson>

That makes no sense. I step on his bad leg and pull his foot toward me, to help him concentrate. The pain is like a zipper opening up in his knee, spilling out broken glass.

"Why?" I say again. "Why did you do this?"

He finally looks at me, and he has the strangest expression on his face. Even through the tears and the pain, he seems to smirk.

<you don't know> <you don't know>

The people around us are saying things. Maybe they're asking questions. They might be telling me to back off. *<what's going on> <think this is real> <someone should do something> <call 911> <has anyone called 911> <is that a real gun?> <god look at his leg> <guy is killing him> <stop> <this might be real>* There is a charge of fear and confusion and anxiety in the atmosphere. I do my best to ignore all of it.

"Tell me," I say. I want the name. I want the reason.

I twist his leg again. Harder this time. It bends in a way it was never meant to bend. The smirk vanishes and he screams.

But I get one word, before he passes out.

<Downvote>

Then I realize one of the voices I'm hearing is not inside my head. It's stronger and louder than all the others. I get that telltale prickle on the back of my neck that comes when someone has a weapon trained on me.

"I said, 'Put your hands up!' *Now!*"

I look up and see a Santa Monica bike cop, his sidearm aimed at me.

He is ordering me to put my hands in the air, behind my head.

I obey. Unlike me, he's got no way of telling the good guys from the bad here, and I don't want to get shot again today. I kneel on the path, next to the gunman's unconscious form, and wait for the cuffs. The adrenaline fades, and my side begins to hurt like hell. I look down and see the blood seeping through my shirt.

And I wonder:

What the hell is Downvote?

///5

The Reid Technique

The cops take me to St. John's in Santa Monica. It's already swamped with the tightly controlled chaos that hits an emergency room after any tragedy. Doctors and nurses move past one another the same way waiters do at a restaurant during the dinner rush. No wasted motions or words. The noise and pain come from the victims and their families. They scream and they cry. Some try to be stoic. Others demand answers at the top of their lungs. But their minds are all the same storm of panic and anxiety; for me, it's like walking through a sheet of cold water and getting drenched to the bone.

There are reporters crowding into the waiting area. The police shove them back, not at all gently. I get whisked past the line with a cop on either side of me.

A moment later, I'm in a small room behind the double doors. A nurse cuts away my ruined shirt, and then a doctor takes a quick look at the wound. A stray round nicked my side and tore a short, bloody gutter in my *latissimus dorsi*. No visible bullet fragments, no arteries hit. She stabs me with a local anesthetic in a syringe, waits the minimum amount of time for it to work, and then staples the wound shut in a quick, staccato sequence. She places a pad over the weeping staples and tells me to keep pressure on it, and then disappears to deal with the real casualties.

After that, I'm left alone for forty-five minutes. I'm not under arrest. Nobody reads me my rights or asks if I want a lawyer.

But a cop stays right outside the door, and I know that he'll put me down hard if I step outside my tiny room.

So I wait.

The panic subsides slowly, the cold tide receding as people are channeled off into operating rooms or the ICU or waiting areas deeper inside the hospital. The nurse returns and jams an IV into my arm, and I begin to get some fluids back. I only realize I've been shaking when I stop.

I scrape what I can from the minds of the people who race past, dealing with the chaos. But there's not a lot of solid information. Even small crime scenes are messy in the first few hours; something as simple as a liquor-store robbery generates five or six different narratives. *The guy had a gun. No, it was two guys. No, it was just one. He was black, he was Mexican, maybe he was Asian. I saw the whole thing. Well, I saw most of it.*

Now imagine that multiplied by three hundred guests, with the glare of celebrity and the TV lights and a couple hundred quick-spreading rumors. Basic facts get twisted up pretty fast.

I've snagged a few theories already: *<someone heard one of the guys say "Allahu Akbar"> <terrorists> <an old boyfriend, pissed off at her> <group of psychotic stalkers, working in teams now> <what is the world coming to>*.

None of it matches up with what I saw, but everyone has their favorite story already fixed in their minds.

Even inside the hospital, I can hear the news choppers hovering in the sky outside. It's got to be like Christmas for the media. This will be bigger than San Bernardino or Orlando. The news channels have to be doing wall-to-wall coverage by now. It's more than just another mass shooting. There's fame and sex and TV involved.

And someone has to be blamed for it.

I made the mistake of putting my head up. Even if the other guests say I'm on the side of the angels—which is unlikely, because nobody sees anything clearly when bullets start flying—I still broke any number of laws. Not least of which was crippling a man in front of witnesses.

If I'm not careful, I could finish the day in a cell.

So I wait, doing my best to look patient, helpful, and most of all, innocent.

Another hour passes. The door opens, and a guy about my age in a suit enters. He wears his credentials on a lanyard so nobody will mistake him for a mere civilian. He looks me up and down, and I scan him at the same time.

I can feel him size me up, and I get a quick read on him from the self-image that we all carry with us, at all times, as a way of reminding ourselves who we are.

Agent Gregory Vincent, from the Los Angeles branch. When I look inside his head, I get a picture of his desk. It's immaculately clean. He doesn't let it pile up with papers or coffee cups. The computer lines up with the monitor, which lines up with the edges of the desk, all at right angles. More than anyplace else, that's his home. He needs to have one space where everything is perfect and orderly, because he deals with chaos every day.

Already I'm a little worried. He's smarter than your average fed, promoted faster than other people with more seniority. More arrogant too. And I'm not sure why he's here. This should be LAPD's case all the way.

Vincent stands next to me. He does not apologize for keeping me waiting. He hands back my ID and wallet and phone, which is a nice gesture, but basically meaningless. I could still be arrested at any moment, and then he'd just take them back.

"Greg Vincent. FBI," he tells me. "I'm told we have you to thank for the capture of a couple of the gunmen. That was admirable."

I don't get admiration from him. I get a wave of suspicion. And dislike. He's run my name and read whatever he could find before he came in here.

But I play along. “I was just doing what anyone else would have done. Got caught in the middle. That’s all.”

“I think you’re being modest,” he says. “We’ve got just a few more questions, and then we’ll get you out of here.”

He’s all smiles. That’s when my alarm bells start ringing. I’d say my chances of leaving this room in cuffs just doubled.

“What do you do for a living, Mr. Smith?” he asks.

“I’m a security consultant,” I reply. That’s what it says on my taxes. Which I pay early and in full, because I do not want to give guys like Vincent an excuse to look deeply into my life.

“Explains why you’re still walking upright and the other guys are in the hospital,” he says. “Impressive.”

“How are they?”

That surprises him. “Do you really care?”

It’s the difference between assault and homicide, so yeah, I care. Out loud, all I say is “I’m curious.”

“Critical but stable condition,” he says. “One guy has a concussion. One guy is breathing through a tube now. And the one you ran down is going to have a limp when he gets out of the hospital. But isn’t there something else you’d like to know?”

“What?” For a moment, I’m baffled.

“You haven’t asked me how the bride is doing.”

Shit. I’ve been thinking so hard about blocking the inevitable backlash that I forgot to act normal. I already know how Kira is doing. I took that from the mind of the nurse. But Vincent’s right—that should have been the first thing I asked.

Now he’s looking at me with even more suspicion. I make an admittedly lame attempt to cover.

“She’s in surgery, is what I heard. Nobody knows how it’s going to come out.”

"Who told you that?"

"One of the other officers. I didn't get his name."

He frowns, but he lets it go.

"Well. About fifteen other people got hit too. Six dead so far. Another in critical condition, aside from Ms. Sadeghi. One of the groom's relatives—his grandfather, I think—had a heart attack. But it could have been much worse. It was very lucky you were there. Where did you learn to handle yourself like that?"

"Army," I say, and leave it at that. He knows there's more to it. But I want to see if he'll push me on it.

He doesn't. He moves on, smoothly. "Where were you stationed?"

"All over."

He nods as if that's satisfactory. "Why were you at the wedding today, Mr. Smith?"

"I was invited."

He waits. I don't add anything else. His face doesn't change, but I can feel his patience ticking down, like the timer on a bomb. He tries again: "By whom were you invited?"

Proper grammar. Very nice. "The father of the bride."

"You a friend of the family?"

"No. I did some work for him a while back."

"What kind of work?"

"Consulting on security issues. Does it really matter?"

"No, I suppose not. It just seems a bit odd that Mr. Sadeghi would ask you to his daughter's wedding. I had a guy install a burglar alarm on my house. I don't invite him to family events."

"Maybe you should talk to Armin about that."

"Oh, I have," he says.

He's lying. Armin is, as far as I can tell from Vincent's short-term memory, planted like an oak outside the operating room, waiting for news about Kira and surrounded by a wall of lawyers. Vincent hasn't been able to get within ten feet of him.

But that doesn't stop him from spinning out his theory.

"Mr. Sadeghi said you were not invited to the wedding. He says you crashed. The security guard says you interfered with his efforts to stop the intruders."

That last bit is true, at least. The security guard did say that. Maybe he even believes it. Guy has to salvage his ego somehow.

"That's not true," I say, mainly for the audio recording. Silence can be taken as agreement.

"Yeah, well, here's what I think, Mr. Smith. I think you are deeply involved in what happened here today. I think you're pulling some kind of shakedown scam. You arranged for your partners to hit this wedding so you could be the hero. And then you got a little rougher than they anticipated because you wanted to keep them from ever talking. Now, I'm not sure what your endgame is, but I know this: you were behind what happened here today. And that means you are looking at attempted murder and conspiracy charges."

Standard law enforcement interrogation is almost all based on something called the Reid Technique. You've seen it done badly on cop shows, which is the way a lot of cops learn it too. The quick-and-dirty version goes like this: Act like you already know everything. Tell the story the way you believe it. Say it with real conviction, as if you've got Gus Grissom and the whole CSI lab and DNA evidence backing you up, right outside the door. Say it with such confidence that you make the suspect believe you've got him completely nailed. And then get him to confirm your theory. Then you've got a confession, and you don't need any of that other evidence.

It's so effective that it leads to completely innocent people confessing to crimes they never committed. But it's a much harder trick to pull when the suspect—in this case, me—can read your mind.

I know that Vincent doesn't believe his own bullshit. He's got nothing on me. This is a half-court shot, aimed in blind hope of getting some answers from me. He's uncomfortably close to desperation.

And I can see that one word again: "Downvote."

So I wait him out for a long minute. Then I look at him with every ounce of sincerity I can muster, trying to project the image of a righteous ex-soldier, a decorated veteran. You could use my face on a recruiting poster when I say, "You're wrong. I had nothing to do with this. And you know it."

He thinks, distinctly and clearly, <*Well, shit*>.

For a half second, he considers screaming and threatening me. I get a glimpse of myself in a holding cell. But he abandons the notion almost as quickly as it flits across his mind. He knows it won't gain him a thing.

He covers his disappointment pretty well. All that shows on his face is a sudden resignation.

Then something interesting happens. He goes off script. He shuts down the audio recorder on his phone. (The one that I can see. The digital recorder in his pocket is still going, of course.) He pulls a chair over to my hospital bed and sits down heavily. He dry-washes his face with his hands and slouches to look a bit more human.

"Sorry," he says. "I had to be sure. Had to push you a little bit. You know how it is."

Bad cop and good cop, all in one package. Must be a federal cost-saving measure. I'm not buying it. "So you believe me? Just like that?"

"Yes." <*no*> <*mixed up in something dirty*> <*just not this*> <*probably*> <*nothing I can prove anyway*> <*maybe I can salvage something here*> "You know how it works. You were an interrogator in the army, weren't you?"

There it is. We're not done. We're really just getting started. He's got bare-bones access to my military file, the version that's been flea-dipped. There's nothing in there that he can use to tie me to this. I should get out of here now. Stand up and walk away. Send Kira some flowers and then shut off my phone for the next month. My job and my expensive lifestyle depend on not ever getting drawn into an active criminal case, or, God forbid, the media.

But I've got to admit, I'm curious now too. And if I get Vincent talking, I can drag far more information out of his brain than he could ever get from me.

"So what really happened out there, then? Who were those guys?"

"Ongoing investigation," he says. "I can't really say more than that."

But he makes no move to get up. He wants me to ask something else.

With just the right amount of carelessness, he asks, "Did he say anything to you? Before you crippled him, I mean."

I know what he's looking for. So I give it to him.

"One of them said something, but it didn't make a lot of sense."

Vincent doesn't move. His face doesn't change. But in his mind, he's eager, sitting on the edge of his seat.

"It sounded like he said 'down vote.'"

"Downvote?"

"Yeah. I think that was it."

I'm not exactly lying. He didn't say it out loud. But he thought it. Close enough.

More than enough, in fact, to trigger a whole flood of images and memories and associations for Vincent. *<Downvote>* *<knew it>* *<bastards>* I do my best to sift through all of them as they fire past.

It all goes too fast for me to get much detail. He's not thinking deeply on any one topic, just skimming across the surface of a bunch of different memories. I get an image of a computer file on his desktop. A collection of police reports and interviews from a dozen different places. Some crime-scene photos of a dead body. And then a familiar name shoots through Vincent's head: *<just like Jason Davis>*.

That gets my attention. Why would this have anything to do with Jason Davis?

I try to push a little deeper, but Vincent's mind is already racing away to other things: if he can get to the gunmen before their lawyers do, if he should take another run at Armin, where he parked his car. *<do they even validate here?>* *<badge usually works but some of these attendants . . .>* And so on.

I decide to drag him back to the topic, see if that shakes anything loose.

"Do you think this might have something to do with that actor who got shot? What was his name again? Jason Davis?"

His eyes widen, just a fraction, but he covers his surprise almost immediately. "Why would you ask that?" he says, stalling a little.

I shrug, as if I couldn't care less. "I just saw something about it on TV," I say. "I thought maybe there's someone gunning for TV stars. Something like that."

"Like a stalker or a serial killer?" he says, and smirks a little. "Nothing like that."

He's lying. His tone says I've asked him the stupidest question he's ever heard. But inside his head, it's a different story altogether.

This is my unfair advantage in any interrogation: the subjects never know they're being interrogated. All I have to do is ask the question, and I get an honest answer, no matter what comes out of their mouths. It's like that old kids' trick where you tell someone to think of anything except a large white rabbit. For the next few seconds, it's nothing but bunnies on the brain.

In Vincent's case, as soon as I mentioned Davis, his mind immediately snapped back to that one word. Downvote.

<he can't know> *<Downvote could have posted it>* *<no I would have seen that>* *<just guessing>* *<better keep him quiet>* *<don't say anything>*

The shootings are related. And I get a glimpse of something else. A file folder on Vincent's computer, filled with data. Marked with the same name. Downvote.

He's ready to leave. His attention has already skated away, even as he hands me his card and asks me to call him if I think of anything else. I'm no longer a suspect in his mind. Just one more random element, and he doesn't have time for those. As far as he's concerned, we're done.

We're not. I don't have the time—or the focus, honestly—to try a deep dive into Vincent's mind right now. But we are going to talk again.

Because now I know: this isn't the first time this has happened.

And from the way Vincent is reacting, it's not going to be the last.

///6

The World Is Not a Safe Place

Once Vincent is gone, it's not long before the attending signs me out. She tells me how to change the dressing on my wound, gives me prescriptions for antibiotics and painkillers, and forgets me the instant she leaves the room.

I put on my suit jacket and pants over the hospital scrub top they've given me in place of my ruined $200 shirt.

My head spins as I realize how much crap I've got piled up against my firewalls. I've got the panic and fear of the wedding, the ordinary tragedies of the ER floating all around me, Vincent's frustration and tension, and I still haven't dealt with the pain I inflicted on the shooters.

And I got shot. Let's not forget that.

It's all coming. It's just sitting there, like a shadow, right behind me.

I should be back at The Standard. I should have the lights out and the door locked and my OxyContin and Scotch ready for the moment it all comes crashing down on me. I should get someplace quiet and safe before the tremors and the pain and everything else begins.

Instead, I turn away from the front doors and wander farther into the hospital, following the signs marked ICU.

I want nothing more than to get away from all this.

But I've got to see Armin first.

///

Armin Sadeghi stands in the waiting area nearest the operating rooms on the second floor. His family is scattered around him, lying over the chairs and couches like survivors of a shipwreck washed in by the tide. They seem too exhausted to even lift their heads.

But Armin stands. Back straight. Glaring at the TV, which is running a constant repeating loop of footage while talking heads debate the meaning of it all. I am certain that his wife, his sons, their wives, have all told him to sit down. To get something to eat. Rest.

Not a chance. Armin will meet whatever news comes out of those doors on his feet.

His bodyguards and his lawyers, as well as a suit from the hospital, all form a committee to meet me when I try to enter the area. *<who's that guy?>* *<stop him>* *<doesn't look like a reporter>* *<one of the guests?>* *<jesus he looks rough>* *<doesn't matter>* *<stop him>* The lawyers and the suit are mouthing apologies, talking about security, while the bodyguards simply form a wall.

Armin looks over and calls them off. They all back away immediately. I'm grateful. The day has been long enough already.

Armin grips my hand and my arm to greet me, a kind of half handshake, half embrace. Despite the fairy tales Vincent was telling, Armin does not suspect me of involvement in this. *<he's hurt>* *<should have hired John for security for this instead of that fat bastard>* *<should have done a lot of things>*

Which is not to say he trusts me. Armin Sadeghi does not really trust anyone. He hasn't since he was twelve years old.

That's when his world tore itself apart.

When Armin was a child, Iran wasn't the bad guy behind the terrorist plot in every action movie. It was a country trying to travel through time from the fourteenth century straight into the twentieth, powered by the oil that seemed to be everywhere under a thin layer of dirt and rock.

Armin's father owned a construction company that built workers' dorms and apartments and glass-and-steel high-rises. His mother wore Chanel dresses, not a hijab. Investors from the West visited their house, which had a swimming pool and air conditioning. In a few years, his father would promise them, Iran was going to be like Arizona with oil rigs.

But not everyone wanted to be dragged kicking and screaming into the present. The Muslim religious authorities thought the Shah was the devil, delivering Iran to a secular hell. A lot of people believed them, because, after all, they were the voice of God. It didn't help that most of the crowds at the mosques were still poor as dirt, while the Shah was sucking nearly all the money from the oil fields directly into his own pockets. And anyone who didn't like the way things were run could expect a visit from the Shah's secret police.

The rage began to boil over into protests and strikes. Seminary students were out in the streets at night, sometimes forcibly correcting anyone they saw violating Islamic law.

Armin knew about this, but only in the sort of abstract way that any kid follows the news. He didn't really believe it would ever touch him.

Until the night it showed up at his front door.

I've been inside Armin's head, and I've seen that night in his mind. Childhood memories have a tendency to grow larger and more exaggerated if they're not forgotten altogether. Armin still carries it very closely, and it has become saturated with all the dread and fear he felt.

There was a pounding at the front door. Armin padded down the stairs to see what was going on. He was the youngest child, but he was also the only son. He felt like it was his responsibility.

He saw his father facing a group of about a dozen angry young men.

They were loud. Accusing. They wanted to know where he stood.

Then they wanted to know why he didn't keep the faith. Why his wife and daughters were allowed to dress the way they did. And most of all, why he had so much when they had so little.

His father stood at the door, arguing with the men. Not pleading. But not yelling back at them either. The students were still just a crowd. Just kids, really, talking big.

But looking for something. An insult. A careless gesture. Anything, really, that could serve as a reason or an excuse.

The moment seemed to stretch for hours to Armin. He doesn't remember exactly what was said, but he does remember that everyone seemed to calm down. His father was about to turn back inside, to close the door.

Then one of the young men pulled Armin's father from inside the house and dragged him out into the courtyard.

Just like that, the men were no longer individuals. They were a mass, a single organism with multiple heads and limbs, acting with one intention. They beat and kicked Armin's father. They shouted insults and obscenities. They tore his clothes. Armin didn't realize he'd moved from the stairs, but he found himself at the door, watching.

One of the young men turned and saw him there. For an instant, Armin saw only the hate shining in his eyes. The young man took a single, lurching step toward the house. Toward Armin.

Armin thought of his mother and his sisters.

For some reason, the young man didn't take another step. Perhaps it was seeing Armin. Perhaps he felt some shame at beating and humiliating a man in front of his son.

Or maybe that was the point.

Whatever the reason, he barked something at his companions, and they all walked away. They didn't run. There was something terrible in that. They were not afraid of being caught. It was as if they wanted people to know what they'd done. Like they were proud.

Armin's father was abandoned in a heap on the ground. Armin and his mother helped his father back inside, and Armin locked the door.

But he knew it was not enough. It was a thin piece of wood. It would not keep the world out.

Not long after that, Armin's father sold everything he could and took his family to America. Armin went from a small mansion in Tehran to living with his parents and four sisters in a motel room in Santa Monica.

His father used what was left of their money to buy a car wash on the edge of Culver City. Armin's English was limited, but good enough to communicate, so he worked the cash register after school.

The Shah fled Iran less than a year later, and the Ayatollah's forces swept into power. The U.S. embassy was captured, and Armin learned to tell the kids at his new school he was Persian if they ever asked where he was from.

His father dropped dead of a heart attack when Armin was seventeen. He was suddenly the patriarch of the family. And he set about building his empire.

The first thing he did was level the car wash and turn it into a strip mall. Then he used the rents from the property to finance other purchases. A used-car lot. Off-brand burger joints. Cheap office space. Gas stations and liquor stores. Payday loan places. All on the edges of the right zip codes. He leveraged himself to his eyeballs, using one property as collateral for the next. He bought the motel where he'd lived when they first arrived in America and turned it into condos. He tore down battered old houses and built minimansions that edged right up to the property line. He kept buying. He never stopped.

And then, when the market soared in the nineties, the little guy who started with a bunch of cheap corner lots was worth close to half a billion dollars.

He never made noise about any of it. You won't find his name on "The Wealthiest Angelenos" in *Los Angeles* magazine, or anything like that.

He lives in Beverly Hills now, in a house with twelve bedrooms and a tennis court. His kids all went to the best private schools on the Westside, despite the looks he and his wife sometimes got from the WASP parents with their blond hair and perfect teeth. He is on the boards of a dozen different foundations and charities and hospitals.

But he's never forgotten the lessons he learned in Iran almost forty years ago. He still picks up change he finds on the street because he says no one is rich enough to walk away from money. He has bank accounts in the Caribbean and Switzerland, and keeps a stack of cash and gold coins in a wall safe in his house. He has a team of private security that he has been building since he moved into his first office, and he pays them well and knows the names of every one of their children.

He is always waiting for someone to come to his front door again.

Armin pulls me away from his family. Kira's fiancé, I notice, is not invited to join the conversation. He is alone at one end of the room, at the bottom of his own well of shock and sadness. He can barely form a legible thought, struck stupid by everything that's happened.

Armin steers me over to a corner to talk privately. His bodyguards move to join us, but the lawyer blocks them. He understands who I am now. And he's guessing that this conversation does not require any witnesses.

He looks at the scrubs I'm wearing. "You are all right?"

"Fine."

"Thank you," he says. "I saw you, you know. Everyone else was running to get away. You ran toward them."

I shrug. "Not too smart."

He almost smiles. "No. Not very smart at all."

I can already see the answer right at the front of his mind, but I am polite enough to ask. "How is she?"

Just summoning the words almost does it, almost breaks that iron self-control. But he chokes it down before he speaks. "They give her a good chance," he says, and clears his throat. If his eyes were not suddenly shining and wet, you'd think he could be talking about the weather.

But, as always, I get the full story. Despite the front he is maintaining, he is ricocheting from one tragedy to another inside his head. His wife is wrapped deep in her own pain, and he is terrified for her, that she will have to face burying a child. His sons, his other daughters, their spouses and their children—he has no idea how to protect them from this, or even how to explain it.

And then his mind goes back to Kira, and his thoughts almost sing with anguish.

She was the youngest. And she always needed more than his other children. More time, more money, more patience than he could give. Unlike his other kids, she'd never known anything but wealth. She never saw the boxy little one-bedroom near Palms where he and his wife lived with their oldest son until Armin had the time and money to find something bigger. She's never ridden in a car more than a few months old, had a live kangaroo at her first birthday party, learned to use a credit card before she was ten.

She did not know where any of it came from. She only expected it to be there. He recognizes that he played a part in this. He was always working, always busy, and she was his littlest girl. He indulged her. But he expected her to understand that none of it was free. That there was a cost to all of it.

They argued more as she got older. He can hear some of his own angry words echoing now, and he would give anything to take them back.

There were times he wanted to shake her physically, to force her to wake up. The world was not a safe place. He would try to say it sometimes, when he thought she was old enough to understand. He'd begin to tell her about Iran, about his own father, and the nights when the world began to burn. He tried to give her some idea of the vast distance between that place and time and the luxury and security she enjoyed now. And yet, how close it still was—how at any moment there could be that knock at the door that would take it all away.

His other children had at least pretended to pay attention when he told them about this. Kira simply rolled her eyes, waved him away, and said, "Whatever, Daddy." She was an American. That was the past. Ancient history. It was beyond her. "You and your stories." And she would get into the sports car he'd paid for, and drive away without checking for traffic.

So often he looked at her and saw a stranger. The way she flung herself into the world, leaped into everything as if there was no way she could ever be hurt, as if there would always be someone to catch her before she hit the ground.

Armin realizes now that even if she never said it out loud, she always thought it would be him. Her father. Who paid for the cars she wrecked. Who bailed her out of jail. Who hired the doctors and the counselors and the lawyers who made sure none of it went on her record. And who hired the man who saved her from the kidnappers.

For a second, I curl into myself, feeling a fraction of the pain and worry Armin carries. I see her again, in flashes of his memories. A little girl, tiny in her father's arms, smiling in her christening dress. Beaming with pride, arms above her head, from the top of the monkey bars at four years old, seeking the highest spot and testing boundaries even then. He can see the tracks of tears running through her makeup, vomit in her hair and on her prom dress, that first time he was called by the police to pick her up. He remembers the overwhelming relief when I brought her home that morning from her kidnappers. She snarled at him and cursed him and called him names, refused his embrace, and screamed bloody murder all the way to rehab. And he had still never been so grateful in his life.

He thought that was the worst it would ever get. He thought it was all finally turning around for her. Sobriety. Fame and fortune. And a marriage. His little girl. He was just old-fashioned enough to believe that this all might finally make her happy.

Armin looks at me and gets it all locked down again without barely a tremor.

"I spoke to an FBI agent," I tell him. "I wanted you to know. There's something else going on here. It's not random."

"What did he say?"

"He didn't say anything."

Armin waves that off. He knows what I mean. *<get on with it>*

"There's a larger investigation going on. I can look into it. Or your lawyers—"

"No." I know what he's going to ask. You don't need to be a psychic to figure it out. "I want the men behind this," he says quietly.

"The men who did this, they're already in jail," I begin.

"Not just them. Whoever was behind them. Whoever was with them. Anyone who helped them. Anyone who *even knew their names*—"

He realizes he's starting to raise his voice. His lawyer looks over at us. Armin stops himself.

"I want you to find them. No matter what happens—"

He stops himself again. He was going to say *to Kira* but it stuck in his throat.

"No matter what else happens. I want them to pay," he says.

I look around the waiting area. He takes my hesitation for reluctance.

"Whatever it costs," he says. "Whatever it takes."

For once in my life, I'm not haggling for money. I didn't walk in here to ask Armin's permission. I came to tell him that I was going to find out who did this. And make them pay.

But I was not prepared for this.

My work, my life, depend on not seeing the pain of others. On causing it, when necessary.

In here, this close to Armin, all I feel is his pain. I am entangled in his whole family's agony, strung across this room, binding them all together in fear and worry and suffering.

I do not want to feel this. I do not want to carry this burden.

I don't know how anyone does. Christ, the faith it must take to have children in this world. I cannot imagine loving anything that much, and then sending it to face the random evil and insanity that swirl around us all every day.

I could walk away. I've got other clients. I've got a safety net.

Except for one thing. Kira was kind to me.

I honestly cannot say that about many people.

So I turn to Armin and I tell him, "No charge."

Armin doesn't say anything. He takes my arm in that same half embrace. His eyes well up again. I try to stifle a completely inappropriate laugh. How twisted has your life become that you're grateful when someone agrees to find the men who shot your daughter?

That's not what he's thinking, though.

He's thinking of Kira, walking down the aisle.

He allowed himself, for that moment, to forget the lessons he learned in Iran. He trusted the ground under his feet.

Then the shooting started.

Now he feels like an idiot.

He should have known better. It is exactly like he always told Kira:

The world is not a safe place. There are people who will hurt you. No one is watching your back. No one is looking out for you.

Except your family.

I leave the hospital through the front entrance. There are a few photographers still hanging around, hoping for a shot of one of the victims or their families. I think *<nobody nobody nobody>* as hard as I can. Most of them barely glance in my direction. One guy lifts his camera, but then says, loud enough for me to hear, "Nobody."

I get an Uber to the hotel, pick up my car, and barely make it back to The Standard before I start to lose it. The valet—who usually gets a good tip from me—thinks <*drunk asshole*> as I stumble past him. I'm limping from the phantom pain in my knee, hunched over to one side from my real bullet wound. I have to lean on the wall of the elevator to stay upright. Putting the key in the door takes the last bit of concentration I've got. Inside the room, I can feel the fear and the panic all start to swamp me. I'm shaking as I crack open two fresh bottles—pills first, then booze. I swallow an amount that will hopefully not land me back in the hospital, and then settle back into a chair to ride it out.

It's not enough. I feel like I'm swimming in the sweat and shock and horror of everyone gathered on that patio. The pain blurs my vision. I reach for the pills again, but I stop myself. Instead, I take Vincent's card out of my pocket and try to focus on the lettering.

I've got work to do in the morning.

///7

Show Them What You Think of Them

I watch CNN while I dial Vincent's number. The news is still all about the shootings. If it weren't for the celebrity factor, it probably wouldn't be the lead story. The final body count is too low. But some genius has already dubbed it "the Red Wedding," and there's a graphic on TV and a hashtag on Twitter.

The shooters have been identified. I catch the names: Robert Baldwin, Myles Andrews, Daniel Goetz. There are photos from their booking shots and social media. Three baby-fat faces with hipster hair.

As I watch, I keep an eye out for my name or face—the police have not released the video from the TV crews, but there are at least a dozen angles on the shooters from different cell phones. Fortunately, in all the chaos, nobody seems to have gotten any action shots of me. I catch the start of an exclusive interview with the bodyguard who jumped me. He's got two black eyes and a splint on his nose from where I head-butted him. People seem to be giving him credit for my actions, and he's humbly willing to accept.

Let him. I don't need the publicity.

Vincent's phone goes to voice mail. I hit mute on the TV and leave a message.

Vincent calls back almost immediately. He says he's surprised to hear from me. My talent doesn't work over electronics—one of the many reasons the 1-800 Psychic Hotlines are bullshit, I've usually got to be within a dozen yards of a person to read them—but it seems genuine. He probably thought I would hide from any more questions.

I tell him that Armin has hired me to look into the shooting, and that maybe we can share some information. He says that sounds like a good idea. We're both lying. I think I just moved back onto his suspect list, or he wants to use me to get to Armin. Could be both. And I don't plan to share any information—just take it.

But hey, most relationships begin with lies, so why should ours be any different?

We meet in the afternoon at a coffee place not far from the Federal Building in Westwood. He's wearing a clean shirt with the same jacket and tie as the day before. Exhaustion spills off him like paint fumes and I don't need to look inside his head to see he hasn't gotten any sleep. He orders a triple espresso boost to his iced blended. I'm going to feel his caffeine jitters on the way home, I know it.

We sit down and he checks my suit. A different Armani today. The one I wore to the wedding had blood on it.

But Vincent is only thinking about the price tag. *<not a knockoff> <got to be $1,500 even if he got it on sale>*

Out loud, he asks, "How's Ms. Sadeghi doing?"

"Last I heard, she was stable." Armin's lawyer passed the information along.

Vincent shakes his head. "Well, please give my best wishes to the family. I'd tell Mr. Sadeghi myself, but I haven't been able to speak with him." He doesn't bother to hide his annoyance. He works for the FBI. He expects his calls to be returned.

Except it doesn't quite work like that in Armin's tax bracket. "Armin's got some trust issues when it comes to the government," I say. "But I can make sure that he'll hear any message you want to give him."

"Which is why you're here, I assume," he says.

"Armin wants to do whatever he can to assist the investigation. I'm here to help facilitate that."

Vincent vents some of his frustration by reeling off a list of items: Times and dates of Kira's movements. Any security-camera footage from the house, in case the shooters were there. Guest list for the wedding. And so on. I make a show of taking out my small notebook and writing them down. I've got no intention of doing any of them, but it gives me time.

This is where I start to go to work. The thing is, searching someone's brain isn't like entering a term into Google. People's minds are messy, disorganized places. Even a type A overachiever like Vincent wanders between a couple dozen topics in his head while we're talking. He feels something caught between his molars, reminds himself to make a dentist's appointment, considers the wording on a warrant on another case, reminds himself to call the LAPD liaison again, toys with the idea of subpoenaing Armin's tax records, and checks out the barista when she bends over to get something from under the counter—all before he reaches the end of his list.

And somewhere in all of that, there's a glimpse of what I really need to know. Downvote. There's the thread. I start to pull.

"You know, I looked up 'Downvote,'" I tell him when he pauses for breath.

He's instantly wary. Defenses go up. His game face goes on. Carefully neutral tone when he says, "Yeah?"

"It's some Internet term. Means to vote against something to reduce its popularity. So what I'm wondering is, why would a guy who just shot up a wedding say that?"

I wait for him to respond. To his credit, Vincent doesn't take the bait.

He's been through the FBI's interrogation training courses. Most people will start talking just to fill the silence. They'll give away their secrets because they seem to be incapable of handling a few seconds of quiet.

Vincent doesn't say anything. But he can't keep from thinking.

The word "Downvote" is the key to big chunk of his mental real estate. I see a computer file with the word DOWNVOTE—when he started it, he didn't know what it meant either. That was almost a year ago. Now it's full of folders and subfolders, articles clipped from websites, crime-scene photos, and online videos.

He thinks about Jason Davis and Kira. There's something in his mind riding along with their names that I can't quite navigate. He doesn't seem to like either of them much. I know people who investigate crimes have to maintain some distance or they'll disappear under the bodies of the victims that pile up in their lives. But this is more than that. There's an antipathy—an actual distaste—for both of them.

I can't see where it's coming from. He's never had any personal experience with them before the shootings. And it doesn't seem to have affected his work in any way.

So I file it away for later and move on.

An Internet site. Hours and hours in his GSA-purchased ergonomic chair in the office staring at the flat screen, looking for something, anything, that will lead to a real-world name or address.

It's all jumbled up. A lot of material there. I need some direction. I push him a little more.

"I know the same people who targeted Kira targeted Jason Davis. I know there's a connection," I say.

"Where did you hear that?" he asks. *<goddamn LAPD> <leaks like an old man's dick>*

I let him think it's the police. "It doesn't matter. What I hear is that there's some kind of Internet group. Someone called Downvote. And it's probably targeting celebrities."

There's a brief flower of panic in his mind at the thought of this news getting around. But none of it shows. "Interesting theory," he says.

I'm close. *<Downvote> <Kira Sadeghi> <going high-profile now>*

He's wondering just how much of this he can afford to tell me.

While he's deciding, he asks, "Private security consulting. How did you get into that?"

I shrug. "Had to do something when I left government service. This is pretty much all I'm qualified for."

He checks my suit again. *<definitely not a knockoff>* He can't help but ask, "How's it pay?"

"You looking for a job? I'm not hiring, but I could make a few calls for you."

He smiles back. *<bite me>* "I'm not quite ready to leave government service myself. I hear it's nice, though. Sitting around in some rich guy's hotel room, living off his credit card, following his mistress around when she goes shopping . . ."

That's what he says. But I can see a whole range of options scrolling through Vincent's head. Everything from leg breaking to contract killing. I'd like to say I'm offended, but it's not an unreasonable assumption.

"Sometimes it's a little more exciting than that."

"Like yesterday."

"Unfortunately, yeah."

He leans in. "What does Armin Sadeghi *really* want you to do, Mr. Smith?"

He's not recording this. I know. So I tell him the truth, because I can always deny it later. And from what I can read in his mind, he's never going to want either of us to repeat this conversation.

"What do you think? He wants the people responsible for this," I say. "And he wants them dead."

Vincent's mind goes very quiet as he chooses his next words.

"I can understand that he must want revenge," he says. "But those men—they're in jail now. In fact, I'm due to interview them tomorrow. He's just going to have to trust the system to do its job."

This is a hard, bright line for him. He will not give me the shooters. I didn't really expect him to.

But there's something else. Something else he's waiting for me to ask. And then I get it: he wants me involved. Not sure exactly why yet, but that's why I'm here.

So I push him a little more, to see where he'll go.

"You and I both know they didn't do this alone," I say. "There are other people out there. I intend to find them."

Vincent maintains the poker face for a second longer, but I see his decision as he makes it. He gives me a small smile and says, "Well. I might be able to help you with that."

"This is going to require a little background, so be patient," he says. "It all started about nine months back. I pulled a case. Hate crime. Something that got kicked over to my desk for possible civil-rights violations. It's the sort of thing we have to do all the time if the victim is in any of the check boxes—you know, minority, gay, trans—totally routine."

In his head, again, I see the file on the screen on the computer on his immaculately clean desk.

A gay-rights activist—not a big name by any means, just a guy who showed up at protests and occasionally threw glitter at Republican politicians—had been beaten into a coma outside a WeHo club. Vincent was supposed to review the police report and decide if there was any need for the Bureau to get involved.

Usually all that meant was a quick read of the basic facts. Name and date and specifics. Everybody in the office had to do one of these, take one for the team now and again. It was important to have the open file. Just in case it did turn out to be a hate crime, or part of a larger pattern, or the victim's friends and family turned up the heat in the media. The FBI never wanted to look like it was ignoring anyone who belonged to any recognizable minority. It was important to have the computer file just in case something really did explode, so the media-relations people could say, "We've opened an inquiry."

But nobody really took this one seriously, Vincent says. "Cops were willing to write it off as a robbery at the time."

He smiles, waiting for me to ask the obvious questions. Sometimes I really hate this. Pretending I'm waiting for him to let me in on the secret when I can see what's coming next. But it's the price I've got to pay for an all-access pass into Vincent's head.

"But it wasn't a robbery," I say.

He nods. "That's right." He waits.

I restrain a sigh and ask, "How do you know?"

Here's where he gets to explain how smart he is, and he can't help but glow a little.

Vincent tells me he noticed a line in the report from one of the victim's friends. The friend said he was sure the victim had been targeted for his activism, because he'd been getting death threats on Facebook.

Vincent had a couple of minutes before he was due for a departmental seminar, and he got curious. He clicked over to the Net and looked up the victim's page. All of the settings were public, so he could see everything that had been posted.

And it was a garbage fire. `DIE U FAG` was the mildest thing he saw. The rest of the messages were even more vicious and badly spelled.

In the real world, the activist was not a big deal. But online, he was huge. Thousands of people followed him. And most of them fucking *hated* him.

He lived to piss off the people who were already clenched-teeth angry over gay rights. He made jokes, he argued, he insulted, he belittled. In return, he got pictures of loaded guns, targets drawn on his face, and misspelled threats.

At this point, Vincent was intrigued, but not necessarily ready to call it a conspiracy. Most of the old-school agents took threats on the Internet about as seriously as crank calls. Those guys barely used email, so the Internet was a distant galaxy to them. Even his coworkers closer to his own age dismissed social media. Many FBI agents are strongly discouraged from having a social-media presence; there's just too much potential to screw up active investigations, or worse, drag the agency into a lawsuit. So a lot of them don't know anything about it. They think it's for posting pictures of your kids or your lunch. A waste of time, in other words.

Vincent knew better. He looked up the accounts that were posting the threats. Most were anonymous. He put in a request for their IP addresses with Facebook—the company has a dedicated support page for law enforcement—and went back to his other cases. When he got the records, he had a few minutes at his desk, so he began searching for some of the email addresses associated with the accounts. Nothing too complicated—just entering the emails and usernames into Google or law enforcement databases and seeing what came back.

An hour later, he found himself deep into message boards on the Net—places like reddit, and 4chan, where people type back and forth about whatever they want.

That's where he found the photos.

One of the people who'd posted a threat on the activist's Facebook page had been dumb enough to use the same username on a message board.

(I've said it before, but it bears repeating: in real life, most criminals are not Lex Luthor.) And on the board, he posted pictures of the gay activist beaten and bloodied on the sidewalk.

These were not crime-scene photos taken after the fact. Vincent checked, because there are cops out there who like to thrill their friends by taking those photos and showing them around. No, these pictures were taken during the beating. They were taken by whoever did the beating. They clearly showed three guys in masks jumping the activist outside the club. People complained about the terrible resolution and the camera angles (LANDSCAPE YOU IDIOTS! ALWAYS LANDSCAPE!) but most of the other posters on the board gave them the virtual equivalent of applause:

yeah man that fag had it coming

probably enjoyed it LOL

too bad you didn't kill the little bitch

Vincent wasn't surprised by this, not really. He'd already spent enough time down in the sewers of the Net. He was getting used to the things that floated around there.

He took down usernames and locations, but he knew there was almost no chance of ever finding these people down in real life. They could post anonymously, leaving almost no digital records. He was about ready to give up.

But then someone typed a response that caused him to pause.

dude, wtf you doing posting from downvote? you know that stuff is supposed to stay on-site, asshole

Downvote. The photos came from Downvote. Whatever that was.

He kept searching.

He found out the hard way that Downvote was the common term for disliking something. There were literally millions of hits. But as he piled through, he narrowed down his results.

And found a website called Downvote.

I get a good look at the site in his memories. It's bare-bones, minimal design, but not at all homemade or generic. There's a weight to it. Everything looks stark and heavy. Close your eyes, and you could still see the words from the screen burned into your retinas.

It wasn't much to look at. I can see it in his head as he tells me all this. No animation or instant-on video or stylish design. It's mostly just a list of names under a big slogan in block letters.

SHOW THEM WHAT YOU THINK OF THEM

It took Vincent a minute to realize what he was seeing. He explains it to me now, though I get the picture in sharp detail from his mind.

"Downvote is a hit list," Vincent says. "The most hated people on the Internet at any given moment."

Downvote had its own message boards, where the members of the site would debate who should be on the big board on the front page. Whoever got the most votes got on the list. Then the Downvoters were encouraged to do something about them—to Downvote them in real life.

Some of the Downvotes were a lot like junior-high pranks. The spokeswoman for a weight-loss company got a hundred pizzas delivered to her home. A banker who was briefly famous for saying poor people should "just get more money" when he appeared on CNBC found himself with all his credit cards hacked and maxed out.

But the other Downvotes were like the beating of the activist. People got hurt.

A loudmouth talk-show host was SWATted—someone calls 911, gives another person's address, and then tells the police he's holding hostages and he plans to kill anyone who comes near the house—which led to an armed response team breaking down his front door with guns drawn. A video-game developer who insulted console gamers on Twitter had his car torched. A female comedian found a pipe bomb waiting for her on her doorstep, which fortunately failed to go off.

All of this was supposed to stay strictly on the Downvote site, but it leaked out onto the message boards. People bragged. They were proud of it.

And, Vincent noticed, it was getting worse.

By scrolling back through the messages, he could see that the site started a little over a year earlier. Back then, it was mostly pizza deliveries. But it escalated quickly. The number of users was going up. People were looking for a place where they could settle scores. They were suggesting more names all the time.

Vincent finishes his drink, sucking down the last of it through his straw, before he says, "I've been monitoring it ever since. I was afraid something like this was going to happen."

I can see the website in his head. The big board with the list of names. Last weekend, Jason Davis said something stupid on Twitter, in response to some random fan complaining about the latest plot twist on his show.

```
Oh please. We make the show so losers like you don't
have to get a life of your own. Crack a window,
fucktard. Get some air.
```

He shot up to number three on Downvote's list. The death threats began, he started carrying a gun, and then he took a shot at an autograph seeker. Downvote loved it. The users of the site began an email campaign to get Davis the most severe penalty possible. He moved up to number one on Downvote's hate list.

Until the news of Kira's wedding broke. Then she bumped him from the top spot.

There are maybe a hundred questions at the front of my mind. So I'm a little surprised when the first thing I ask Vincent is "Why the hell didn't you warn her?"

He looks confused. "You mean Kira Sadeghi?"

"Yes," I say tightly.

He must see the anger on my face, because he gets defensive. "Hey," he says. "This is not my fault. We were monitoring the situation, as I said. We have a lot of cases to pursue. We use our resources as best we can."

"Her name was in big letters on a website, and that wasn't enough?" I don't bother to mask my sarcasm. "I thought you guys were listening to all our phone calls and tracking everything we did on the Net. Do you actually need the bad guys to send you an invitation now too?"

He considers saying something really impolite. I'm going to write that off to the lack of sleep.

"The site isn't just out there for anyone to see. It's on the Dark Net. Do you know how much material is hidden there?" *<dick>* *<do you even know what it is?>*

I do, actually. I've hung around with enough tech CEOs and attended enough of their meetings to pick up some of this stuff. The Dark Net is the name for the underside of the Internet. Every time we go online and type a search term into Google, or like something on Facebook, we think we're seeing the whole World Wide Web. It's in the name, right?

Not even close. Something like 90 percent of the Internet is hidden, accessible only by special software called Tor, a browser that enables secure, encrypted web access. These websites are private and unlisted, completely invisible unless you know exactly how to find them.

And down there, in the depths where nobody is looking, the Net is crawling with all kinds of unpleasant things. Sites that sell drugs or child porn or weapons, or all three. Users are completely untraceable by standard methods. They can swap bootleg movies or bomb-making recipes, or hire hit men, and nobody can track them.

Vincent is saying Downvote is one of those sites, down there in the dark. And there's no way to find out who's behind it either.

He did what he could. He gave the site address to the FBI's tech nerds, who told him he might as well ask Santa for a pony. The actual people sending the messages could be anywhere in the world. Untraceable, more or less.

"It could be based on a server in Russia or China or in Burbank," Vincent says. "We've got no way of knowing."

His frustration is smoke floating in the air around him.

And then I see it, behind the careful spin coming out of his mouth. He tried. He did. He keeps saying "we," but it's not really a team effort. It's just him.

It's replaying in his head: the meeting where they turned him down. He piled all his research into his computer folder and took it to his supervisors. He made his case in a presentation in one of the conference rooms. He had PowerPoint and everything.

His bosses were skeptical, to say the least. They thought it was a video game. A joke. They thought the pictures of the activist were Photoshopped.

The SAIC—a guy who needed help getting documents to print on the office network—was still up to his eyeballs in the aftermath of San Bernardino. He had congressmen threatening his budget, wondering why the

FBI wasn't busting sleeper cells like they did on *Homeland* or *24*. "People talk a lot of shit on the Net," the SAIC told Vincent. "But at the end of the day, it's usually some lard-ass who'll never leave his parents' basement."

Even now, with Kira's shooting, his bosses are still skeptical. They're more interested in the terrorism angle. Maybe Kira's very existence was an insult to some jihadi lunatic. They are dug in against his theory now, because if they admit it, then they have to admit they ignored a potential threat.

Vincent can feel the case slipping away from him. He needs something they can't ignore.

And he's running out of time.

Someone in the media is going to make the connection between all of these crimes, or someone from Downvote is just going to send an email to the *New York Times* or put up a public website that announces the whole thing.

Because once the word about Downvote goes public, it's going to spread like Ebola. It's the perfect story. It combines paranoia about the Internet with jealousy and fame. It's reality TV with a body count instead of ratings.

Vincent is doing his best, but he knows he can't keep the lid on it much longer.

If he doesn't find a way to stop them, everyone will know about Downvote soon. And these dipshits will finally get what they've always wanted. They'll be famous.

Even worse, they'll find a whole new target audience. A whole new world of players who will want to join their game.

More people will die. He knows it.

And almost as important, the case will certainly be taken away from him and given to a multi-agency task force with some big swinging dick from Washington at the top of the org chart. Any chance to make a name for himself will disappear in the scrum of bodies the FBI will throw at the problem.

He has to crack Downvote open before that happens. This is why he's here, talking to me. He thinks maybe if I go blundering around, I might shake something loose. Then he might get the evidence necessary to get his supervisor on board. Get some resources. And run the investigation himself as the lead agent.

He sees himself bringing it to his boss: *<If they're targeting celebrities now, it's really going to hit the fan.>* *<Hate to say I told you so, boss, but I told you so . . .>*

In other words, he's trying to use me.

But like I said before, I'm using him too. And I've already got everything I need.

"Well, good luck," I say, and stand up. "Thanks for the coffee."

He looks confused. "What?"

"I'll relay your requests to Mr. Sadeghi. I know he'll want to do everything he can to help."

"All right," Vincent says. He's instantly suspicious. His radar is telling him something just went wrong—he really is a smart guy—but he doesn't know what. There was more he wanted to say. He has ideas, a hunch, leads. He was going to point me at them, like a trained dog.

But I don't really care. He saw me taking notes. He just didn't know they were about more than what he was saying out loud.

"Be sure you stay in touch," he says. He stands and walks out of the coffee shop with me. His mind is churning.

Before we go our separate ways, he can't help asking, "So what are you going to do?"

I shrug. "I'm not sure," I say. "I mean, if the FBI can't stop these guys, I don't know how I can."

Now he suspects I'm just screwing with him. I smile and shake his hand.

"But I'll try to think of something," I tell him.

///8

Clark Kent Was Right

Our brains are busy little places, processing millions of bits of information every minute. That's a lot of work, so they cheat wherever they can to save time. They ignore anomalies and fill in the same background details whenever possible. They can be blind and deaf to things that are right in front of our faces. People see what they expect to see. They operate on autopilot until something comes along to jolt them out of it. That's one reason why when a driver plows over an elderly grandmother in a crosswalk, the first thing he always says is "I didn't see her!"

With my talent, I can exploit those vulnerabilities in our cognitive infrastructure, the same way a hacker can exploit openings in computer code. I can bypass what their eyes are telling their brains. I can hide in plain sight.

Which is why I'm walking into one of the largest jails in the nation with nothing more than a blank piece of paper for ID.

The shooters are being held at the Twin Towers facility downtown. It's run by the L.A. Sheriff's Department, and holds about twenty thousand inmates at any given time, either waiting for trial or serving out their misdemeanor sentences. You might see it in the background on the news when a celeb is released from jail for their latest DUI.

The Twin Towers include the medical facilities for the prisoners. And from what I read in Vincent's thoughts, they're all still recovering from what I did to them.

I'm trying not to be too proud of that. There are guys I used to know who would have put them in the morgue, not the hospital.

Then again, if I'd killed them, I wouldn't have a chance to question them now. So, silver lining, I guess.

I'm wearing a cheap suit and glasses—my Clark Kent disguise—as I join the line of people waiting to go back into the jail on official business: attorneys waiting to see their clients, cops working cases and getting statements or evidence.

And FBI agents about to interview the suspects in the latest mass shooting.

The line moves, and the sheriff's deputy behind the check-in window finally calls me forward.

A quick scan tells me she's already tired at ten thirty in the morning, doesn't sleep well due to anxiety and apnea, and is more than a little irritated at her husband, who left for work without getting the kids dressed for school. Bored, drowsy, and distracted. Perfect for me.

I hold up my blank papers and tell her I'm FBI agent Greg Vincent. I'm here to see the suspects from the Sadeghi case. I list them off by name, along with their prisoner numbers and the name of the sheriff's chief deputy who's authorized my visit, all taken out of Vincent's memory.

I can feel a slight spike of interest from the deputy—her name is Ronda—when she hears the names of the shooters. *<those assholes>* *<shot up that wedding>* *<unbelievable>* But her sense of outrage has been worn down by the steady stream of ugliness she's seen on the job. People do horrible shit to one another all the time; other people get paid to lock them up or put them back on the street. Mostly what she feels now is a dull cynicism.

She barely glances at my papers. I project, as hard as I can, the image of legal forms and proper ID. *<nothing unusual here>* *<back to work>* *<totally normal>*

She barely even sees them. She hands them back and taps a few keys on her keyboard. I'm about to turn for the metal detectors when she suddenly stops and frowns. "Wait," she says.

Not a good sign. This whole trick of mine depends on people sticking to their routines. Anything unusual wakes up the conscious thought processes, and those are a whole lot harder for me to hack.

I try to look both calm and slightly annoyed, as if this were just one more bureaucratic obstacle preventing me from serving the cause of justice. "What?"

"You're early," she says, like I did this on purpose to screw with her. She points at her screen. "Two of the prisoners aren't available. Says here Baldwin is with his lawyer and Andrews is in with the doctor."

Well, shit. Should have realized there might be some scheduling problems. I shrug, like this is most obvious thing in the world. "Yeah. So? I'm here to see Goetz."

She narrows her eyes. "You're here to talk to Goetz." Her tone is flat, but I can see suspicion lighting up her brain.

I see it inside her mind just before I say anything else.

Goetz is the guy I punched in the throat. He can't talk. He nearly choked to death on the damage I did to his windpipe before a paramedic did an emergency tracheotomy in the ambulance. He's still breathing through a tube.

So I give her an irritated look and say, "Well, not *talk* to him. But yes, I'm here to interview him."

She scowls. "How do you do that, anyway?

I do my best impression of an FBI agent, which is to say, I put a full serving of arrogance into my voice: "He can still write, you know."

I might have pushed it. For a moment, she considers asking to see my papers again.

But she feels the pressure of the people behind me, the impatient sighs, the glares, and the shifting. Whatever her bosses tell her in her evaluations, she knows her job is to keep that line moving.

So she waves me on. For a moment, she thought her day had almost gotten interesting. But she sinks back into boredom as soon as I step away.

I walk through the metal detectors and then I'm escorted into the medical wing by another deputy.

Let's find out what Mr. Goetz knows.

Goetz is laid up in a bed in the medical wing of the jail. It looks almost like a regular hospital, except for the locked doors and the metal furniture bolted to the floors. My escort lets me in to see him, tells me to knock when I'm done, and leaves. His face was carefully blank the whole time, but he was practically spitting with contempt inside. *<swear to God, it was up to me I'd finish the job on this one> <donate the organs> <maybe do some good with the spare parts> <pinch off the tube, let him choke>*

I'm tempted to do the same thing. I look at Goetz in the bed. There's a tube running out of his throat, and the hissing and pumping of machines. His hipster haircut is greasy and lank, and he's hollow-cheeked and dark-eyed. He seems helpless and shriveled. And yet I find I want to step on him, hear his bones crack like a cockroach under my heel.

I shove it away. It won't help. I need the information. So I plaster a fake smile on my face and step closer to the bed.

"Mr. Goetz," I say. "I'm with the FBI. I was hoping you'd be willing to talk with me."

He gives me a sullen glance before looking away again. His thoughts are a repeating loop. *<who gives a shit> <totally fucked anyway> <what does it matter?>*

He doesn't recognize me. That's not too surprising. Stress and adrenaline usually interfere with forming memories. There's too much input into the brain at once, and everything gets lost in the chaos.

And the glasses help. Say what you will about Clark Kent, but he was always right about this: one single distracting detail can make an entire disguise.

I can feel the cushion of painkillers between him and the world. The staff has taken good care of him. He has a small dry-erase board on the bedside table and he grabs it.

wheres my lawyer

He's more curious than suspicious at this point. The drugs are taking the edge right off, making him stupid.

"I'm here to offer you a deal, Mr. Goetz. But if you'd rather I talk to your lawyer, we can always wait until you've been arraigned. Of course, that could take a while. Weeks, maybe."

He shrugs and waves me over. *<what the fuck else do I have to do?> <asshole> <don't even know who you people are>*

what u want, he scrawls.

"I thought we could talk about the incident."

why

I think about every episode of *Law & Order* I've ever seen, and throw whatever legal jargon I can at him. "Maybe there's some detail you've forgotten to mention. Perhaps there's someone else you can name. Something I can use to convince my bosses to offer you a plea bargain."

He makes a rasping noise that I realize is his version of laughter now. *<yeah right> <like that would help>*

"I'm not going to lie to you, Mr. Goetz," I lie. "You are in a lot of trouble. But there's a chance, if you know anything at all that might provide some kind of explanation or reason for your actions . . ."

He rasps again and raises his shoulders in an exaggerated shrug. *<caught on camera> <whole world saw> <totally fucked>* He pictures prison: a bunch of scenes from movies and TV shows and bad jokes about rape in the showers. His thoughts rapidly spiral into despair like water down a drain.

That doesn't help me. I need to steer him back to the shooting.

"Is there anything you can say? Anyone else who was involved?"

That only confuses him. *<what?>* He looks at me blankly.

"Maybe it wasn't entirely your plan? Maybe you were scared. You were afraid of getting hurt. Maybe you were only going along with your friends?"

He looks away and I feel a flare of wounded pride. He considers blaming Baldwin and Andrews. *<they're probably going to do the same thing to me>* But it stings a little. *<I was first>* *<my idea>* *<I was the first one>*

Jesus Christ, he actually wants credit for this.

"Why did you do this? Why did you shoot Kira Sadeghi?"

He turns and makes a face when I mention her name. But it's exactly the right question, as it turns out. It triggers a whole chain of memories as I get a good, long look inside his head.

And it's like a horror movie in there.

He is still filled with rage at Kira. A woman he knew only from his TV screen and her Twitter account. Even now there are scenes from *Tehrangeles* playing in his head like a montage from the show. Kira dancing in a club. Kira kissing her best friend's boyfriend. Kira posing seductively against a wall. Kira laughing at some random guy trying to chat her up. In Goetz's memory, these images all glow like they're radioactive.

And somewhere along the line, he began to take this personally. He went from a casual viewer of the show—he never would have called himself a fan—to watching episodes over and over, building a mental catalog of Kira's crimes.

All of this for someone he never met.

I steel myself and try to untangle the mess of bad wiring inside this guy's skull, to find the place where he started to go off the deep end.

It's hard to describe, but there is a definite starting point to his obsession. Before all this started, Goetz was a customer-service rep for a cable-TV company. He spent his days in a warehouse-like building in El Segundo answering irate calls from people who wanted to know why they couldn't get their pay-per-view to work. He didn't even have his own desk. He'd just slot into whatever cubicle was open, stacked in row after row along the great, empty floor. At night, he'd go home to a tiny apartment he shared with two other guys and flip on his computer. About the only perk he got from work was a discount on his broadband.

He spent a lot of time on the message boards, railing against everything in his world that sucked. Someone posted a clip from *Tehrangeles*—something like "You won't believe what this girl does next!" And there was Kira. Frozen at the moment she was about to spill out of her bikini top in a hot tub, her face caught in an expression of pure delight.

He clicked. Saw the clip. Saw her laughing. Looking too happy. Too rich. Too much.

He couldn't laugh at her, like he could most of the people on those stupid shows. And he certainly wasn't laughing with her. She lived on a different planet than he did. All he felt, right then, looking at her, was small.

He kept clicking.

From there, it started growing like a tumor. I know Kira is supposed to be the bad girl of the show, but in Goetz's head, he recalls being bombarded with images and stories about her shitty behavior.

Worse, they all seem keyed to hit exactly the wrong notes with him. He was alone, struggling at his crappy job, spending 70 percent of his income on rent, barely able to afford pizza and beer when he did go out. He would see Kira in a $3,000 dress, making out with a guy in a club he could never get into, then dropping that guy for another one. It began to feel, to him, like she was rubbing his nose in his own sad excuse for a life.

He examined video from each episode like it was the Zapruder film, looking for evidence that would prove she was an evil bitch. His roommates got bored with it. They stopped talking to him. Didn't matter. He found plenty of other people who would agree with him. He began spending even more time online, complaining about her on the message boards, in comment sections, anywhere he could find a place.

Then he found Downvote.

He was already using Tor to access the Dark Net. Most of the time he downloaded porn that he couldn't get on the aboveground torrent sites. But a link on one of his message boards led him to Downvote.

There he found a whole community of people very much like him: extremely pissed off, and constantly howling for blood.

Kira had her own subsection on Downvote. People would argue about her, post video clips and articles, and elaborate fantasies about what they'd do to her if they got the chance. They lobbied to get her on "the big board"—Downvote's front page. Once she was there, Goetz was sure someone would do something about her. Put her in her place. Teach her a lesson.

He found other Downvoters who agreed with him. Pretty soon he was spending all his time in arguments, trying to get her into the top ten.

Then she finally made it. He felt vindicated. Now everyone agreed with him, everyone would see that she was as loathsome as he'd always thought.

Only it wasn't enough. Nothing happened. Her name just sat there—sometimes it went up, sometimes it went down. She stayed on the board—he downvoted her every day, doing his part—but it wasn't like anyone was about to cancel her show.

It didn't cost her anything. That's what really galled him. She didn't even know they existed, all these people who hated her.

She had to know.

So one evening he typed the words "Someone should do something about that bitch" into his computer.

Easily a dozen other people responded with more or less the same message: "Like what?"

"We should ruin her wedding," he typed back. The news was out by then. Goetz couldn't miss it. His newsfeeds were crammed with mentions of Kira, pictures of Kira, Kira's greatest hits from the show.

"Yeah, we should crash it," one of the other Downvoters wrote back.

"We totally should."

"We should fucking ruin it," another wrote.

"We should fucking ruin *her,*" one other guy typed.

And that's when Goetz had the idea. He could show her. He could show them all.

Of the dozen or so who chatted with him online that night, most dropped away immediately when he mentioned getting guns. Just logged out and never came back. Goetz didn't care. He thought they were cowards.

Five hung around. They all talked a good game. One guy was in Canada, though, so he was out. Two of the others just rubbed him the wrong way. He didn't think he could count on them if it came down to a real firefight.

But Baldwin and Andrews—one lived in Henderson, Nevada, and the other was in Riverside—they were on board. They loved the idea. They all met up and made a plan. They filled out their forms and bought their guns. They ordered their fake waiter costumes online. They mapped out the site of the wedding and drove there together and parked Baldwin's shitty little Mazda hatchback at a parking meter near the beach.

They walked up to the hotel from the public walkway and wandered right past the fat security guard.

They hid by the deck until they heard the "Wedding March."

Then they jumped out and started shooting, and people fell down.

Goetz expected he'd be sick. Or nervous. Maybe even a little guilty.

Instead, all he felt when he saw Kira fall was a sense of wonder. He'd done something. He'd proven she could be touched, that they really did exist in the same world. No matter what else happened, for that split second, he mattered.

He'd shown her.

<*bitch had it coming*> bubbles through his mind, even now.

I find myself staring at his breathing tube. It would take almost no effort at all to crimp it. Then it would be only a matter of seconds—not even minutes—to watch him suffocate.

Then I remember: everything in here is recorded. There are cameras in every hallway, every cell, every medical bay. There is a long digital trail of my presence here. In the past, I've walked five feet in front of guards with automatic rifles in broad daylight, and afterward, they would swear they'd been looking at nothing but empty air. I can fool human beings into seeing stuff that isn't there.

Cameras and computers, not so much. I'm good, but I'm not good enough to talk my way out of a murder committed on video.

So I shake my head and forcibly break contact. Look away and take a deep breath. I realize my hands have clenched into fists.

Goetz is not completely stupid. He is watching me more carefully now. He saw the sudden rage and how I forced myself to remain calm. He knows something is off here. His mind has shifted from self-pity to self-preservation. Better late than never.

He writes on the board again.

get out want my lawyer

"This is the only chance you've got for a deal," I tell him, pulling out the fake smile. My face feels like rubber. It doesn't put him at ease.

He takes the board back, scribbles some more.

what's ur name

He underlines it several times. Glaring at me the whole time.

<*who the fuck are you, dude?*> <*look familiar*>

Decision time. He can't yell for help, but he does have a button that will summon the nurse on duty in the pod, and the deputies along with her. My blank papers will not withstand that kind of heightened scrutiny. I could still get out of here, but not without hurting someone, and I don't want to do that.

It's time to go. I stand up.

"It seems like you need your rest," I say. "We'll continue this another time."

I knock on the door and wait for the deputy. Goetz is on full alert now, however. He taps the board again, points at me, gestures furiously. *<who the fuck are you?> <you trying to trick me?> <answer me> <not going to get away with this>*

The deputy is taking his sweet time getting me out, and Goetz is only getting more agitated. He'd be up and out of bed if it wouldn't dislodge his tube. He's mouthing obscenities. In his head, I hear them at full volume.

It's just a little more than I'm prepared to take.

I step back toward the bed and push him down into the mattress. I put my face close to his. He sees me behind the glasses for the first time. I feel the sudden shock of recognition. He suddenly remembers where he's seen me before.

<oh shit> <oh no> <it's him>

"That's right," I say quietly. "It's me."

He reaches for the call button. I grab his wrist and pin it down. He struggles, but not much.

"You want to live, Mr. Goetz? Tell me who's behind this. Tell me about Downvote."

Panic in his brain. Like a rat gnawing at its tail pinned in a trap. He can't talk, and he can't reach the tablet to write because I'm holding him down.

But I can get what I need direct from the source.

The problem is, it doesn't make much sense. He doesn't know what the hell I'm talking about.

<behind it?> <Downvote? What about Downvote?> <what the fuck, dude> <arm hurts> <stop> <it's a website it's just there> <nobody's behind it> <just me and the guys> <my idea> <please let me go>

"Hey," the deputy says, from behind me. "What are you doing?"

I stand up. Smile again. Hopefully more convincingly this time.

"He seems a little agitated," I say. "Maybe he needs to rest. I'll come back later."

The deputy takes a look at Goetz, who radiates relief, but otherwise keeps his face blank. The deputy stands on the edge of a decision for a long moment, teetering back and forth between suspicion and indifference.

In the end, indifference wins. Bad shit happens in these jails all the time. There's the usual menu of gang violence, rape, and beatings. And over in the men's central jail, some of the deputies were so notorious for beating prisoners that they were more like a gang themselves. The former sheriff resigned under indictment for lying about it, and one of his top under-sheriffs was just convicted of federal corruption charges for covering it up. Now everyone has to be even more careful. There have been so many investigations, one after another, that anyone could be a federal informant. Prisoner, deputy, staffer—doesn't matter. Anybody could be a snitch.

The deputy knows: you want to keep your job, you keep your head down, you keep your mouth shut.

So he pretends he hasn't seen a thing.

"You coming?" he asks.

I nod, and go to the door.

But before I leave, I look back at Goetz. "Don't worry," I tell him. "I'll see you again."

I admit, I take a lot of joy in the wave of fear that rolls off him as I walk out.

///

My arrogant little victory dance is short-lived. The deputy takes me back to the lobby by a different route, and we pass one of the exam rooms where a prisoner from the seventh floor is being treated.

I forgot. This is not only one of the largest jails in the country, it's also the largest mental health facility in the world. That's because it's the holding pen for every head case who gets arrested in Los Angeles County. At any given moment, there are about two thousand people with some kind of mental illness in Twin Towers. Everyone placed on a seventy-two-hour hold by their concerned relatives, every suicidal vet, every addict who's melted his brain, every crazy homeless person picked up for jerking off in public.

My talent means I soak up thoughts like a sponge. I get migraine headaches just from being around people who are supposed to be normal.

But splashing around a giant pool of schizophrenia and brain damage is a thousand times worse. I've been near people who have completely lost it before: PTSD cases who have finally buckled under the weight of their memories, prisoners whose sanity has broken against the walls of their cells and torture, and those celebrity stalkers I mentioned before, the ones who suddenly discover a blinding truth that never occurred to them before.

After I've spent enough time in their presence, their perspective starts to infect mine. It feels like there's sand under my feet on a steep incline, and I'm sliding helplessly toward something I can't quite see. Everything looks . . . *bent,* somehow, like the angles of the world are slightly off, meeting in the wrong places. It takes almost physical effort for me to pull out of their heads.

The seventh floor, as it turns out, is where the really severely disturbed patients in the Towers are kept. They are dressed in heavy blue gowns, designed not to rip or tear so that they can't be used to make a noose.

I know all this in a second because it comes blasting into my head, along with the pure dose of insanity from the man being held down by three deputies and a nurse.

I'm rooted to the spot, watching. He looks elderly, but is thrashing against them with inhuman strength. I can feel the last remnants of his self-image—the little personal ID card we all carry around in our brains—and I see that he's barely into his forties, but he's been living hard for a long time.

The nurse is trying to hit him with a dose of Thorazine that looks big enough to take down a horse. The inmate sees the needle and somehow manages to shove one of the deputies—who's built like he pours steroids over his Frosted Flakes for breakfast every day—across the room. The nurse is knocked back as well.

The inside of his head is a black-cloud thunderstorm, with occasional flashes of pain like lightning. He looks at the faces around him. He sees them, but he sees something behind them as well, reptilian pupils in their eyes, scales at the edges of their skin. Demons. Stink of human flesh on their breath. He knows—absolutely *knows*—that the needle is filled with a radioactive cancer virus that is going to infect his soul so that it can be consumed by the demons, so they can shut down his light—

I'm yanked away suddenly. I almost raise my fist to lash out when I realize it's the deputy, dragging me down the corridor.

"You find that entertaining?" he snaps. "Come on."

I was standing there for only a few seconds. It felt like forever. It was like quicksand, sucking me down.

I find myself twitching and try to focus on the thoughts of the deputy. *<fucking gawker>* *<staring at that son of a bitch>* *<not a zoo, for Christ's sake>*

He's angry, and he thinks I'm scum, and he can't wait to be rid of me.

But at least he's sane.

///9

The Future of Money

Outside the jail, I take a moment and collect myself. By which I mean I find my pill bottle inside my jacket and immediately pop it open. Two diazepam down the hatch. Deep breaths.

This is one of my great fears: that someday I will lose it like they have. That the walls I have built against all the noise and chatter will finally break down from all of the accumulated damage, and I will be swamped in other people's thoughts. That I will lose my way among all the random and competing voices.

Because I've seen it from the inside, and it looks far too easy to me. It's never just a sudden snap, like a tether giving way. Nobody ever wakes up and decides to be crazy. It is a long, slow, gradual process, a series of steps down a never-ending staircase, or a hillside slowly collapsing into a heap under a steady rain. A man starts by thinking that maybe there's some explanation for his persistent cough; he does a Web search and finds something about chemtrails. And a year later, he's holding up a cardboard sign outside the White House, demanding the truth about aliens.

The first bad idea looks so innocuous at the time. Most people stop there. Most people have at least one irrational belief. But for some people, it leads to another, and another, until they are in the middle of a wilderness where they are convinced they are the only ones who know the path to truth.

When I get wrapped in too close to the thoughts of others, I have a hard time not following that path. I have to pull myself back, or risk becoming just as lost.

And it scares the hell out of me.

The drugs begin to work. Once I feel calm enough, I try to sort through all the conflicting impressions I read in Goetz's mind.

It's all a jumbled mess. I got a whole stream of information pissing out of him along with the fear. Through all of it, though, I felt something. It's like a splinter stuck just beneath the surface of the skin, with no way to get it out. It's incredibly strange, but I would swear he had help. It was like something was pushing him toward Kira.

His Facebook feeds, his Twitter account, his news sites, they all began to show him more and more of Kira. And the more he clicked on her, the bigger she became in his life.

Part of this is the inevitable feedback loop of the Internet now. I'm no tech genius, but even I know that the Web shows you more of the things you already look at. You enter the term "Kira Sadeghi" into Google, and you're tagged with that data. You carry that tag around to all the other websites you visit, and they all start showing you more stuff related to Kira Sadeghi in a desperate bid to get your attention.

But this is different, somehow. This is more than that.

I'm not offering him any excuses. He made his choices and pulled the trigger. Even though he is guilty, he still does not feel guilty. Or ashamed. Or even a trace of remorse. He feels sorry for himself above all. For that alone, he deserves whatever he gets.

But it certainly felt like something was steering him toward her. From inside his head, it almost felt inevitable.

I'm finally beginning to calm down. The panic is fading. The pills are swimming happily in my bloodstream now, and I feel the chemicals physically forcing my pulse and breathing back to normal levels.

I'm about to head to my car when a strong hand grabs my shoulder and spins me around. I was so out of it I didn't even feel anyone's eyes on me.

"What the fuck do you think you're doing?"

I look up and there's Agent Gregory Vincent. And he is not happy.

I can see from the briefest glimpse into his mind that I am already busted, but I try to smile my way through this anyway.

"Agent Vincent, good to see you—"

"Don't," he says, pointing a warning finger at me. "You are this close to a cell right now."

I drop the smile. "On what charge?"

"Impersonating a federal agent," he snaps. "Funny thing, I was about to go in and interview the prisoners from the Sadeghi wedding, and then the deputy tells me that I'd already checked in. And one of the prisoners is scribbling notes about a guy who wanted to kill him. Then, by the most incredible coincidence, when I checked the security video . . ."

I can see where this is going, and sarcasm is really not Vincent's strong suit. So I yawn and stretch and say, "All right. You got me. I was in there. Trying to get some more information. It's my job. You want to bust me, let's get going. Armin will have me bailed out before five."

<son of a bitch> He's seriously considering putting cuffs on me. But there's an overriding wave of curiosity that's stronger than his anger. He wants answers more than he wants to punish me.

"So how did you pull this off?" he demands. He shows me the papers I signed to get into the Twin Towers. They include his signature, his ID number, his case numbers—in short, all the official chicken scratchings that verify his status as a fed. Not to mention the prisoner numbers, their pod and cell locations, and all the other data that convinced the deputies I had every right to be inside the jail.

It goes without saying that I shouldn't have any of that information. But I dug it from his head.

"Where did you get all of this?" he says, shaking the papers in my face. "Have you hacked into my laptop? That is a serious federal crime, Smith—"

"I'm good with numbers. Saw all that on the paperwork you brought to coffee, and I memorized it—"

"Bullshit. It never left my bag. You never had the chance."

This is what I get for being so cocky. I thought I'd be long gone before Vincent came around to the jail. Now I'm vulnerable. And he knows it.

"You're not going to arrest me," I say.

He glares. "You seem pretty sure of that."

"You want something else. Otherwise, you'd have me in a cell already." I point at the jail. "I mean, we're here anyway."

He nods, slowly. He's still angry, and confused, but he's making a decision. It doesn't really matter how I got all that paperwork. He's got a use for me. He still needs something—or someone—to break open his case.

And now there's no way I can say no.

"So," I say, "you want to tell me over coffee, or are we just going to keep standing out here?"

He's really close to punching me in the face.

But he resists the urge, then straightens his jacket and stalks away.

Coffee it is, then.

We sit at a table at the closest Starbucks. Much less friendly this time. He's still glaring at me. Still thinking *<prick>* at me. But then he takes a sip of his coffee, breathes deeply, and says the name he wants me to hear.

"Aaric Stack."

It takes me a moment to place it. Then I snag it. Tech billionaire. Software developer. Currently in some legal trouble, but I can't remember exactly what.

Then I pluck it from Vincent's head. "The guy behind Bankster?"

Vincent makes a face. "He says he's not, but we all know that's bullshit."

I remember most of it now. I read something about this in *Bloomberg Businessweek*, and Vincent's memories fill in for what I can't recall.

The background first: Bankster is a user-friendly, completely untraceable app that enables people to send money back and forth anonymously over the Net.

It's basically the Facebook version of Bitcoin. Not to get too technical, but Bitcoin is a way to transfer funds electronically using a string of data that keeps the identities of both the sender and the recipient a secret. It's a nearly perfectly encrypted system to create and send digital cash all over the world.

The problem with Bitcoin is that it's too difficult for the average Facebook user. It requires a digital wallet, plus some knowledge of coding and encryption. Then you have to find an online Bitcoin exchange that you can trust. One of the most famous online Bitcoin exchanges collapsed after it announced $473 million of its deposits were either lost or stolen. Even if the exchange doesn't fall apart on its own, the value of a Bitcoin itself jumps around like a kid without his Ritalin. Monitoring it makes watching the stock market look simple by comparison. In other words, buying Bitcoin is a chore. Like the earliest PCs, it's still too complicated and too expensive for a mass audience.

But to use Bankster, all you have to do is download the app from one of a hundred different sites and enter a credit-card number. For a small percentage, Bankster will transfer funds electronically between two accounts and encrypt the transaction so it cannot be traced or hacked. And it hides the transfer in the noise of millions of credit-card and financial transactions moving across the globe every second. On the other end, anyplace on the planet, the data is decrypted, and automatically deposited on the recipient's credit card. The record of the transaction deletes itself upon completion, like a Snapchat session.

Which makes it perfect as a payment method for online drug deals, child porn, and gun sales, among other things. The Department of Justice opened an investigation into Bankster, calling it "PayPal for the black market."

This is where it gets interesting. Aaric Stack is a programmer. A tech genius. And a billionaire. He freely admits he came up with the code that enables Bankster to work. He published it, for free, on several websites. The Bankster people took his work and ran with it, but he's got nothing to do with them. He just thought it was an interesting problem, and he believes that digital currency is the future of money.

Now, however, the U.S. Attorney's Office wants him to undo his work. He's facing a legal order to break his own encryption and give the government a door into every transaction Bankster has ever processed.

Stack has refused, so far. He says it's a matter of principle: he doesn't want the government to have the power to see what people are buying and selling. He's said that the ability to spend money might be the last right anyone respects.

The feds want to put Stack in jail for contempt until he decides to be a little more flexible about his principles. The judge has blocked them from enforcing their subpoena while the lawyers argue it out.

That makes Stack, at least technically, a wanted man. There is a federal subpoena waiting in U.S. District Court in Los Angeles for Aaric Stack in the case of *U.S. v. Bankster.*

But right now Stack lives full-time on his yacht, the *Nautilus,* which is currently using GPS to remain a constant twelve nautical miles off the coastline, out in international waters. He was on his boat for a weekend cruise when he first got word of the subpoena. As soon as he got the call from his lawyers, he aimed the *Nautilus* out onto the high seas, beyond the reach of U.S. law, but still close enough for one of his choppers to bring him takeout from San Francisco's best restaurants. And he's stayed there ever since, a man with a satellite Internet link but no nation.

The feds have been content to leave him floating outside their jurisdiction. Stack isn't your average fugitive, after all. He's got money and lawyers, and he's famous enough for the media to be interested if anything bad happens to him.

"And you think Stack is also behind Downvote?" I ask Vincent. "Why?"

"Our tech people noticed some of the same code in the software for Downvote and Bankster."

"Sounds a little thin to me."

"Yeah, well, that's what my bosses think too. Financial crimes has this one, and they don't want to share. And I've told you that Downvote isn't exactly a priority for the FBI. So I can't get to him right now."

"And I can?"

"If you don't want me to throw your ass in jail, you will."

Vincent smiles at me. It's not a pleasant smile.

"Well, when you put it that way," I say, "how can I say no?"

/// 10

Before the Sharks Come

Sara Fitch is a lovely person. Most of the time.

Honestly, she is. We are sitting about half a foot from each other in the leather seats of Aaric Stack's private chopper, on our way to meet him on his yacht. I've been with her for over an hour now, which is more than enough time for me to sift through her thoughts and memories.

You might think your dirtiest secrets or your worst habits or your secret piles of crazy are buried deep inside, way down under layers of guilt and repression, but the mind doesn't always work like that. With most people, the guilt and the weird and the crazy run through everything like a fudge ripple in ice cream. It doesn't take much time or effort at all for me to get the flavor.

And I can say without hesitation that Sara Fitch is a thoroughly good person. You want to know her worst secrets? The evil hidden behind her nearly perfect exterior?

There are times she doesn't tip 20 percent, and she always slams the door on those kids who sell school candy because she doesn't think it's safe for them to be out wandering in strange neighborhoods like that.

That's about it. She got into her job for the right reasons. She likes to help others. She feels bad for the homeless, for stray cats and dogs, and works hard to be kind even when things are exploding around her. What's more, she has a quality that's easy to recognize but hard to define: to me, it almost looks like a shine coming off her. People like her and trust her because they can see it too, even if they lack my talent. It is probably recognition of the simple fact that she appreciates and enjoys her life, and wants to do the right thing.

I instinctively like her a lot, even if she is carrying a Glock 19 in a rig under her jacket and a Smith & Wesson M&P in her bag. Both have more than enough stopping power to put me down easily at this distance.

I can't say I blame her. Sara is Stack's executive protection specialist—his bodyguard. That's why she's carrying the weaponry. Most billionaires have at least one, even if the general public has no idea who they are.

And she's pretty sure I came here to kill her boss.

She may be right. Depends on how our meeting goes.

As soon as Vincent gave me the name, I did some research on Aaric Stack.

I used to disdain that kind of dull, on-screen homework. I was never much for mission briefings when I was doing covert work either. I believed I could grab whatever I needed from my targets' heads—my version of cramming the night before a test.

But on my last big job, I learned the hard way that you can miss important facts, especially when you are dealing with people like Stack, who generate more information than they can comfortably remember, just by existing.

Now I do my homework.

Stack is one of those eccentric geniuses who seem to stumble into exactly the right opportunities as they wander around randomly. The only son of a Bakersfield preacher—Stack's first name is from the Bible, it means "rule with mercy"—and the product of a seemingly idyllic home life. He dropped out of high school and hit the road at sixteen. In interviews, he never really talks about this, saying only he was curious about what was out there beyond farms and oil fields. He made his way to San Francisco, where he got work in a PC repair shop, and despite a lack of any kind of training or degree, began designing and programming computers. One of the shop's customers turned out to be an exec at Sun Microsystems, and the two of them got to talking. He must have said the right things, because within a year he was working for the computer company in its embedded systems division. He began writing code—insanely complex, incredibly smart code. He was recruited by other tech firms and began skipping from one high-paying job to the next, collecting stock options as he went.

Then the first dot-com crash hit, and the tech companies either collapsed or began firing people. Stack, with no degree and no contract, was one of the first people dumped in the layoffs.

But Stack had already cashed out his options—later, he said he was just lucky, he'd been planning to buy a boat—and suddenly had a lot of free time on his hands. He started to play around with the idea of self-correcting, self-programming software, and began researching artificial intelligence.

One day he noticed that he spent most of his time every morning clearing spam out of his inbox. There were spam filters out there, but they rarely seemed to work. Stack would get a spam email promising him an erection like an oak tree, and would click a button to add the sender to his spam filter. But the next morning, there would be a dozen more ads for herbal Viagra and horny housewives and six-pack abs. The spambots—automated software that churned out millions of messages per hour—were too prolific. The spam filters were not smart enough to catch every single cheap ad. Too many of them still looked like regular email.

Stack began to wonder: How could he teach his spam filter to tell the difference between spam and real human communication?

Six months later, he'd created an AI toolkit that stopped almost all spam from reaching his inbox. His software could distinguish between an email sent by a bot and a real person 99.9 percent of the time—a kind of reverse Turing test. He called it GNIRUT.

Eighteen months later, Google bought GNIRUT for $500 million in stock and worked it into the next version of Gmail. Stack took half of the payout and invested it in a bunch of start-ups. At the time he said he felt guilty about having so much money and wanted to help other programmers get their ideas off the ground. One of those companies was Facebook.

Today he's worth about $5 billion. If he felt guilty about being rich before, I imagine he's deeply tormented now.

I had to admit, Vincent was probably right. He looked like a good candidate for the creator of Downvote.

Aside from the lack of any proof.

Of course, I could get that proof easily. All I had to do was get into a room with him. That was going to be the tricky part.

I figured there were two options: a commando-style raid on his yacht, involving some kind of minisubmarine, or the direct approach.

Even though I look pretty damn good in a wet suit, I figured the direct approach was easier. So I made a phone call first. I left a message with his attorneys in San Francisco, telling them I was looking into something that Mr. Stack might be able to help me with. Very polite and courteous.

I didn't expect a return call. I especially did not expect to hear from Stack himself.

"John Smith?"

"Speaking."

"This is Aaric Stack. I was hoping we could talk."

"Go ahead. I'm listening."

"I meant in person. I'd like to have a face-to-face meeting with you. In fact, I'll pay you for your time. I'll give you a hundred thousand as a retainer, up front, just for the meeting."

That, I admit, caught my attention.

"I'm afraid I am already on a job, Mr. Stack, so I can't take on any new clients at the moment."

"I know," he said. "You're working for Armin Sadeghi. You're trying to find out who shot his daughter. How is she, by the way?"

"She's still in a medically induced coma, from what I hear," I say. "In fact, that was what I wanted to talk to you about."

There was a long pause. "I know," he said. "You want to ask me about Downvote."

I hesitated. There are times I really wish my talent worked over the phone. All I could think to ask was "What can you tell me about it?"

He gave a heavy sigh. "Well," he said, "I think I might be responsible for it."

So I said yes to the meeting. I drove up the Five and met Sara Fitch at a private helipad on the North Shore, where we got into Stack's helicopter for the run out to the yacht.

She's wearing standard business attire, good bag, sensible shoes, minimal makeup. And the guns, of course.

She's been perfectly pleasant on the surface, but over and over in her head, she keeps thinking the same thing.

<so stupid> <so stupid> <so stupid> <why not just paint a target on Aaric while I'm at it?>

Like I said before, she's usually a lot sunnier than she feels right now. She's one of those genuinely resilient, optimistic people who manage to bounce back from whatever hits her. I don't meet too many of them. It's an odd sensation for me. It's like her mind has the faint scent of fresh linens.

But she doesn't see any silver lining here today. If it was up to her, we'd be doing this meeting over FaceTime. Or not at all.

For her, it's simple. Her job is to keep Stack safe. I am a potential threat to that safety, because I harbor the belief—possibly justified—that Stack helped create a situation that put a friend of mine in the hospital. And killed a half-dozen innocent people, and wounded almost two dozen more.

I can sense the frustration coming off her like steam. I can't blame her. If Stack were my client, I wouldn't let someone like me within a hundred miles of him.

But Stack insisted. He seems to think he can talk to me. Convince me. Or buy me.

He's still her boss. So despite her best instincts, we're about to land on his yacht.

I read about it, but even I was unprepared to see it in person—and I've spent a lot of time around rich people and their toys.

For starters, "boat" doesn't begin to describe it. Even the word "yacht" is too small. It's more like a cruise ship. An aircraft carrier. Or, more accurately, a hotel put on its side and made to float.

It's 460 feet long—or about forty-three stories, which is the same height as Caesars Palace in Las Vegas. There are two helipads on deck, and an Olympic-size swimming pool. And, like a baby nestled in the arms of its mother, there's a smaller yacht—a mere forty-footer—docked at the back of the *Nautilus*. I've read that the entire thing can be steered from a flat black touchscreen the size of an iPad; the usual captain and crew have been replaced by fully automated systems run by a software engine designed by Stack himself.

It looks invulnerable. You can see nothing but ocean for miles in any direction. From here, Stack could fire up his engines and head for any number of nonextradition treaty countries. Or he could just stay out here, floating in luxury.

Still, having been involved in more than a few black-bag renditions, I know there's nothing that would really stop the government from just grabbing Stack if it wants. The Justice Department can always drop a team of U.S. marshals on his deck, put him in cuffs, and then argue the legal niceties later.

A guy as smart as Stack has to know this too. He must realize he can't bob out here in the surf forever.

Which is probably one big reason I'm here.

He needs a solution before the sharks come to get him.

The helicopter lands on the *Nautilus*'s forward pad like it's been drawn in on a string. Not an easy trick in the middle of the ocean. Whatever Stack's paying the pilot, it's not enough. Sara exits the chopper ahead of me, but waits to escort me down the staircase into the yacht's lounge.

That's when she decides to frisk me. "Raise your arms, please," she says.

I try not to take it personally, but I also want to establish some boundaries.

"You know, you invited me."

That stops her in her tracks. "I didn't," she says shortly. "Aaric did."

"Figure of speech. What I meant was, if you really don't want me here, I don't have to be here."

She hesitates. Her job is to control the situation, and she's given up a lot already. She considers saying *fuck it* and canceling the meeting altogether.

But this is what Stack wants, and she told him she'd do her best to make it happen. It's more than an order from a boss. It's actual trust. She believes he knows what he is doing.

She steps back slightly. Raises her hands in surrender.

And she gives me a warning.

"You had better not hurt him," she says. There is something plaintive and vulnerable in it. I don't get a single note of sexual attachment or romantic feeling from her—she is not involved with Stack that way—but this is more than professional for her.

I don't remember ever having this much affection for any of my clients, and I am actually a little envious. Stack has risen a notch in my estimation if he can inspire this kind of feeling. It's nice to be reminded that for some people, loyalty is more than a paycheck.

Not that it will slow me down if he had anything to do with the attack on Kira, of course.

I give her my best smile and say, "You have nothing to worry about."

That does nothing to put her mind at ease. She thinks about her guns again. Then begins leading me toward her boss.

Despite what I've read, the *Nautilus* isn't entirely unmanned. There are casually dressed crew members waiting for us. They keep an easy distance. They've got smiles on their faces, but I can see that Sara has briefed them to watch out for me. They're ready to jump at me if she gives the word.

Sara walks me past them, keeping her hands free, tension ratcheted up inside.

I get a good look around the *Nautilus*. It's massive, and massively impressive. Being inside feels like getting hit with a gilded hammer over and over. Sara walks me past a formal dining room, a small movie theater, a library lined floor to ceiling with books, and a racquetball court. Off to one side is what can only be called a trophy room. I get a glimpse of geek treasures like Captain America's shield, a portal gun, the Right Hand of Doom, a transporter pod. It's the only area on the boat that seems to have any personality. Everything else looks like it was ordered straight out of a decorator's catalog.

We turn down another corridor, and then Sara comes to a surprisingly small and ordinary-looking door. She presses a button on the wall. There's a chime, and a voice from the other side says, "Come in."

Despite the yacht's size, Stack's office is tiny—a little round room crammed to capacity with computers, screens, cables, and, behind a curved table that circles him like a belt, Stack himself.

I do my best to cover my surprise, but Stack has changed drastically from the pictures I've seen. The photos that accompany his Wikipedia page and news articles showed a typical geek: soft in the middle and around the edges, a smiling round face on a doughy body.

Now he looks like a walking skeleton. He has burned himself down to a wire-frame version of his former self, all sharp angles and hollow cheekbones. His formerly frizzy hair is shaved to stubble on his scalp, and his neck looks like a pipe cleaner supporting his head.

He is starving. Hunger has become his default state. I feel a void the size of a bowling ball in his stomach. There is half of a single protein bar on the desk next to him. He takes a small nibble and folds it in its wrapper again. He feels a thrill of victory and control as he swallows, even as the void inside him echoes with even greater hunger. He stands and greets us, smiling.

Sara approaches the desk and leans over to kiss him on the cheek. He smiles even more widely, and I get pure affection for her coming from him. Nothing sexual, which I find odd because, well, I've seen her. In most straight men, it's never far from our thoughts. But that part of him seems to be buried deep.

She introduces me, and Stack offers his hand. We shake, and it's like holding a handful of pencils. I scan him, like I do most people when we first meet.

I get the slightly dizzying impression of a stratosphere-high IQ. He's not the first genius I've met, and I've learned the hard way that I might be able to read their minds, but I can't always understand them. However, their actual memories and feelings are usually much easier. Nobody's very smart when it comes down to the raw emotions curled up close to the limbic system, where we're all still reeling between our hurts and wants and needs, some going back to infancy.

For the most part, Stack is calm. I met a billionaire investor and software designer not too long ago whose mind was like a deep freeze, all cold calculation. Stack is a big stuffed teddy bear compared to him. He uses his considerable intellect to focus on the here and now, to anchor himself in the present moment.

Still, I can see an old scab, way down deep. I know better than to pick at it, but along with the hunger and the design of the room, his damage is pretty obvious.

Sara takes a post by the door. She has no intention of leaving. Standard bodyguard protocol: never leave the client unattended.

Stack smiles at her. "It's okay," he says. "You can go."

"No," she says. "I can't."

Stack is flattered. But he's not worried. He laughs. "I told Sara you probably wouldn't try to kill me until after you'd heard my offer," he says. "Otherwise, how would you get paid?" He waves her away. "It's fine. Really. Give us a minute."

Sara bristles at being both dismissed and discussed between the two men as if she wasn't in the room.

"It's a bad idea," she says to Stack.

I stay quiet. I could easily say something smartass—and honest—here about how I'm already close enough to do whatever damage I want. But I get no fear from Stack. No trace of a guilty conscience. If anything, he seems to want to be helpful. So I don't want to antagonize either of them.

Sara fights with herself for another moment, then gives me a warning look. "Behave," she says, and points a finger at me. Then she leaves.

Once the door is closed, Stack shrugs in a sort of apology. "She takes my safety a lot more seriously than I do," he says.

"You should be grateful," I say, meaning it. "That's going to keep you alive."

He smiles again. "Yeah, well, we'll see," he says. He's thinking of federal prison, mainly, but I still don't get any guilt. Just a kind of resignation.

Then he waves me to the only other seat, a simple chair that could have been bought in bulk at IKEA. I sit down.

"Thank you for coming," he says. He is bright and cheerful, despite the problems mounting for him back onshore.

"Like you said, you're paying for it," I tell him.

He nods. "I want you to know something right up front," he says. "I know about you."

By which he means he's heard about me, and my abilities. And my reputation.

That makes sense. I get most of my work by word of mouth and gossip among people in Stack's tax bracket. Some of them start out skeptical, but I've got a fairly convincing track record.

"So you know what I can do."

"I've heard about it," he says. "I've even seen a copy of your CIA file."

"You know, the word 'classified' just doesn't mean what it used to."

"Come on. You are one of the covert world's worst-kept secrets. There are guys who pass your file around like it's a bootleg copy of the next Marvel script. You can't be surprised."

I can't say I am. The truth about me—and the operatives like me, Cantrell's other special-ed kids—has been out there for years. There have been books, magazine articles, documentaries, cable TV specials, even congressional hearings: *the truth about America's psychic soldier program, revealed at last*. If you look hard enough, you can find the line items on the budgets that funded us.

But nobody believes it's true. Serious grown-ups aren't supposed to believe in ESP, even if they check their horoscopes every day. It's a kind of built-in cover. And for my clients, it's a kind of additional layer of exclusivity. They get firsthand knowledge of something that the common herd thinks is nothing more than an urban legend.

The smile fades. "I hope you don't mind," he says, "but I would like to conduct a small—well, I hate to use the word 'test,' but—"

"You want to make sure I really can do what I say I can do."

"Exactly. I hope you'll understand it's not a lack of trust. I am genuinely fascinated as to how someone like you works. So I've designed a simple protocol that should establish a baseline by which—"

I'm sure he has. He loves doing stuff like that. But we've both got better things to do. So I skip ahead.

"I could tell you that you were playing a beta of a new game from a friend of yours at Blizzard before I entered the room. Gaming always relaxes you before a big meeting. Or I could give you the name of the lawyer who called you this morning to discuss the latest developments with the federal case—he was supposed to call at ten, but he was almost twenty minutes late—and I could tell you he said that the judge is leaning toward forcing you to make a personal appearance."

Stack looks surprised, but reflexively comes up with alternative explanations. *<could have monitored my email>* *<hacked my computer>* *<could have tapped the call>* He's about to mouth those objections out loud. He really wants to use his test protocol.

"But if that doesn't convince you, I could always tell you what happened when you were five years old," I say.

Stack recoils as much as he is able behind the desk in the small space.

Tears well up in his eyes, and I get a sharp, painful glimpse of the wound deep in his core. He has done something wrong. He has been banned from the family table again and shut in a dark room. There are footsteps in the hallway, and I can feel his fear and dread as the door opens and his father is silhouetted in the light from the hall—

And then he slams it shut before any more memories can intrude. He breathes in deeply, practicing techniques he's learned from a dozen therapists and yoga instructors and gurus.

"I'd really rather not," I tell him.

"Okay," he says. "That's enough. I believe you. I appreciate you not going into detail. That is kind of you."

I'd love to take the points but I can't. "Not especially," I say. "I don't want to experience your memories." Even secondhand pain hurts. I've got enough of my own.

"That's fair. It's not your burden," he says. "And I wouldn't wish it on you. I think we can say you've passed the test."

I nod. We're done with the preliminaries. "So why am I here?"

There it is, right at the front of his head. That one word again.

"Downvote," he says. It sounds like an echo to me. "I know you're looking for the guy behind it."

"I am," I say. "There's a federal agent named Vincent who thinks it might be you."

He shakes his head hard. "No," he says. "It's not me."

He's not lying. It doesn't matter that he knows I can read minds. Even if he tried to hide it, I'd still be able to see the truth in his head. Even if he had a split-personality disorder or some deeply repressed memory, I'd still be able to see the place where his memories had been torn and stitched over. People can lie to themselves all the time. But never to me.

But there is something he wants to confess.

"But that's why I wanted you here. I do think I bear some responsibility—"

There is a great tidal surge of memory and guilt. I see emails, instant messages, late-night chat sessions; hundreds of screenshots all scrolling through Stack's memories.

"You know him."

Stack nods. "I worked with him. For a long time."

He pauses. I know what he's going to say next, but I let him get it out. He needs to say it out loud.

"And I think I helped him build Downvote."

///11

It's Easier to Make It a Weapon

I hold up a hand to keep Stack from saying anything else. "If you're about to confess to me, I should warn you. I'm not a lawyer or a priest. If I get pulled in front of a judge—"

"You think I don't know that?" he asks. Stack doesn't roll his eyes at me, but there's a brief blast of scorn from him all the same. It's like a burst of hot air from a hair dryer, quickly snapped off. He's spent years trying to scour any trace of arrogance or superiority from his soul, working toward his own vision of peace. *<positive intent>* *<didn't mean anything by it>* *<breathe>* Still, it slips through sometimes. Being smart was the only advantage he had once, and now, if someone questions his intelligence—even indirectly, as I just did—those defenses come back. Sometimes the clichés are true. Especially the one about old habits.

"I know you are just trying to help," he says. *<positive intent>* *<breathe>* "But really, it doesn't matter. I think you'll see why, if you let me explain."

I nod. True, I could grab everything Stack is about to say direct from his head. But I can't download his intelligence. I need the Easy Reader version if I'm going to comprehend what happened. So I want him to translate into plain English.

He settles into his chair and gears up. "First, how much do you know about the Net? Coding? Massive social networks? Ever read any Jaron Lanier?"

I smile patiently. "I use email," I tell him. "The rest of the time I'm usually pretty busy in the real world."

He sighs heavily. "Oh God, a digital Philistine. This is going to be worse than pitching investors." But he's smiling. He really does love explaining this stuff. "Don't you know by now? The Net *is* the real world. Everything out there is just a pale shadow."

"Yeah, I've heard that before. I still haven't seen anyone get killed because of a computer program."

The smile vanishes, and a dark shadow passes through his mind. The memory of an image on his screen. A dead body. He shoves it away quickly, and goes back into his story.

He tells me he was looking around for his next project. He'd spent enough time being an idle billionaire playboy. He had his yacht, he had a personal chef and a hot female bodyguard. He felt like he'd hit most of the check marks on his personal list of life goals. So his intellectual curiosity began to grow again. Just like he did with spam emails, he began with something he found personally annoying.

"I wondered why people are always such colossal dicks to one another online," he says.

"Really?" I say. "I hadn't noticed."

My sarcasm whistles past his head like a fastball. "Take a look at the comments section on any news story. Or go on Twitter or Facebook. You give people a chance to say whatever they want without consequences and they almost always turn vicious. Even the so-called nice people. People who won't correct the waiter when they get the order wrong. They'll sit there and eat food they didn't order rather than have an unpleasant conversation. But you get them on a computer—"

"And they're not polite anymore. Right."

"Oh, it's worse than that. A lot worse."

And then he hits a few buttons and the screens all around me light up with the site itself. Downvote.

It's the first time I've seen it out in reality, and not in someone's memory. On the front page is the name of the site, followed by the slogans:

SHOW THEM WHAT YOU THINK OF THEM

HOLD THEM ACCOUNTABLE

MAKE THEM PAY

Then there is the Big Board—the list of the most hated people on the Internet, as decided by the people who come to Downvote. Some I recognize—the president, of course, and a couple actors and actresses—but many I don't. Clicking on their names, Stack shows that each comes with a small biography, a collection of everything that can be gleaned from the Net about them by the Downvoters: Facebook photos, profile information, even home and work addresses and cell-phone numbers. They could be anyone. Anywhere.

Beyond the front page are the message boards, where the Downvoters argue for their choices.

As I said, I'm not a big social media guy. I spend enough time in people's heads as it is, getting everything they've got live and unfiltered. Aside from pictures of their cats, I figured I'd already seen whatever they could possibly show me.

But even I'm surprised by the sheer level of unfocused rage that pours out of the screen.

Wormwood2311: what a waste of skin.

PresidentBusiness19: If I see this fag in the street, I will pull my Glock from its concealed-carry holster and give him a few new holes!

HeavingStalking says: goddamn cucks wasting our vital heritage makes me ashamed to be an American.

DashGorgon: It's the Jews controlling the media, shoving these fuckin ragheads down our throats. can't wait to see them all choking the gas chambers.

And it always comes back to rape. Dozens of rape threats. This was from a string of messages about an actress who had sued a hacker who stole a bunch of nude selfies from her phone:

Fuck that bitch. I'm not going to stop spreading her disgusting nudes around and making sure her life is a living hell until she either kills yourself or I rape her to death.

i hope she gets raped

only question is will she be raped first or killed first

ill do it imma kill her and then rape her

i swear i would put this bitch 6 feet deep

I've done some unquestionably evil things. I've killed. I've tortured. I can say I was just following orders or doing a job, or even that they were worse than me, but I can't change the facts. I've hurt people.

But even if I don't have much of a conscience, I have limits.

These people blow past them. They talk about violating people like they're ordering something through the drive-through window.

And they have no goddamn idea what they are talking about. I wonder if any of them have ever experienced actual pain. If they know what it does to you just to watch real violence happen, just to be close to it. If they know the difference between video games and spy movies and real life.

Or if they are just that dead inside.

I'm certain none of these people see this, but it is like a suicide hotline. Every one of these posts is a cry for help: *I'm sad, I'm angry, I'm disappointed my life isn't as good as someone else's, there's nothing I like on TV, and I'm bored.*

I get to see this all the time—every dirty thought, every deeply hidden prejudice, every secret hate. There is a constant throb of barely contained rage going on in the minds of almost every person around me. I see what's going on behind the polite smiles.

But I don't have any choice about the crap that comes streaming into my brain from all the angry, disappointed people around me. I don't know why anyone would do this to themselves voluntarily.

I search for the words. "That's pretty awful," I say.

"Yeah," Stack agrees. "You get death threats, rape threats, and racist slurs. And then they get inventive. And I kept wondering why. When I began programming, we all thought computers would make us better people. That we'd get better at communicating. Not worse."

"You were wrong."

"But I wanted to know why. So I started doing research. I went onto the message boards and into the forums. I figured that was the best place to start. And I kept asking, 'Hey, why are so many people such dicks when they're on a computer?'"

He smiles. I can see some of the responses in his head. *<fuck u lol> <toughen up fag> <don't like it then turn off your computer you fucking pussy>*

"At the very least, I got some firsthand experience. But I didn't give up. And pretty soon I started to get responses from some other programmers who wondered the same thing. One of them called himself Godwin. We messaged back and forth for hours. We both wanted to know: Why did so much of the Internet turn into junior high school? That's never what any of us intended when we started."

I get another flash of a painful memory from Stack. In the hallway of his school, a group of jocks shoving him aside, spilling his books onto the floor, in a casual display of their teenage might and invulnerability. The last days of jock culture in America, when the word "geek" was still an insult and guys like Stack had to hide their comic books or get the crap kicked out of them by the football team. But then the Internet changed everything. It became cool to be smart. No matter how weird your fetish or how specific your taste, you could find someone else out there who shared it. The Internet connected everyone in one big, worldwide family.

At least, that was how it was supposed to work. In reality, the bullies still existed online.

"So Godwin and I began to talk about how we could make people better. How we could push them into behaving online."

I must look skeptical, because Stack stops and asks, "You don't think it's possible, do you?"

I consider all the ways I could answer that question, but I decide to be honest. "In my experience, people are who they are," I tell him. "They don't change."

He smirks a little. "You sure about that?"

I give him a look. I spend all my time inside other people's heads. I've tried pushing their thoughts into some kind of order through sheer force of will. And I've seen how they insist on barreling down their own personal course of destruction, no matter how many roadblocks are in the way.

"Pretty sure," I say.

"Ah, but you're wrong," he says, and he spins one of the screens around to show me a bunch of charts and graphs. "I knew we could change people's minds. You just have to apply the right pressure. Look at what Facebook did a couple of years ago. They made people feel sad by adding depressing news stories to their news feeds. And they prodded people into voting on election day by including 'I Voted' buttons on their pages. And it worked. It's a technique called massive emotional contagion. It's possible to spread an emotional state or a mood over social media—just like a computer virus, only it affects the users, not the computers. In other words, Facebook was willfully screwing with the heads of their users—and then they bragged about how it worked. They published papers on it. And that's just what they admitted to. What happens if a piece of legislation comes up in Congress that Mark Zuckerberg doesn't like? Or if there's a presidential candidate he wants to see in the White House? What does Facebook start pushing to its users then?"

"You're saying people can be steered. Pushed into behaving certain ways."

"Exactly. Godwin and I figured out we could do the same thing. Only we could go even further. We could make people act nice by spreading different kinds of emotional contagion. We wanted to develop an algorithm that would do just that. We needed a way to force them into being better versions of themselves."

He looks a little guilty here, and I sense a small amount of discomfort. In his moment of hesitation, I can see what he did. I don't have his technical genius, and I certainly don't understand the lines of code stringing through his mind, but I get the intent.

"You created a virus," I say.

He looks surprised. "No!" he says. Then he reconsiders. "Well. I wouldn't call it a virus, exactly."

"What would you call it?"

"Stealth software. A tiny little package of code. Small enough to be contained in a cookie from a website. Once you clicked on the site, it would download itself onto your computer, and it would start showing you nice things. It would add itself to your social media feeds, and begin scouring the Net for good stuff. Happy families. Puppies and kittens. Firefighters rescuing babies. You know. Things that would make you more positive. Emotional contagion, but in a good way."

"Sunshine and lollipops and rainbows," I say. "This sounds like a great advertising trick. But I don't see how you're supposed to make it into a weapon."

He rolls his eyes, and impatience simmers in him. "Are you serious? It's *easier* to make it a weapon. That was where we started."

I wait. He realizes what just came out of his mouth. *<whoops>*

"I don't mean we started out designing a weapon. It really was supposed to be benign," he says. "But first, we had to look at what drives people. What pushes them into action. And that's where you run into the limits of the hardware. You should know exactly what I mean."

"The human brain," I say. "Yeah. I'm familiar."

"Right, of course," he says, remembering who he's talking to. "Well, that was the point. For everything we've done in the last couple of centuries, we're still talking about a lump of tissue designed by evolution to keep an ape alive. Our forebrain—the part that's supposed to do all our finer thinking, that's supposed to control our basic impulses—that's like a new upgrade, in terms of human evolution, maybe two hundred and fifty million years old. Practically still fresh from the factory. Our emotions, though—they're wired down much deeper, close to the spinal cord. That's the part that handles all the stuff we need to deal with to survive. And that's the part that takes over when we feel threatened. That part of our brain is still the big boss when it comes to setting priorities. Fear. Greed. Hunger. Lust. We had to learn how to design our software to trigger those basic emotions first, before we could move on to the nicer ones."

Despite what I saw at Kira's wedding—and inside the minds of the shooters—I'm not convinced. He's moved into an area I do know something about, from my time in the army and the CIA. Part of my training involved looking deep into what makes people behave, and what makes them follow orders. Because I was expected to do both, but I was also expected to use my talents to make other people do the same thing. I needed to know how the operating system inside people's heads worked, and how it could be manipulated. And it's not as easy as Stack makes it sound.

"I don't buy it," I tell him. "It takes a lot of work to make one soldier do what he's told. Months of training. Group dynamics that reward teamwork and conformity. A rigidly enforced hierarchy with constant supervision and monitoring. That's what any army is, when you get right down to it. And it still breaks down all the time. People disobey orders. They slack off. They go AWOL. There are soldiers who put down their guns in the middle of combat rather than shoot a kid, no matter what it might cost them. Or they'll wander off into Taliban territory because they believe everyone else around them is wrong. But you're certain you can get people to dance like puppets on strings with a few Facebook posts."

Stack smiles, as if I've just proven his point. I can hear him say *<aha!>* in his head, like Sherlock explaining the bloody obvious to Watson.

"That's the beauty of it," he says. "We didn't *need* people to follow orders. Whoever gets exposed to this will go out and do what I want because they think it's their own idea. For better or worse, the Internet is our nervous system now. Someone pokes us on social media, we lash out like we're actually hurt. I present them with the right input, and they react. All we had to do is play on their emotions. Fear. Anger. Hate. I'm not building an army. I'm opening a floodgate."

I am still not convinced. "So what are they going to do? Most of them won't get up out of their chairs. You know this. They might send an angry email. And then they'll go back to looking for porn or watching Netflix."

The irritation flares up again, and he loses his temper. "Oh yeah? Well, I know it works, because we did it!"

Then he stops. But I've already seen it.

I get a name. <*Gary Holmes*>

"Who's Gary Holmes?" I ask, and suddenly I see guilt blossom inside Stack. I get several images. A guy in the crowd at a baseball game, holding a foul ball. A kid with the unmistakable shaved head of a cancer patient. And it comes back to me. I'd forgotten the name, but not the story.

Stack looks away. And I get that image again.

A dead body. Holmes, his corpse like something washed up by the tide, bloated and dead-eyed in a cheap apartment.

And suddenly it's clear to me. "You tested it."

Stack looks down at the surface of his desk and sinks into himself. Despite his age and wealth, I feel like I'm seeing a child sitting in his seat right now. I hear echoes of a second grader when he speaks again.

"I thought we had to know," he says quietly.

Stack talks, but it comes spooling out of his memories quicker. Gary Holmes was in the crowd at a D-backs game last summer when Paul Goldschmidt knocked a foul up into the stands in the eighth inning. The camera followed the ball as it came down, right toward the waiting glove of eleven-year-old Justin Richards. Everyone around him backed off to let the kid have it.

Except Holmes. Who hauled himself out of his seat two rows away and used his 290-pound bulk to knock Justin aside, sending him flying over the railing. He then snagged the ball and did a victory dance.

The entire stadium saw it on the Jumbotron and booed. Holmes did not react with grace. He flipped the crowd off. Repeatedly. He spat on the people in the stands nearest to him. He grabbed his crotch. He was taking down his pants to moon the crowd by the time security got to him. The clip was played repeatedly on *SportsCenter* that night, and the rest of the country got to see him too.

It got worse. It turned out that Justin was at the game as part of a Make-A-Wish group of pediatric cancer patients. Doctors gave him maybe a year.

Holmes could have ended it there by just apologizing and giving the kid the stupid ball, but he refused. When a local TV reporter asked him why he'd knocked an eleven-year-old senseless for a foul ball, he decided that this would be his fifteen minutes. "Hey," he said, "there are winners and losers in this world. He's got cancer? I got the ball. Life's tough."

It went viral. He went on CNN and dug himself even deeper. ("Look, all I'm saying is that if he really wanted the ball, he shoulda fought harder for it.") For a couple of days, Gary Holmes was the most hated man in America.

And then the Kardashians did something or there was another mass shooting. People found something else to care about. They moved on.

"What did you do?" I ask Stack.

He hesitates again. His clean ideas and good intentions have taken a dive right into the muck.

"We thought—I thought—he would be a good test case. I figured we could get people to rally around him, make him give the foul ball back. So we entered him into the program. Sent it out into the wild. People who clicked on the news story would get more and more news about him. And they would be motivated to do something about it. I thought we could shame him. If enough people got angry—"

He stops.

"What makes you so sure your program had something to do with his death?"

"I didn't. I mean, not at first. He didn't give the ball back. In fact, he just seemed to get worse. He tried to become a celebrity. He got an agent. Then he dropped out of the news. I figured the software needed more tweaking. Godwin and I went back to work on it. Then I got a news alert a couple of months later. He was dead."

The police thought it was a simple home invasion. Holmes lost his job, got divorced, moved to L.A. for some reality-TV thing that never worked out—and then moved back to a really shitty neighborhood in Phoenix. The media pulled out the clip of him knocking the cancer kid senseless again, and nobody really mourned.

Except Stack. He wondered if their software had something to do with it. He scoured the Internet for clues.

Stack found a photo of Holmes's dead body that was posted on a message board, along with a boast from an anonymous user: YOU'RE OUT.

That was all the confirmation Stack needed. He was sure his program had led to this.

"I told Godwin we couldn't do this anymore," he says now. "He was angry. He said we really had something important. Valuable. We had to keep going. I told him no. I wanted to wipe out every copy of the code. Clearly we didn't know what we were dealing with. And I thought that was going to be the end of it."

I see the text messages and emails in his memories. Lots of back-and-forth. But in the end, Godwin agreed. He said he'd erase his copies of the program. Stack went back to focusing on his anonymous payment application. He thought it was over.

And suddenly I get it. For all his intelligence, he couldn't see through someone else's lies.

"Godwin took the code, didn't he?" I ask, even though I already know the answer.

In response, Stack sags a little more in his seat. He points at the screens.

"It's in here," he says. "As soon as I heard about this online, I checked. It's hidden in the site. Every visitor gets that code we designed together."

He taps a few more buttons, spins the screen to show me again. A list.

"Look. Atlanta, Georgia. Local weatherman gets the crap kicked out of him after getting busted for a DUI near a school zone. Gay-rights activist in Los Angeles put into the ICU. Radio talk-show host gets a bomb threat. Woman in D.C. caught flipping off the camera at a veterans' memorial has her credit rating and her tires slashed. Mom in Iowa who slapped her kid in a grocery store gets fired, gets a visit from child services, gets rear-ended while out driving. Jason Davis is attacked by a stalker while he's walking his dog."

"And Kira Sadeghi," I remind him.

Stack nods. "And Kira Sadeghi. Every one of those people was on Downvote. Celebrities are easiest to target. They're already out there, in front of the public. But you can make someone into a celebrity too. Think about all those people who have lost their jobs because they posted something stupid on Facebook or Twitter. For a couple of hours or a couple of days, they're worse than Hitler. Anyone could be a target. It doesn't even matter if it's true. The online mob will take them down."

I remember everything I pulled from Goetz's head, how he was repeatedly pummeled with images and clips of Kira. The algorithm found him, identified him, and kept feeding him fuel for his rage.

He wasn't alone. And now I realize, he wasn't the only one either.

This is why Vincent had developed such hostility toward Kira and Jason Davis after visiting Downvote. He didn't realize it, but he'd been targeted by the software too. It had started pushing every negative fact it could find toward him. He got to see them at their worst every time he clicked on his computer. Of course, he didn't take his sidearm and start shooting at them because Vincent is, more or less, stable and sane. But someone who's already on the borderline . . .

"Lone gunmen," I say, taking the words right out of his mind. "Borderline personalities. People who are at the breaking point."

"The crazies," Stack says, nodding. "The ones who are looking for a reason, for something to fix on because their minds are already coming apart. There are a surprising number of them out there at any given moment. And when it all comes together for them, they've finally got someone to blame for everything miserable in their lives. They'll jump out from behind the computer and go after the bad guys. They've finally got a target."

Now I can see it the way he does, the picture that's suspended crystal clear in his head. It looks like one of those maps from a movie where the zombie virus spreads, or the missiles are flying in a World War III simulation. A red spot appears in San Francisco or Iowa City or Jacksonville. Red lines leap across the map. More red spots wherever they land. And then, when the map is covered in red, there are sudden explosions, thousands of miles away from the original outbreaks.

"Emotional contagion," Stack says. "Like you said. A virus. And it's getting worse. Most of the people won't do anything, of course. But they'll spread the message. They might send an email. Or share the idea along their networks. And if it's the right idea—if it hits just the right notes—then it's going to hit critical mass. Millions of people will see it. And in most cases, I only need a few to go out and do something about it."

We both sit for a moment after that. Stack, with his guilt. Me, I'm just trying to put it all together.

After a long moment, I finally ask the obvious question.

"So what do you want me to do about it?"

Stack unwraps his half of a protein bar again. Takes another tiny nibble. Wraps it up and places it back on the desk. God, he's hungry.

"You know I've got my own problems with the federal government right now," he says. "I know this is going to sound selfish. I'm not guilty of what they think I've done. But I could give them something else, something that would stop people from getting really hurt—"

"You want to trade Godwin to the feds. Get yourself off the hook, get them to focus on him."

I see his defenses go up. "It's not just about saving myself," he insists. "Godwin has to be stopped."

"Fine," I say. I don't really care about his justifications or his excuses to himself. As long as he gives me the guy who put Kira in the hospital. "Tell me where to find him. I'll handle it from there."

He smiles. There's a little dance of amusement in his brain. "Well. That's where we run into a problem," he says.

And I see it. I scan all the memories I can find. Same answer.

"You don't *know* his real name?"

He shrugs. "We only ever collaborated online. That's how I do ninety-nine percent of all my work now. He could have been a guy in a wheelchair or a twelve-year-old girl in a trailer park, for all I cared. His ideas were what mattered."

"You worked with him. You built an entire software platform with him," I say. "And you never once got his actual name?"

I'm slightly incredulous. Not that I don't believe him. I just don't believe people can operate this way. No wonder he can't go to the feds with this. Or even his lawyers. It's not the worst excuse I've ever heard, but it's close.

"You really don't work in tech, do you?" Stack asks, and he's actually grinning now. "I couldn't tell you the real names of most of the people I talk to every day. I have no idea what they look like. Or if they're male or female or something else entirely. They're screen names to me. I know their voices from what they type. I could identify any of them from a few lines of code or text. But they could walk right by me in the street and I'd never even glance at them."

I give him a long look. I don't find this nearly as amusing as he does.

He must see something in my face, because inside his head, it's suddenly all shields up, and he's leaning back hard on his belief in his superior intellect. "This is how the world works now," he insists. "Ideas are more important than what you look like, or where you're from. That's all just meat. The ideas are what matter. I would think that someone like you would understand that."

I take a long look around at his high-tech womb, the tight little space he's carved out for himself at the center of his floating fortress.

And then I look back at him. "Until someone from the real world decides to reach out and touch you. I think you would understand that."

He shrinks from me, mentally and physically. But he nods.

/// 12

I Need You to Be Smarter

Sara rides back with me in the helicopter. Her mind is a little less troubled than before, but it's hardly a calm blue ocean. She's pleased that Stack was unharmed when I stepped out of his office, but she's still got something she wants to say to me.

"You taking the job?" she asks.

"I'm not sure," I tell her. It's the truth. I don't know if Stack will really help me find Godwin or not. It's a good lead. And he's got resources that Armin can't match. But his offer comes with strings attached. One of which is sitting right next to me.

"If you're going to work for us—" she begins.

"*With* you," I say. "Not for you. With you."

"Either way. We need to set some ground rules first. I know some of the things you've done," she says.

"You know what I can do?" I ask her.

"I know what you *say* you can do," she answers carefully. Of course, she's also got the standard, more honest response: *<such a load>* *<but what if it's not?>* *<yeah then he'd be reading my mind right now>*.

"That's right, I am," I tell her. "I really can read minds. I thought you'd want to know that up front. I find it saves time."

She stares at me for a second. *<son of a bitch>*

"Yeah. A lot of people have that reaction."

While she's digesting that, I scan her mind to find out what she knows about me.

I learn that Stack shared my file with her. In addition to the file, she's also done her due diligence. Executive protection is still a fairly small field. There are a lot of people who claim to have CIA and Special Forces backgrounds, and Sara has had a lot of experience checking into that. She was able to reach out to a lot of people who have worked with me, and got more information from people she knows in the military.

She's assembled a fairly complete picture of me, and the view from inside her head isn't exactly flattering. It's as if there is smoke all around me, a kind of darkness I carry. There are numbers in her mind: my body count, a tally of lives lost because of me, either directly or indirectly. There is a former tech CEO who now goes into seizures whenever he tries to sit in front of a computer. A corpse found on the roof of a mall in Dubai. And further back, a list of names of people who got on the wrong side of the War on Terror.

I am a little impressed that she's still willing to sit this close to me. I am not sure I would do that, given some of the stuff on my résumé.

And that is why she wants to talk to me.

"Listen. Here's the way it is," she says. *<okay>* *<stick to the subject>* *<focus>* "You are not in the military anymore. And you are not being hired as a hit man. We do not want to see people diving off rooftops. Or getting blown to pieces on the Santa Monica pier. This is our one non-negotiable condition. No killing."

I can't say I enjoy how she's looking at me right now. I'd like to say she's wrong. I'd like to mount some kind of defense of myself here. I'd like to say, I have done only what I've had to do to protect myself and my clients. And that I never enjoyed it. That would be the professional response.

But it wouldn't be true.

Perhaps predictably, I get a little angry. And I try to turn it back on her.

"What do you think you do for a living?" I ask her. "If someone were to take a shot at Stack, would you just sit there? Or would you shoot back?" She was prepared to put a bullet in me if I threatened him, after all.

But she doesn't seem at all bothered by the question. In fact, she's got an answer all ready for me.

"Look. In this world, there are sheep, and there are wolves. You're a sheep—hey, you're a good person, a solid citizen. You keep your head down and do your taxes on time. But you're easy prey for the wolves. Those are the people who prey on the sheep. The people who are willing to break the rules of the pasture and hurt and kill so they can take whatever they want. So you have to have sheepdogs. People who can do the same things the wolves can, but who choose not to—unless they have to. Someone to protect the sheep. Show their fangs to keep the wolves at bay."

I've heard this before. It's popular with a lot of Special Forces types. I've never bought it. "And that's you?" I ask.

"That's me. And that's you too, if we're going to work together."

"So I can bark, but not bite?"

She frowns. "Don't play dumb with me," she says. "Do what you have to, but no more than that. Someone tries to hurt you, you figure it out, but whatever you do, you will not leave a trail of bodies that goes back to my boss."

"So it's about public relations, not morality. You don't want him to look bad."

Her frown deepens only a little, but I can feel a real spike of animosity under her self-control. For the first time, I've made her angry. "No. It's about morality. Aaric believes in making the world a better place. But he's not talking about religion or politics. For him, it's math. He's worked it out to the last decimal place, and the equations only balance if we stop killing each other. He's going to help make it happen."

"You mean, you really believe in this social-networking software of his? You think it can push people into being better?"

"I believe in *him*. He is smarter than I am. And he's smarter than you. So I don't care if you think it's bullshit. We cannot allow this guy Godwin and Downvote to pervert what Aaric has been trying to do. That is my bottom line. And that goes for you too."

"And what happens if we do run into people who want to hurt us? Someone else who's all fired up from Downvote and ready to rack up a body count?"

"You're supposed to be this incredible living weapon, right? Well, then prove it. If we get in trouble, you find another way. I need you to be smarter. You will follow the rules. Or you can go back to cleaning rich people's toilets."

There's another, more practical reason she doesn't want me to kill Godwin. Stack needs him, needs to trade Godwin to the feds, and that won't work if we deliver a corpse.

The main problem with that is, I just want Godwin to pay. If things get difficult, then it's going to be a lot easier to kill him than capture him. Maybe it shouldn't be, but it is.

Still, if she were making the argument that we have to take Godwin alive because it's the only thing that will keep her boss out of jail, it would make more sense to me.

But for Sara, it's really as simple as doing the right thing.

I check her for deception. Performance. The mental signs of salesmanship, the parts of the brain that start humming when someone is saying something they don't quite believe, when they're trying to fake sincerity.

But she has no doubt. She says it's not religion or patriotism, but it sure feels like it. It's that same certainty I get from some believers. Not the ones who have never been tested. It's easy to be certain about Jesus or America when you're nineteen and you've never prayed for anything but a date to the prom. I mean the believers who have seen friends die and watched family suffer, and have realized that their place in the plan doesn't mean unlimited happiness and rainbows. They have seen the world, and the ugliness it contains, and yet they still believe that their way is the surest path to salvation, whether it be democracy or Christianity or Buddha.

Sometimes I envy those people. It would be nice to have an answer, any answer, instead of blindly groping around in the dark. That's where I find myself most of the time. I know more than most people ever will. I have access to all their secrets. And because of that, I have never found an answer I trusted. There is always another truth, a hidden motive, something just below the surface waiting to be revealed.

But there are times I would like to believe.

"All right," I tell her. "If I take the job, we'll do it your way."

She nods. "Damn right you will," she says, but she's smiling now. She knew I'd say yes. Because she has faith.

We'll see how far that takes us both.

///13

I've Thought About You

We land back at the heliport. I'm supposed to go to my hotel so I can think over Stack's offer. Sara is still not sure if she can trust me, or work with me. I'm not particularly offended. I have the same concerns about her.

We walk from the landing pad to the office, a tiny building that fronts the parking lot, at the middle of the concrete apron on the edge facing the bay. The wash from the rotors is still drowning out everything else around us as we step inside.

We walk straight through the small building—it smells of gourmet coffee and kerosene—and then step out the front door into the fenced parking lot. Sara turns from me toward her executive SUV. She's a little relieved to be parting ways. It's not much fun to have to watch what you're thinking every second. I'm planning to find the nearest McDonalds's and order everything off the Extra Value Meal Menu; being around Stack and his constant hunger has left me absolutely starving.

That's when I pick up the thoughts of the woman waiting to kill us.

She's hidden behind a truck about a dozen yards away, and she rushes out, firing from an Ingram MAC-10. There was almost no hesitation between seeing us and the action. I barely get a glimpse of a woman in gym clothes, ponytail bobbing up and down. She could be a jogger out for a run, on her way to her Pilates class, except for the converted automatic weapon in her hands. She's trying her best to get to us before we can react.

Even with my advance warning, I barely have a few seconds to lift Sara up and take her down behind the SUV.

Sara has a momentary burst of surprise *<what the hell>* and then she hears the bullets thud against the body of the car at our backs. The SUV is armored against everything up to a rocket launcher. The bullets' momentum is sapped by the heavy ceramic plates under the vehicle's metal skin. We might as well be behind a vault door.

As soon as I release her, Sara doesn't waste any more time on shock. She just accepts it and smothers any fear with a practiced calm. She pulls out both of her guns, then waits for the other woman's barrage to stop. She plans to pop up and lay down covering fire, giving me enough time to get inside the SUV. Then she plans to follow, and drive us right out of here, to safety.

Good plan. She's done it before, lots of times. It's the safest, smartest move.

But I don't feel much like retreating right now.

I find the shooter's mind above the stuttering sound of her weapon. Surprising. You don't get many female assassins, whatever the movies tell you. But she handles the MAC-10 like a pro. It feels familiar in her hands. Hours and hours of practice. From her mind, I get a quick download, flash impressions. *<don't let up> <don't give him a moment> <shoot the second you see him> <doesn't seem so tough> <circle around> <nail them both>*

She's walking—grit crunching under the soles of her fashion sneakers—coming around on our right. I can feel her thoughts moving, like a blip on radar. The MAC-10 grows lighter in her hand as she keeps spraying bullets. She's got to reload—there.

She pops the empty clip, not as smooth as she'd like, brings up a fresh one.

Sara opens her mouth to tell me to get into the SUV.

But I'm already moving toward the shooter by then, sprinting from behind the vehicle as fast as I can. As I cross the asphalt between us, I pick something nice and debilitating from the menu. Let's see how she likes the sensation of a compound fracture in her lower right ulna.

Not much at all, as it turns out. Her right arm jerks, her fingers splay out, and she drops the gun. I see—and feel—the pain etched on her face under her designer sunglasses. She turns to face me, shocked as I close the gap.

I get close enough to put the heel of my hand into her face. Not terribly gentlemanly, I know, but then it's not very ladylike to open fire without a proper introduction either. I see the blackness interrupting her vision like a too-long blink. There's a burst of frustration from behind me. *<goddammit, Smith, MOVE>* Sara is up now, aiming both guns like Wyatt Earp, and I'm in the way.

But she holds her fire. I follow the punch with an elbow strike to the shooter's head. She's already on her way down, but I am taking no chances. I help her by sweeping her legs out and shoving her to the ground.

She's on her back, dazed and confused, bleeding freely from the nose and mouth. But she still manages to shoot her leg up in a kick aimed at my knee. I step back in time, because I saw it coming, but just barely. She's very quick. And very angry.

So maybe I'm a little rougher than necessary when I put my foot on her throat.

Sara is at my side in a moment, gun pointed at the shooter's head. The fight goes out of her in an instant. I see it mirrored in her mind—an absolute recognition that Sara is not screwing around, that she will pull the trigger. She recognizes that she's caught, and she's got no desire to catch a bullet in the face.

I step off her neck and then lean down. I relieve her of the knife she's got under the spandex and the backup piece in her belt pouch.

"I didn't even see her," Sara says. She's breathing heavily, the adrenaline still running through her. But the gun doesn't waver a millimeter.

"Neither did I."

"You are both dead," the shooter snuffles out through her damaged nose. It would probably be scarier if she didn't sound like she had a bad cold.

"Oh, shut up, Jezebel," I tell her. Jezebel Todd. Perfect name for a Bond girl or a hit woman. Her parents practically aimed her down this career path.

She looks surprised. So does Sara.

"Did you find her ID?" Sara asks.

I give her a look. And she remembers. *<Oh. Right.>*

"Yeah," I say. "Not just a fun trick at parties."

Sara turns her attention back to our would-be killer. Points the Glock right at her nose. "Who sent you?"

Jezebel has her clever retort—*<fuck you>*—all lined up, but I've already got the answer. Her mind swings open like a cheap screen door.

"She doesn't know," I tell her. "Cutout hire. Email, encrypted cash transfer. She does it all the time." Jezebel Todd. Twenty-nine years old. An honest-to-God, old-fashioned contract killer. Reasonable rates, 15K to 35K, depending on the job. Nobody sees her coming. Nobody expects their killer to be an attractive young woman with an open smile and a perfectly matched outfit. I get a glimpse of some of her previous work. People all over the place, living too long by someone else's measurement. A businessman in Tacoma, walking into his hotel room. The owner of a restaurant in San Diego, two in the back of the head by the Dumpsters. A woman, a Realtor, taking Jezebel on a tour of a two-bedroom, strangled. Family photos in the Realtor's purse, as Jezebel stole her cash and credit cards afterward.

I'm hit with blinding rage, out of nowhere. I lift the MAC-10 from the ground. I've got it resting on her forehead almost before I know what I'm doing. "You piece of shit, she had *kids*."

Jezebel's arrogance and anger vanishes. She gapes at me, terror streaming off her thoughts.

"Whoa, whoa, whoa!" Sara shouts. *<Christ what did I just tell you?>* *<no killing>* *<stop>* *<please>* She points her own weapon skyward as she shouts at me. Whatever she's done to us, Sara's not prepared for me to murder this woman right in front of her. "Smith, don't!" *<please>* *<don't do this>*

I hesitate. I'm looking right into Jezebel. I've barely scratched the surface of her memories, but now all she can think about is dying. And she has the nerve to be surprised. After all she's done, she never really thought it would happen to her.

The moment stretches, impossibly long. I can hear sirens in the background. Someone has called the cops. I am mostly just curious what it will do to me, at this range. The pain and the shock and the sudden absence of life. It always drags me down, a little, into the sudden vacuum where a life used to be. It's like looking into darkness, and sometimes I fear I will not come back.

But this time, I'm tempted to take the chance.

<oh god> *<I think he's gonna>* *<oh god no>* *<please>*

Then, as if from a great distance, I hear something else.

Jezebel's phone, ringing in her belt pouch.

It's enough to wake me up.

I remove the gun from her head and take her phone out of the pouch.

"One sec," I say to her. "Gotta take this."

I stand up and leave Jezebel at the end of Sara's gun. I check the caller. It's listed as DOWNVOTE with an all-zero number.

I spend a second weighing the pros and cons of answering, and then figure what the hell.

"I'm afraid the person you are trying to reach cannot come to the phone right now," I say. "But if you'd like to leave your name and number, I'll be sure to deliver a message."

"That's funny," a smooth male voice replies. It sounds like something out of a commercial for a luxury car. No hesitation. Not a hint of stress. Very cool. Very Blofeld. "Not hilarious. But pretty funny, all things considered."

"Mr. Godwin, I presume," I say.

"You can call me that if you want."

"I could also call you Dipshit. Does Dipshit work better for you? It has such a nice ring to it."

A slight pause. "You're not going to make me angry, John."

It's true. He doesn't sound angry. I could probably work on that, but the sirens are getting louder, and Sara is beaming distress and confusion and, most of all, impatience at me. I've got maybe a couple more minutes. *<police are coming> <what are you doing?> <not the time for a chat>*

So I should probably get to the point.

"Fine. You're Godwin. You're behind Downvote. Which means you're responsible for what happened to Kira Sadeghi. And that means I am coming for you—"

He interrupts me. His tone is not quite angry. More like aggressively bored. "Oh, can we just *not* do this, *please*? We don't have a lot of time here, so can we just *cut the shit*? I know all about how scary you are, Mr. Smith. I've heard all about the man, the myth, the legend. You've got quite the reputation. But I am asking you to be smart. To stop for a moment and think. You've spoken to Stack. To the feds. I know this. Doesn't that tell you something? Doesn't it say that I am watching for contingencies, even ones like you?"

Something bothers me about the voice, and suddenly I realize what it is: all Godwin's words are being filtered through a voice-masking program—

and not through one of those cheap voice-synthesizer jobs that makes the caller sound like a gangster in witness protection either. Rather, all the idiosyncrasies, all the human parts of speech—not just the tone, but the pauses, the cadence, the *um*s and *ah*s and pauses that make up a person's style of speaking—are all gone, sanded down by some very intelligent piece of software. It's like talking to a machine doing a very good imitation of a human being.

"I'm offering you the chance to walk away," he says. "I don't want to get into a pissing match with you. There's no profit in it for either of us. You and I can both have long and happy lives. Just walk away now. Do whatever it is you do for fun. I really do not care. Just move on. Be smart."

"Or what? You'll kill me? People have tried. Recently, in fact."

The filtering software masks what might have been a laugh. Instead, it comes out as a burst of static, an electronic cough. "You mean the woman you probably just shot? Please. I only hired her so you'd pick up this call. She barely counts as a warning. You've never met anyone quite like me before. I don't believe anyone else has really taken you seriously before, John. Nobody really believes in what you can do. Nobody knows what you really are."

I laugh a little at that. The adrenaline is still surging through me, and I'm feeling pretty invincible. "And you do?"

"Well, to be fair, I'm a lot smarter than the other people you've met. And I've thought about you."

"Oh, stop. You're going to make me blush."

The electronic voice suddenly goes cold and distant, as if it bounced off Mars before coming through the phone.

"You don't really give a damn about Kira Sadeghi, John," Godwin says. "I know that. You're just looking for an excuse. A way to prove you're human. Because, in the simplest possible terms, you are not one of us. Sure, you look like us. You even try to act like us—your jokes, your attitude, your obsession with things like good clothes and good food—but those are only things you've seen on TV. Read in magazines. Protective morphology, they call it. You know the truth. There is something missing inside of you. You've never had a friend. You've never had a woman in your life who looks at you with anything like love."

"You're wrong," I snap. It gets out before I can stop it.

"No. I told you. I know what you are," Godwin says. "And so do you. You've never felt like one of us because, deep down, where it counts, you're nothing close to human. Our private moments, our hidden thoughts and desires and hurts—that's what makes us who we are. And you strip them away without even trying. You know our secrets just by walking into the same room as us. You meddle in our deepest places, and then you walk right out again, as if nothing has happened. You are an existential threat, John. Honestly, if people stopped to think about it—I mean, *really think* about it—they'd have you executed on the spot. They would end your life before you damage us any further."

The synthesized voice gives this the sound of an official pronouncement—a verdict on my fitness to be among humans, and it's clear that I have been found wanting.

"That's why you're so hung up on avenging that Z-list slut. You want to pretend you actually care about people."

Sara snaps to get my attention. "Smith," she says, and points. There is a patrol car, followed closely by an ambulance, approaching.

Almost out of time. I need to get something from Godwin while I still can. "Listen—"

"No," Godwin says. "You listen. This is your only chance. Or you get to learn what humanity is really capable of."

He hangs up before I can come up with a snappy comeback to that. I'm not quite sure what I would have said to him anyway.

Suddenly none of this seems very funny anymore.

///

The police do their best, considering we're not much help at all. Sara tells them the barest minimum possible. We arrived, she started shooting. The end. The officers decide that Jezebel Todd—who, as it turns out, has her own wanted poster and an FBI alert tagged to her—must have thought I was Stack, and was out to either shoot him or kidnap him. A hired gun, looking for a rich target. Makes sense. More or less. I help push the idea into their brains as much as I can. I tell them I'm a security consultant, and that I was meeting with Stack for just this reason.

It seems a hell of a lot simpler than the truth. I keep Jezebel's phone in my pocket, and neither Sara nor I mention the call. There's no way that involving the cops in Downvote will make any of our lives easier. Vincent might disagree, but screw him, he's in L.A. and I'm here.

Still, it takes hours to untangle ourselves from the crime scene. Jezebel is taken away long before the police finish with us. She's regained some of her composure and attitude by the time they put her in a patrol car. She even winks and grins at me through the blood around her mouth. I'd be able to see it on her face even if I couldn't read it in her mind.

<I'm coming for you, sweetheart> <this is nothing> <never going to touch me for everything I've really done> <be seeing you soon> <you condescending prick>

Then they slam the door on her and drive away. I make a mental note to find out if she makes bail. I might even pay it myself, just to be waiting on the street.

It's almost evening by the time we sign our statements and the cops go away. They impound the bullet-riddled SUV as evidence.

We're finally alone, sitting in the heliport's small office, drinking the coffee that was left in the pot. It smelled a lot better than it tastes.

Sara takes a deep breath, blanking her mind, releasing the tension. Then she snaps back, all business.

"All right," she says. "What was that call about?"

"Just a second," I say. I use my talent to scan around us. The heliport's manager is outside, smoking a cigarette. He's thinking hard about quitting and moving to Iowa. *<crop-dusting> <they do that there, right?> <any-place they don't shoot at you> <good lord>* But no one is eavesdropping.

"Godwin," I tell her. And then I give her the highlights: walk away now, terrible vengeance, face my wrath, and so on.

"How did he find you? Did you bring him to us? Was he following you?"

There is a blare of alarm all through her nervous system, a feeling like a parent's fear for the safety of a child. She's worried about Stack again.

"Actually," I say, "he followed you."

That stops her short. But it's what I got from Jezebel Todd's memories. She'd been told not to follow me. Which was smart on Godwin's part, because I would feel it as soon as someone started focusing on me. Instead, she followed Sara. She put a tracking device on the SUV, saw it park at the heliport, and then just waited for us to come back from the yacht.

Sara scowls. She doesn't like hearing it. *<sloppy> <stupid> <should have known>* She replays the sound of the gunfire, the feeling of surprise and anger that came over her when I knocked her behind the SUV. *<should have seen it coming> <should have seen him coming>*

But it really wasn't her fault. It's hard to imagine an enemy around every corner. It's exhausting to be on continual alert, always looking for an attack. To always be on guard. Nobody can do that every minute of the day. At some point, you have to let your defenses down.

Unless you're me, of course. I've got my wired-in proximity alarms, the radar in my head that tells me whenever someone even thinks about doing me harm.

Maybe this is what Godwin was talking about, the distance between me and the rest of you. Because as I listen in on Sara's internal monologue, I can't imagine what else she could have done to protect herself. Sometimes I just don't know how you regular people manage to stay alive.

"Don't beat yourself up," I tell her. "You're not a spy. You don't spend your life looking over your shoulder. Ninety percent of the time, you've got no way of knowing if someone is behind you in a crowd."

She grits her teeth. "Would you please not do that?"

"Do what?"

"Talk to me without me saying anything."

Oh. Right. "Sorry. It happens."

That was a mistake. I need a drink and my pills. I can feel the damage I did to Jezebel creeping up on me. Not to mention the memories of what she's done to other people. I wonder exactly how much Scotch it's going to take to keep her victims from crawling into my dreams.

"Whatever," Sara says, a note of irritation in her voice as she forcibly derails that train of thought. "He thought you'd come to see Aaric, because he knew Aaric is one of the only people who can give me a lead on him. That means he must be pretty worried about you, if he's got a hired killer ready just in case you show up."

"No," I say. I turn and look at her. Ordinarily, I'd like to believe that. I'd love to be so impressive that the bad guy trembles at the mere possibility of my crossing his path. But after my conversation with Godwin, I don't think so. "He seems like he's got a plan. And he's prepared to do whatever it takes to keep anyone from messing with it."

"But why?" she asks. "Why go to all this effort? All this expense? What does he get out of all this? What is he planning?"

I think about the software voice speaking Godwin's words. *Nobody has ever really thought about you before. Not like I have.*

"I don't know," I admit. "But I think I'm just another contingency to be managed. I don't think he's scared of me at all."

That's not what she wants to hear. *<well that's just great>*

We're both silent for a moment after that. Sara keeps thinking about what she could have done to prevent Jezebel from ambushing us. I try to figure out what Godwin gains from all of this.

Neither of us comes up with any answers.

"So what do we do now?" Sara finally asks.

I stand up. "For starters," I say, "call the chopper back here. We need to go back to the boat and tell your boss I'm taking the job."

///14

This Is Still America

We meet with Stack again on the *Nautilus,* and I formally agree to work for him. We shake hands and everything. Seems a little redundant, since someone has already tried to shoot me, but it makes Stack feel better.

We then spend a few hours mapping out our strategy. It's late, and we are still coming down from the shooting, but the clock is ticking now. Godwin has had months to get his plans together. We're playing catch-up.

Stack has something, however. He's so excited he barely registers Sara's shock and exhaustion. In this moment, he's too interested in what he's found. *<I'm fine thanks for asking> <dodged a few bullets but all in a day's work, right?>* Sara forgives him for it, mostly. But it's not every day she nearly takes a bullet for her boss, and she would have liked a little more recognition.

Not going to happen tonight. Stack has already been trying to pick up the digital bread crumbs of Downvote, and he's practically bouncing in his chair, waiting to explain what he's learned.

"All right, Downvote is a Dark Net site, right?" Stack begins, going slow for my benefit. "That means it's as good as invisible. No way to trace its IP address to a location in the real world. But the website has to live someplace, right? The data has to be stored on a server somewhere. And the people who work on the site have to be able to access it. Like Godwin."

"So how do we track that?" Sara asks. I'm glad she did. I don't want to look like the only one who doesn't know how the Internet works.

"Ordinarily, we can't," Stack says. "The home server could be anywhere in the world. It could be a box running off an AOL dial-up connection in Sri Lanka. Everything on the Dark Net runs through a host of proxy servers—the traffic bounces literally all over the Internet before it reaches your computer. Totally untraceable."

"Except it's not," I say. This is not a guess. I can see Stack's satisfaction glowing through him from across the room.

"Not for us," he says. He smiles. He's pleased with himself. This is what he loves. Figuring it out. Solving problems. Finding the answers. Vincent said this wasn't possible, but it's not exactly surprising to me that the billionaire software genius might know a few tricks that the FBI's IT department doesn't.

"I've been running a simple, brute-force attack on Downvote for days, looking for possible ways inside," Stack says. "And I think I've got something. Downvote is getting popular, and Godwin can't keep it running all by himself. He's got help. And some of that help . . . well, they're not as diligent as Godwin is about covering their tracks. He's leaking data every time he accesses the site. I intercepted some packets between the site and a remote computer, and I was able to sniff out an IP address."

Sara and I wait patiently for the translation.

"Houston," Stack says. "One of the people who works on Downvote lives in Houston."

A little over nine hours later, Sara and I are parked in a subdivision that was new ten years ago but is now starting to show some wear and tear. Paint chipping on some of the houses. A few of the lawns not so well groomed.

We chartered a private flight out of San Francisco on Sara's corporate

Amex, and were in Houston almost before the sun rose. Since then, Sara and I have been sitting in our rental car, staring at her laptop.

The streets are empty. Nobody home in the middle of the day.

Well, almost nobody. Sara watches the screen of her laptop intently. Stack wrote a program for us: it's tracked the Downvote user down to a specific address, and alerts us as soon as he goes online. We see all his activity on our screen in real time.

So we've been watching Downvote pretty much nonstop the entire time we've been in the car, tracking the user when he gets on the site.

From Sara's laptop, there's a pinging noise, and a light appears on a map.

"That's him," she says. "He's just logged in."

She says "he," even though all we've really got is a screen name: Redrum. His avatar on a dozen different boards is a pirate with a bloody knife clenched in his teeth. Technically, it could be anyone—man, woman, or other. It's like the old joke: on the Internet, no one knows you're a dog.

Except we know this is a guy, because we've been watching him the whole time we've been here, and he is nothing but a fountain of shit toward women. In the past two hours, he's set up over a dozen new Twitter accounts and usernames to attack a female reporter for ESPN. So far, he's sent her over a hundred messages—and pictures and texts and videos—almost all variations on the same theme: *"Kill yourself." "Jew bitch." "You'd have made a good lampshade." "Can't wait until you get raped." "Fuck you." "Die you dyke." "Nobody will cry at your funeral."*

And on like that.

The reporter's crime? She wrote an article about his favorite baseball team that he didn't like.

Sara has watched them all pile up, her mouth drawn into a thin, grim line. I promised I'd stay out of her head, but I still check on her mental state every now and then. Nothing specific, just taking a moment to gauge her internal temperature. She warned me about killing, but I am actually a little concerned about what she might do to this guy in person. We need him to survive long enough to get a lead on Godwin, after all.

We are pretty sure Redrum's real name is Tom Moffett. Matches the name on the mortgage that we got from public records. He's thirty-seven, self-employed, freelance software consultant. Used to be an IT guy at a mortgage broker right before it imploded, and he's been working at home ever since.

"You ready?" Sara asks.

I nod. I think we've been careful enough. Nobody else is watching the house. Nobody is expecting us.

"Let's go," I say.

We drive around the corner and pull to a stop on the street right in front of the house. Not exactly subtle, but we figure that if he's looking at the screen, he won't be watching out the front window for anyone. And I need to be this close to scan the interior. We're about at the limits of my range.

I get a focused presence in one room. A stream of letters, the fluid feeling of motion as someone types very, very quickly. A body a little heavier than it should be, left behind in the flow of his work on the machine.

That's how he thinks of it. The machine. Like he's handling a jackhammer or a cement mixer. I can just barely see what's going through his head—a string of code, moving and switching lines, putting together a Web page—

<such bullshit, totally beneath me, but hey, if they want to pay for shit, they can get shit> <I told them what they needed> <cheap out if they want to>

His frustration is a tangible thing, piled up inside his guts. It feels like a sack of pennies, bright and shiny and seemingly endless, no matter how many of them he spends on all the stupid, lying, whining, *cheating, whoring, fucking morons*—

Sara places her hand, gently, on my arm. And I'm back.

"John? I asked if you got anything?"

I drag my mind away and answer her. It's definitely Moffett in the house. "Yeah. He's inside. Alone. Nobody else in his short-term memory. He's not expecting a thing. Should be no problem."

We walk right up to the front door. Like respectable visitors. Or Jehovah's Witnesses. Nothing to worry about.

On the other hand, this is Texas, where people have been known to purchase antitank missiles for home defense, so a little caution is probably warranted.

Sara stands by the front door with her gun drawn and behind one leg. I cue up a particularly nasty sensation of a spinal fracture and prepare to shove it into Moffett's mind.

We have to be quick. Stack warned us that Moffett probably has a fail-safe on his machine, ready to wipe the hard drive clean at the press of a button. "Coders usually aren't stupid," Stack said. "I mean, they can be, but not about coding. He knows he's got incriminating stuff on that computer. He'll have a self-destruct button."

So here's the dilemma. We can kick down the door, and risk him hitting the button and erasing everything we need. Or we can ring the doorbell, and risk him shutting everything down behind encryption it will take us a million years to unlock.

I look up, and see a webcam staring back down at us. I check inside Moffett's head again. The same string of code.

"He's still plugged into Downvote?" I ask quietly.

Sara checks her phone, like she's looking at her email. Stack put the tracking app on there too. "Yes," she says.

"That's not what he's working on," I say. "He's doing something else."

"Sloppy," she says. "He should log out."

"Let's ring the bell," I decide. "He'll leave it running."

She considers it. Nods, and presses the button by the door.

I can feel his attention on us immediately. As I've said, my talent doesn't work through electronics. But I can see Moffett, in my mind, looking at a window that's just opened on his screen. The webcam. It's wirelessly linked to his computer. Cheap DIY security. Fifty bucks at Home Depot.

I get a pulse of frustration. *<goddamn fucking fuckers>* *<look like real-estate agents again>* *<fucking told them last time>* I feel him haul himself out of his secondhand Aeron chair. Step into a pair of flip-flops that have the same logo as his tracksuit. Stomp toward the door, muttering to himself.

Most important, he doesn't shut down his computer. Or log out.

"He thinks we're Realtors," I mutter quietly, in case the camera is wired for sound.

He opens the door.

Tom Moffett. Shorter than he appears in his own mind. Hair retreating quickly to the back of his skull. Goatee. Eyes blinking rapidly in the sudden daylight.

"What?" he snaps.

Sara decides, right there, to improvise. "Hello, sir. We're with Greater Texas Realty, and we were wondering if you might be interested in putting your home on the market."

She gives him her best smile. Most men—hell, most women—would soften at least a little at that. She plans to ask to tour the house, to price it out for sale, and to get us inside that way.

Not a bad plan, really.

But Moffett is only looking for targets for his anger. And we've presented him with perfectly acceptable victims.

"You fucking people. How many fucking times do I have to fucking tell you? I am not fucking interested in fucking selling! Jesus Christ, are you too fucking dense to read the sign that says *no* fucking *solicitors*? Or did your husband not slap any sense into you this morning? I swear to fucking God, I have had it with this bullshit, you stupid fucking *bitch*—"

This is how he thinks it will go. We want to sell his house, so we'll have to put up with his shit. Common courtesy will keep us from reacting with anything more than hurt feelings.

But this is not what is really happening.

I get a flash of all the abuse Sara has witnessed on the screen as it scrolls through her memories. And she pivots and decides, <*Screw it*>.

She punches Moffett hard in the chest, simultaneously depriving him of air for his next sentence and shoving him back into the house.

He stumbles and falls flat on his ass. We're inside the house in a second. I slam the door behind us.

He glares at us from the floor. "What the *fuck* do you think you're doing?"

Sara shows him the gun. "Shut up," she says. "Please."

He goes from belligerent to terrified in a split second, barely any shifting of mental gears at all.

"I'm sorry," he blurts. "Please, there's no money in the house, just take whatever you want and go."

In his mind, he's absurdly grateful that his wife and their daughter aren't home. He's so frightened for them. It makes me soften toward him a little. Worst part of my talent: the ability to see everything from the other guy's perspective.

I think of Kira. It erases any sympathy pretty quick.

"Where's the computer?" Sara asks. Then she sees it. A big desktop model in what must serve as his office and a playroom at the same time.

I look at the toys scattered on the floor and realize he set it up like this so he can multitask. He can type up a dozen rape threats on his computer while his daughter plays a few feet away. Modern parenting.

We leave Moffett cowering on the floor and walk over to the computer. Sara looks at the screen and takes out a thumb drive. This is something else Stack prepared for us: it's preloaded with a program that will hijack the hard drive and send a copy of everything to a remote server.

Only Sara frowns as she looks at the screen. "This isn't Downvote," she says.

I take a look too. This is the project he was working on—his actual job, designing a website.

Sara taps the mouse, moves a few windows, but there's nothing active on the screen that has anything to do with Downvote.

She checks her phone again. "But he's still logged in . . ."

I hear Moffett move behind me and pick up his thoughts at the same time. He heard Sara say "Downvote" and his mind lit up like a Christmas tree with an entirely different set of fears.

He's scrambling over to a table in the breakfast nook, and I realize our mistake instantly. He doesn't keep Downvote on his home computer. Of course he doesn't.

Moffett is moving toward a laptop sitting on the table. That's where he keeps his really secret stuff: his hacking toolkits, his porn, and everything he's got connected to Downvote.

He'd rather risk a bullet from Sara than have us find out what's on there.

I'm sprinting across the room toward him, but he's a step ahead. He slams the laptop shut just before I can snag it.

I shove him away from the table, and he hits the floor again. But now he's a little less scared.

"Who the hell are you people?" he shouts at me. "If you're cops, you need a warrant! I want a lawyer! This is still America!"

"Oh, shut up," I tell him. I crack open the laptop again.

There's a simple login screen. The name is filled in, but the password field is blank.

"Dammit," I hiss. Sara has crossed the room behind me. She looks over my shoulder.

"Well, crap," she says. "You couldn't reach him?"

"Hey, you could have shot him in the leg. Then he wouldn't have been so quick."

"I thought you could paralyze him with your brain or something."

"I try to avoid that when I can."

Moffett's confusion—and anger—is only growing. He seems to pick up on the fact that he's not going to die in the next couple of minutes. So the belligerence is emerging from wherever it went to hide a few seconds ago.

"You're not even cops, are you?" he snarls. "You'd better get the hell out of my house, or I'm calling 911—"

I turn to him and kneel down. "No," I say. "You won't."

He's a little quieter now that I'm within arm's reach. But he's still bubbling with rage. "Oh yeah? Why won't I?"

"For one thing, she still has a gun. And for another, you don't want anyone remotely related to law enforcement looking at what's on that laptop, do you?"

He hesitates. I can see the bluff forming like fog rolling in.

"There's nothing illegal on there," he says. "I don't care who sees it."

"Really? You want to explain Downvote to the police? You ready for that?"

He thrusts out his chin, like he's daring me to throw a punch. "Pretty sure that breaking and entering and assault with a deadly weapon is worse than anything I've got on there."

"Does your wife know?" I ask, and the sudden blare of alarm from him gives me the answer. "You want to explain Downvote to her?"

He crumbles. "Look," he says, "it was just a joke, it didn't mean anything. Why are you taking this so seriously? Why are you picking on me?"

"Joke's over. People are getting hurt," I tell him.

<yeah no shit Sherlock> *<that's the point>* "I don't know anything about that."

Sara, who's still staring at the login screen, interrupts.

"We don't have time for this," she says. "I'm sure he's got it triggered to wipe the hard drive if we enter the wrong password. I've got a guy we can call, a hacker, he can probably be here in an hour or two with his kit—"

"Yeah, we could do that," I say. "Or we could just ask."

I turn back to Moffett. "What's your password?"

"Eat me," he snaps. But it flashes into his mind: *<T0KY0St)rm> <Warn1ng-10k-Sot0t>*.

I stand up and search the kitchen counter for a pen and paper. Then I write down the string of characters and numbers for Sara.

She's about to start typing, despite the skepticism on her face and in her thoughts. Then I stop her. "Hold up," I say. I ask Moffett: "Any other booby traps? Anything else we need to enter to get into the machine?"

"Booby traps?" He snorts, pure contempt rolling off him. But inside: *<dammit> <knew I should have installed another layer of encryption> <doesn't matter> <laptop's going to brick itself once they enter the wrong password> <is this guy crazy or what?> <seems crazy>*.

"We're good," I tell Sara. She types the password.

Moffett grins. The screen goes blue for a second.

And then the laptop chimes and opens up for us. She smiles.

"That is actually very cool. You're turning out to be a pretty handy guy, Mr. Smith."

"More than just a pretty face," I say.

Moffett, meanwhile, is awestruck. "How the fuck did you do that?" he wants to know.

"Magic," I say as Sara plugs in the thumb drive and begins sucking down all the data. "Now. Let's have a little talk. I want you to tell me everything you know about Godwin."

There is a spike of pure terror from him. He goes paler than when I mentioned his wife. That was wound up in shame and embarrassment, but those are survivable. This goes down all the way to the brain stem, where fight-or-flight lives, the part that gets triggered when our brains decide we're in real mortal danger.

Godwin scares Moffett out of any of his poses and personas. He's no longer the suburban dad or the online troll or the secret hacker. He's just a guy feeling very exposed and alone.

And so, of course, he clamps his mouth shut as tight as he can and shakes his head. *<no way>* *<not a chance>* *<he's killed people!>*

"He's killed people?" I repeat, and Moffett's eyes go wide again. "Who? What are you talking about?"

"What? How did you—?" Moffett is confused, because of course he's not actually talking at all, but I'm able to see it in his memories as it pops up.

Moffett is one of five different sysadmins running Downvote. He's been on the board for over a year, which makes him a veteran. He posted all the time, talked about his computer skills, suggested fixes and upgrades for the site on the message boards. Godwin recruited him by an encrypted email to start doing some of that work, then gradually gave him more responsibility, and more access.

But it came with a warning too. Not long after he gave Moffett the access codes to Downvote's secure server, he sent an email with a video clip.

I can see it in Moffett's mind clearly: a skinny kid in a black T-shirt, getting beaten by two big guys wearing biker gear. The clip had been edited to show only the highlights. They used chains, their fists, and boots. In the end, the kid was little more than a stain on the floor.

"That's what happened to the last person who betrayed me," Godwin typed in an instant message to Moffett. "Just keep that in mind."

And he has. It is as vivid now as the day he first saw it. Moffett is pretty sure he's a dead man because we've gotten in here and cracked his laptop.

"How does he get bikers to stomp people for him?" I ask, and Moffett is completely freaked out now. He's got no idea how I can see what was in his head, so he jumps to a much more rational conclusion.

"You guys are feds, aren't you?" he says. "I want witness protection. I want a new identity. And security! For me and my family!"

Sara looks at me. I shrug. Anything that will keep him talking—and thinking—is good.

"Why don't you tell me what you have to offer," I say, kneeling down to face him, "and then we'll see what we can do?"

"He's an actual criminal," Moffett hisses. "I mean, I thought he was just in it for the fun and games, but he has a whole bunch of Dark Net sites out there. He moves drugs, money, fake IDs, all kinds of stuff. That's how he gets the bikers. He pays them in meth."

"And you've got proof of him doing this?" Sara asks, shifting effortlessly into cop mode. She's enjoying this. She loves watching *Law & Order* marathons on cable.

Moffett laughs, almost hysterically. *<are you kidding?>* *<idiot>* "Of course not! He moves everything through other people! He sends the drugs via FedEx! The bikers have never met him! Hell, I've never met him! We do everything over chat and message boards."

"So you put together the site's leaderboard. You keep track of the totals. You update it periodically. And you keep the site secure. Monitor the message boards, make sure nobody is making anything too public."

He nods, but just barely.

"Does any of the money go through you?" Sara asks. *<maybe we can track the funds>*

"No," Moffett says. "It all goes through Bankster. Totally encrypted."

"The PayPal of the black market," I say to Sara. "So glad someone invented that."

She makes a face at me. <*shut up*>

"So does Godwin pay you for your work, at least?" she asks.

"No," he says. He keeps his face blank. But I get a flash image from his mind of a priority mail envelope, delivered every other Tuesday. Packed with cash. Even better than Bankster.

I give him a hard look. He shrinks down farther.

"Well. A little. It's mostly a volunteer effort." <*did it for free at first*> <*people need to be taught a lesson*>

This is what's really baffling to me. And though we don't actually need to know, I ask him the question anyway: "Why?"

That stops him cold. He blinks. "Why what?"

"Why make this site? Why Downvote? Why invest all the time and money and effort?"

"Because otherwise they would just get away with it," he says, like he's talking to a four-year-old.

"Get away with what?"

Again, he looks at me like I'm from another planet. But now there's an added layer of contempt.

"*Everything*," he says.

In the end, we leave Moffett in his living room as soon as we've finished copying his hard drive. There's nothing more we need from him, and there's nothing I can do that will scare him more than Godwin does. We let him go on thinking we're feds. It's easier that way.

Back at the hotel room, I watch as Sara uploads the whole of Moffett's hard drive to Stack on his boat. Stack's cadaverous face stares back at both of us from the screen of Sara's laptop over a video link.

I can hear him tapping a few keys over the laptop's speakers, and then he breaks into a grin.

"Yes. We've got the login to his servers," Stack says.

"Which means what?" I ask. I am getting a little bored with all the tech stuff. I know it's necessary, but I'm anxious to get moving again.

On-screen, Stack's grin grows wider. "It means we can access the server, and we can intercept the signals as they're coming in. We know where it is."

"We've got the actual, physical address for Godwin?"

On-screen, Stack's grin vanishes. Sara looks at me, a kind of pity on her face and in her mind. "Not quite," she says.

I should have known it wouldn't be that easy. "Then what do we have?"

"We know where Downvote is located. We've found the server where Godwin keeps the site. Godwin can still access it from literally anywhere in the world. We need to intercept the traffic from him the next time he logs into Downvote. Which means you need to get physical access to the server itself if we're going to find him."

"So where are we going?"

"Reykjavík," Stack says.

"Iceland?"

"Do you know another one?" Sara asks, sort of amused.

"I'll keep working it from this end," Stack says. "Maybe I can find something else in the hard drive. You two, travel safe."

His screen closes.

Another digital bread crumb on the trail. One more lead to follow. No wonder Godwin sounded so confident. He's at the end of a million-mile maze. I turn to go to my room and start packing.

Sara doesn't pay attention as I leave. She's already clicking over to Amazon, talking to herself. "I wonder if we can get same-day delivery here," she says. "There's no way we're going to be able to buy winter clothes in Texas in May . . ."

///

As soon as I'm away from Sara, I take out my phone and dial a number. The encryption delays the connection slightly.

A voice that sounds like the owner is ten minutes late for his throat cancer diagnosis answers: "Jimmy's 44 Club."

"Hey. You guys still have Monkey Knife Fight on tap?"

A pause. "Nah, not this week. We got Chupacabras and Regal Select."

"Let me give you my number, you call me when you get it back."

"Yeah, sure."

The bartender takes my number and hangs up. I get just inside the door of my room when my phone rings again.

It's Cantrell.

"That was fast," I say. "I thought maybe I'd have a chance to order room service. Get down to the pool."

"You don't want to swim in a hotel pool," Cantrell says, his voice full of its usual shitkicker twang. "You know how many kids pee in those things?"

"Still, I didn't think I was on your priority list."

Cantrell chuckles. I can practically see him put his feet up on his desk and grin. "John, I have learned that it is best not to leave you unattended for any great length of time."

Cantrell was my recruiter, my handler, and my mentor when I was using my talent for God and country. He taught me about spycraft, how to drink good Scotch, and sent me all over the planet to crack open the minds of terrorists and pluck out their secrets. He was the head of the CIA's top-secret psychic soldier program—they called us Cantrell's special-ed kids behind our backs, which is kind of stupid, because we could read minds, after all—and for several years, I was the most reliable weapon in his arsenal.

If I've had enough to drink, I would probably tell you he's the closest thing to a father I've ever had.

And of course, he betrayed me and lied to me, which led to my leaving the Agency and going private.

But that doesn't mean we can't still use each other.

Like right now I need hard data that can't be found on the Internet. Cantrell still lives in the world where information exists as rumor and innuendo and hearsay. These are the kinds of stories that are rarely ever put down on paper, let alone typed into a computer database.

If anyone knows anything about Godwin, it's Cantrell. Or he'll be able to find out.

I give him the bare minimum at first. "I'm investigating something and a name has come up. A hacker who's branched out and become a genuine crime boss. I've heard about contract hits with bikers, meth sales, drugs, money laundering . . . You know. The usual delights."

"This investigation of yours have anything to do with that shooting at the wedding?"

"You keeping track of me?"

"Always," he says. "But in this case, I got flagged when some federal agent pulled your file. Named you as witness and person of interest at the scene." Cantrell is a private contractor now too, but he still maintains links with the Agency. And anything to do with the old program usually gets sent to him.

"It's related," I admit.

"Got a name for me?"

"Godwin is his online alias."

"Oh, that narrows it down."

But I hear something in his tone. If I had not spent years with him, I wouldn't have picked up on it. "You've heard of him," I say.

"Well, yeah, bits and pieces," Cantrell says. And he tells me what he knows.

Godwin is currently a nagging, recurring presence at the edge of several international drug enforcement investigations. "Organized crime needs good computer programmers just as much as legitimate businesses these days," Cantrell says. "Probably even more."

But Godwin is never the main target, Cantrell tells me, because he's smart enough not to become too big, or too public.

"He's not an idiot like that Silk Road dipshit, putting his name out everywhere and embarrassing the federal government by giving interviews," Cantrell says. "He's found his sweet spot, and he sticks with it."

Godwin is known as a service provider. He sits in the middle, like a fat spider in a web, and does the logistical work for the criminals above and below him.

There's no record of him before he started out with the Eastern European mobs, mostly Romanian, ripping millions of credit-card numbers from horny guys visiting cam girl sites. Then he branched out into online drug sales, using the mobs as suppliers to U.S. customers. He's contracted biker gangs for collections and enforcement, like Moffett says, hiring them over encrypted email and message boards, and paying them with regular bags of meth and cash FedEx'd to anonymous PO boxes all over America.

"So where can I find him?"

"That I can't help you with," Cantrell says. "I can reach out to my contacts at the DEA if it's important, but I'm pretty sure they don't know dick either. That's the thing about this Internet you kids love so much. Guy could be anywhere. Could be in Hawaii getting a tan on the beach, or he could be next door to you in your hotel."

"That's what I hear. Well, if you can think of anything—"

"I'll be sure to be in touch," Cantrell says. There's a pause and I can hear him chewing on one of those cigars he keeps in his desk. "Still. Kind of surprising he'd send somebody to shoot up a TV wedding. Seems stupid and direct for him. Can't imagine he'd want to actually put his fingerprints on something that public and noisy."

I can't help feeling proud at knowing something Cantrell doesn't. "Yeah, well, he doesn't exactly have his finger on the trigger," I say. "It's more like he's working a remote control. He's using social media to push people into position. On-demand mayhem via the Internet. Like Pokémon Go, but with bloodshed."

"Bullshit," Cantrell says flatly. "How's that even supposed to work?"

I explain a little bit about social contagion, and the software that Stack designed, when I realize Cantrell has been way too quiet. Instead of interrupting me with dirty jokes or insults, he's listening intently.

And too late, I shut up.

"Interesting," Cantrell says into the sudden silence. "Software that pushes people around. Turns crowds into weapons. What a neat little toy he's got there."

I am kicking myself mentally. Of course Cantrell would see a use in this.

"He's not going to have any more fun with it," I say. "Not after I find him."

"Oh, I've got faith in you, John," Cantrell says. "I'm sure you will track him down. In fact, you should stay in touch on this one. I think maybe I can help you out with it. In a big way."

"I can handle it on my own, thanks."

"John, come on now. Never be too proud to ask for help from a friend."

"I'll be sure to keep that in mind," I tell him, and hang up as fast as I can after that.

Stupid. It's hard to get out of old patterns. I still want to impress the teacher, and I end up giving Cantrell valuable intel.

I know he's probably already thinking about how much the Agency would pay for something like Godwin's software. Millions, without blinking an eye. I know because they spent far more than that on the projects that trained me. The idea of controlling people, steering them in whatever direction they need, has been an obsession of the CIA since the MK-ULTRA experiments back in the fifties. At its heart, that's what the Agency is for: making sure people behave in exactly the way they're supposed to.

And I don't have to imagine what they would do with that kind of power. I've caught the live act. I'm not a fan.

/// 15

You've Got the Wrong Guy

We start to run into problems the very next day.

First, we arrive at the airport and discover the charter to Iceland that Sara has arranged has been canceled. I know, I know, cry me a river, I don't get to put my ass down in the leather seat of a private jet. But it bugs me, and not just because it throws off our schedule. We've got to get to Reykjavík fast, before Godwin can send anyone to wipe his remote servers. I know we cannot depend on Moffett to stay quiet, no matter how much we scared him. Every hour counts right now.

But what really bothers me is that the operator in the private terminal tells us that we were the ones who canceled the reservation.

"Impossible," Sara tells him for the fourth time. "I never talked to anyone from your firm."

The man at the counter gives us a polite, concierge-level smile, but doesn't budge. "I can only tell you what I see here on my screen. Your charter was released after a phone call from a Miss Sara Fitch—"

"That's me. But I never—"

"—and so we allowed another party to use the plane. They left early this morning." <*not my fault you screwed up, sweetie*> "I am terribly sorry."

"Fine," Sara says, fuming. "Are there any other charters available? Anything at all?"

"Not if you want to leave the Houston area today, I'm afraid," the man says, his voice oozing with sympathy. "I do see that there is a commercial flight to JFK leaving in less than an hour, if you hurry. You could make a connection there." *<tough shit, you rich pricks>*

Sara scowls, but we don't waste any more time arguing.

We turn and head for the doors so we can get to the main terminals.

"What do you think?" Sara asks.

"Hard to believe someone else got our jet that fast. Seems like everyone is flying private these days."

She turns her scowl on me. Not the time for humor, I guess. "You know what I mean. Do you think it's Godwin? Screwing with us?"

I honestly don't know. It would be child's play for someone like Godwin to cancel the flight with a keystroke or two. But it seems so . . . pointless. "He's already sent someone to shoot at us," I say. "Canceling our flight? That's like a prank phone call. Maybe he's not as smart as we think he is."

"Aaric said Godwin was at least as smart as him," Sara says. "Which means, yeah: he's a hell of a lot smarter than we think he is. I'm not sure we can even imagine how smart he is."

Well. That's reassuring. Sara's mind clouds with worry for a moment, and it's contagious. I feel like I've just been outmaneuvered, and I don't even know how yet.

But we head for the ticket counter and get our last-minute seats to JFK. Because at this point, what else are we going to do?

This is the other reason I prefer flying private. For me, airports are like being crammed in a factory farm, but I'm the only animal who knows how it's all going to end.

People are everywhere, and I can feel every bit of their anger, their boredom, their frustration, their pain, and their sadness. The mile-long TSA line is like a twisted spine sending signals of pain and rage right through me. People come to the airport with their hangovers, their undigested meals, and their unresolved feelings. *<should have said something> <going to miss her so much> <why can't Daddy live with us anymore?> <could have at least waved good-bye> <please don't go> <just go> <so tired>*

Not to mention the fear. *<what if the plane crashes?> <what if someone steals my car?> <what if that's the last time I ever see him?> <what if . . .>*

I'm already paranoid enough, looking out for another hit man from Godwin without all this emotional static.

But aside from the obscene price of our last-minute tickets, we haven't had any other problems. Sara makes a quick run over to the gift shop for a charger pack for her phone, leaving me waiting in line at the counter to gate-check our bags. I'd love to slide over to the nearest bar and chase a couple of pills with a quick Scotch, but we don't have that kind of time. I'll have to wait until we get into our first-class seats.

My phone buzzes in my jacket. Priority message. I have only a few people on my VIP list, so I take it out and check.

It's a file from Cantrell. He managed to get a photo of Godwin from his contacts at the DEA. It's a mug shot of Godwin's last arrest, years ago in Manila. It's dim and grainy—it looks like the copy of a fax of a fax—but it's better than anything we had before.

In the photo, he's square-jawed and unsmiling. High forehead, thick hair cut high and tight. A weird flat gray to his eyes that comes across even with the poor quality of the picture. I know I am projecting here, but he looks utterly bored. Confident, even.

He had reason to be. Cantrell's note tells me that he was arrested on a drug charge but never convicted. He sat out three months in a cell waiting for the trial. Then all the witnesses against him, including one of the cops, either disappeared or changed their stories. His attorneys got the charges dropped. He walked out of the jail and hasn't appeared in an official court record anywhere since.

Cantrell closes his email by saying, "Let me know if you want my help with this one. Could be very lucrative."

Yeah. Thanks but no thanks. I pocket my phone again and start looking around for Sara. Our flight begins boarding in ten minutes. The agent at the gate calls me forward, and I haul our luggage up to the counter.

I've just negotiated all the tagging and bagging when I feel the telltale prickle of someone's attention on me.

I turn and see a guy in his twenties framing me in the shot of his iPhone. Fortunately, not someone lining up a gun. But still. I raise my hand to my face and turn away just before he snaps his picture.

I get a blast of anger and disappointment from him. *<son of a bitch>* Then he moves around, changing positions, trying again.

I keep my back to him and try to probe a little deeper to figure out what he's doing. I've been under surveillance before, but it's usually never this obvious.

All I'm getting is an increasing amount of frustration as he circles around, trying for a picture. Plus, my attention is divided—the gate agent is asking me something as she hands me our luggage tags.

"Excuse me?" I ask.

She sighs heavily, and now I get her frustration aimed at me as well. "I said, did you want to add a frequent flyer number? Or upgrade to our gold member rewards program?" *<wake up> <jerk> <not like I enjoy repeating this crap over and over>*

"No, no thank you," I reply, and try to focus on the cameraman again, who is now somewhere to my left.

I turn my head to get a look at him, and that's when the other guy rushes out of the crowd and sucker-punches me.

I manage to pull back and roll with it, so it doesn't land very hard—but it still rattles my brain around.

This almost never happens. I can usually see a punch coming long before it's thrown. I can't remember the last time I got tagged, especially not in public.

So that's probably why I just stand there, stupidly, for a long moment, looking at my attacker.

It's a different guy, also in his twenties, wearing a polo shirt and shorts and flip-flops, an aging frat boy going a little flabby. He's enraged but uncertain. I didn't fall down, and now he's wondering what the hell to do next.

I have no idea why he hit me. And the stream of words coming from his mind is no help at all.

<cocksucker> <had it coming> <now what?>

He's clearly an amateur, which is lucky for me since I'm standing in place like a moron, waiting for him to hit me again.

The gate agent is stunned into silence, and the other people around me are frozen too. Everybody's waiting to see what happens next.

Then someone else in the crowd locks on me and says, "Hey, hey—*it's him!*" I turn and see a fat guy in a Cowboys jersey break out of the crowd. His mind is a night sky full of fireworks, nothing but sound and big lights going off and a picture of me with a target on my face. He rushes me and tries to take me down with a flying tackle.

I sidestep him neatly and he hits the counter hard enough to crack the cheap particleboard. I turn back to my first attacker, Polo Shirt. I scrape his name out of his head *<Matthew>* before I ask him, "Dude, what the hell?"

But he just holds up his phone, like one of Moses's tablets, and turns to the crowd and yells, "It's the guy! Get this prick!"

And he turns to throw another punch.

Fine. I'll get the answers later.

I grab his wrist and drag him into an elbow strike and he drops to the grubby carpeting right next to my roller bag. This sends a charge through the crowd, and a couple other people move toward me, like they've got targeting systems locked.

<it's him> <it's him> <that's the guy> <him? here? really?> <that's him!>

I'm reading the same thoughts from several people now, accompanied by a massive surge of adrenaline, some kind of shock of recognition.

I can feel it, all around me, like a charge in the air before lightning strikes.

I'm suddenly at the center of a circle of people, and they're all looking at me like I'm their worst enemy.

<it's him> <bastard> <can't get away with that>

<Smith?>

I look up and see Sara, confused and frightened. I shake my head, telling her to keep back.

"It's him!" someone yells.

"What the hell do you think you were doing?" another guy yells, from the back of the crowd.

The locks on polite, everyday behavior are beginning to come undone. Being part of a crowd is giving them courage. They suddenly have a target, an outlet for their frustration. The cabdriver who took them the wrong way to the airport. The kids at home who are never grateful enough for all their parents' hard work. The boss who always manages to work an insult into every conversation.

It's all coming out now. They hate me so much I can feel it like a sunburn.

"Who the hell do you think you are, buddy?" another voice, again from the back of the crowd.

I think of what Stack said. How people will do and say things in groups they would never consider if they were on their own.

I have to be careful. I have to say exactly the right thing now.

"Look," I say, my voice as calm as a hostage negotiator. "You've got the wrong guy."

Wrong thing, as it turns out. Their faces all turn to snarls, and a man in a Hooters trucker cap screams, "Get him!"

And they charge.

They're operating on instinct. On anger and endorphins. They know they have the numbers—dozens of them, one of me—and they are all feeling brave and righteous. They will excise me like a cancer.

Just like that, they have gone from a crowd to a mob. And I suddenly have a new understanding of what the term "flashmob" means. In a matter of minutes—seconds—they have become a swarm, a flock, a stampede.

Bodies hit me like a wave. I find myself shoved up against the counter. Two guys are yelling at me, pawing at me, trying to rip my suit off or punch me. A woman is swinging her purse, trying to clobber me on the head with it. The gate agent is shrieking into a phone, panic blazing from her. Airport cops are on the edge of the crowd, but there are too many bodies in the way.

I can't tell minds or bodies apart. Just a mass of undifferentiated rage.

And I find that Stack was right again: it is contagious. Especially for me.

My blood pressure spikes. My teeth clench, along with my fists. I manage to stay on my feet. All I want, for a moment, is to begin hurting people. To use every cheap move and dirty trick I've ever learned to break their bones, crack their skulls, disable and deform them, make them pay.

It would be so easy to cripple them, inside and out. I could give them nightmares that would have them in therapy for years. I could fold this one's knee back, and he'd walk with a limp for the rest of his life. I could punch this one in the throat and watch as he choked on his own windpipe. I could make this one live through a car crash or a gunshot wound or a knife to the chest—

No.

It's not them, I tell myself. It's not them. It's Godwin. Whoever he is. Wherever he is. It's him.

I suck down a deep breath. Move into a defensive posture, mentally and physically. Guard my head and my body, and bat their hands away as they reach for me. They are too close to me and each other. They are doing more damage to themselves than to me. The two men pinning me to the counter are already out of breath.

Rage can be exhausting if you don't do your cardio. They will be out of steam in a moment. All I have to do is wait them out. I can survive this. I can.

Then the buckle on a woman's purse catches me below the eye and opens a cut on my cheek. Blood starts to run. I flinch, and that gives one of the men an opening to catch me with a punch across my left eye.

And suddenly I have had *enough* of this shit.

I grab one man's hand and bend it toward his wrist and he yelps and squeals. I feel his pain, sharp and bright. I take it and hold it, then fling it out into another man, where it stabs him like a shiny needle he feels in the same place.

But I'm under control, I tell myself. I do exactly what I need to do to get them to back off. Nothing else.

They both try to stagger away from me. Instead, they bounce against the crowd yelling behind them.

In those moments, it's like they wake up. They look around and see what they are doing.

Their rage is suddenly replaced by fear. They're in the center of something big and ugly, but they are no longer a part of it.

<oh my god> <what am I doing?> <help> <never meant this>

They pull back from the brink. Just like I do.

But you can't call time-out in the middle of a mob.

I can't use any of my mind tricks on this many people at once, especially when they're operating on the level of lizard-brain instinct. I need something else, some way to wake them all up. I look to my left and see it: a fire alarm set into the nearest wall.

I grab the purse from the woman's hand. She's suddenly appalled. *<how rude!>* Her wallet was in there, her checkbook, her phone, with her pictures of her grandkids. She remembers them, and in that split second, she snaps out of it, and she's no longer part of the mob either.

I take the purse and fling it at the alarm switch as hard as I can.

It hits like a fastball and a siren begins to wail, along with a loud buzzing noise. Sprinklers in the ceiling open up, and water begins to drench everyone in the terminal.

It's the perfect cold shower. People step back, blinking, shouting with surprise. The rage curdles fast. They feel sick and guilty.

I get that too. It feels like nausea.

The cops reach me then. They're the only ones in the crowd who are still angry. I've got no idea how to explain this.

Fortunately, Sara is there. She handles it. She saw the whole thing, Officers. People just went crazy and attacked.

She points out the first two guys—Polo Shirt and the Cameraman. They are trying very hard to be nonchalant, walking slowly away from the mass of bodies.

The cops turn their anger on them, slam them up against the wall and start shouting questions. In the meantime, someone finally turns off the sprinklers. We all stand around, dripping wet and faintly ridiculous.

It takes about twenty minutes of this before we finally get to the root cause of the whole riot.

Polo Shirt—real name, Matthew Harbaugh—holds up his phone.

It's from his Facebook feed. There's a picture of a man in a suit. My face—grainy, probably chopped from some surveillance camera video—has been painstakingly Photoshopped onto the body.

He's pissing on the American flag.

The headline: YOU WON'T BELIEVE HOW THIS RICH LIBERAL GOT AWAY WITH THIS!

The story hardly matters. In Texas, this is a death-penalty offense. Which explains why this group of otherwise ordinary people were just looking for an excuse to beat the shit out of me.

I am amazed at Godwin's work, at his speed. He didn't even have to put me up on Downvote. He just had to plant the seed.

For the next few minutes, the cops snarl at me instead of anyone in the mob. I've just gone from victim to suspect. *<maybe we need to search his luggage> <rich bastard> <probably drugs> <something> <man, if I had him alone for a few minutes>*

Those are some of the milder thoughts. They're actually doing their best to lock their anger down, to keep it behind the thin blue line. They are cops, after all.

But it's hard.

So I keep explaining, patiently and calmly, that it's not me in the photo. That I didn't do anything like that. That I am a veteran myself. And so on.

Finally, Sara unspools the whole mess by tapping on the story on the phone. It leads exactly nowhere—one of those anonymous Internet memes that doesn't seem to have a source, that appears to generate spontaneously, like mildew in a shower.

"John Smith," she says to the cops. "I mean, really? It could be anybody. It's fake."

They both scowl at the phone for a long time. They look at each other. *<what now?> <can't charge him> <have to let him go>*

They're not sure they want to believe that the story is a fake. But they see this as the quickest way to end this with the least amount of paperwork.

"Man. Sure looks like you, though. I can see why they wanted to kill you," one of the cops says. He looks at the picture and then at me again. He shakes his head. "You can hardly blame them."

"I thought you never got hit," Sara says. She looks at me from her little pod in first class, across the aisle from mine. Her hair is still wet even though we both had time to change into dry clothes. She's trying to be playful. To laugh off the experience. It's a pretty common reaction after something frightening or shocking, and it speaks well to her mental health and resilience.

I'm not quite there yet.

The cut below my eye has stopped bleeding. But my jaw still hurts, and I've got blood on my new, dry shirt, so I'm not seeing the humor.

It should go without saying that we had to take a later flight. The police decided to let me off with a warning, even though I was the one attacked. It helped considerably when I said I didn't want to press charges. The people in the mob separated and went back to being themselves, on their way to their final destinations with a story to tell when they arrived. *You'll never believe what happened at the airport . . . Oh yeah. I even punched him. Guy had it coming, what can I say?*

At least it's quiet now. Most of the people in first class have pulled down their shades, put on sleeping masks, and taken drugs to knock themselves out. Something happens when you yank a human being thirty-two thousand feet into the air. At some deep, almost cellular level, everyone in a plane knows their fate is no longer in their hands. For at least a couple of hours, they are free of gravity and all the cares and worries back on the ground.

Sara's still waiting for an answer.

"Too much going on," I tell her. "One guy trying to get my picture, dealing with the gate agent—"

"Oh sure." She's smirking. Amusement dances in her mind.

"There was a crowd too. I've told you I'm not great with crowds."

"Right, it's like your kryptonite." Now she's smiling.

"I'm not offering excuses here." I try to keep the annoyance out of my voice. "Just reasons."

"Of course not," she says. "It was a fluke thing. I'm sure it happens to a lot of guys with psychic powers and Special Forces training."

I just scowl at her and turn away, which nearly makes her laugh out loud.

"Well. We know Godwin is aware of what we're doing," she says. "That was tailor-made to get you attacked."

"You think?" I pick up my drink again.

I'm on my fifth Scotch. It still barely takes the edge off what I caught from that crowd—from the mob. They chose to let go, and let the primal, animal part of their brain do the driving.

They never see it like that, of course. That's the excuse we always use. When the bodies are on the floor and the damage is done, people like to say that they lost control. "I didn't know what I was doing." "It just happened." "I just saw red and it was over in a flash."

Bullshit. I've been inside your heads. I have seen how it works. I know. And so do you, if you're honest with yourself. When you're about to yell at your kid. Or right before you step on the gas to cut off that car in traffic. Or you pull back your leg to kick the dog. There's always a second when you can stop, when you teeter on the edge of a decision. I have watched this, in real time, seen the thoughts form and freeze, seen the pathways emerge in your neurons before they fire. For that instant, you're like someone at the top of a cliff, looking down at the ground, far below. You know what will happen, just as surely as you know how gravity works.

It doesn't matter. Almost all of you choose to jump anyway. You are choosing to do the wrong thing. And you are so grateful, because most of the time you have to smile and say please and thank you. You have to drive between the yellow lines and follow the speed limit. You have to be patient and tolerant, or at least fake it. Until, finally, when you're tired, when you've had a bad day or a bounced check, something happens. Your kid breaks the rules one more time, or someone cuts you off, or the dog pisses on the rug. And you've finally got a reason. You are justified.

You let go. For that moment, you are flying free, doing exactly what you wanted to do, without restraint. I've seen it. Your minds are filled with what can only be called joy. You get to lash out, and for that microsecond in your brain, you bathe in happiness and pretend that you live in a world without consequences.

Then your child cries, the dog yelps in pain, or you hear the crunch of plastic and metal as your car collides with another.

You come crashing back to earth. And you say, "I just lost it."

But I know the truth. There's always a choice.

Sara seems to realize that we're not bantering anymore. I feel a wave of genuine concern. "Hey. You okay?" she asks.

"I'm fine," I say, a little more sharply than I intend. She recoils, looks back at her iPad. I'm glad. I don't want to talk right now. Because, of course, I am lying through my teeth. I am pretty far away from fine.

I am shaking a little, and doing my best to hide it. My life depends on control. And everyone in that mob, everyone who attacked me—they chose to surrender control.

My kryptonite, Sara just called it. She doesn't know how right she is.

We're going up against someone who can manipulate crowds of people with my greatest weakness—who could tip me right over the edge, into madness.

I didn't tell Sara this, but as soon as the police were done with us, my phone buzzed.

It was a text. Godwin, of course.

`I warned you,` it reads. `That's not even the worst I can do to you. That's just the beginning.`

I shut the phone off, as if that would help. And I've spent all the time since thinking about running away and hiding, just so I do not have to look over the edge at what I saw in those people's minds again.

But I can't.

I can say this job is for Kira. Or for the paychecks from Armin or Stack, or even the promise of whatever money Godwin's got piled up in his secret hideout.

The fact is, I have to stop him now. Because I cannot have someone out there who can do this to me.

I will not have it.

/// 16

She's Not Supposed to Tell Anyone It Was Jay-Z. But It Was Jay-Z.

We land at Keflavík International Airport, which is blindingly clean, all high-polished wooden floors and chrome. It's like the best-managed IKEA store on earth.

Everyone is polite. Iceland is basically a small city with an entire country around it—330,000 people on an island about the size of the state of Virginia. So almost everyone knows each other, or knows someone who knows someone. It's like a very large extended family.

We have a hired car and driver to take us to the hotel. The temperature outside is in the forties and the sun is high in the sky. This is as good as the weather gets here, and people are still moving around on the streets, headed for Reykjavík's clubs. But we just spent eight hours inside a metal tube after dealing with a screaming mob. That's worse than your usual jet lag. We head to our rooms.

I am a little worried about Sara. My talent will wake me up if anyone tries to break into my hotel room. I'll get the warning from their bad intentions in plenty of time to be ready.

She doesn't have that luxury. In the hallway, before she heads into her room, I turn and ask her, "You going to be okay tonight? Alone?"

She gives me a look. *<is he hitting on me? now?>*

"I'm not hitting on you. But after what happened before, we might have visitors."

She's not sure she believes that. I'm not sure I blame her. *<it's been a while>* I can't resist chasing that thought. She doesn't have many relationships. She's usually with Stack 24-7, because he doesn't trust anyone else, and because she doesn't trust many other people to watch him either. Her last boyfriend was a year ago, and she thinks of him now. A tall, dark cipher. Useless for pretty much anything but occasional physical relief. His features are blurry. She doesn't really remember what he looks like.

So for a split second, she considers it. I'm pleased to see I'm not completely repellent to her after all.

But then she remembers she's a professional.

<no> <hasn't been that long>

She decides she's too tired to think about any of this anymore. She shows me her handbag, which still holds her Smith & Wesson.

Iceland allows tourists to bring in their own firearms with a special permit, and Sara had Stack's attorneys grease the process for us before we arrived. I probably could have picked something up or just used my talent to smuggle our weapons in—but it's nice to have permission.

"Thanks for asking," she says. "But I'm fine. And I'm sure you can take care of yourself."

She heads into her room, the door closing behind her with a firm and final click.

The next morning, I head to the hotel gym.

I don't really enjoy sweating next to business-class travelers desperately trying to work off their hangovers and expense-account dinners. But unlike those guys, I'm not on the elliptical trying to run away from an upcoming heart attack. I've got people waiting to end my story a lot quicker than that.

And I've found, as I'm rounding the corner on thirty, that the condition I earned in basic training requires more and more upkeep. If I don't invest at least an hour every day in routine maintenance, I get slow, and there have been too many times when a second or two is all the advantage I get. So I figure I can put up with the barely functional equipment and CNBC's morning blather on all the TVs.

Eventually, of course, it won't be enough. I'm going to get old, and it won't matter how many reps I do, or miles I run every morning. I'll be too slow at the wrong time. I won't react quickly enough, even with my talent, and there will be someone waiting to take advantage of that. It doesn't take a psychic to see that coming. The question is, am I going to know when it's time to quit, or will I fool myself into thinking I've got just enough luck left for another job?

I'd like to think I will walk away voluntarily before that happens, but right now the signs aren't encouraging.

Sara is already there when I enter. She's running on the treadmill, moving like a machine, cool and smooth and relentless. She's barely breathing hard.

Her mind is almost as perfect—calm and empty of everything, except for brief flashes from the outside world: the early Mozart symphonies coming through her headphones, the time remaining on the display, and an occasional word that blurts out from the talking heads on the TV.

Then she notices me. She has a small surge of happiness at the sight, an uncomplicated moment of joy, like a kid who's just seen a friend in the school lunchroom. She smiles and waves.

I suddenly feel better than I have in weeks. I tell myself not to be an idiot, but it's still a better high than the pill I took to deal with my usual morning headache.

I take the treadmill next to her and I try to match her pace for a while before giving up. She's faster than I am. She could keep going at that rate for another hour, easy.

There's a surge of pride inside her head—small but unmistakable—when she sees me adjust my treadmill to slow down. She likes winning. She's used to being underestimated. Executive protection—or let's call it what it is, bodyguarding—is an alpha-male, testosterone-soaked business. On the job, she's met a lot of ex-military, ex-cops, ex-FBI. All guys. All who think she's inherently unqualified for her job.

And it's not just men in the business. When she tells people what she does for a living, even the fat slob who services her car—the guy who hasn't done a sit-up since high school, who's never been in a fight in his life—figures he could take her.

She's gotten that same attitude ever since she walked into her first firearms certification course. The instructor looked her over before saying, "What are you doing here? You're a girl."

The other people in the class—all men—laughed. Truth be told, she didn't really want to be there. She was sixteen. Her dad, an army vet, insisted she know how to use all the guns he kept in their house, and signed her up for the course. It wasn't how she wanted to spend her Saturdays, so he bribed her with the promise of buying her a used car.

But once she heard the meatheads laugh at her, she got pissed. She must have spent a thousand pounds of brass that summer. By the time she was target shooting for her final evaluation, she was hitting her targets inside the ten ring every time.

There was no moment of respect from her instructor. He never gave her a high five or told her she was the best he'd ever seen, or even that she shot pretty good for a girl. He just scowled and marked her off, her dad bought her the car, and that should have been the end of it.

Instead, she realized she had a talent, that the idea of protecting people spoke to her, and so she got her criminal justice degree and applied for the New York Police Department. She earned top marks on her entrance exam, and she was photogenic, so she was quickly shuttled over to the security detail as a trainee. She was supposed to follow the mayor, the commissioner, and other top brass around in public, to keep them safe at high-profile events. She was supposed to balance out the uglier, older veterans on the squad—represent a little diversity for the cameras.

I can see a clear memory, never far from the front of her thoughts, of how that went down on her first day on the job. Some of the older guys from the NYPD's elite detective division objected to her presence. One in particular, a big fat guy with a thick Bronx accent, squared off against her. At six feet four inches, he had eight inches and maybe a hundred and fifty pounds on her. He lifted weights and worked out twice a month with a former MMA champ. "Suppose I'm the man, and I get shot," he asked, "how's a little thing like you going to move me?"

Sara looked up at him and told him, "Believe me: if I need to get you out of a room, one way or another, I will get you out of that room."

He laughed at her. He put one hand on her shoulder and pulled her close. He asked her again—breath tainted with burned coffee and cheap bourbon: "How's a little thing like you going to move me?"

She locked her fingers around his wrist and fired her knee into his groin. He went white and curled in half. She ducked under him and lifted with her legs, and fireman-carried him up and down the room while the rest of the cops laughed.

Nobody gave her any crap after that. She knows she's not supposed to be too proud of that moment. But it shines in her head with its own special light.

Most of the time, however, Sara found she was more like a mom with body armor than a hired gun. Just getting the mayor or a city councilman in and out of a boring two-hour luncheon speech took about sixty hours of prep work. She had to check the venue, including the bathrooms, for bombs, cameras, and listening devices. She had to watch the people entering, not just for weapons, but for glitter and cream pies in case they wanted to be YouTube heroes. She had to run deep background checks on the entire catering staff to make sure none of them had a mental imbalance that would cause them to put laxatives in the soup.

She began to work a lot with private security companies, alongside former Navy SEALs, Army Rangers, and guys who'd been on the FBI's special response teams. They lived to kick down doors and crack heads.

That was how she learned that bodyguarding isn't about being the biggest swinging dick in the room. The SEALs and the other action figures were bored out of their minds. They got sloppy. Made mistakes. Several of them quit. Bottom line, they were not people trained to keep people alive. They were trained to kill. There was a small part of each of them that was looking forward to a fight.

Sara figured out that if you're ever caught in a situation where you have to pull your gun to keep someone safe, you've already failed. Ninety percent of the time, protecting someone is about knowing where the nearest exit is. By the time trouble hits, you should already be long gone.

Which isn't to say she was above the occasional action-hero moves herself. She was working a detail alongside the mayor during a music festival in Central Park. Private security was there too, protecting the headliner. (She's not supposed to tell anyone it was Jay-Z. But it was Jay-Z.) They were moving together, quickly, out of the park and toward a waiting limo when a crowd of fans went nuts and broke through a barricade and headed right for them. They were cut off from the limo, and half the mayor's detail and the private guys were swamped by the crowd. Sara was left alone with the mayor and Jay-Z. She grabbed them both and shoved them along, running for a police cruiser with the doors open, blocking an access road.

She pushed them inside, got behind the wheel, and jumped a lawn and a sidewalk getting them out of the park, then headed the wrong way down a one-way street to get them to the closest police substation, which was standard protocol.

Jay-Z laughed most of the way. The mayor checked his phone for messages like it was any other day.

Her supervisor wasn't thrilled when she reached the station, but the head of Jay-Z's detail—a guy who ran a multinational, high-security client protection service—handed her his card.

That's when she learned that some private protection consultants could make over $100,000 a year to start. So she got a job with that firm and immediately went to work, mostly guarding C-suite execs from Fortune 500 firms.

Not long after that, Stack hired her. He heard some people from Amazon singing her praises, and his fortune had just passed into ludicrous territory.

He needed her to feel safe. And she needed to believe that she was doing something more important than just keeping a rich guy from getting mugged. Stack told her his plan to make the world a better place through technology, and she was sold.

Now, when Stack goes out for a meeting or to make a speech—it doesn't happen much these days, but it still happens—they assume she's his assistant or his PR handler or his girlfriend. She fades into the background. Becomes part of the scenery. No one sees her. So they never see it coming if she has to pull her Glock from the concealed-carry holster in the back of her skirt.

She's still willing to show off on occasion, however. Like now, she just turned the treadmill up as high as it can go and finished her morning run at a sprint, while I'm still trying to catch my breath.

She's only lightly glowing with sweat as she steps off the machine. The gym has a free weight set. "Spot me?" she asks. I help her rack a bar. She's able to keep talking while pressing nearly twice her body weight.

As usual, she's got an agenda on her mind. She tries to sound conversational when she begins speaking, but I can see she's going down a list in her head.

"A lot of people thought you were retired when I started asking about you," she says. "Hiding out on your own private island off Seattle, watching the seagulls, catching fish for your supper."

"I didn't catch any fish. But other than that, yeah, that was my life. I'm surprised people cared."

She gives me a look from under the bar. <*come on*> "It's not that big a community. You know that. You've got a reputation."

"Really? What do people say?"

She grins. "You don't know already?"

"It only works when I'm close. Can't tell what people are saying about me long distance."

She thinks about how to phrase it. <*con man*> <*full of shit*> <*violent*> <*spooky*> <*weird*> <*dangerous*>

"There are a lot of people who claim to be ex-CIA. Or ex–Special Forces," she says, hoisting the bar with a small grunt. "Not many who say they can read minds, though. But you can see how that might lead to some skepticism. Some people think you're running some kind of scam. But some people—the ones I spoke to, before I set up our meeting—they know you can do some interesting things. Like the Eckerd job. Or OmniVore. They don't think you're a con artist. They just think you're dangerous."

Well, at least she was polite.

"Dangerous. That's flattering, I suppose."

"What do you expect? Given some of your clients . . ."

She leaves it there, but I can see who she's talking about. People like Nikolai's father. Clients who might expect a permanent solution to their problems. Which would make me a very expensive hired thug.

I can't really argue with that, though, so I just watch her lift the bar again.

She finishes her set, then sits up and looks at me from the bench, one eyebrow arched, her expression camera-ready.

"I also heard there was a woman on that island with you," she says.

I shrug. "There was. She left."

She smiles. "I bet. What happened?"

I've asked myself the same question. It seemed like I had everything I wanted. A retreat from all of you people and the constant high-pitched whine of your thoughts. A solid cushion in the bank. Even a woman who'd taken a bullet for me and came and found me again anyway.

Kelsey had worked with me. She was assigned to help me by my client. She knew what I was, and accepted me for it.

But nothing lasts. That's the thing. I began to worry about the size of the cushion in the bank. I missed the feel of sitting in a private jet. I spent a lot of time wandering around the house, wondering what to do with myself.

So I began taking jobs again. And that upset Kelsey. Not so much that she said anything. But she didn't have to. Even if I couldn't see the thoughts marching across her brain, I would watch her unconsciously rub her shoulder where the bullet hit her. She could still feel an echo of the pain.

She got angry, but she kept it inside. It didn't all come spilling out until she found out what I'd done to one of her former coworkers, and how I'd gotten the nest egg sitting in my money market account. He'd made a mistake that nearly got me and Kelsey both killed. He was the reason she'd been shot. So I bankrupted him.

It was all perfectly legal. And I figured I had a good reason.

But that was too much for her. She knew this guy. Had worked with him for years. And even though he'd betrayed her, she couldn't live with my idea of justice. She didn't want to be part of that.

I knew she'd made her decision when she kissed me good-bye one morning as I left for a job. I knew she'd start packing her bags as soon as the boat took me away.

I left anyway.

When I came back, there wasn't even a note. But then, she knew I didn't need one.

The island house seemed too empty after that. And I noticed for the first time that Seattle is really incredibly gray.

Not long after that, I moved myself into the suite at The Standard. I told myself it was for work, that I needed to be back in L.A. for the jobs.

"Different priorities," is what I finally tell Sara. "We wanted different things. Usual story."

"Maybe," Sara says. "Then again, maybe you're just not very good at happily-ever-after."

Again, I can't really argue with that.

///17

Security Is Our Top Priority

Before we go out to the server farm, I pull my own gun out of my luggage. I've been scanning around us all day, checking for any of Godwin's hired help or the signs of another flashmob. Nobody's pinged my radar so far, so maybe he doesn't know we're coming here.

And Iceland is, statistically speaking, one of the safest places in the world. Despite all of those murder mysteries set in the cold reaches of Scandinavian countries, there's almost no violent crime in Iceland. Homicide is practically nonexistent. Most of the time the cops don't even carry guns.

Still, I remember what happened the last time I left my gun at home. I load a clip into the Walther, put it in the holster under my jacket, and head to the car.

The data center stands—like so much else around here—on a vast, empty plain. The online brochure says it used to be a NATO facility, but it's been totally retrofitted and upgraded. Even so, it's possible to look at it and see the last outpost at the end of the world—a final remnant of civilization after whatever Apocalypse eventually manages to bring us down.

Reykjavík is known worldwide as a haven for data. The cold temperatures mean that the server farms don't have to waste as much money on air conditioning to keep the computers from overheating. And they also benefit from the cheap geothermal power that runs just underneath Iceland's frozen ground.

I've been in server farms back in the States before. The ones I've seen are little more than warehouses filled with row after row of computers, stacked and racked and humming quietly as data pours through them.

But this place has spent some money on the customer experience. The building is an architect's dream—all clean lines and sharp angles—with giant panes of glass and mirror-finish floors in the lobby. Despite the vast emptiness just outside, Mr. Einar Magnusson, the data center's manager, is smiling and cheerful. He's like a breath mint in human form—crisp and fresh and clean, bright green eyes filled with delight as he greets us.

Sara has led him to believe that Stack might be interested in investing heavily in data storage, and Magnusson is already counting the money in his mind. He's glad to take us on a tour of the facility, eager to show off.

He opens a locked door with a key, a thumbprint, and a retinal scan. "Security is, of course, our top priority," Magnusson says. "No unauthorized personnel can access our facility, and we have multiple redundant systems in place to ensure that there are never any breaches of our data."

Then he holds the door for us and gestures for us to walk right in.

We get our first look at the server farm. In its own way, it is almost beautiful.

The light is low. Blade servers, all fitted with glowing blue LEDs, stretch for what seems like miles in every direction. There is an unearthly hum as the data of a billion people—their emails, Web searches, movies, photos, and naked pictures—fly through the room on their way from one corner of the globe to another.

Our original plan might have just hit a snag, however. Sara was supposed to distract Magnusson by asking a slew of technical questions while I found the server for Downvote and then copied its data onto a portable hard drive.

Did I mention that what we're doing isn't strictly legal?

Yeah, it's not.

As part of its drive to boost its economy with the money from these data centers, Iceland's government takes the privacy of their clients very seriously. It usually requires a warrant and a diplomatic request from the U.S. government to crack open one of these servers.

We don't have those. So Sara and I were hoping to get in and out of here as quickly and quietly as possible.

Unfortunately, this isn't like anything we were expecting. I thought there'd be something like a map. Or maybe even a sign.

Seems a little foolish now.

So, Plan B. Get it from Magnusson. Sara is already well into her questions. I interrupt. "How do you keep track of it all?" I ask, putting a little more awe into my voice than is strictly necessary.

Magnusson's expression doesn't change, but inside his mind, he's spitting mad. He was enjoying being the focus of Sara's attention.

"What?" he says, perhaps a little more sharply than he intended.

"How do you know whose data belongs in which place?" I say, keeping the gee-whiz tone.

Magnusson smiles, and a layer of condescension slides down over his thoughts. "It's actually quite simple. Our clients are organized by their IP addresses. We have dynamic switching capability, so it is quite an easy thing to expand server capacity beyond the initial blades as needed—"

"Yeah, but isn't there some kind of, I don't know, guide? I mean, how do you ever find what you're looking for?"

He does not quite roll his eyes, but it's a close thing. "We maintain a constantly updated directory," he says, and points to a simple desktop terminal on a nearby table.

"Very cool," I say. "Would you demonstrate?"

Magnusson smiles, and this time it's almost genuine. He's happy to show me how easy it is to answer my question, since it only makes him look smarter in front of Sara.

"Certainly," he says, and walks over the keyboard and begins typing away. He enters his password, which I snag as his fingers dance across the keys—November1234, that's just sloppy, probably the default and he's never changed it—and then enters a string of numbers to find a specific server.

A map immediately comes up on the screen, with a green line leading from our location to the server rack.

"You see?" he says. "Child's play. All you have to do is enter the name of the client, or the IP address, and we can find the location in seconds."

"Outstanding," I say. "Thanks so much."

And then I hit him with the sensation of an overwhelmingly full bladder.

Childish, I know, but he's almost like a substitute teacher. I can't help torturing him. Besides, we do need him out of the way, and this is probably the most painless method to do that.

He holds out for an admirably long time. He tries to keep his mind on his sales pitch to Sara, but eventually his eyes start to cross. "Excuse me," he says quickly, and heads for the door. "Please do not touch anything," he adds, just before he starts to sprint to the lobby. "I will be right back."

As soon as the door clicks shut behind him, I head back to the terminal, enter in his password, and then type in the IP address of Downvote's server.

A map pops up on the screen, just like before, only this time leading us downstairs three levels and to the back of the facility. Of course it wouldn't be close by.

Sara frowns. "Let's get going."

"Magnusson won't be gone long," I tell her.

She makes a face. "If he comes back before we do, we'll tell him we slipped away for a quickie. We're kinky like that."

Before I can dig any deeper into that, she's moving quickly toward the metal stairwell at the center of the floor.

There are levels and levels of racks of computers, all with the same eerie blue glow. Sara and I keep checking the numbers on top of the rows. Everything looks alike. It would be easy to get lost down here. That end-of-the-world feeling just keeps getting stronger.

Despite having what is an undeniably spooky talent, I'm not usually much for omens or vibes. But I can't help feeling like something is wrong here. I tell myself I'm just being paranoid—having a mob attack you will do that—and nothing is bouncing off my radar. We're totally alone down here.

We find the row of servers we're looking for, and head down, checking the boxes as we go. We find the box with the Downvote server inside, and Sara opens her bag. She's got a compact sixteen-terabyte Samsung drive—which ought to be enough to suck whatever data we need out of Downvote's server. She hooks it up with a fiber-optic cable, activates a special software package that Stack prepared for us, and starts transferring the information.

Then I think I hear something.

I scan our surroundings. Nothing. The only thoughts I'm picking up are Sara's. *<come on come on>* *<watched pot never boils, toasters never pop, and nothing ever downloads as fast as you want it to>*

Nobody else. It's possible I heard Magnusson come back into the data center—he's far enough away that I wouldn't hear his thoughts—but he would probably start calling for us.

Still, I could have sworn . . .

A second later, I know I hear something. The sound of something moving on the floor. Probably a mouse or a rat or a lemming or whatever they have in Iceland.

Only this sounded much bigger.

I stop listening with my talent. And start listening with my ears.

I remember something from my days of Special Forces training. When the operators would teach us how to move. How they emphasized being quiet, but not too quiet. How the wrong kind of silence was almost as big a giveaway as the wrong kind of noise.

This is the wrong kind of quiet.

I start walking slowly down the row of servers, toward the noise. Sara looks up at me, sharply. I gesture for her to stay silent.

I don't pull my gun. I mean, that would be paranoid. Nobody alive can sneak up on me.

I'm sure I'm going to feel like an idiot when I look around the corner and find nothing.

The guy hits me just as I stick my head out from behind the server racks.

It's a good, solid punch, with lots of weight behind it, and I bounce off a rack of servers before I hit the floor.

Despite the spots dancing in front of my eyes and the ringing in my ears, I still don't quite believe it when I look up and see a man, dressed all in black, wearing mirrored goggles and a ski mask, standing above me.

All I can think is, *Totally fucking impossible*.

Then I'm rolling out of the way as he tries to stomp on my head.

He just barely misses me. I scramble away from him as fast as I can, but I'm crab-walking and he's on his feet.

I finally remember: Sara.

"SARA!" I shout.

No response. I'm about to scream again, but he catches up to me and swings a kick that lands right in my ribs, knocking me flat on my back again, taking the wind right out of my lungs.

I didn't see it coming. I didn't see anything coming.

Usually I never lose a fight because I can see all my opponent's moves before he makes them. But I'm getting no thoughts from him at all. As far as my talent is concerned, there's nobody there. I'm getting my ass kicked by a ghost.

He puts another kick into my side as I lie on the ground. The surprise is almost as bad as the pain. But when he winds up to do it again, I manage to get over my shock enough to catch his leg.

All right then, I think. Let's do this the old-fashioned way.

I haul him off balance, and he has to twist and turn away from me to keep from getting dragged down to my level. I use the space to hop to my feet, ignoring the pain in my head and my sides. He's way ahead on points, and I want to even the score.

I throw a punch that he dodges easily, but I catch him with the kick that follows it. He grunts, but that's the only sound he's made so far.

I throw another combination of punches. He dodges and blocks them—he knows what he's doing—but I keep up the pressure, and he can't counter fast enough.

I finally drive a hard left past his defenses, and I hear something crunch under the ski mask as I connect.

It's eerie, being this close to someone and not knowing what they're thinking.

On the plus side, however, when I hit him, I get none of his pain. None at all.

It's like a Get Out of Jail Free card. I throw myself into the fight, advancing on him, punching, kicking, grabbing, just to see what I can get away with.

Which, as it turns out, is what he was waiting for. He lets me get over my feet and overextended, and then grabs my wrist and yanks back. Within a second, he's got me wrapped up in a complex choke hold.

Exactly the kind of trap I would never usually fall for, except it feels like I've got a paper bag over my head. I'm fighting like an amateur here.

I'm losing oxygen fast, I've got no chance of breaking the hold, and this goddamn ninja is still barely breathing hard.

So I swallow my pride and pull my gun.

I will tell myself later that I didn't really want to shoot this guy because I want to know how he's able to silence his thoughts. Or some crap like that. But the truth is, I really thought I could take him hand-to-hand.

As soon as he sees the gun come out from under my jacket, he ratchets up the pressure on my throat. I get a little dizzy, but it's not fast enough. I can still aim the gun over my shoulder in the general direction of his head.

He breaks the hold and shoves me away into one of the metal racks before I have a chance to pull the trigger. So at least I know he's not stupid. Or bulletproof.

I suck down fresh air and turn, aiming the gun at the same time, but he's already ducked behind another rack of servers.

I run after him, but it's like he's vanished. There are too many twists and corners and blind spots. He could be five feet away from me or a hundred yards. I have no way of knowing.

For one of the few times in my life, I'm forced to rely on my ears and eyes like everyone else.

I can't say I'm enjoying it.

"SARA," I shout again.

Still no answer. But I can hear her thoughts now that someone isn't pounding a steady drumbeat on my skull.

<Smith> <he's still here> <hope you can hear this> <saw him near Downvote server> <moving north up the server row>

She's being smarter than I am. Keeping her mouth shut. I move quickly and quietly toward the spot where I left her.

She's not there anymore. I can feel her close by, however. She's hiding. I put myself in her head for a second, and I feel that she's already got her gun out. Smart move.

I figure our ninja must be unarmed, or he would have shot me instead of fighting. And while it's possible there are other people in the world who can stay completely off my radar, it's not likely they're hiding in here with us right now. Which means we've got him outnumbered.

Then I turn the corner and see the ninja and learn that at least one of my assumptions is wrong.

He's got an H&K submachine pistol in one hand.

He sees me at almost the exact same moment. He's already aiming.

"Get down, Sara!" I shout as I dive for cover. Bullets spray and ricochet through the stacks of metal. Sparks fly as lead tears through silicon and cable. Something flies past my hair, then I feel a burning sensation across my ear, and I know I've been hit by shrapnel.

I stay down, eyes closed.

The rattle of gunfire stops suddenly. My ears are still ringing.

I lift my head cautiously. I still can't see a damn thing.

But I can hear Sara's thoughts. *<is it over?>* *<is Smith still alive?>* *<who the hell was that guy?>*

I want to call out to her, to tell her he's gone, but I realize I have no idea if that's true.

I can't see. My hearing's shot. I can't call out to Sara without giving away my position. We could wait down here for hours as he stalks around the rows and picks us off.

Patience has never been my strong suit.

I crawl as fast as I can to the back of the room. Then I haul myself into a crouch, like a sprinter starting from the blocks of a track meet, and I begin running down the aisle at the end of all the racks.

Gun up, clearing each row as fast as possible, finger on the trigger, ready to pull at the first sight of a man in black.

I get to the end of the room. Nothing. I double back and do it again. Each time, expecting a bullet to come out of nowhere and kill me.

I'm just past where I find Sara, half hidden behind a row of shot-up servers. She has her gun out as well.

We manage not to kill each other.

Then, working together, we clear the rest of the room.

Empty.

He's gone.

Like I said before, Iceland is usually a peaceful place. People leave their kids unattended on the street, their keys in their cars.

So the police aren't terribly happy about us bringing a war zone to their nice, quiet country. There is a fully armed antiterrorist strike force waiting for us when we finally reach the surface. They have their weapons out and aimed at us from a firing line just inside the lobby.

Mr. Magnusson called them. He will not smile at us again at any time during our visit.

We are not idiots, so we have already placed our guns on the floor of the lobby and our hands on our heads. Then we spend an uncomfortable amount of time zip-cuffed on our stomachs after that, even though, again, we are technically the victims here. But nobody is taking any chances.

While we're waiting for this all to get settled, I pull the facts from Magnusson's head. He went to the bathroom, where he spent a long, uncomfortable time, until he heard gunfire. He called the police, who responded with overwhelming force. Nobody wants a repeat of what Anders Breivik did in Norway. He and the other staff hid in his office until the cops arrived and pulled them out.

The ninja, whoever he was, is nowhere to be found.

I'm grateful to see that he shows up on the security feeds, at least. It turns out to be what keeps us from going to jail. After the police examine the video, they realize that we are . . . well, not exactly innocent, but at least acting in self-defense.

Fortunately, the cameras do not show us cracking open Downvote's server and downloading its data. The angles are all wrong for that. We tell the police—and Magnusson—that we got bored waiting for him and went looking around. Magnusson doesn't want to buy it. He pushes for us to be charged with something—anything.

"Millions of dollars in damages!" he shrieks. "God only knows how much data was lost! Our clients—and my people—me—we could have been killed!"

I don't really blame him for flying apart. This is no kind of fun, even when you're trained for it. There's a high, sharp buzz saw of rage and helplessness cutting through his mind every few seconds, tearing any composure he might have into pieces.

Sara, however, invokes the power of Stack's money and lawyers. That focuses his thoughts again pretty quickly.

Because here's the other thing the security video shows: ordinarily, it should have been impossible for the ninja to get inside the data center after Magnusson left. All of those redundant security measures, right?

Except he walked right in. Magnusson, on his way out to the bathroom, left the outer door blocked open.

Presumably so he could hurry back after taking a piss.

Magnusson's outraged protests die in his throat as we all watch the video: he blocks the door open and scurries out of view. The ninja walks in through the lobby entrance, totally casual. A security guard approaches him slowly—and then the ninja pulls out the H&K, and everyone in the lobby goes diving for cover. The ninja walks through the open door, on his way downstairs looking for us.

"Security is your top priority?" Sara asks. "John, didn't you hear Mr. Magnusson say that before? Along with something about how no unauthorized personnel can access the facility?"

Magnusson chokes out an apology to Sara, but I'm not really listening.

I keep watching the video, looking for some other clue. The ninja is obviously linked to Godwin and Downvote, but I have no idea how. Ordinarily I wouldn't have to guess. I'd just know, from his own brain. Instead I have to stare at a screen and hope he holds up a sign.

A few minutes pass as he fights with me downstairs and shoots at us. Then the lobby security cameras show him walking calmly out the front doors again, just moments before the police storm inside. It's almost as if he was invisible to them. Hiding in plain sight. Walking away in all the confusion.

It looks, in fact, a lot like a trick I might pull.

In the end, the police let us go. Nobody is particularly happy about it, but we do have permits for our weapons, and there is no Icelandic law against being shot at.

It is much later as we drive back to our hotel, even if the sun is still out.

In the passenger seat, Sara opens her bag and shows me the hard drive.

"We got almost all of it. Unfortunately, he came looking for me before the transfer was completed. I barely had time to disconnect and hide."

"Do you think he was after the server too? Trying to wipe it before we could get it?"

I know this is what she thinks, because I can read it at the top of her mind. But I'm trying to be polite.

"Yeah," she says. "But if he was, he did it the hard way."

I get an image from inside her head, a memory: the Downvote server box, shattered and riddled with bullet holes.

"He shot it up?"

"Either by accident when he was aiming at you, or on purpose," Sara says. "The site is still up, though. I already checked. It must have switched to another server automatically. And we have no idea where that one is.

With any luck, we got enough data for Aaric to track him down before I had to pull the plug."

Then something occurs to her. "So who was he?"

I pause. I'm almost embarrassed to admit it out loud. "I don't know," I say.

She gives me a look. "But you were there. You should know everything he did."

"I should, yeah."

She lets that sit for a moment, waiting for me. More or less patiently. *<so what happened?> <what's going on?>*

I decide that the truth is the only way to go.

"I couldn't read him," I tell her. "At all."

"What? What does that mean?"

I rub my eyes. I can feel irritation and confusion bubble up from her. It doesn't help my headache. "It was like a blank space. Nothing there."

"And that's never happened before?"

"Never."

"Never?" I don't need my talent to pick up on her skepticism.

I turn and look at her. "No. Never," I say flatly.

"Come on, surely there have been times you couldn't read someone. I mean, didn't you just tell me that it's not always easy to figure out what's going on inside someone's head? That's there's a lot of stuff in there?"

"It's not the same thing," I say as I struggle to explain it, both to her and to myself. Yes, there have been people who are difficult to read. People who are just smarter than I am, as I've said, or people who are much, much stupider. People whose thought processes are deformed by some kind of mental illness, like that patient back at the jail. There have been times I've been overloaded with information, and I've had to work to pick out the relevant bits. There are people who are adept at guarding their thoughts, like Cantrell. He would mask his secrets behind well-rehearsed mental routines, like shopping lists or memorized scenes from dirty movies. And there have been times when a head injury or a concussion has muffled the usual stream of thoughts all around me.

But this was completely different. At all of those times, I could still pick up something. I may not have understood it, or read it as clearly as usual, but there was still something there. Even if it was just static. There was a response.

Not with this guy. "It was like—if you went to enter a search on Google, and the Internet was completely down," I tell Sara.

"I didn't think that was possible for you," she says.

"Me either," I say. I try to find some way of telling her how completely alien this was for me. "He was in the building. He was just a few feet away from me. But if I hadn't seen him—with my eyes—I never would have known."

She tries to stifle a small note of amusement. "Yeah, that's how it is for most people. All the time. It's called being normal."

That's not how I would describe it. A dozen different words go through my head. Blind. Deaf. Ignorant.

Helpless.

Out loud, all I say is "It's not as much fun as I thought it would be."

///18

I Prefer the Honesty

I watch Sara dance in the midst of a knot of impossibly beautiful Icelanders, their bodies caught like sculptures in the strobe, some kind of electronic-techno crap pumping out of the club's speakers. I am not much of a music critic—to me, it's all just noise. But even I can say that this barely qualifies. It's more like a porn soundtrack as the people on the floor writhe and twist and contort themselves. Only the presence of clothing is preventing actual pregnancies out there.

Sara was too keyed up to lock herself up in her hotel room, and despite my arguments, she insisted on going out. Reykjavík is known for its nightlife, so she had lots of choices for entertainment. She also said she didn't need a babysitter or a bodyguard, but I decided to tag along anyway. I've been watching the crowd all night, running through the surface thoughts of everyone here on the off chance that Godwin has more hired help waiting for us. We are unarmed, because the police confiscated our weapons. (With a polite promise to return them on our way out of the country, which they hoped would be very soon.)

So far, from what I can see, nobody wants to do Sara any harm. Well—at least not intentionally, although some of the positions they're picturing don't look very comfortable.

Sara bounces up to me after shoving her way through the crowd of drunk Icelanders. The alcohol in her bloodstream fizzes in her brain, and she lands almost facedown on the bar.

"Whoa," she says, pushing herself back up with a big happy grin. "More vodka. Now."

"Not sure that's a great idea."

"Oh come on," she says. "Don't be such a Gloomy Gus."

I can't help it. I laugh. "A Gloomy Gus?"

"You are always, like, such a downer," she says, enunciating her words very carefully. "Seriously. Is your life that bad?"

I laugh again, but for a different reason this time. "You've definitely had too much vodka. You don't remember what happened today?"

She waves that off. "Of course I do," she says, impatient. "I'm not talking about that. People start shooting at you and you're practically happy. I mean, you're always walking around with the weight of the world."

"You should see what I see."

Another hand wave. She barely hears me. "Right, right," she says. "People have dirty minds. What else is new."

I take another quick scan of the crowd. "You want me to tell you what people are thinking right now?" I ask. "You want to know what a dozen of those men in this bar thought when they saw you go by?"

It comes out a little uglier than I intended. But Sara shrugs it off. "Nothing to do with me," she says. "It's in their heads. Let them think what they want. That's their world. It doesn't have to be a part of mine."

"You manage threats for a living," I snap back at her. "You cannot believe that. What if one of those guys tries to make himself a part of your world?"

She smirks at me, and there's a sudden clarity behind her eyes, despite all the vodka. "Then he probably won't like the result," she says. "But until then, it's not my problem."

She is utterly calm. Totally confident. It takes me a second to recognize the feeling that shoots through me. Envy.

"Well, it's always my problem," I say. It sounded a little less petulant in my head.

"Yeah, and you know what? They're always going to be there. No matter what you do."

I thought she was an adrenaline junkie. A lot of people in this line of work are. They want to go up against the big threats. They like the high stakes of protecting another life. Nothing is routine when there's a chance that someone could die if you don't do your job right.

Now I see that I was wrong. She is not an addict. Sure, she loves the thrill. She would be an utter wreck if she didn't get some reward out of the jolt that comes from facing down an imminent threat.

But that's not what keeps her going, at her core. I can see it there, a tiny little sun blazing at the center of her mind. She's a genuine optimist. She believes. Believes in her capability to handle the world. Believes that it will get better, with applied effort. Believes that Stack is worth saving, and by extension, so are the people who will benefit from his genius.

Looking at that tiny little sun, basking in its warmth, is like a holiday on an alien planet for me. For an instant, I wonder what it would be like to live there.

"So what do you suggest?" I ask. I genuinely want to know.

She leans in close, still smiling. "Let's dance," she says.

And she spins back out onto the floor. A dozen people watch her, all filled with lust and admiration and simple joy, just from being near.

I can't help smiling too.

But I don't dance.

I'm almost ready to relax, to let my guard down. It might be the vodka. But then I catch a ripple as it runs through the crowd. It somehow feels like an echo, reverberating through dozens of different skulls at once. The same basic idea, with the same emotional response, washing over the crowd like a wave.

I realize that the tone I just heard is not another electronic beep from the DJ's speakers. It's the sound of every phone in the club pinging with an alert from their social media services.

All of the Icelanders cast their perfect features down to the screens in their hands. Their sharp cheekbones are illuminated by the light.

I check my phone. Nothing. This is not a good sign. Iceland is almost as wired for social media as the United States. A club full of young people—this is basically Godwin's target demographic. I can't believe I didn't think of it before we came in here.

(And of course, I really do know what I was thinking when I came in here, too anxious and hopeful, thinking with my dick as usual. Stupid.)

I am already moving toward Sara, trying to get to her in the center of the crowd, which has stopped moving to the music. There are already ugly looks being thrown.

Just not in my direction for a change.

I grab one of the phones away from a young man who's looking at it in disgust. He squawks something in his native language, but I'm already moving deeper into the crowd.

It's Sara. Or, it's close enough. Another Photoshop composite.

She holds a stack of Icelandic currency with a big smile on her face. It's on fire.

This one was for European audiences, so it's a little more sophisticated than the meme that Godwin invented for me.

Icelanders are a pretty laid-back group, as a whole, I think—you have to have some emotional stability to deal with the weather alone—but they are sensitive about their economy. Back when the big collapse hit, Iceland had overextended itself by buying businesses all over the world, gaining billions in debt, and eventually defaulting on pretty much all of it. They took it a little more seriously here than we did in America, where everyone got to keep their jobs. There were mass protests and bankers and politicians went to jail.

I don't read Icelandic, but the message on the phone has hit a hot button in the minds of everyone around me. Something about Sara being one of the rich American bankers who profited off their country's humiliation.

She's suddenly Public Enemy Number One out there. The crowd closes around her like a fist.

I drop the stolen phone on the floor as mine suddenly beeps with a text message.

`I took a bit of time with this one. Just for her. See how she likes it.`

Godwin.

I start shoving my way through the sweating dancers, trying to get closer. Nobody wants to move. Some mental persuasion helps them. I don't think about the repercussions for myself. I serve up pain in every flavor: broken legs, back spasms, stomach cramps, cattle prods, whatever it takes to get them to move.

I am about a dozen feet away when I finally see Sara again. She's at the center of a scrum of young men, all of them shouting at her in Icelandic. "*Útlendingur!*" someone screams. I don't know the language, but the intent sings out from their minds.

<foreigner> <arrogant American bitch> <fuckers think they can come here and do whatever they want>

There's a big, heavily muscled dance-floor god looming over her, pushing and shoving at her. She has her hands up. Her expression is patient. She tries to back away, but the crowd shoves her forward again. The big guy forms a fist with his right hand.

I'm firing up something painful for him—maybe a nightmare, maybe a seizure—when Sara saves me the trouble. She dodges his slow, clumsy punch and knocks his arm aside with a sharp block.

He bellows and swings again. And she beats him stupid.

She is magnificent. No other word. Hand-to-hand, she takes the guy down like she's swinging an ax into a tree. Openhanded blows to his neck and gut. Kicks to his knees and ankles. Six-plus feet of Icelandic outrage falls to the floor in pieces.

That gives the other men in the mob pause. I can feel their anger start to break apart, quicker than back in Houston. That rage. That surrender to a bigger, simpler feeling. It starts to wash back as they see that there might be a personal consequence for their actions, that their victim is not as helpless as they thought.

But it works only for those who can see it. The others behind them are still just a mob. And they are shoving forward, drunk, angry, shouting. There's no handy sprinkler system to cool them down this time. And I'm starting to get caught up in it again. Feeling the rage. Wanting to do harm. To fight back. To make someone pay.

So I think hard.

Consequences. That snapped a couple of them out of it. People get angry, they forget their actions have consequences. Or they just don't care.

Let's see if I can remind them.

This is going to be tricky. I am not good with crowds. But this isn't really a crowd, is it? It's a mob. And mobs are notoriously single-minded.

I reach out. Find that humming string of outrage, connecting all of them. And pull on it, straight into the mass that they've become. A direct line into all of them at once.

It suddenly occurs to me that I have never done anything like this before. I could be looking at a stroke or a complete mental breakdown.

But it's too late now. We are surrounded. And I'm in their minds. All of their minds.

I light them up. I overload the pregenual anterior cingulate cortex in all of them. That's the part of the brain that is responsible for detecting errors, for embarrassment and guilt and shame.

For a brief instant, in every one of their heads, it's as if there is a searchlight from a police chopper fixed on them, showing the whole world what they are doing. They are all exposed in that bright light, on display. For a second, it's like the whole world is watching them. Judging them.

Imagine having God or your grandmother catch you with one hand in the cookie jar and the other on your privates. That's what they all feel now.

That stops most of them cold. They snap out of it. *<my god>* *<what am I doing>* *<so ashamed>* *<that's not me>* *<never would have>* *<never meant to>*

Some of them, however, could give a damn. They are pushing past the ones who are frozen with shame, still snarling. They know what they are doing. And they are perfectly content to keep doing it.

But there are a lot fewer of them. And it's easier for me to pick them off, one by one, with pain and suffering I draw from my mental deck. This one with the bottle in his hand gets crippling gastrointestinal distress. That woman with her nails like claws suddenly finds herself unable to move her legs and falls flat on her face. The guy with the shaved head still screeching about foreigners chokes as his lungs suddenly tighten.

Now we've got a clear shot at the door. This time, we're not waiting around for the police. We're just getting the hell out of here.

Sara, despite everything, is smiling as she takes my hand and we run.

<My hero> she thinks, and the thought is both genuine and topped with a thick layer of sarcasm and irony.

But what the hell, I'll take it.

///

After we lose the angry Icelanders, we sprint, breathless, all the way into our hotel, me still clutching Sara's hand even though the danger is long past. There is no one behind us—I sensed it when they gave up, several blocks ago—but we don't let go.

Most of her buzz has evaporated, burned off by the sudden adrenaline rush and the sprint through the cold street. There are a lot of conflicting thoughts running through her head at top speed now.

She thinks of Stack. But not for any of the reasons I would have guessed.

The knot that binds them finally loosens enough for me to see how it was tied. I get a clear look into her memories.

She was raised on Long Island, a nice, middle-class girl from a nice family. She had a cousin, a young man who was terribly abused by his stepfather, a mean drunk. Her dad's sister—his mother—didn't want to go to the cops. But when her cousin collapsed at school with the pain from a broken collarbone, her dad was done being tolerant. He didn't rush over and beat the man to death, although that was probably his first instinct. Instead, he showed up at the doctor's office and simply brought him home. To Sara's home. He told his sister and her husband that it was out of their hands. His nephew was living with them now.

And if his stepfather ever showed up again, then her dad promised to cripple him.

She remembers her cousin weeping and thrashing in the night in the spare bedroom. He had problems even before the beatings began, and he was broken in a lot of ways. It was not always easy having him around. But she thought he was getting better.

Then, a year later, when her cousin was fourteen, he simply left. Walked away from all of them with the money in his wallet and a duffel full of clothes. Didn't leave so much as a note.

To this day, she has no idea what happened to him.

When she met Stack, she saw the same damage in him. He found himself revealing his own abuse, his own beatings at the hands of his father. How he was starved, sometimes for days, for minor violations of the family rules. How any interest in girls or sex or anything Stack's father considered ungodly would lead to horrible retribution. She knows how deep those wounds go because she lived under the same roof with someone who also suffered them. It also didn't escape her notice that he ran away from home at the same age as her cousin.

They fit. She needed someone to rescue. And he needed someone to protect him.

Mostly, Sara thinks about the awful waste of Stack's life. He has more money than most people can even imagine. But he is still confined by his father's strictures.

She remembers the last time he was on dry land. She accompanied him to a business meeting, and then he decided to get dinner. That in itself was unusual, because he usually just survived on those protein bars. They ate at one of those fifties diner places, burgers and fries and oldies on a real jukebox. Stack ate his burger and even most of his fries, and did not look even a little guilty. The waitress offered him a hot fudge sundae for dessert. It came with the meal, she said. No extra charge.

He sat there, and she could see him struggle. He practically vibrated in his seat; he wanted it. She wanted to tell him, *It's just a stupid dessert. Go ahead and get it.*

But he wouldn't. He just couldn't get past whatever cage had been built inside his head.

And now he's looking at time in a real prison, despite all his genius and his money. Despite everything he has, she thinks about how little time he's actually spent as a free man.

Sara is thinking hard about that. About how tomorrow is never what you expect. How people can vanish right in front of your eyes.

<been a year> <life is short> <people trying to kill us> <stupid> <not professional> <screw professional> <a whole freaking year> <life is short>

She's watching me closely. I can feel it. As soon as we are in the elevator, I barely catch my breath before our eyes meet. Sara's are shining with something wild and she does not look away. She's made her decision.

<now> <now> <now> It's like a drumbeat, in rhythm with her heart.

"Now?" I ask, because even though I can hear her thoughts, there are times when I am a wildly optimistic listener.

"Now," she says, and pins me back against the wall of the elevator even as I move toward her. Her mouth is on mine, her tongue pressing, exploring, tasting. She's got my jacket off and I'm pulling at her blouse as the elevator doors ding.

We pause for breath, look up, and rush past the elderly couple waiting patiently for us to leave the elevator. They both give us little smiles, and then they share a little memory of an elevator of their own, many years before.

I don't really care. I am fumbling with the key card, doing my best to open the hotel room door without surrendering a square inch of contact with Sara. The (goddamn) lock finally clicks, and we go tumbling into the room.

She is on top of me on the bed. She pops the buttons off my shirt and then tears her own off as well, followed quickly by the bra. For a moment, I simply look at her, above me. I want to pause and burn the image in my brain.

But her thoughts are still a drumbeat. *<now> <now> <now> <now>*

So I flip her on her side and pull her skirt and panties down. She gets my suit pants off me by pulling and kicking.

<now> <now> <now>

Then I am inside her, in her mind and body, together. We are desperate together, rushing, pushing, moving, kissing.

<now> <now> <now>

Until finally we collapse into each other. For a moment, I am just panting, trying to catch my breath. She curls into me.

What seems like almost no time later, she lifts her chin and looks up at me. Her eyes are still bright. I hear her thought, loud and clear.

<again>

I wake long before Sara. She is deeply unconscious and facedown in the hotel's thick comforter and pillows while I go through my usual morning routine.

First I hit the floor and curl into a ball while my brain replays all the pain and injuries I inflicted with my mental tricks last night. The worst is a phantom pain in my side, which I realize is a leftover from where Sara hit the big guy last night and cracked one of his ribs. I sweat it out until my muscles unclench enough for me to reach my bottle of OxyContin. I dry-swallow two and sweat some more until they start to work. After that, I get up and stagger to the bathroom, where I grab the Vicodin and diazepam and the Paxil from my shaving kit and gulp those down to help the Oxy. I shudder under the sudden weight of a lingering feeling of guilt left behind by touching the minds of the mob. So I crank the knobs to hot in the shower and stand there until my meds start to work in harmony and all I feel is the water.

Thirty minutes later, I am dressed, looking reasonably human, and drinking coffee delivered by room service. It's not until I click on the TV and open the blinds that Sara finally stirs from her coma.

For a brief second, she's disoriented. There's that moment of hotel room panic, and then memory and habit kick in, and she forces herself to breathe deeply and normally. She lifts her head—I get a nasty sloshing feeling, about 10 percent of her hangover—and looks at me through one eye. The other is still gummed shut with sleep.

"Morning," I say, handing over the coffee and half of one of my Vicodins.

She accepts both. There's very little that's verbal going through her head at the moment. I'm not surprised. After everything that's happened in the last couple of days, it's totally natural to want to stop thinking for a while.

"Thank you," she says. "What time is it?"

"Almost noon, Greenwich Mean Time."

She smiles. "You know, I've heard that for years, and this is the first time I think I've ever really understood it."

She pauses. She sees herself in the hotel room mirror, and a jolt of embarrassment runs through her. She remembers some of the things we did last night. She felt free, blew past her usual inhibitions. But in the morning light, they're clamping down again. Along with the hangover that's squeezing her temples like a vise.

"Ah, listen. This is not—usually—me," she says.

"I know," I say.

<of course you do> <got a front-row view> <jeez> "Right. Sure. I'm not trying to say we did anything wrong—"

"Seemed like we did most of it right. Not to brag."

I almost get her to laugh with that one, but she stomps down on her amusement. She wants to finish what she's saying.

"I'm just saying that I don't usually act like this."

"Well. You have had a lot of people shooting at you lately."

She looks at me carefully. I can see her measuring, weighing, judging. I get a glimpse of myself through her eyes. That weird shock of recognition. It never really goes away.

In her mind, I look too calm. Too put together.

"Doesn't seem to bother you that much," she says.

"I've had a lot more practice."

"You're telling me you get used to it? People trying to kill you?"

She is asking me for a lot of reasons. So I consider the question carefully before I answer.

"For me, that's when the world makes the most sense," I tell her. "That's when the masks drop. At least no one is playacting anymore."

"And you get to hit back," she says.

"Yes."

"You like that part?"

"I prefer the honesty."

Then we both hear something out of the burble of meaningless words from the TV.

CNN is the background noise in every business-class hotel and airport in the world. It's almost soothing, the endless scroll of death and disasters and politicians screeching at one another, because it's always there and never seems to change. So it's easy to ignore most of the time, until you hear certain key words that break through the drone. Words like "mass shooting" or "attack" or "terrorism."

Or, in this case, "Downvote."

Sara looks up, now fully alert. I turn around to see the screen. It's right there, spelled out across the bottom of the screen: IS A WEBSITE TARGETING INNOCENT VICTIMS FOR MURDER?

"Oh no," Sara says. She finds the remote and quickly turns it up. The volume rises just in time for us to hear Wolf Blitzer waffling over images of a house marked off by crime-scene tape.

"—appears that a random threat was called in to police by someone claiming to be holding hostages inside the house, a tactic called SWAT-ting. It's used all the time by people online, but what makes it different this time is that a website has taken credit for the entire shooting. It's called

Downvote, and it is a hit list of celebrities and random people from social media who have become targets of an online mob—"

The story is brutal: police in Atlanta were alerted to a possible hostage situation by a 911 call. But the house where they showed up belonged to a local attorney known for his annoying personal-injury ads. His thirteen-year-old daughter heard someone at the door and was knocked unconscious by a cop carrying a battering ram. The attorney's wife was hit by a tear-gas canister fired into the house, which exploded and gave her and their younger daughter third-degree burns. The attorney himself was shot in the back when it appeared he was reaching for a gun. It turned out to be his phone.

All because someone didn't like his ads on television, which promised big payouts in the name of justice. The bullet hit him in the spine.

Along the bottom of the screen, viewer comments on Twitter are scrolling past. The one that catches my eye is `HAHAHA!!! Who's he going to sue for that?`

Then, there it is. The familiar front page of Downvote, listing names of targets. Wolf helpfully informs us that we are watching the site in real time. "As you can see here, literally millions of people are now voting and adding names to the board, people that they want to be hurt, to be punished, and even killed. We have a report that this site may be connected to the mass shooting in Santa Monica recently, where reality-TV star Kira Sadeghi was grievously wounded—"

Back in Los Angeles, I bet Vincent just got his task force. Too damned late to do anyone any good.

Downvote just went public. Godwin's experiment in antisocial media is out in the wild now. And the whole world is rushing to see, adding more people, putting more eyeballs on the site. Spreading the contagion.

What was it Stack said? "I don't have to raise an army. I just have to open a floodgate."

My phone rings. I don't even have to look at the caller ID.

"This is your fault, you know," Godwin says.

I tap the speaker icon so Sara can hear. "How do you figure?" I ask.

"I was willing to let the site stay on the Dark Net before you began poking around. For at least a few more months. You forced me to move up my timetable. So every extra casualty, every new kill, that's all thanks to you."

"So turn it off. Prove you're really the good guy here. Shut it down."

There's a pause, and then the static chuckle. "No. I don't think we'll be doing that."

Sara has cast off her hangover and the blankets and is tapping furiously at her computer now. She's trying to reach Stack, to get him online so he can trace the call or Godwin's Web traffic.

She's also still naked, which is kind of distracting.

"I know you tried to take out my server," Godwin says. "Moffett contacted me as soon as you left his house. That's why I was ready for you."

Not that ready, I think. But he doesn't seem to know that we managed to access the server despite his hired ninja. He's just arrogant enough to assume that because the server went offline, he managed to stop us.

"Right. Because you could give a damn about anyone who gets hurt. So don't tell me this is my fault, Godwin. You started this. But I will finish it."

"You talk like a movie poster, you know that?" Godwin says. If not for the voice synthesizer, I'd swear I could hear the irritation in his voice. He sounds pissed off, but in the same way you get angry at the waiter who brings you the wrong drink.

Sara gestures to me. She's got Stack on the laptop now. Text only, which is fortunate, because I'm pretty sure his head might explode if the camera was on.

I read through the messages quickly.

```
stack: was able to get most of the data from the server
stack: still can't track him directly
stack: he's still bouncing his traffic all over the Net
stack: but I've got his backup server's location
stack: he's definitely using it right now for this call
  can see the traffic going right to you
stack: keep him talking going to try tracing it back
  to him
```

"What is it going to take for you to stop harassing me?" Godwin asks. "You should know by now that I can get to you anywhere. You honestly think you can keep dodging and weaving? You think you're that lucky?"

It hits me right then. Godwin didn't call to gloat. He called to bitch and moan. This is all annoying him. He wants me to stop, but only because he doesn't want to have to deal with this anymore.

Suddenly I'm very interested in looking inside Godwin's head, if only to try to track down the source of all that arrogance.

But at least I know how to keep him talking.

"It sounds to me like you're frightened," I say. "It sounds like you want this all to go away. Like you realize what an enormous mistake you've made."

Another static burst. Laughter. But he doesn't hang up.

I keep going. "Sorry. There is no reset button for you. You screwed up. You were stupid. And now you're going to have to pay for it."

I think it must be the word "stupid" that does it, because even with the voice modulator, I hear real emotion, real anger, in his voice when he responds.

"You think—" He pauses. "You think I'm—" Another pause. "You idiot. You think your cheap little freak-show talent is going to keep you safe? I told you that you did not want me to concentrate on you. I gave you every chance to walk away. Now it's too late. Now I'm making you a priority."

```
stack: got him
```

I see the message and smile.

"I look forward to it," I say, and hang up.

Let him stew with that for a while. He's going to see me. Sooner than he thinks.

/// 19

I'm Here for Bogdan

We got a police escort to the Reykjavík airport. It was not an honor or even a courtesy. More like a bouncer seeing us to the door. An unsmiling police lieutenant named Jonsson personally escorted us to the steps of the Gulfstream Sara chartered. His mind was colder than the frozen tarmac we were walking on, and the only glimmer of happiness he felt was when we began to close the plane's hatch. I took a quick peek inside his thoughts, and found out he'd been made aware of the near riot at the club near our hotel. He knew we were involved, but decided the best course of action was simply to get rid of us as fast as possible. Still, it chafed his sense of order and responsibility. Unsurprisingly, he did not invite us to come back anytime soon.

He returned our guns, at least.

Sara spends the flight napping, still feeling the effects of the vodka poisoning her system. I am grateful for that. As soon as she falls asleep, I finally stop getting the fumes of her hangover through my own brain.

While she sleeps I make the mistake of turning on CNN again.

"A high school cheerleader in a suburb of Chicago has been forced to flee her home after being targeted by what's being called the antisocial media site, Downvote. The sixteen-year-old victim was tagged as a 'mean girl' and 'stuck-up' on the site, and nearly a million people began repeating rape and death threats against her across the Internet. After her address was posted to the site, her home was hit by gunfire in what police say was a drive-by shooting sometime around three A.M. She and her family were then taken into protective custody, and the house was then mobbed. People shoved past police barricades and began tearing the family's possessions apart. We have video of that as it happened. Now, I want to warn our more sensitive viewers, this segment will contain graphic language—"

I tried clicking on another channel, but just as Vincent had feared back in L.A., Downvote has gone viral. Over on MSNBC, Rachel Maddow is trying to give her audience the big picture.

"The website known as Downvote has declared open season on everyone. Anyone can be added to the list of names on the site, and if they receive enough votes, they can become the target of massive, organized online mobs. Victims have found their credit ratings hacked, their emails released in public, their addresses revealed, and been bombarded with threats. Some have even experienced actual violence—"

It's even made Fox News.

"Los Angeles police say a pipe bomb was thrown over the fence of the residence of actor Kyle Slater after he reached number one on Downvote's Internet hit list. Slater plays the bad-boy senior on the hit Fox show *Pathways,* but is perhaps best known for his messy public breakup with singer Alana Sweet last month. The Justice Department says it has now opened an investigation into Downvote and is working to track down the owners of the website—"

I shut the TV down and try to think. One question keeps nagging at me: Why? Why is Godwin doing this?

As far as I can tell, he hasn't demanded any kind of payoff from the people who are named on the site. Stack has been monitoring all of Godwin's Web traffic, so we should know. He's not blackmailing any of the celebrities who have been Downvoted. He's not offering to protect anyone from the online mob he's created.

It seems like he's content to simply let it rage, to keep burning, to see how far the fire will spread.

Even though I've never read a thought inside his head, this doesn't seem like the Godwin I know. Godwin is a criminal. He's a schemer. He's utterly convinced of his own superiority.

And in everything I've learned about him, I've yet to see him do anything without some kind of profit.

But this—this is just anarchy. This is just opening the floodgates, like Stack said.

There has to be a motive. There has to be a reason.

I just have to figure out what it is before anyone else gets killed.

Especially me.

Reykjavík to Bucharest seems like a short hop compared to the flight from Houston. Just five hours across Europe and we're at Henri Coandă International Airport. We submit to a cursory inspection by the customs agents. I use my talent to help them overlook the guns. I intercept the visual input when their eyes fall on the familiar metal carrying cases, and then reroute it away from the areas of their brains where it would be recognized. They look right at the weapons, but they don't see them. They just give us both a brief grimace and hand back our passports. Welcome to Romania. Enjoy your stay.

A bribe probably would have been just as effective, but I hate to waste money.

Then we're out the doors of the airport and into a waiting Land Rover, arranged by Stack or one of his assistants. I'm on constant alert now, scanning the crowd for anyone taking any interest in us whatsoever. I refuse to be caught off guard again.

We've got one advantage over Godwin, at least. We know where he's been, but he doesn't know we're here.

Sara boots up the GPS, but I turn it off just as quickly. She's still irritable from the hangover and the lack of sleep, so her look says it all. *<what the hell, Smith?>*

I take out a map and remind her that GPS can be hacked and tracked. She scowls, but starts the car and begins asking for directions. "I feel like we're back in the twentieth century," she growls. "You better know where we're going."

I do, actually. I've been through here several times before, usually in a CIA-owned plane, usually with a guy in the back wearing a black hood over his head. Romania is home to several black-site prisons—the places where we take the detainees and terrorists that we don't want on any official records. The Romanians were hard-line Communists in the Cold War, but famine and bone-grinding poverty converted them to capitalism pretty quickly after the Soviet Union collapsed. Despite an average wage of less than a thousand bucks a month, they're considered one of Europe's success stories. They take everybody's money these days.

I've got no idea how much the CIA paid in rent for the little building in Bucharest where we took our prisoners. It looked like a DMV and was surrounded by ordinary government offices. But that's where I did some of my best work with Cantrell, digging secrets out of the minds of terrorists. I hacked into the brains of men who financed sleeper cells, who sold nerve-gas samples to the highest bidder, who beheaded journalists, who convinced mentally disabled kids to strap on suicide vests and run through U.S. and Israeli checkpoints.

Unfortunately, today we're not dealing with anyone that nice.

Romania is also where Godwin began to really make money, and he did it by working with the Romanian Mafia.

I don't know the specifics—Cantrell didn't give me that much detail—

but I can see what a great match Godwin and the Romanians made for each other.

According to what I've learned from Cantrell, Godwin works mainly with the Boian clan, who specialize in two things: cybercrime and human trafficking.

When it comes to cybercrime, Romania was something of a pioneer in the field. In the days of the Cold War, Romania was home to a lot of mathematicians and computer coders. After the Communists fell, many of those guys found they could make a lot more money in computer crime than in solving equations. Today, Romania has literally the fastest Internet connection speed in Europe, and in some places, the highest download speed in the world. It also has very little oversight and regulation. That's why it's known worldwide as a hub for criminal hackers. The hacker who broke into George W. Bush's private files lived here. If you've seen any of Bush's paintings, you've got that guy to thank.

I can see Godwin setting up shop, happy as a pig in shit.

Cybercrime sounds clean and almost painless. It's ATM skimming, moving money around different accounts to avoid taxes or hide drug profits. It's Internet scams that steal credit-card numbers or hack into private files for financial information. Sure, you might have to call your bank and get new cards, but nobody really gets hurt, do they?

Except when they do.

Because occasionally, the cybercrime intersects with the Boian clan's other business: the human-trafficking side of the operation.

And that is definitely brutal.

Okay. I admit it. On all my business trips, I've looked at my share of porn. The pay-per-view stuff in the hotels, and the never-ending stream that flows through my laptop from the Net. So I don't need someone to explain to me what a cam girl is. I am aware there are women of all ages who sit in front of their computers and do things for money. Some of them work together in apartments and shared houses. Some of them go to warehouses that are divided into cubicles, where they change into lingerie or swimsuits like a uniform, do their shift, and then clock out afterward and go back to their real lives. Some of them smile and laugh about it, make their rent, and then move on.

And some of them are penned up like veal, threatened with beatings and rape, and have their earnings stolen out from under them by the people running the shows.

Like the Boian clan. The Romanian Mafia owns a lot of cam warehouses because they are great fronts for laundering money. That's where Godwin comes in. He converts the earnings from drugs, prostitution, gunrunning—anything on the black market—into the credits used to buy time for the cam girls' sex shows. Then he cashes those credits back out as profits to the shell corporation that owns the cam-girl site and sends them back to the criminals, minus his fee. The money becomes clean and almost legitimate.

But that requires a lot of cam girls sitting in front of their computers around the clock to make it work. The Mafia brings them in with promises of big, easy paychecks—which means something in a place where so many people are barely surviving. Once they're inside, they find it's not that easy to get out.

The Boian clan has a bad reputation. I did some research on the plane ride, and I found out why Godwin would use them. Like the biker gangs he hired back in the States, the Boians are known for a fondness for amphetamines and brutality. Recently they covered the driver of a cigarette truck in gasoline and lit him on fire when he resisted a hijacking. Then Godwin posted a video of the man as he burned to a pirate video site with the title "Got a light?"

Nobody has tried to play hero with the Boian clan since.

That said, I'm not actually that worried about these guys. Godwin uses them to scare people, and yes, they're willing to break bones and inflict pain.

But once you get past that, you start to see how limited they really are.

Something you have to understand about gangsters: they're under tremendous amounts of stress. The halfway intelligent ones have realized that they are essentially chronically unemployed and constantly in search of a new job that will, most likely, either put them in jail or kill them. They know they've painted themselves into a corner in their lives, but they know there's no window at their back. So they just keep doing the same thing, hoping that one of these times the big score will land, and they might be able to retire to Mesa, Arizona, or someplace. But since they can count on one hand the number of people they know who have made it past their fortieth birthday, they aren't really depending on it. They're aging twice as fast as civilians because of all the pressure, and their attention is always divided.

And the stupid ones, the ones who haven't figured this out? They're challenged just navigating all the ordinary obstacles in their lives on a day-to-day basis. That's why they became criminals in the first place. They couldn't think of anything better.

This is why I love going up against thugs. They're easy. Like Vasily's crew back in L.A. They're a light workout. It does amazing things for my self-esteem. I mean, I've made some stupid mistakes and sometimes wake up filled with regret at my choices. But I can always tell myself, thank God I haven't sunk this low.

Well, not yet, anyway.

We find the warehouse quickly, using the coordinates that Stack snagged from Godwin on the phone call. It's a squat, cinder-block building on the outskirts of Bucharest, down a stretch of badly paved road at the edge of an industrial district. The economic miracle hasn't reached this part of town yet: it's still all gray concrete, eroded by years of neglect.

The street is deserted except for a caveman in a leather jacket who looks almost as solid as the wall he's leaning against. All it takes is the briefest of scans to know that his primary purpose is not to keep people like us from getting inside.

He is there to keep the women inside from getting out.

I can feel it from my seat in the Land Rover when we park. It's like a physical weight, a pressure in the air. I can't make out anything clearly at this distance, but I sense the minds of the people inside, and my teeth immediately clench. I feel constricted. Caged. Trapped.

Sara notices my shift in demeanor immediately. She's learned to pick up on this, because my mood swings have been a pretty good early-warning system for keeping us alive so far.

"You okay?" she asks.

"No," I reply. "Do me a favor? Wait here."

I get out of the Rover without waiting for her reply and start walking toward the slab of meat at the door.

The slab—his name is Andrei—looks only mildly interested. They get visitors here from time to time. He's not on high alert. He thinks he can handle whatever comes his way.

I figure I will try it the easy way first. I walk right up to him. I have to tilt my neck a little to look him in the eye. He waits for me to speak.

I tell him, in English, "Godwin sent for me."

Which is true, more or less.

I get the confusion coming off him. It's not the language he doesn't understand. He speaks broken English as well as anyone else in Europe. He just doesn't recognize the name. And then I see why, inside his mind.

<Bogdan>

They call him Bogdan here. From *bog*, the Slavic word for "God" and *dan*, for "given."

God-given. Somehow that makes me clench my teeth even harder.

"Bogdan," I correct myself. "I'm here for Bogdan."

He shrugs. <*Who gives a shit?*> comes off him loud and clear. "Not here," he says.

"Then let me talk to whoever knows where he is," I say.

He frowns now. The thought and the words are almost simultaneous. He's bored and irritable. "And who the fuck are you?" he asks.

I'm close enough now to the door to feel some of the minds inside. Several are fogged by an amount of drugs even I find impressive. Others are bored. Others are anxious. Scared. Afraid of what might happen if they do not make their quota for the shift.

Then there are the minds of the men. Three of them, inside—the keepers, they call themselves. Bored, like Andrei the giant here. Bored and getting ugly. One of them has a thought. About that new girl, the one who just started in the last cubicle on the left.

<*yeah got to get them young*> <*before they get ideas*> <*start acting bitchy*>

That's about where I decide I've had it.

"You know what?" I say to Andrei, smiling brightly. "Never mind."

I hit him with the nastiest memory I can summon from my mind. A 40 percent third-degree burn I got from a soldier who'd been trapped in the wreckage of a flaming Humvee in Iraq. He barely survived.

Andrei screams as he feels his flesh blacken and crack, then curls into a ball on the ground.

I pound on the door while he keeps screaming. I sense alarm on the other side, the approach of another one of the keepers. This one's name is Iancu. He yanks the door open quickly, gun in hand, and sees Andrei writhing on the ground, gapes stupidly for a moment—

And then shrieks himself when his legs fall away under him as I shut down the nerve pathways from his brain to the sacral plexus at the base of his spine.

I am going to regret both of these moves later. But not now. Now, even though I feel the pain and the panic blazing off the two men like bright sunlight, it seems entirely justified.

I reach down and scoop up the gun that Iancu dropped when his legs turned to jelly. I don't think I'll need it, but I don't want to leave it for him.

I march down the entryway. Most of the building is empty space, divided by the same kind of cubicles you see in every open-plan office in the world. There are sheets hung over each one, forming little tents. The only real room is a small, built-out kitchen that has a large picture window to watch the cube farm. Along one wall is a row of server racks, more computing power than this place possibly needs, even with every lonely and horny guy in the world jacking in to watch the shows.

I can hear sounds. Stilted English. Breathy, theatrical moans. Bad Europop from cheap speakers.

In my head, I pick up nothing but the same boredom and fear and anxiety I sensed outside, only worse now. I feel like crawling out of my own skin.

I pass one of the cubes on my way to the kitchen, moving fast. I catch a glimpse of one of the girls. She cannot be more than fifteen in her star-spangled bikini. She looks up at me, her eyes rimmed with enough eyeshadow to look like a raccoon.

The last two keepers rush from the kitchen area, where they were sitting. The first one doesn't hesitate, doesn't ask stupid questions. Just launches himself at me.

It doesn't help him. He gets about halfway across the concrete floor to me and drops like he's just been shot in the back.

Which he thinks he has. That was my own memory. Up close and personal. I hope he appreciates it.

That leaves the last one, the keeper named Miron, the one who was thinking about the new girl. He, at least, remembered his gun. He almost gets it centered on me before he sees—impossible as it is—eight metric tons of Mercedes Atego truck bearing down on him, horn blaring, about to turn him into roadkill.

He screams and throws up his arms, waiting for the impact.

I hit him instead. First in the gut, right under the sternum, knocking all the air out of him. Then I punch him in the head as he folds up. He remains on his feet, so I do it again. And again. And again.

He's down on the floor with his friends after a few more hits. I kick him once. Just to be sure. Then again, just to be cruel. The truck, if it had been real, would have hit him only once.

I sense Sara behind me before I hear her.

"Jesus Christ, John," she says. She is looking around at the whole setup, the men on the ground, the bloody wreck of Miron at my feet.

"They were . . ." I search for the right words.

She shakes her head, and I know she gets it. *<I know>* She's not angry or frightened by my actions. If anything, she's only stunned by the sudden ferocity.

I suck down a deep, calming breath. It helps. Not much, but it helps.

"Not part of the job, I know," I say.

"You were pretty quick," she says. "I think we can spare the time."

She takes her laptop bag and the cables over to the servers. She has this down to a practiced routine now. A few moments, and she's got Godwin's data humming into her machine, Stack's programs hunting for every trace of him in the system.

That has the side effect of shutting down the cameras and the network. A few of the women—and the girls—have emerged from their cubes, watching us carefully.

They see the mess I've made of their keepers. I get a lot of mixed feelings.

<deserved it> <the pig> <will they take it out on us?> <blame us for this> <who is that?> <Americans?> <what now?>

One woman, a little older than the rest, a veteran at nineteen or twenty, comes tottering out in her high heels, a cheap silk wrap tied hastily around her.

"What have you done?" she demands.

"This place is closed," I tell her simply. "We've shut it down."

She looks shocked. She glances over at the men on the ground, who are starting to moan and move around. She has no sympathy for them. *<bastards> <see how you like being knocked around>*

But it doesn't change the fact that I've just come in and upset the entire order of the little universe in this building.

"Where the fuck are we supposed to go now?" she asks, spitting the words out in her thick accent.

"I don't know," I say.

"Then what good are you?" she snaps back.

I don't have an answer for her. I don't pretend that this was a rescue mission. That I've made anything that much better.

But there are some things you simply cannot let happen. No matter what. Looking at the woman, I try to find a way to say that out loud, to bridge the gap.

"Smith," Sara says, rescuing me from saying something stupid. She points at the screen of her machine. "I think we've got something here."

I come over to her and peer over her shoulder. It's mostly gibberish to me, but I recognize a few of the names on the files as they are loaded into her laptop. They're labeled with DOWNVOTE.

<this is it> <source code> <brains of the operation>

"This is Godwin's source code?" I ask, just to make sure.

She makes an impatient noise. "This is his everything. Pretty sure we've found all his backups here. He didn't expect anyone to get to these servers."

"Can we shut down the site from here?"

She shakes her head. "No. It will just kick over to another server, like it did last time."

Not what I wanted to hear. I need to hurt Godwin. Do some damage. This doesn't seem like a weapon. This seems like clerical work.

"Can we at least find him from this?"

Sara shrugs. "Maybe," she says. "Maybe not. But if we get this to Aaric, he can start undoing some of the damage. He can figure out a way to start counteracting the code that's out there already. He might even be able to get some evidence against Godwin that he can give to the FBI, if Godwin left any financial information or documents on here."

Sara is a lot more excited about this than I am, reminding me once again that we have different goals here. She wants to save Stack. The main problem with that is I just want Godwin to pay. And if things get difficult, then it's going to be a lot easier to kill him than capture him.

I shove the thought away. It doesn't matter unless we can find him.

"What about Godwin?" I ask. "He was supposed to be here."

She shrugs. "He probably was. This seems to be his main data center. But we'll have to give everything to Aaric before we can be sure."

She looks at me, and must see the frustration on my face.

"It's another piece," she says, in a consoling tone. "We're putting it all together. We're going to get the data we need to take him down. We will."

Right, right. And they got Al Capone on tax evasion.

I cross the room, away from her, back to Miron, who is groaning on the floor.

I bend over and pull him into a sitting position. *"Unde este Bogdan?"* I demand in bad Romanian. (I can also ask where the bathroom is and order a beer. Everything else, I need my talent to translate.)

Miron looks at me, dazed and concussed. *"Nu stiu,"* he mumbles through a split lip.

I scan what passes for his thoughts. He's not lying. He's got no idea.

I see in his memories that Godwin was here yesterday. Using his computer, transferring data much the same way Sara is now. But he left. And he didn't tell Miron or anyone else where he was going.

Dammit.

I hit Miron again, and he flops over like a fish. It doesn't make me feel a whole lot better.

"Smith!" Sara says. I look up.

She's glaring at me as she gathers up the laptop and our cables. *<you've hit him enough> <got to get control> <sometimes I wonder> <no better than a thug himself>*

That irritates me, both for Sara's passing judgment on me and for the fact that she's probably right. I step away from Miron, leaving him to bleed.

We're at a dead end. There's nothing more we can do here. So Sara and I head out the front door.

The cam girls are crowding out alongside us with whatever possessions they've got gathered under their arms. I give all the cash I have on me to the ones who are closest, shove it at them, really. We offer them a ride in the SUV, but they walk away without looking back.

Despite my frustration, I try to take some satisfaction in shutting the place down.

This is not an unqualified win. I know that. But these were bad guys doing bad things. And sometimes, when you get the chance to stop people like that, you take it.

Maybe we're no closer to Godwin, but at least we managed to do that.

That feeling of accomplishment lasts all the way to the end of the road. Then we see the police cars waiting for us, lights and sirens flashing.

///20

The Only Bait in Town

There's not a lot to say about a Romanian jail cell. I try to imagine giving it a review on hotels.com or something like that, and all I've got so far is: "Relatively clean. Toilet works. Smells of bleach rather than urine, blood, or vomit."

Compared to some of the other cells I've seen, I'd have to give it five stars.

As soon as the Romanian police brought me and Sara to this substation, they split us apart. Sara was swiftly and politely taken away by a pair of female guards, while I was escorted by a group of five men down a separate corridor.

They were all edgy around me, giving me plenty of space as they walked me through the booking procedure. I scraped what I could from their brains, but they hadn't been told very much by their superiors. Just that I had interfered with a local business and assaulted its employees. They weren't stupid men, however, and they knew which business and which employees. So they were aware of who I'd taken down already, and they were treating me with caution.

I wasn't about to make any trouble. I didn't see the point yet. So far, everything was being handled properly. Nobody had any thoughts about taking me into a back room and pulling out the batons to teach me a lesson, or any crap like that. Whatever deal the cops had with the local Mafia, it didn't extend to beatings and torture.

At least, not yet.

So I decided to wait it out. I figured that eventually someone was going to have to figure out what to do with us. If they were smart, they would let us go, because we presented far too big a problem if they tried to deal with us through official channels. I'm not sure what the charge would be for breaking up a human-trafficking ring, and it might be a little difficult to find witnesses willing to testify against us.

Besides, as soon as Sara gets on the phone to Stack, I suspect this is all going to vanish in a sudden flurry of lawyers and money. Then we're back to tracking Godwin. I know we hurt him today. I have a sense that we've got some vital intel on Sara's laptop now.

I lean back on the thin foam mattress that covers the steel bench in the corner (review edited to add: "They really worked to add comfort, even on a budget") and try to relax. My only other companion in this wing of the jail is a young man who is trying to sleep off a beating and a truly impressive amount of alcohol. From the brief flashes of memory, I can see that his evening in the bars last night ended with a challenge to fight any man in the place. It didn't end well. But he's a few cells away, so his pain doesn't intrude on me too much.

We're going to be here for a night at the most. I figure I may as well get some sleep.

It's only when I sense a familiar mind walking down the corridor toward the cells that I realize something has gone wrong.

There are a couple of guards with him. They roust the hungover kid out of his cell with a few shouts and curses, because of course he doesn't want anyone overhearing our conversation. Then they leave us alone.

I take a few deep, calming breaths without opening my eyes. I want to be cool and centered for this conversation. Because it is always a test with him. It's like playing chess and poker at the same time.

He stands at the bars of the cell. I can feel him there, waiting. Let him. He can make the first move.

I don't even have to wait that long before I hear Cantrell's shitkicker drawl calling my name.

"Come on, John," he says. "I know you're awake."

I open my eyes, and there he is. Looking like he's barely aged a day since we first met. Considering the number of people who spend their waking hours plotting against him, you'd think he would have a few more wrinkles.

But no. All I see are a couple more laugh lines around the eyes. Cantrell really does enjoy his work.

He is wearing a suit today, not a uniform. It's a standard, forgettable off-the-rack number, nothing flashy. He blends in, just one more American businessman doing business in the New Europe.

But wherever he is, and whatever it says on his ID, Cantrell is always a spy. He may not be on the official payroll anymore, but he is always connected to the Agency, or, as he likes to put it, "the full might and majesty of the all-highest." He could pull out his phone and order a drone strike or get a direct line to the White House.

I take a pass at his mind, but Cantrell was the founder and director of the top-secret psychic-soldier project that trained me. He spent years learning how to guard his thoughts from operatives like me.

So all I get is a repeated loop of an Eagles song. <*"You can't hide your lyin' eyes"*>

I stand up to face him. It's only polite. He gives me his used-car salesman's smile, and I know that I'm already screwed.

"So. Did you put me in here?" I ask.

He laughs to buy time, but he drops his guard enough for me to see the truth. <*no*> <*wish I'd thought of it*>

"I admit, I was following you after your phone call."

"You know I hate that."

"Toughen up, buttercup. You can't drop intel like that and expect me to stay home and watch *Monday Night Football*. We've still got very good relations with SRI"—the Serviciul Român de Informații, the Romanian intelligence service—"so when you filed your flight plan out of Iceland, I was on my way. But I was only planning to keep an eye on you. You were the one who decided to start kicking mobsters in the teeth."

I don't like his tone. "You know what they were doing to those girls?"

A little wisp of frustration escapes him. <*oh for God's sake*> "Probably the same thing they were doing for years before you got here, and the same thing they'll do tomorrow without you." <*grow up*>

I let that pass, and he continues.

"Turns out the local cops have a deal with the owners of that warehouse you hit," he says. "An alarm goes off, they're supposed to come a-running. There have been some recruitment and retention issues with their employees."

Which means that occasionally the women make a run for it, or other Mafia clans try to push their way in and take over.

"Frankly, they don't know what to do with you," Cantrell says. "You're not hooked into the local power structure, you're not working for anyone they know, and they haven't got a clue why you're here."

"I'm surprised Godwin hasn't told them yet."

"There's a lot of things Godwin doesn't tell people. He works on a need-to-know basis, it seems."

"Yeah, I had a boss like that once."

"Sounds like a smart man."

"Kind of a pain in the ass, actually."

Cantrell laughs, crinkling the lines around his eyes some more. It's genuine. I don't get any more annoyance or irritation off him. Which means he's really certain that he's so far ahead of me I can never catch up.

"Well, thanks for visiting," I say, and sit back down. "I'm sure you've got better things to do than hang around here."

Cantrell keeps smiling. "John," he says, "cut the shit. You are looking at a long stretch in a Romanian prison, which makes this place look like the Royal Hawaiian. It's time for us to talk."

"I don't think so. I've got a client back in the States with a couple billion dollars. Once he hears about this, we're out of here and back to work."

Cantrell waits. Lets me read his thoughts.

"Oh bullshit," I say, not believing it.

He reaches inside his jacket pocket and pulls out a folded section of newspaper. The *Wall Street Journal,* international edition. An actual *paper* newspaper. He's old-school like that, and he does love his props.

He hands me the article through the bars. I only have to skim the headlines, because I got the news right from his brain.

SOFTWARE DEVELOPER ARRESTED ON MEGA-YACHT

And, below that: *Gov't Claims He Is Key to Millions of Criminal Transactions on the Web.*

Well. Looks like Sara and I aren't going to be rescued by Stack anytime soon.

I briefly wonder if she knows about this, and how she's taking it.

Then I focus on Cantrell again. Now he's playing Jimmy Buffett in his head. <"*. . . and you're the only bait in town*"> But his sense of victory is like a soft glow all around him.

"Nobody else is coming to bail you out, son," he says. "So it's probably in your interest for us to talk."

"What do you want?" I ask, even though I don't have to be a telepath to know the answer. Still, it never hurts to observe the formalities.

Cantrell looks slightly wounded. "It's not about what I want, John. It's about what Godwin wants. I am not sure you've really considered the bigger questions here. Why do you think he's doing this? Why run a site like Downvote at all? What does he get out of it?"

I have to admit, that's been bugging me from the start. I do not know what motivates Godwin. It's easy to throw around terms like "sociopath" when discussing people like him. But it's not often very accurate. We've all seen the same movies, so we all like to think that we can diagnose an antisocial personality disorder from a few scraps of information. In truth, a classic sociopath is really rare, and not usually someone you'd call a great success. A person who can think only of himself, who cannot empathize with others, who lacks any real sense of consequences—that's not someone who makes a good supervillain. More often than not, those are the guys doing time for aggravated assault or stealing a couple hundred bucks from a convenience store.

So it doesn't make sense that Godwin would go to all the trouble of setting up Downvote just to hurt random people. Especially when you consider that his entire career up until now has been all about the careful accumulation of illegal wealth, far away from the attention of the wider world.

Cantrell waits patiently while I grind through all this one more time, and then decides to take pity on me and give me the answer.

"It's a product demo, John," he says.

And suddenly it makes sense. Godwin has designed Downvote to show the world what his software package can do. How it can motivate people to rage and fear and even violence with only a few keystrokes. All of the victims of Downvote are nothing to him but advertising. Like any other start-up, he is building his brand.

Which means—

"He's got a buyer lined up," I say.

<*Took you long enough*> Cantrell thinks. I'm pretty sure I was meant to overhear that. Out loud, he says, "Exactly. And now think about it. Who would be interested in a software package that could steer massive groups of people without their knowledge? Who would want a technology that could direct the behavior of entire populations in a way that they would never know they were being manipulated? Who'd want to be able to create enemies and scapegoats and put them in front of the mob whenever they need a distraction?"

I don't take much time with that little quiz. "You."

He smirks. <*walked right into that one*> "I won't deny I'm interested, but I'm not Godwin's target audience. The Agency didn't even know about this until you brought it to my attention. Think bigger. Lots bigger."

Not just the CIA, or any other government agency, then.

Then it hits me. "China."

He nods. "You've got a nation filled with people becoming unimaginably rich overnight while others are still dirt poor and starving. The whole country is accelerating into the twenty-first century at Warp Factor Ten, with a government that's desperately trying to manage almost two billion people who could lurch in any direction at any time. So you can see how something like Godwin's little social program would be of interest."

He's right. I'm embarrassed that it's taken me this long to figure it out.

"And you can understand why the Agency might not want that sort of technology to be out there in the world, in the hands of a foreign power, without having some kind of ability to counter it," Cantrell adds.

I give him a look, but he does his best to keep a straight face. "You mean the Agency wants it so they can use it themselves."

"When did you get to be such a cynic, John?" <*of course we want it for ourselves*> <*don't be a child*>

"So is that the deal? You spring me out of here, I get the software package from Godwin, and keep it away from the Chinese?"

"Saving the day for the USA and Chevrolet, Mom and apple pie," he says. "And we'd pay you a hell of a lot of money, too."

"How much?"

He holds up five fingers. I read the rest in his mind.

"Million?"

He shrugs. "What can I say? Some people up above are very impressed so far. You know how excited the Agency gets about all that mind-control crap. I don't think some of those guys have ever gotten over MK-ULTRA."

"Pretty generous offer." Which makes me suspicious as hell. Cantrell is singing Gordon Lightfoot tunes to himself now, which doesn't help. <*". . . 'bout a ghost from a wishing well"*> "What happens if I pass?"

"John, I know you're extra-strength tough. I trained you to handle worse than some pansy Eurotrash prison. But your new lady friend over in the women's section. You sure she's up for it?"

"She's tougher than I am," I shoot back, no hesitation. But I am glad Cantrell can't read minds, because it feels as if someone just drove a spike into my gut.

"I'm sure she is," Cantrell says. "Still. Is that how she really wants to fill her schedule for the next three to five years? I can't say I know her, but I'm almost certain she's got other plans."

He takes a step back from the bars, as if to walk away, but we both know it's just for show.

"Even if I agree," I tell him, "without Stack, we don't know where to find Godwin. We can't track him, even with the information we've got now."

Cantrell waves like that's no big deal. "I told you where he's going already: China."

"Last time I checked, that was a pretty big place."

He smirks again. He really loves this. "Oh, didn't I tell you? I already know where he's meeting his Chinese contact."

Like a magician, from another pocket—I told you he loves his props—Cantrell produces a small folder. He opens it. It's an invitation to a party. The address reads Severn Road, Hong Kong.

Cantrell folds the card away and looks me in the eye.

"So. Enough chitchat. You in or out, John?"

I nod, and Cantrell hollers for the guard. He radiates a total lack of surprise. As I said, he walked in here knowing he'd already won.

"You hungry?" he asks. "You remember that place we used to go for lunch? We should see if it's still open."

The guard comes and unlocks the cell. Like Cantrell said, the Agency still has a lot of influence around here.

It looks like I've got one more client to add to my list now.

I retrieve Sara from the jail two hours later. Cantrell and I had some further details of our arrangement to hammer out. And I didn't want her to meet him, or even know about him. I don't want her to know just how divided my loyalties are at the moment. I still need her help to get this job done.

So while she waited in a cell I had lunch with Cantrell at that place we used to go. I fully admit that this was a dick move.

Fortunately, she emerges from the holding area a little rumpled but otherwise fine. We're getting our effects back from the police clerk when I break the bad news about Stack.

Fear and concern suddenly drench her thoughts, followed closely by guilt. *<how did this happen?> <he was supposed to be safe> <should have been there> <he's got to be terrified>*

I take her laptop case and put it into my bag while she gets on her phone. She tries to reach someone back in the States who can give her some information about Stack. With the time difference—it's not quite five in the morning in Seattle—it's not easy. She finally remembers she has the home number of one of Stack's attorneys, but he's not much help. He says that the feds had promised him nothing would happen until the next hearing in court. Then, according to the staff on the boat, they were boarded by U.S. marshals who stepped off a Coast Guard cutter with a subpoena in hand. It was totally out of bounds, he says. But he admits there's not a lot they can do about it.

I can hear Sara's end of the conversation as well her thoughts. She only gets angrier. *<useless>* *<told us this would never happen>* *<wrong about everything>*

The lawyer says that Stack is in a federal holding facility somewhere on the West Coast. He promises to call her as soon as he has a meeting scheduled. But he tells her they're dealing with Stack as a federal witness, and that means he doesn't have the same rights as a federal prisoner. It could be a while.

In the meantime, all of Stack's corporate accounts are frozen. There's no charter jet waiting for us at the airport now, no line of credit to access anymore. He suggests she use her personal credit card to get home, and she'll probably be reimbursed when this has all been cleared up.

Sara hangs up. I know better than to say anything. I take her to the Romanian version of Starbucks to get her something to drink and eat.

All she can do for the next half hour or so is read the news feeds about Stack on her phone, looking for whatever information she can find.

"Oh, this is such a load of *crap*. They say he wandered back into U.S. territorial waters, and there just happened to be a Coast Guard ship waiting nearby. The *Nautilus* is completely computer controlled. It couldn't wander off course if everyone on board was drunk and stoned. They crossed the line and grabbed him."

"Probably, yeah."

It has occurred to me that Cantrell exerted some pressure behind the scenes to get Stack in custody so that I'd have more incentive to work for him. Because that's what spies do. They cheat, they steal, and they lie. Sara is smart enough to figure this out too, which is another reason I didn't want them to meet.

Then we notice CNN International on one of the TV screens hanging in the background of the café. The anchor says the word, and it catches us both off guard again, though it really shouldn't.

"The antisocial media site Downvote strikes again. Today, the head of a major investment bank was nearly shot after his name appeared at the top of the website's hit list. Police say a lone gunman identified as James Dale Miller approached Stanley Deakins of the Coldwater Group as he left his Park Avenue apartment building. Miller opened fire with a small handgun, but Mr. Deakins's security detail was able to wrestle him to the ground before Deakins was harmed. Deakins, you may remember, called higher taxes on the rich a form of Nazism in a speech last year, and said that the rich were a new minority who deserved civil rights protections. Four bystanders, including a seventy-six-year-old woman, were hit by stray bullets and are listed in critical condition—"

Sara turns away. "Jesus Christ. We have got to stop this."

"We will," I tell her.

"How?"

It is not usually in Sara's nature to feel helpless. But it comes crashing out of her like a wave with that one word. She doesn't have to say any of the rest out loud. I know it all, even as it scrolls in an anxious list down through her mind. *<no money>* *<no transportation>* *<no clues>* *<no idea where to go next>*

"I reached out to some old contacts," I tell her. "I have a lead. Godwin is on his way to Hong Kong."

She is so glad to hear this she doesn't even question how I know it. I've done some fairly miraculous things already, so maybe I've built up some credit.

Then her mood crashes again suddenly. "How are we going to get there? I can't access any of the money Aaric set aside for us, and my corporate Amex won't work—"

"Don't worry. I've got money. I can pay for it."

"You'd do that?" she asks, and she's so grateful it shames me. She is looking at me like I'm some kind of hero. No sarcasm or irony this time.

I feel something uncomfortably close to guilt as I look back at her. But then I remind myself that's what spies do. They cheat, they steal, and they lie.

///21

Chaos and Opportunity

Hong Kong Art Basel is held in the Hong Kong Convention and Exhibition Centre, a massive structure perched at the edge of Victoria Harbour. It looks like a spacecraft parked at the edge of the water, and the aliens simply left it there while they went shopping.

Inside, the halls are crowded with buyers from all over the world. With stock markets veering wildly and interest rates in negative territory, everyone is looking for a safe place to stash their cash. Art, at least, has some chance of going up, which is more than you can say for money in a bank account. And this way, you get something to look at for a few years while you wait for your investment to pay off. HK Art Basel has become a favorite spot for Chinese businessmen. They want to convert their new wealth to solid assets as quickly as possible.

But the real action is at the private parties held around the event. That's where the off-the-books deals are made, where the collective wealth of the guests could finance a Mars expedition.

And it's where Godwin is supposed to close his deal with his Chinese contact. That's why Sara and I are headed for the highest spot on the island.

Our driver takes us up Severn Road, which twists and winds its way toward the top of Victoria Peak. If you're looking for the most expensive real estate on earth, forget Manhattan. This is Hong Kong, where people will live in spaces as small as sixteen square feet marked out by chicken wire. The homes here go for about ten grand a square foot. So a view from the Peak means you have literally made it above eight million other people who are all packed and squirming together in the city below.

Sara looks remarkable. She's wearing a Valentino dress that we bought off the rack at Hong Kong International Airport but seems made for her. She went pale at the price tag, but I convinced her it was the only way to fit in at this party and put it on my card. I look shabby next to her in my best suit. I feel strangely like we're on our way to prom. As I've said before, I am an idiot. This is work.

Sara's mind is churning with anxiety. Her mind keeps darting back to her Glock, which is in her clutch purse. She wishes she could have brought the S&W too.

I pulled the same invisibility trick with the customs inspectors who searched us at the airport, even though they were much more thorough than the ones in Romania. I had to mentally steer their eyes past the pieces of the guns, which I'd broken down into their parts and hidden in various places in our luggage. The Chinese authorities are fairly strict about that sort of thing, especially here.

Since taking Hong Kong back almost twenty years ago, China has been slowly tightening the reins on the city, reminding everyone who lives here who's in charge. Critics of the government have been disappeared, only to turn up on the mainland, pleading for forgiveness in videotaped confessions. The police have been cracking down, throwing people in jail without charges, starting with the lawyers who would ordinarily work against this kind of tactic. That hasn't gone over very well with the people still laboring under the belief that Hong Kong should be a democracy. There have been protests with thousands of people in the streets, hunger strikes, and calls for international action.

Complicating matters is the fact that Hong Kong is still a capitalist's wet dream, producing billions of dollars from the sheer ambition and sweat of its inhabitants. Nobody wants to interrupt that flow of wealth, or risk their access to China and its money.

We arrive at a modernist cube that seems to emerge from the hillside straight into the sky. There is a garage at the base of the house, where the valets take keys as Mercedes and Ferraris and Lamborghinis line up, their engines growling impatiently.

As we pull up, all I can feel is a surge of anticipation in the minds of the guests. It's almost like a cocaine high, or the predatory anticipation I feel when I've visited stock markets and investment banks on the day of a big deal. There's a potential in the air, like the gathering of static before a lightning strike.

An older man with a head of beautiful white hair is arguing with the valet trying to move his classic Bentley. "No, no," he says firmly, as if training a dog. "It stays right here. I'm only going to be a moment, and I am terribly sorry to say I absolutely do not trust you to take it down the hill and back—"

Sara and I step out and make our way to the entrance. There are security guards, but no one is checking invitations or IDs. If you don't belong, these people will know almost instantly. And it is a long drop down the hill.

We walk up a staircase to the main floor of the house. The wood is all dark paneling, thickly lacquered, creating deep pools of mirrored light on the walls and floors. There are some tasteful pieces scattered here and there, mostly antiques from Hong Kong's colonial period, at odds with the home's exterior design.

But the main attraction is the view. There is a magnificent plate-glass window that displays the entire harbor and city below. From this point, it seems as if the house is floating on thin air above the entire island. As Sara and I get closer, peering down, we can see that it's not far from the truth. This section of the house is cantilevered out over a sheer face of the peak, with nothing between us and the next house built onto the hill, what looks like a thousand feet down.

Sara walks away from me to search for Godwin. I promise to keep track of her in case she sees him. With any luck, we can take him by surprise and get him out of here before he knows what's happening.

Servants with trays of champagne and insanely expensive food cut around me. I wander through the crowd, picking up the usual delights and complaints of the true global elite.

The room is the same as so many others I've been in, all over the globe, with crowds just like this one. Perfectly chilled, filtered air, the same subtle mix of cleansers and polish and expensive soaps. The only thing that really changes are the outfits.

These are people who are almost never uncomfortable, who have entire systems devoted to moving them from place to place with the least amount of friction possible. They are transferred from cushioned seats in town cars to folding beds in the airplane, escorted by polite handlers with discreet weaponry hidden under custom-tailored jackets. They are fed before they are hungry, given wraps and jackets before they get cold, and tucked into thousand-thread-count sheets at the end of their days. I wonder if anyone here has actually felt his stomach grumble in years.

But if something happens to upset the careful equilibrium of their lives, then stand well back. They get volcanically pissed, and no one in a hundred-foot radius is safe from the explosion. The reaction is almost always the same, springing from their minds with the outraged squeal of a toddler badly in need of a snack and a nap: "I am not paying for *this*."

When I'm feeling generous, I understand the frustration, because I know where it comes from. I have worked at this level, around these people, for enough time to know that they are simply adapting to their circumstances. Almost everyone here isn't just a person anymore; he or she is a machine for moving money around the globe. They make it and they spend it in amounts that would be obscene to anyone who still has to balance her own checkbook at the end of the month. They power entire companies—hell, in some cases, entire economies—with their decisions in rooms like this one.

But they're not machines. They're still people, and people are fragile and fallible. On some level it must be terrifying to wake up in a different country every few days, even if it is in a luxury suite with a view. We are not that far removed from people who lived their entire lives within thirty miles of the place they were born, who never saw different stars in the sky at night. The new global elite may have private jets to shoot them all over the planet, but they can't outrun the basics of biology and history. Human beings haven't evolved substantially for about two hundred thousand years. That means we haven't had a real upgrade to our software or our hardware since before we learned how to plant crops.

Unless you count aberrations like me, of course.

Aside from that obvious exception, we're still basically cavemen who have managed to change the world instead of adapting to it. And at some bone-deep level, we're going to get a little irritable and paranoid without a familiar place to call home, or at least a wall to put behind our backs.

Most of the people at this level respond by turning into little windup dolls. They have to check all the marks on their schedule, make each appointment on time, hit the gym and the bar every day, roll their calls, generate *x* number of dollars or euros or whatever by the month's end. They stay busy so they never have to think about the sheer isolation and strangeness of their lives. They have an endless to-do list, and that's enough to keep the Reaper on the other side of the door.

The ones who move billions of dollars around—the men and women who are not just glorified traveling salesmen—they think about it. I know.

I have been inside their heads. They wonder what it all means, sometimes. When the Ambien isn't working, and their thoughts leak out as they look at a clock at 3:00 A.M. and they don't quite remember what time zone they're in, they wonder: What the hell am I doing here?

At moments like that, they are just like any of us. They want to go home.

I keep scanning the crowd. Sara is across the room. Neither of us sees Godwin, or even anyone who resembles the grainy older photo we got.

Then a Chinese man steps forward. He looks a little younger than me, but that could just be clean living and regular exercise. He's handsome, and smiles with white, even teeth. He's just about my height, so we are almost exactly eye to eye as he introduces himself.

And I cannot read his mind at all.

"Hello," he says, offering a slight bow and a handshake at the same time. "My name is Zhang San."

I smile back and take his hand in mine. "We've met," I reply.

A few days ago. In Iceland, where he fired off an H&K submachine pistol and tried to kill me.

He laughs as if I've just said the funniest thing he's ever heard.

Back when I was working for the CIA, I always heard rumors that the Chinese had their own version of our special-ed kids. The Chinese government would never allow anyone else to gain a strategic advantage that they didn't have as well. So, if we had a bunch of psychic soldiers, and the Russians had their own program, then you could be sure China would have one too. While Cantrell and the CIA specialized in finding natural talents like mine and developing them, there were stories that the Chinese government wasn't content to wait for random freaks to pop up. Researchers began taking large groups of children and training them in remote viewing and other psychic techniques. The program was designed to awaken EHF or "Exceptional Human Function." Reports were mixed:

some of the kids were allegedly able to read minds, move physical objects with their thoughts, see through solid objects with a kind of X-ray vision, calculate faster than a computer. I also heard about black labs, genetic manipulation, drug experimentation, but nothing that was ever verified.

We never met any of the EHF kids in the field. At least, not that I ever heard. I was too busy in Iraq and Afghanistan and Eastern Europe. I came across a couple of relics of the Soviet era once or twice. But never anyone from China's program.

Until now.

Zhang must be one of the EHF kids, all grown up. His age fits. I've been around other psychics before—in the CIA program where Cantrell trained us—but I've never had this happen before. I was always able to read them, and they could read me. Usually it caused headaches, tension, and a grating on one another's nerves, like we were stuck in some kind of feedback loop. If we spent too long in the same room, arguments and fights would break out over the stupidest, pettiest stuff. It was like chewing tinfoil. Cantrell kept us as separate as possible for just that reason.

Zhang, however, seems utterly delighted to see me. His grin does not waver and he looks at me as if I am a long-lost friend.

It's not as much fun for me. I don't feel any pain, but I'm still trying to deal with the sensation of a blank space right in front of me, an emptiness where he stands. Usually I am sorting through a flood of information when I am this close to another person. With Zhang, it's a black hole. And it's throwing me off my game.

"So I take it Godwin's not going to join us?"

He finally stops shaking my hand. "I'm afraid not. As soon as your passports were scanned by customs, Mr. Godwin decided he had better things to do. We've rescheduled our meeting."

Stupid. Should have realized if the Chinese government was involved, then of course they'd be watching for our passports.

This leaves me at something of a loss, however. Ordinarily, I'd make my next move based on what I read out of Zhang's mind. But that's not an option.

I think he's having the same problem. We both stand there for a moment, saying nothing.

Then Zhang asks, "Tell me, would you like a drink?" His English is flawless. Far better than my Mandarin or Cantonese, or, for that matter, any of the other languages I sort-of speak.

God yes, would I like a drink. And since it looks like we're actually going to have to talk, like ordinary human beings, going to the bar seems like a great idea.

The bartender ignores five people waiting in line to greet Zhang. "What would you like?" he asks with another smile. "Whiskey," I tell him, and his grin grows even wider. He cannot possibly be enjoying this as much as it seems.

I take a moment to try to read whatever clues I can from his appearance, since I can't just pluck the answers from his head.

His suit is bespoke, a perfect fit, probably from one of Hong Kong's famous tailors, though I don't recognize any distinctive cut or stitching. It's just slim enough that I'm fairly sure he's not carrying a weapon, but the weight in his pocket could be an exceptionally small pistol.

The staff is deferential to him, which means he carries some authority around this place, but he doesn't seem to have any official role. He does not wear a badge or lanyard or anything else that tags him as a functionary. If anything, he seems like a tech mogul at the center of his own launch party; everyone is always polite to the guy paying the bills.

The bartender serves our drinks—whiskey for me, something clear with ice for him—and we step away from the crowd. I let him lead us over to a pair of comfortable chairs, set near a corner.

We both have our backs to a wall and sit at an angle from each other, not quite face-to-face but so that we can watch the whole room.

He raises his glass in a toast.

"To chaos and opportunity," he says.

"I always heard that those mean the same thing in Chinese," I reply.

He tries not to smirk. Almost manages it. "That's a misconception, I'm afraid. But it does make a nice fortune cookie."

I raise my glass back to him. "Here's to nice fortune cookies, then."

We drink. And watch each other for a moment. And I still get absolutely nothing.

It must be the same for him, because he laughs and says, "It's extraordinary, isn't it?"

"Not the word I'd use."

"But that's what's so extraordinary about it," he says, leaning close. "Usually, I would know exactly what word you would use. I wouldn't even have to ask. I'd simply know. Instead, we have to play this guessing game. It's really just . . ."

He sees the look on my face, and realizes this isn't going over very well with his audience. He sobers up a little and bows slightly again.

"It's a new experience for me," he says. "You can see why they get into so much trouble. Always having to figure out what they're actually saying to each other."

I don't have to ask who he's talking about. He means normal people. People without our particular talents. Mere mortals like you.

"I don't know," I say. "I've always managed to find trouble pretty well on my own."

"I've heard that about you."

"Yeah? Well, I haven't heard jackshit about you."

That makes him laugh again. "What can I tell you? There's a price that comes with fame."

He sounds almost like Cantrell there. Scolding me. *"You know spies are supposed to keep things secret, right?"* he once said.

"I don't want you to feel disadvantaged," Zhang says. "Ask me whatever you want. Let's get to know each other."

Jesus. This is the weirdest first date I've ever been on, and that's saying something.

"You're EHF, aren't you?"

"I was," he says. "Most of us have moved on, into other arenas of public service."

"And now you're working for Godwin."

He makes a face. "I wouldn't put it that way. I would say we have mutual goals. More like a partnership between private enterprise and the government."

"Right. You guys do a lot of that."

"Well. Let's not forget, we are still Communists."

"Have you seen what Downvote is doing? You're happy with that body count?"

Zhang shrugs. "I've worked with worse people."

"So what do you get out of it?"

"I'm afraid I cannot tell you that."

"Then why were you in Reykjavík?"

"I should think that was fairly obvious."

"I mean aside from trying to kill me."

He waves that off. "Please. If I'd wanted to kill you, you'd be dead. You need to practice your hand-to-hand skills more. I think you've grown lazy, relying on your other abilities."

"You're right. I should have just shot you."

"That would have been a mistake. I'm not your enemy."

"Doing a great impression of one so far."

His smile has faded by now. We both take another drink. I pull my pill bottle from the inside of my jacket. I look over and realize that he tensed up for a moment.

I show him the bottle. "Nothing lethal, I swear."

"For the headaches?" he asks.

I nod. "You want one?"

He shakes his head and takes out his own bottle. "I've got my own."

We chase our pills with another drink. The rest of the party begins to crowd in on me. Zhang feels it too. He looks around the room and grimaces.

"Too many people in here. Are you picking that up?"

I nod and point. "The man in the blue suit. He's wearing some kind of codpiece, I think."

He pinches the bridge of his nose. "Some people's idea of a good time."

"I'd be more concerned about the art dealer over by the big red painting," I say. "Her heart is hammering. Any more cocaine in the bathroom and she's looking at a cardiac arrest."

"If she gets caught with cocaine here, she's looking at a seven-year prison sentence," Zhang says. "We take it a bit more seriously than you do."

I'm suddenly glad I've got a prescription for my pills. Then I sense a sudden shriek of panic, held inside only by severely rigid self-control.

I look over at an older Chinese businessman, his face utterly calm as he watches the screen of his phone. "That man just found out he's facing a margin call when the market opens," I say.

"Who?" Zhang says sharply, looking up. I point out the buyer. *<where will I get the money?> <nothing left to sell>*

"Interesting," Zhang says. "I had no idea he was that overextended." He takes out his phone and makes a note.

"So what else can you do?" I ask. "Aside from reading people. I heard some of you EHF kids could move things with your minds."

He chuckles. "I heard that about the Russians too."

"It would be pretty cool, though."

"Oh, absolutely. But I suspect you and I have similar skills. It might be why we cancel each other out so completely."

This is surprisingly friendly. I've never known anyone I could compare notes with like this before. I'm tempted to ask him if he knows how our abilities work. Where they come from. I get the feeling he might have some answers. But at the same time, I'm trying to remind myself that we are not on the same side, despite our similarities.

Still, I wonder if this is what a real conversation is like, among normal people.

"I have a question for you," he says. "Why do you still do this? Why are you running around as an errand boy for other people? Surely, by now, you could have your own company. Your own empire. You could be richer than the men who hire you."

"What, and give up show business?"

"I'm quite serious. There is a great deal of money out there for people with our talents. All it takes is the willingness to move to the center, away from the fringe."

"Is that what you're doing now? Working for Godwin?"

"*With* him," Zhang says, a bit of an edge in his voice now. "Not for him."

"I prefer to choose my clients. I don't really want to spend that much time in the center. Seems like too much of a target to me."

He looks disappointed. "You are still thinking the way they trained you to think. As a soldier. Or a servant. You're still trying to do a job that you are no longer qualified for."

"What's that supposed to mean?"

He grimaces. Trying to find the right words. He seems like he genuinely wants me to understand him.

"Not too long ago, there were tens of thousands of protesters clogging the streets here. Waving flags and shouting their slogans. That sort of thing can make the men in power nervous. But they can't send in guns and soldiers anymore. Not since Tiananmen. You can't run a man down with a tank. It's bad for business. Sends the wrong message. Still, you can't have these children blocking the streets and interfering with things, and most of all, refusing to do what they are told. That's even worse for business."

"Spoken like a true Communist."

He waves that off, refusing to let me distract him. "We have a country of over a billion people. Just to keep the majority of them fed and sheltered requires an extraordinary amount of effort and planning and intelligence. It is, perhaps, the most complex and delicate machine in history. And if it's disrupted, millions will die."

"So you keep the machine running smoothly? Make sure nobody throws a stick in the gears?"

Zhang shakes his head again. "No. That's what I'm saying. You and I were both trained to do that, but that was a long time ago," he says. "Now we are an obsolete system. Crowd control and social pacification for the twentieth century, not the twenty-first. The people who built us have either retired or moved on to the next generation. We are too visible, even with our talents. We're too unpredictable. They want something shinier and better. They want machine precision. Quantifiable results. They want software. They want drones and algorithms and artificial intelligence. Hard to believe, isn't it? Did you ever think we would be the ones who'd lose our jobs to automation?"

He gives me a significant look. I know he's trying to tell me something here. But I'm not good at subtext. I've spent too long knowing exactly what people mean.

"You think Downvote means you can retire? That you won't have to keep doing your job?"

Zhang has an almost wistful look on his face when he replies. "I sincerely hope so," he says. "But I don't think you would feel the same way. Are you capable of retirement?"

Not so far, apparently. But I don't want to admit that to him. Instead, I shrug and tell him, "If they can get a robot to do what I did, then that's fine by me. I don't miss it."

"Then why are you still doing it? What do you possibly get from this?"

I don't have a good answer for him there. Then I think of Kira.

"Somebody has to pay."

"Someone always pays," Zhang says. "That's the only remaining truth of this world. The trick is to be the one who gets paid."

"Is that what you're doing now? Getting paid?"

"More than you are, I suspect," Zhang says. "You could make a great deal more profit from this by simply walking away."

"Oh well, if you put it that way. Sure. I'll head back to the hotel. Pack my bags. I'll be on the next flight. Honest."

He laughs, genuinely delighted again. "You're not even trying," he says. "You really should listen to me, Smith. We are talking about the greater good here. If it's your life against millions, the math is not in your favor."

"Look," I say, putting down my drink and facing him. "I appreciate the warning. Really. I do. But we both know I'm not going to stop. So whatever you've got planned, go ahead and do it. It will save me time and you the frustration."

Zhang smiles and finishes his own drink. Then he stands, buttons his impeccable suit jacket, and gives me a slight bow again. "It's been interesting talking to you, Smith."

"You too, Zhang," I reply.

He walks away without another word.

Sara approaches quickly from across the room. She was watching the entire time, and I can feel the curiosity emanating from her like static electricity.

"Who was that?" she asks quietly.

"His name is Zhang San," I tell her. "That was the guy who shot at us in Reykjavík."

"What?" *<the hell, Smith>*

She manages to stay calm as I explain our conversation. At least as much of it as I understood. He's definitely playing a longer game than I can see.

"There were Chinese psychic soldiers too?" For a second, I feel Sara's dizziness as she thinks, quite distinctly and clearly, *<This is my life now, Jesus Christ>.*

"Similar program. Started younger, though. Even his name. It's the Chinese equivalent of John Smith. It's a placeholder name. Just like mine."

"So you mean he's like you?"

I catch a glimpse of Zhang as he stands at the door of the party. He sees me. He says something to a security guard at his side, who turns and locks eyes with me.

Then he gives me a friendly wave. And leaves.

The security guard, meanwhile, turns and starts heading toward Sara and me.

"No," I tell Sara. "I don't think so."

For starters, he's smarter than I am. Dammit.

Now I know why Zhang had his friendly little chat with me.

He was buying time, letting his people get into position. Anybody could have seen that coming.

It's a trap. Of course it's a trap.

I see it like a diagram on a whiteboard, now that Zhang has given the word to his men. The security guards know their plan. There are four of them. The one at the front door picks up another friend and they come at us from the front. The other two are behind us, coming through the crowd, boxing us in.

I get numbers, data, phone calls, instructions, all jumbled in their memories. But the overall strategy is pretty easy to read: they are going to kidnap us and take us out of here.

Zhang is long gone by now. Doesn't want to get any of this on his nice suit. I can't blame him. If I'd been smarter, if I'd been thinking ahead, Sara and I would have been out the door as soon as I recognized him. Instead, I sat down and had drinks with the guy.

Zhang was right: I've gotten lazy, relying on my talent. I'll be sure to address that if we don't end up in a Chinese black-site prison before the end of the night.

I look around the room, my mind racing, looking for any possibilities. There are no other ways out, except for that plate-glass window over the thousand-foot drop. I can do a lot of things, but I can't fly.

The two headed toward Sara and me are halfway across the room now. The other two are still behind us, letting other people pass, but ready to move if we turn and make a run for it.

"John . . ." Sara says, just the barest hint of panic in her voice. "Those guys—"

"I know. Give me a second."

I try to come up with a brilliant plan. Pretty much fail. Come up with a half-assed escape route instead. That will have to do. This is going to get ugly and public. No other way around it.

So we might as well get it started.

But first, I decide to take a page from Godwin's playbook. Let's see how Zhang's men react to a flashmob themselves.

I say to Sara, "When I start moving, follow me and stay close. Don't get distracted, don't worry about whatever you see. Just stick with me."

I'm grateful that she trusts me enough now to simply nod, despite the misgivings running beneath the surface.

Then I take a deep breath, try to find a moment of calm somewhere inside myself. Remember the feeling of touching all those minds at once in Reykjavík. Extend myself as far as I can go.

It occurs to me that this could go bad in any number of ways, but by then, it's too late. I'm plugged into the entire party. Feeling all the thoughts and sensations of the guests like a network, with signals humming along invisible cables between everyone here.

> *<cannot get a decent return> <robbed him blind> <what he deserves for marrying a twenty-year-old who dresses like a stripper> <I mean, really, who is stupid enough to buy that> <might as well invest in Florida swampland at this point> <Good Lord, are you really wearing that this year?> <I am so goddamn tired> <bought for eighty flipped for three hundred and fifty in one day> <isn't that the guy who stabbed the curator at that gallery?> <can't believe anyone paid that for fucking Popsicle sticks, but hey if it sells, it sells> <oh, hasn't she come up in the world now> <Incan ceremonial head masks> <is that James Franco?> <call it what it is: a beauty contest> <ugh awful it looked so much nicer on the Internet>*

In my mind, I reach out for one of those cables, and I send an image along it, a picture from my mind. Godwin specializes in hate and anger. For this crowd, I create the perfect fear.

Several people will later swear that their phones buzzed with an emergency alert on the screen, the kind the authorities use when there's a kidnapped child.

Except in this case, it says there's been a terrorist attack in Hong Kong.

```
ALERT ALERT ALERT—TERRORIST ATTACK—POSSIBLE "DIRTY BOMB"
DETONATED NEAR HARBOUR—BIOLOGICAL AND/OR CHEMICAL AGENT—
AUTHORITIES BEGIN EVACUATION—
```

They don't panic, even though they feel a charge of shock and anxiety. They do their best to keep their faces blank.

But they start to move for the exits, or to collect their spouses or their lovers or their lawyers.

And they begin to whisper the news to one another.

The news spreads fast. I hear it everywhere, in their minds, and in quiet tones. *<chemical attack> <terrorists> <ISIS?> <get out> <get out> <got to GET OUT OF HERE>*

I hear a half-dozen people on their phones, hissing at the pilots of their private jets: "Get us in the air as soon as possible—don't ask me why, just do it!"

The security detail, which was cutting smoothly through the crowd toward us, is suddenly bogged down by dozens of people all moving in different directions, nobody willing to yield.

I grab Sara's hand and start pushing toward the door along with half of the other guests. Good manners are barely prevailing, more because no one wants to alert anyone else to what's going on. Everyone here wants to be first out the door. Information is power, after all. I figure we have a few moments, at best, before the pushing and shoving starts.

The first security guard scowls and begins body-checking his way toward us. People yelp in protest, but then back away when they see his size and his scowl. He crosses the remaining distance between us in a few long strides.

He reaches out for me. "You," he snaps. "Come with me."

I reach into my memories and draw out the feeling of a punctured lung. Got that off an Iraq vet who took a round in the chest.

And I put it right into the front of his mind, stabbing it there like a knife.

His eyes go wide. He gasps for breath, falling almost to his knees. For a second, it's like there's a boulder trapped inside his chest, pressing against him, taking up all the space where the oxygen should be.

Sara sees it, knows the signals well enough by now, and we move faster through the crowd.

Now the panic is beginning. The man who has fallen, gasping, plays right into the fears I planted. "He can't breathe," someone says, an edge of hysteria in his voice. "He can't *breathe*!"

<oh god> <the chemicals> <is it here? already?> <do I smell something?> <choking, am I choking?>

I wonder if this was the smartest move. Too late now. Just have to ride it out.

People are moving as fast as they can now, carrying us along with them. Sara's heels click rapidly on the tile floor.

But the guys at the door aren't fooled. They've been warned. I can see it in their minds. They know not to trust their eyes or their feelings or anything else going on around them.

They let the other guests stream out past them, keeping their eyes locked on Sara and me. They both go for their guns.

There is no plan. They are simply going to stop us, and if we don't stop, they're going to shoot us.

I almost admire their focus and commitment. They're not going to take any chances. They don't waste time on disbelief, like so many of the goons I've gone up against before, because they've worked with Zhang, so they know what he can do. They don't care about the party or the witnesses. They've got a job, and they're just going to do what it takes. They'll worry about the mess later.

All right, then. No need to be gentle.

I reach inside the first man's brain and interrupt the connection between his inner ear and his nervous system, shorting out his sense of equilibrium instantly. His eyes roll, he makes a valiant effort, but he immediately collapses.

I get a tiny amount of what he's seeing. Up just became down, the walls flipped position, and his stomach tied itself in knots. For him it was like gravity reversing itself. He clutches the floor like it's his mother.

My own foot nearly slides out from under me, but Sara is right there, perfect timing, and she takes my arm and steers me toward the door, still heading straight at the other guard even though he's got his gun out.

I'm not sure what I've done to deserve this kind of trust, but I'm damn sure going to earn it now.

I can't risk anything that will leave me too helpless—God only knows what's waiting outside for us—but we need this guy down and out quickly.

I jump into his head and hit the ventrolateral preoptic nucleus, a tiny region in the pons, right between the midbrain and the medulla oblongata. The orexin neurons there regulate sleep like a light switch. And I imagine I'm slamming a sledgehammer into it.

In other words, I just gave him narcolepsy.

His eyes flutter like he's been hit with a dart gun. The tension ebbs from his body like an uncoiled spring. He's fighting it, but the gun droops in his fingers, which have suddenly gone slack.

I'm feeling a little drowsy myself, but I shake it off and summon everything I can and put it into a palm strike into his face.

He falls backward, almost comically, feet flying up in the air. The gun drops to the floor. We barrel past him and out the door.

People are shouting as we hurry out the door and down the entryway's stairs. There's no one waiting for us—until we get outside.

The crowd breaks apart as we move outside. The valet is suddenly besieged on all sides, guests arguing, shouting, offering wads of cash along with their tickets, each of them with the firm belief that they are the most important and therefore should be helped first.

Meanwhile, I see four more goons scrambling away from an idling van to intercept us. They were expecting us to come out quietly; I can read the surprise in all of them. But they're catching up with the plot pretty well.

Then we see the Bentley, still sitting where the white-haired man left it, right by the valet stand.

Sara latches on to the idea at the same time I do. We sprint for the car.

I snatch the keys from the pegboard and dive inside the big old beast. It must be from the fifties, easily. The front seat is like a leather couch and the instrument panel looks like something a World War II flying ace would see just before he sighted his guns on the Luftwaffe. I slam the door and reach for the wheel and remember that I'm in Hong Kong and this thing was built when England was still an empire and everything is on the other side. Fortunately, Sara is already there. She grabs the keys and the wheel, which is big enough to fit on a sailboat, and cranks the engine to life. She's a better driver than I am anyway. (Tactical and Defensive Driving Course for Close Protection Officers, instructor, four years.)

The security detail is moving toward us, but they're suddenly swamped by people from the house, demanding help, shouting over one another, wanting to know what's being done here. They expect answers, because they pay people like these men, and they are used to getting what they pay for.

I can sense the indecision in the minds of the security detail. They all have their guns under their jackets, but they don't know if they should pull them in public like this. The guests are all people who matter. It would cause some problems if one of them caught a stray bullet.

The guards begin to shout in angry Chinese and English as Sara slams the Bentley into reverse. We are blocked in by a Porsche. There's a crunch and the squeal of rubber as Sara uses the Bentley's rear bumper to sweep it out of the way.

We still don't have room to turn around, and Sara doesn't want to stop, or even slow down. So she keeps it in reverse, and aims the car butt-first right at the crowd in the driveway.

She revs the engine and jams the horn once in warning, and people turn and scramble out of our path.

The security detail is the last to move. The front fender clips one of them as we pass and he flies away, spinning like a top. I get a twinge of his pain, a muffled snap as he breaks a leg. Then we're moving down the driveway backward and way too fast.

The security team's van is still blocking the exit back onto Severn. Sara slams right into it. The Bentley shudders and we both bounce hard inside the car, but the van skitters out of our way like a shopping cart.

And then we're hurtling in reverse down Severn Road. It's too narrow to make a fast K-turn, and Sara doesn't want to let up on the accelerator.

I feel someone lining up a shot and understand why. A hole appears in the windshield, followed by another. Apparently the guards got over their indecision. We've reached the shooting portion of our evening.

Sara is halfway turned around in the driver's seat, neck craned, trying desperately to keep the Bentley on the road. The engine is screeching at the very limit of reverse gear, and gravity is doing its best to drag us down even faster.

"Are they following?" Sara shouts over the whine of the motor.

Suddenly the van, with its crumpled front end, comes screaming around the curve just above us.

She glances back and we nearly go over the edge.

"Just drive!" I shout at her, and she focuses on the road again.

By the time I look through the windshield again, one of the guards is leaning out the window, aiming carefully with his pistol.

The Bentley twists and veers another hairpin turn just as he fires. I can hear the bullets as they hit the old Bentley's all-steel chassis.

Thank God for classic cars, built back in the Iron Age. If this was a newer model, the shots would have torn right through the plastic and into us.

"Shoot back!" Sara yells, and I realize her gun is in my lap now.

I lean out of the window and nearly get a concussion for my trouble as the Bentley swerves again and my head bangs against the doorframe. Another volley of shots from the van and our windshield shatters completely.

Sara is doing her best to keep the big engine block between us and our pursuers, but they've got the advantage over us. They just have to throw more bullets, or drive us off the hill.

I will never make a shot under these conditions. They have to get lucky only once.

So I decide, screw this.

I pull my head back inside the car. Calm myself as best I can. Ignore the swerving and the squealing of brakes and the screech of the tires.

I feel myself lock on to the mind of the driver in the van. Feel his concentration, sharp as a blade, as he follows us down the road.

I blind him. I blank the signal from his optic nerves to his brain. Everything goes dark.

He screams—I can't hear it with my ears, but it echoes through my mind—and slams both feet on his brakes.

I open my eyes in time to see the van nearly leave the road, almost pirouetting on two tires as it struggles against physics. It comes down with a bang, and then skids into a complete three-sixty, totally out of control when it hits the retaining wall on the side of the hill.

I can feel the bones break on impact. None of those guys were wearing seat belts.

Sara lets out a yell of triumph, slams the Bentley to a halt, and then jams the gearshift quickly into drive, barely losing any momentum at all.

We are almost home free, just about to join the main road back down the Peak into the city.

Sara makes a skidding right turn onto the road when I sense it, too late.

<HOLD ON> <HIT IT>

Something moving toward us at over fifty miles per hour, breaking into my thoughts too fast to do anything.

I look up and see the car just before it slams into the side of the Bentley.

Without airbags or seat belts, we're both thrown around the inside of the car like eggs in a falling carton.

I hear Sara say my name. Then the roof flies up and hits me in the face, and everything goes black.

///22

A Pretty Good Night

I blink, trying to clear the darkness out of my eyes. My first thought is that I'm lucky—however bad the crash was, at least I'm not dead.

And then I try to shift my head, a wave of nausea rushes through me, and I'm suddenly not so sure about that.

My mind is still fuzzy and thick. It takes me a moment to realize I'm outside and the sky above is dark. I can't move my hands or feet. Then I hear voices.

"Hurry up. He's coming to, he's coming to."

"Going as fast I can . . ."

"Hurry up!"

"Hey! You want to do this, man?"

Water. I hear something like waves, slapping against the sides of a boat. So the rolling isn't just in my head. I'm on a wooden deck. I smell diesel-scented air. There's something tugging at my legs. I try to pull away, and someone yanks on my feet. My head hits the deck again, and my vision dances with spots. I feel like I'm going to throw up, but I manage to keep it inside.

I look around and see that I'm on a boat, somewhere out in Victoria Harbour. I can still see the lights of the city, but they're wobbling and blurry in the distance. We are far away from any other boats.

I feel something tugging at my ankles again, and I realize that one of the hired goons is tying something to my legs.

It's an anchor. He's wrapping my feet with some kind of cord.

This is bad. This is really bad.

I don't need my talent to know what they've got planned. They heave me over the side, tied to the anchor, and I'm done.

I close my eyes and try to suck down a deep breath. Everything spins again. I just need a minute to recover. That's all I need.

I'm not going to get it. Strong hands lift me up. I can't even get their names from their minds, or anything about them. My brains are still too scrambled. I'm going to have to do this with brute force alone.

Problem is, I don't have much of that either at the moment. But I've got to try.

I start kicking furiously, but they've already got the cord looped around my feet.

"Aren't you done yet?"

"Can't get the knot tied if he keeps moving."

I can feel the cord cinch tightly around my ankles. If he knots that thing to me, I'm truly dead. No way I can untie it before I drown.

So I take my best shot. I thrash and buck and kick. One guy drops me, banging my head on the deck again. The second guy tightens his grip while the third guy kneels on my legs. They have me laid out and helpless, like a fish they've just landed.

I keep struggling. I feel a little slack in the cord. It's the best I'm likely to get.

I use everything I've got and hinge upward from the middle. The first guy moves back, just in time to avoid my skull cracking into his. The guy on my legs does not. His eyes go wide, and I head-butt him right in the nose. I hear bone snap. He falls back, holding his face, bleeding and shouting in pain.

My head spins again from the impact. Everything flickers for a moment, but I manage to stay awake.

The first guy comes at me from the side. I flatten out again, and he nearly goes right over me. I hear a whisking noise, and realize he's got a blade. He missed slashing me by inches.

The guy on my feet is still struggling to tie off the line. I'd like to give him a nightmare, or split his brain open with some phantom memory of pain, but I can't concentrate. I've got one move here.

I pull my legs away from him and manage to roll to my feet.

I stand there, snarling, "Come on, you bastards!"

They laugh. They find my last stand hilarious.

I can't blame them. I'm bound hand and foot, stumbling on the deck of a boat in the middle of the ocean, my talent gone, completely unarmed. Not exactly my scariest moment.

But I lunge at the first asshole anyway.

By reflex, he comes up with the knife. And I turn just in time to take it in my shoulder instead of my neck.

You'd think, with everything else going on at the moment, it wouldn't hurt so much. But it does.

I stagger back, but the knife stays put, buried deep in my flesh.

Then the edge of the boat hits the back of my knees, and I fall over.

I hit with a splash. I'm hoping he didn't have a chance to tie off the line.

For a second, I float, struggling to tread water with my feet and hands bound, the cold water rapidly sucking the strength right out of me.

Then something yanks me and drags me straight down.

The anchor.

Looks like he managed to get it tied to me after all.

Now it's just a math problem. How far can I descend while attached to the anchor before the air in my lungs runs out?

I don't waste time trying to figure it out. I was never any good at math without a calculator.

Instead, I work on getting the knife out of my shoulder.

I can just get at it with my mouth, but it resists. It's stuck in there deep. I try not to think about the darkness closing in on me all around, the pressure building in my ears and in my head. My lungs are burning already. The math is getting worse every second.

Doesn't matter. Focus.

I pull the knife free with my teeth. A warm spurt rushes into my face. My blood.

Doesn't matter. Focus.

I fold myself in half. Manage to get the knife from my teeth to my hand. Flip it. Slice through the rope on my wrist, take a big piece of meat off the edge of my palm at the same time. Another warm spurt of blood. No time to be careful. Thank God the asshole kept his blade sharp.

Then I'm sawing away at the cord pulling me into the depths.

This is one of my nightmares. Being dragged down into the dark. I relive it every time after I kill someone, or when the pain and the fear get too thick against my defenses. There is a hole in the world that opens up every time someone goes out of it, and it always pulls on me. I see it every time. The abyss, waiting to take me. To take me out of this life. To where it is still and quiet and dark. Where I belong.

But not yet. Not yet.

Focus, dammit.

The cord is tougher than the stuff on my wrists. Maybe some kind of high-test fishing line. I keep sawing away, but it stays straight as an arrow in flight.

And then, amazingly, finally, it snaps. I stop flying toward the bottom of the ocean. For a second, I am suspended in the middle of all the black water, unmoving.

Another math problem. Can I make the surface with the air I've got left in my lungs, or have I already passed the point of no return?

I can barely see a dim light above. A spotlight playing over the waves. Has to be them, on the boat. They're looking for me. If I head for it, I'm going right back to the men who tried to kill me.

But I've got no choice. I don't have enough air to go anywhere else, and if I tried, I could easily get lost out here.

So I kick hard and swim for the surface.

Compared to my descent, it seems to take forever. I am no longer a bullet aimed at the bottom of the ocean but a piece of sodden garbage.

My left arm drags, courtesy of the knife wound.

Doesn't matter. I kick and pull as hard as I can. I release the used-up air in my lungs. I fight against every instinct I have to refill them.

The light above still looks a thousand yards away.

I'm almost done. My left arm stops moving.

Doesn't matter. Focus.

I am stuck in place. The light wobbles and seems closer. But I'm out of the last bubbles of oxygen in my bloodstream. I've got nothing left.

I stretch and crane my neck. Kick with everything I have.

I feel a different kind of cold on my skin.

Air.

I put my face up, barely strong enough to break the surface. I manage to suck down a greedy lungful before another wave washes over me.

And just like that, my talent returns. The men are still here. I know their thoughts. I know them.

It takes every bit of discipline I've ever learned to stay still. To remain just at the surface, breathing as quietly as I can, floating there in the dark. The spotlight passes by every few seconds, but there's a lot of water out here.

The men in the boat are watching for me. Arguing among themselves.

"He's gone."

"Another five minutes." That's the first guy's voice. I know him now.

"We should get out of here."

"You got a date? Five more minutes." *<lazy pricks> <we'll go when I say we go> <going to get a bonus for this> <finally get the hell out of this goddamn city and back to the States>*

His name is Nolan. Dennis Nolan. He's in charge of the other two, but only because he was hired first. He's ex-military, likes to tell people he was Special Forces, but he wasn't. He's been doing thug work for almost five years, since he was dishonorably discharged. (Assault on a superior officer in the Philippines. Drank away his last paycheck in Thailand. Been bouncing around the East ever since.)

They go silent again, but I can sense the dissatisfaction coming off the other two. *<can't see a damn thing> <stupid> <the guy is dead> <cold out here> <waste of time> <shouldn't be here>*

The second guy is also ex-military, Iraq and Afghanistan. Alex Perez. Former Marine. Another dishonorable discharge. Barely submerged death wish. Drinking buddies with Nolan in Thailand. Followed him here. Seemed like a good way to find somebody who would kill him. Hasn't been that lucky yet.

The last one is Sherman. Jeff Sherman. Another American stuck in Hong Kong. Wandered over a half-dozen years ago with a vague plan to become an MMA cage-match fighter, got in the hole with a local loan shark, now does whatever he can to make his interest payments. Met Nolan in a bar eighteen months ago and became part of his crew.

Thank God Nolan is so invested in proving he's the dominant male of their little pack. If they had left, I'd really be dead. My body is going numb. The water is cold and I'm bleeding and I'm probably already in shock. I am not going to make it if I swim. That boat is my only way back to shore.

The trick, of course, is getting on board without them trying to kill me all over again.

Times like this I really wish I could control minds. Then I'd just swim up and order them to bring me on board, fetch a couple of warm blankets and maybe some good Scotch if they had any, and tell them to drown themselves after they delivered me to the nearest hospital.

But I can't. So it's time to see what else I can pull out of my toolbox.

I ease myself closer to the boat, using my good arm. I try to get inside the head of Perez, who's on the spotlight. He's pretty focused on his job, but I manage to read him.

<nothing> <waste of time> <was that something?> <no> <nothing> <nothing>

Dammit. He's more or less competent. He might think this is a stupid idea, but he's still doing his job. Scanning each section of the ocean in a grid formation. He hasn't found me yet, but there's no way I can get past him without putting my face in the pattern at some point.

And time is on his side here. If I wait them out, I still drown.

I need a way to distract him, and I don't have a lot of juice for this.

So I try something a little more subtle. I pick around his memories until I find something pleasant. A day on a beach. In Thailand, drinking ninety-proof rum cut with lime juice. He met a girl, running away from her life as a student at USC, seeing the world. She was golden blond and tanned brown and tight as a rubber band. They screwed all night long in her cheap hotel room until her roommate came home in the early morning hours. She saw their bodies sandwiched together on the narrow bed, naked and sweating, and without a word lifted her dress over her head and joined them.

Yeah, that was a pretty good night.

While he's busy reliving it, the spotlight moves automatically over the water without him seeing a thing. I slosh and heave myself through the waves until I make my way right up alongside the boat.

I tread water by the hull, staying as quiet as I can. I'm right beneath them. They're standing a few feet above my head, looking over the railing.

I find Nolan's mind.

I'd like to do something really nasty to him, but I can't muster the strength, and I'm not sure I can take the pain of the feedback. So I go with something (relatively) simple. I push a picture into his mind of an enormous shark emerging from the water, just like that scene in *Jaws*, all teeth and blood and hunger. Inside his brain, it's suddenly Shark Week.

Like most people would, he panics.

"Holy shit!" he screams at the top of his lungs. He flails about wildly.

It takes a lot of balance and coordination to stand on a boat, even in calm waters. Nolan waves his arms for support. The other two guys slap them away. They don't like him that much, and anyway, they are keyed up and hostile. Any hand flying in their direction, they're going to see as a threat.

Nolan goes over the edge and into the water.

I'm probably going to have nightmares about sharks later, but it's entirely worth it as I hear him scream for help, splashing wildly, convinced he's about to become dinner.

Now the other two are looking for a life preserver or a rope or anything as Nolan keeps thrashing and panicking. When I sense them inside the boat's small cabin, I make my move.

I haul myself over the railing and onto the deck.

I land like a dead fish. Zero points for grace and style.

At first, the other two think it's Nolan. Then they process what they're seeing. I don't have the time or energy to mess with their heads to prevent it.

They bellow and race toward me.

Sherman races forward and plants his foot to deliver a kick that would do a punter in the NFL proud.

But I've still got the knife.

I roll over and slam it into his boot.

The pain is a fire alarm screaming in his head. He tries to check his kick and ends up falling backward, doing some real damage to his joints as the knife keeps his foot nailed to the deck.

Perez stumbles, trying to get past him. I decide that he can share his buddy's pain. I light up his synapses with the feeling of a knife wound and the hyperextended tendons.

He screeches and flops down, grabbing at his foot and leg like there's a shark chewing on them.

Nolan, half drowned, finally gets a hand on the boat, and he's coming up over the side. Unlike the other two, he's smart enough to be quiet.

But I can hear his thoughts just the same. He's got nothing good in mind for me.

So I yank the knife from the other guy's foot and haul myself up just in time to turn and face him.

He's looking at the knife, thinking of how he's going to get it away from me. I dance backward, over the other two, who are still spastic with pain on the deck.

I keep the knife in my good hand, facing him at an angle. The other two slowly haul themselves to their feet. They'll get it together soon. Again, time is on their side here. It's three against one, and I'm in sad shape.

My mind races, trying to pull up just the right combination of moves and mind tricks that will cripple them without costing me too much. Disposal of the bodies is easy enough—just into the drink, like they planned for me. But even once I pull that off, there's still the boat ride back. I'm leaking fluids all over the place, and I could easily pass out before I get to shore. The odds are not stacking up in my favor.

I think of Sara. What she said earlier. And for once in my life, I do the smart thing.

"How much are they paying you?" I ask.

The number pops up in Nolan's brain like it's on a cash register: <*$10,000*>.

I can hardly believe it. "Ten grand? Ten thousand dollars? Seriously?"

Nolan looks sheepish. "U.S.," he blurts. "Not HK."

"Jesus Christ," I say. "I'll triple it."

That stops all three of them cold. "What?"

"Stop this shit, get me back to land, and I'll pay all three of you triple what you're getting now."

They're reluctant. They look at each other. None of them wants to say it, but they can't see a reason not to accept my offer.

Nolan finally speaks. "How do we know we can trust you?"

"Well, if I don't give you the money, you can always try to kill me again."

They look at one another again. Nolan raises his eyebrows. The other guys shrug.

"All right," Nolan says. "You've got a deal."

I've already lowered the knife. "I know."

The ride back to shore is almost ridiculously friendly after that. They produce a bottle of cheap whiskey and we all treat our wounds with generous shots. I realize I am more banged up from the car crash than I thought. My ribs are aching, something twinges painfully in one leg, and half my teeth feel loose in their sockets.

I pull the entire scheme easily from their minds. It's actually pretty smart for its simplicity. Godwin hired them to watch the party and to pick us up in case I managed to pull one of my usual daring escapes from Zhang's men. Once we started down the hill, one of the security detail called them and let them know we were coming. They knew I was supposed to be dangerous at close range. So they improvised and hit us with a car.

I scan their memories and see they left Sara behind because they had no instructions for her. She was half conscious at the time and bleeding from a cut on her head, but didn't look too bad otherwise.

When I call her cell, she picks up, half panicked and half outraged. I'm surprised by the amount of relief I feel.

"Where are you?"

"Where am I?" she snaps. "Where the hell are you?"

"Took a boat ride. Are you all right?"

"I'm fine. Paramedics showed. The people at the party called emergency services, there were all kinds of panic attacks and heart problems among the guests. I just got out of the emergency room."

"They looked at your head?"

"Smith, I said I'm fine. What the hell is going on?"

I tell her what I need and where to meet me.

"Where the hell am I supposed to get—"

"My bag, back at the hotel. There's a black Amex in the lining of the top compartment. Pin number is four-five-nine-seven, password is 'kentallard,' all one word." I spell it for her. "Hit the ATM."

"Do ATMs even have that much cash?"

"They do here. See you soon."

I hang up and take the bottle as it's passed to me again.

Perez turns out to have some combat medic training and manages to patch up the knife wound and bandage my other cuts with the supplies he finds in the boat's first-aid kit. He recommends I see a real doctor as soon as I can. "There is some aggressive stuff out in that water," he says. "You are going to need a big dose of antibiotics."

Sara is waiting for us when we get to the dock—a small dark slip in a crowded marina. One arm is in a sling. In her free hand, she has a small shopping bag with the Valentino logo. She also has company. Two very big guys clearly wearing body armor under their shirts. They glare at all of us on the boat, all kinds of bad intent coming off them.

Sara isn't much friendlier. Along with her dark thoughts, I pick up that she's called in a few favors. The big guys are bodyguards who work for an international security firm. They're in town as part of a detail guarding a boy band on tour. Sara knows their boss, and after I made my call to her, she decided she needed some backup before carting $90,000 in cash down to the docks in the middle of the night.

She hands over the Valentino bag to Nolan, who feels a cascade of relief when he sees the cash inside. *<thank god> <enough to get home> <get the hell out of here> <start over>*

He reaches for me, and I can feel Sara and her sidekicks tense. But Nolan only wants to shake my hand.

"Thanks," he says. "I mean it. Thanks."

Getting a sincere thank-you from the guy who was paid to throw me into the harbor. It's not the weirdest thing that's happened to me this month, but it's definitely in the top five.

Still. Aside from trying to kill me, he's not a completely bad guy. So I just shrug and shake his hand, and tell him, "Don't mention it."

I step onto the dock, and they immediately kick their boat into reverse and motor away from us.

Sara lets them get back out into the harbor before she turns on me. "What the hell is wrong with you?"

I look at her and the two big guys. "Well, for starters, I need a lot of antibiotics."

Sara is volcanically pissed by the time we get back to the hotel. We took a slight detour to a small medical clinic that one of her bodyguard buddies knew about—he'd delivered an aging rock star there once after a nearly lethal combination of Viagra and cocaine—and I got patched up properly. The doctor, who seemed barely awake the entire time, ripped open the makeshift dressing on the new knife wound and sealed it again with surgical glue. Then he shot me up with what looked like a horse-size syringe.

"What's in there?" I asked him.

He just gave me a blank look. <*Medicine, you idiot*> was the only answer I could glean from his mind.

There must have been some painkillers in the mix, though, because despite Sara's anger, I'm feeling pretty good.

She dismisses her friends. They've got to get back to the boy band anyway. And she manages to keep her anger bottled up for the long elevator ride up to my room.

Which really makes no difference to me, of course. <*son of a bitch*> <*stupid, arrogant, condescending, careless*> <*going to get us both killed*> <*just show up with $90,000 in cash on a dock in the middle of the night*>

"Hey," I say. "It wasn't my idea to get kidnapped."

She glares at me. <*supposed to be better than that*> The elevator dings as the doors open, and I follow her down the hall to my room. She uses her key, and doesn't begin yelling at me until the door is securely closed behind us and we're behind the double-insulated walls.

"How could you let this happen?" she begins, and continues from there. I give her my best listening face for a while, but then I head over to the bar and fill a glass.

Sara goes silent as I drink. But her thoughts feel like they could peel the skin off my face.

She takes a deep breath, and then boils it all down to the bottom line. "People are getting hurt and getting killed. Aaric is in federal custody. We are supposed to solve this problem. We do not have time for you to play pirate with your new friends on the boat. You are supposed to be better than that."

Nobody is ever just one thing at any one time. We're all struggling with multiple thoughts and emotions that set up competing agendas inside us. Our minds can be like a chaotic session of the United Nations, with delegates arguing loudly against each other as they all try to be heard, to have their concerns addressed first.

Right now Sara has clamped a layer of self-control over her anger, which is sitting on top of her fear and her anxiety and her sense of duty and responsibility. But beneath all that, I can feel a sense of worry. And relief. She was frightened when I disappeared, terrified that I might have been picked off by Godwin, and despite everything, she is glad I am back.

That's probably what tips me over the edge.

"How do you think this ends?" I ask her.

The question stops her for a moment. "What?"

"When we do get Godwin. We're going to catch up to him. It's only a matter of time. What do you think happens when we do?"

"We take him back to the States, we turn him over to the feds—"

"Grow up," I say, as coldly as I can manage. "He has been killing people for years to protect himself and his business. He will not go quietly. At best, we bring him back in a body bag."

"No," she says. "That's what you want, but it doesn't have to be like that. You can bring him back alive. I have seen what you can do. I know it."

"And what if I don't want to?"

<stubborn> *<asshole>* "Then you're an idiot. You really think that it's going to matter to Kira Sadeghi if you kill Godwin?"

"It matters to me."

"What does that get you?"

"Two things," I shoot back. "Money. And revenge."

"And that's all you want?"

"That's enough."

"You are so full of shit. Why don't you ever do anything to help people? I look at everything I've seen you are capable of—and then I think about everything that I know is out there. The number of people who lie. Cheat. Steal. Kill. And get away with it, because nobody can prove it, or nobody knows about it. Except you. You could do something about it."

I've heard variations on this theme before. From Cantrell. Do your duty. God and country. I stopped buying into it a while ago. Still annoys me, though.

"Like what? You tell me, what should I do?"

"Anything," she snaps. "Anything at all. Step up. Think of all those psychics that say they can find missing people—"

"Frauds."

"—but *you're not*. You could do that. You could give them answers. Closure."

"You think it's that easy?" I shoot back at her, really close to actually losing it now. "You think you have any idea what it's like?"

"Enlighten me," she snaps.

I take a second. And then I decide, what the hell, and I give her one small crumb of the truth.

"It's getting worse," I say.

That stops her. "What do you mean?"

"The pain. In my head. Everything I pick up from everyone else. It's all been getting worse. Everything I do to other people has a cost. I get part of it back. And the cost just keeps going up, every time."

Until this moment, I didn't really want to admit it, even to myself. But it's true. The feedback, the cost of using my talent—it's all been increasing steadily over the past few months, ever since I went back to work. When I was doing black ops, I could shrug off a mission with a good hard drunk and a few hours' sleep. A couple of years ago, it took a few pills. Now it takes half the damned bottle and I still feel like I'm going to go into seizures after I spend too long slogging through other people's minds.

"You have no idea what it's like," I tell her. "You think people want answers? Bullshit. They want to hang on to their illusions. Because sometimes that's all they've got. And more importantly, do you think I want to wade into that swamp? Do you have any idea what it's like, feeling that kind of pain? That kind of hopelessness? I do. And it's enough to make me want to slit my goddamn wrists. I've felt other people's pain my entire life, and it only ever ends one way. That's the only closure I've ever seen."

That rocks her back—I can feel the shift, like she's standing on a boat that's been hit by a wave—but she's not giving up. Not yet. "Maybe you can change that," she insists. "Maybe you are the only one who can change that. You are smart and resourceful. You can figure out five different ways to cripple someone, you can damn well find a way to help them."

"Yeah? What if I've decided that you people deserve whatever you choose?"

She stops. Blinks. I just managed to surprise her. "'You people'?"

"All of you," I say, my voice much rougher than I expected. "Every one of you. I used to think you just didn't see it. The times you hurt each other, lied to each other, betrayed each other. Without a second thought. I used to think you just didn't know. But then it kept happening. I saw it over and over and over."

I did. I can't put it all into words, but over the years I saw it all. And not just the shit in the war zones or on the secret missions. This was years before Cantrell and the CIA found me.

I am talking about the stupid, small, everyday crimes I saw before I was eleven. Husbands and wives lying to each other like a second language. The guy at the cash register swiping twenties from the drawer. His boss, shaving hours off his time card every week. Foster parents preying on the children they were paid to raise. Dull-eyed policemen too bored and too lazy to do more than take a report and ignore the facts right in front of them.

"I learned a long time ago," I tell her. "This is the way you want to be.

It's not that you don't know what you're doing. It's that you just don't give a damn."

"No. You don't get to say that," she says. "Not everyone is like that. There are good people out there—genuinely good people."

I see a list forming. Her grandmother, her mother and father, a few brave cops she's known, and Aaric Stack. Of course. Her personal saints.

I am tempted to start picking through her head for their flaws. I could tell her some of the thoughts I fished out of Stack's mind. Just to win the argument.

But some measure of sanity stops me. I am not that big a bastard.

I take a deep breath. "Maybe you're right," I say. "Maybe I just haven't been hanging out with the right crowd my entire life."

She flares with anger. "Don't," she says. "Don't try to laugh this off. You don't get to write off the entire world. You've got a gift. You can do more than just hurt people."

I shrug. "What can I say? It's what I'm good at."

"You're wrong," she says simply. "I refuse to believe that."

She has such faith. She really is such a good person.

So that's what I decide to use against her, of course.

"You called yourself a sheepdog before," I remind her. "That's how you think of yourself. I know. So tell me: What happens to the sheep after you guard them?"

"What?" Her head is filled with cartoon pictures for a moment. I've thrown her off track, and for some reason, it's caused her to think of those old Looney Tunes episodes where the wolf and the sheepdog work together.

"Sheep get slaughtered," I remind her. "They get turned into meat and leather and sold."

"What the hell are you talking about?"

"We're all just meat, in the end. We're only worth what anyone is willing to pay for us."

She looks at me with something like horror running through her mind.

<oh my god>

That is exactly the moment she gives up on me.

She doesn't say anything out loud, but I catch the blistering exhaust of her frustration as she leaves the room, slamming the door behind her.

I stand there for a moment and finish my drink.

That was harder than I thought it would be.

I walk over to the closet and get my bag. It takes only a few minutes to pack.

I pass by Sara's room as I leave. I can still feel her anger and frustration, all the way to the elevator.

Twenty stories straight down, and I'm in a taxi to the airport.

///23

That's My Other Superpower

Traveling to Laos from Hong Kong is relatively easy, but hardly luxurious. For starters, I don't have access to Stack's chartered Gulfstream anymore. Which means I fly commercial, and I learn firsthand that despite the stereotypical—and probably racist—assumptions people make about the Buddha-like calm of people from the Far East, I can tell you that it's almost as bad as dealing with an airport full of angry Americans.

I wind up on an ancient but spotlessly clean turboprop out of Luang Prabang after connecting through Bangkok. That's going to get me as close as possible to my destination.

I check my watch, and figure that Sara has gotten my email by now. Basically, I said thanks for the laughs and I quit. I would have sent a text, but that's pushing the envelope, even for me. With any luck, she'll stay in Hong Kong while she figures out her next move.

And I can finish this without putting her in any more danger.

Because I didn't just swap bad jokes and war stories with my pirate buddies on the boat, as Sara called them. I also took all that time to dredge through their memories to find out how they were hired, and everything they knew about Godwin.

I learned that Nolan has actually seen him face-to-face. He's been doing jobs for Godwin for a couple of years now, ever since they first met in a hot and damp bar near Godwin's regular base of operations.

A bar in Laos.

I have to admit: Laos is a pretty genius hideout for someone like him. It's remote and incredibly poor and wildly corrupt. Any government interest is easily diverted with a few bribes—pocket change for Godwin. There's also the fact that the U.S. dropped about 2.5 million tons of bombs on Laos during the Vietnam War—or one bomb load every eight minutes, more than all the explosives dropped in World War II. Those little gifts just keep on giving, with the unexploded leftovers maiming kids who go out in the fields looking for scrap metal. That means Americans aren't always seen as helpful and friendly visitors, so there's very little in the way of official cooperation with international law enforcement. And finally, the country borders China, which tends to be fairly protective of its own backyard. As long as Godwin does his business on the other side of the planet, in Europe and the U.S., and doesn't piss off the Chinese, he's safe there.

Nolan went back to Godwin's bar all the time to get paid and beg for more work from Godwin. The directions were practically etched in his memory.

Which led me to one of those moral dilemmas that I am so deeply uncomfortable with. I knew that if I told Sara about Laos and Godwin, she'd want to saddle up and ride after him again, like we've been doing all the way across the planet. She is tough and she is smart and she is determined to save her boss's narrow ass from the federal government by bringing back the bad guy, roped up and thrown over the back of her horse.

I wasn't exactly comfortable with that, but I had enough faith in her abilities and mine to accept the risk. She's a professional. I wasn't about to insult her by saying she's not up to the job. Even after we started sleeping together, I trusted her to have my back, and to watch her own. Because I'm a gentleman like that.

Then we met Zhang San. And that changed everything.

Zhang—despite his charming smile—is far too dangerous for Sara. Hell, he's probably too dangerous for me. He's at least as capable as I am, if not more. He nearly put us both into a Chinese prison just to get us out of the way. If we go up against him again, there is almost no way that Sara doesn't get hurt.

And when I looked into her mind and saw she was actually concerned about me—that she was worried about me when I went missing—I decided that I couldn't live with that chance, even if she could.

I had to find a way to get away from Zhang, and from Sara, and make my run at Godwin directly. Just me. Nobody else.

So I did what I do best: I said some cruel and stupid things, and I pushed away someone who was trying to stay close to me.

Aside from reading minds, that's my other superpower.

The Lao Airlines flight attendant interrupts my wallowing in self-pity. She tells us we're about to begin our descent. She goes through the entire routine in four different languages and probably makes less per hour than a kid working a paper route back in the States.

Luang Prabang Airport is modern glass and steel surrounded by scrubby green fields and trees. The old airport was replaced a couple of years back, and the new one looks as if it could have been imported in shrink-wrap from any midsize city in the American heartland. There are plastic chairs and digital reader boards and air conditioning.

As soon as I am off the plane, I begin scanning the minds of everyone within a hundred yards. I get nothing but the usual weariness and anxiety and frustration of people on the move as I pay the equivalent of twenty bucks for my entrance visa. But I don't let down my guard. Even if I think I've taken Godwin by surprise coming here, I've learned that he's better at tracking me than I am at hunting him. I stay on full alert, like I am walking through a combat zone.

I stop and put the case with Sara's laptop into a rental locker at the airport. It has all of Godwin's secrets, including the backup code for Downvote. I do not want Godwin to get it back if he does manage to get me.

When I leave the chilled air and step into the thick humidity outside, I don't get so much as a glimmer of suspicion. Nobody is looking at me. The only attention I draw is from people who are happy to see a tourist—any tourist—willing to spend money.

It's not until I get out of my cab at my hotel that I pick up the sniper.

It's a small hotel on the street near the Dara Market, about as close as this place comes to a bustling city center. People are stacked around me. A group of children crowd in close, several of them with missing limbs: nubs and stubs of arms and legs, souvenirs of their attempts to salvage scrap metal from the unexploded ordnance out there. I feel their need like quicksand around me. What I've got in my pockets is more than any of them will see in a year. I am too tired to worry about keeping them in a cycle of dependency or damaging their natural initiative. I hand out all the cash I've got, which, of course, only brings more kids.

Then I pick up the telltale prickle on the back of my neck that means someone has locked on to me.

It's such an amateurish move that I'm almost embarrassed for Godwin. I can sense eyes on me and backtrack all the way into the brain of the person holding the rifle. This is one of the first tricks I ever learned when the CIA helped me weaponize my talent.

I step behind a pillar—the kids follow, of course—and feel the sniper lose the shot. I'm about to hack my way into his mind and plant something that will wreck him with nightmares for years when my phone rings.

I recognize the fake electronic voice immediately. This, at least, is impressive. I ditched my old phone and picked up a new burner at the airport. He got the new number in record time.

"Tell me, how did you know which hotel I'd pick? I didn't make a reservation."

"I didn't," he says. "I have men at each of the tourist traps. I figured one of them would spot you."

"You didn't have to go to all that trouble."

"No trouble," he says. "I have plenty of help here. They were looking for something to do. Best to keep them occupied."

Something finally occurs to me. "How did you know I was coming?"

"I sent Nolan after you. He knows where I am. I assumed you'd know too. I told you, John. I've thought about you."

I sit with that for a second. Despite how smart I thought I was, Godwin *knew I was coming*. I suddenly feel a lot more exposed.

"Well, I hate to disappoint you, but I am a bit jet-lagged, so I'm just going to head inside and take a nap. We can pick this up later."

"You're not going to walk away."

I force a laugh. "Unless he can see me through solid concrete, I'm pretty sure I am."

"I'm told you can see what my shooter is seeing," Godwin says. "Is that true?"

For some reason, I feel a slight chill at that, despite the swamp-like heat in the air. "Yes," I say. "That's true."

"Take a look through my man's eyes, then. Go ahead. I promise he won't do anything without my word."

So I slide into the sniper's mind and look out through his eyes. I see his point of view through the rifle's scope, feel the weight of the gun in my arms.

He's focused on the pillar of the hotel that I'm using to hide. I hear something in his ear. Godwin's electronic voice, giving an order. "Now," he says.

The scope moves away, onto one of the children. Small. A little girl. Cleft palate. Holding a begging bowl.

Then the scope moves again, and settles on another one of the kids. Right arm missing from below the elbow. Dirty Spider-Man T-shirt from some well-meaning charity back in the States somewhere. Can't be more than seven or eight years old.

Then another kid. A boy. Hair flopping over one eye. Reaching for me with one hand, squalling like a baby bird for more cash. Another kid. Hobbling along on a handmade crutch and one leg, the other one severed at the knee.

Finally the scope comes to rest on the youngest child in the crowd, who has to be five years old at the most. He is too young to look sad or miserable. He's smiling, openmouthed, at all the excitement as the kids crowd around me.

The scope stays centered right on his forehead.

I get the message. Even before Godwin's voice comes over the phone again.

"You understand now?" he says. "I know you've beaten snipers before. Maybe you can jump into my shooter's head and change his mind. Maybe get him to drop the gun. Or some other stunt. But I think he can still get a shot off first. I know you're willing to risk your own life. The question is, are you willing to bet that boy's life on it?"

"You wouldn't," I say, but I'm only saying it out of tradition.

There is the by-now-familiar electronic cough that means Godwin is laughing at me. Again. Of course he would. He's done worse for less. "You come quietly with us. Or that kid dies here for you."

I can still see through the shooter's eyes. The crosshairs remain on the child as if painted in place.

"What makes you think I care?"

"Maybe you don't. Maybe I've misjudged you, John. But I know some of what you suffered as a child. And I know that you cannot stand to see any other kids suffer."

My mouth has gone quite dry. I have to swallow before I reply. "Yeah. But I hate to see myself suffer even more."

"You're stalling."

No shit, I'm stalling. I am not used to someone outthinking me like this. I'm trying to work out the best possible way to debilitate the gunman so that he doesn't even have a chance to twitch his trigger finger.

Godwin speaks over the phone again. "I hate to be that guy, but I am on a schedule here. So I'm going to count down from five. Then his brains go all over his playmates."

I wrench my mind away from the gunman. Look at the kid with my own eyes. He's completely oblivious. I try to will him to run away. No chance. He sees the other kids getting cash and he wants his turn.

"Five."

I go with Godwin, I end up in a shallow grave somewhere in the jungle. I'll be nothing but bone fragments in a couple of weeks. Decomposition works fast out there. All those bugs and scavengers. Godwin wins. He wins everything. My whole pointless life is over, and he wins. That's the really galling part.

"Four."

And what do I owe this kid anyway? Jesus, who says I have to save every stray out there? He's living in Laos. His odds are not good for a long, healthy life. What, is he going to grow up to cure cancer or something?

"Three."

Dammit.

"Two."

"All right," I say into the phone. "You've got me. Whatever you want. Whatever you say. You win."

"Well. Yeah."

He hangs up. I check the gunman's line of sight, inside his mind again. It's still steady on the boy.

Then I am forced out into the world again as I notice two men coming toward me in the street. Both grizzled white guys, cut from the same cloth as Nolan and his two friends in Hong Kong. Expats who stay away from the United States not because they can't go back, but because they've found a license to do whatever they want outside of its borders. The worst kind of tourists: the ones who stay.

They shove their way through the children and flank me. One on each side. Before I get more than a surface read—<*quickly*> <*quickly*> <*do it now*>—one of them jams a hidden pistol in my ribs while the other pokes something sharp through the cloth of my shirt into my arm.

I feel it almost immediately. They must have used an injector gun. Some kind of mix of ketamine and Demerol and God knows what else.

I start to sag, and they grab my arms and begin marching me along. The kids curse and complain and whine as they drag me away. I get one last look at the boy through my rapidly blurring vision. He notices this time. Gives me a big goofy smile.

Jesus, kid. You'd better grow up to cure cancer.

And then everything goes dim.

///24

The God of Win

When I wake up, I am still a little fuzzy from the drugs but otherwise fine. No hangover, no headache, no pain. All my limbs in the right places. I've woken up in worse shape after a night of what I'd call fun. If I live through this, I will have to get the recipe for that particular cocktail of drugs. I mean, really. I haven't felt anything that smooth since I left the CIA. (The government, it should come as no surprise, has all the best drugs.)

I am tied down. Long packing straps pin me to a table in what looks like a prefab wooden building, somewhere hot and damp. If I had to guess, I'd say I'm still in Laos. I can't sit up, so I turn my head.

There are the broken frames of slot machines, looking like robots that have been gutted, their interiors spilled in front of them on the floor as they have been dismantled for whatever was inside. The flat screens of video poker machines look back at me like a series of black mirrors. A moldering bar runs along the back wall.

I turn my head the other way, and there is Godwin. Sitting not ten feet away from me, in the open door of the building. It is a brilliant, bright day outside, and he is little more than a shadow against the glare. He sits in profile to me, crouched on a stool in front of a small wooden table. It takes me a moment to recognize that it's a blackjack table—stained with mildew in places, scored with nicks and scratches.

Godwin is slightly older than I'd thought. A dark-haired man in his late forties, wearing a loose sport shirt and khakis—the kind you buy for hiking through the wilderness, not the kind they sell at the Gap. He looks like the host of some Survival Channel show that never made it big.

I've never seen him before, or even heard his real voice, but I can read him clearly. And there is no doubt. It's him.

The man behind Downvote. Finally.

He pays no attention to me, focusing almost totally on the card game in front of him. Drawing cards from an old deck with mismatched colors and placing them down in rows.

He's playing solitaire. By hand. Does anyone even know how to do that anymore?

Then I look a little deeper, and I see. I start to see who Godwin really is.

He was born in Australia, outside Perth. Father a refinery worker. Mother a housewife. A fairly normal upbringing, until his father couldn't handle his liquor anymore. He got fired from one job after another, then finally took off and left the family for good. Godwin has no idea where he is now, or if he's even alive.

His mother took care of the kids as best she could. Hotel maid, secretary, clerk in some government office. There were a series of boyfriends and stepfathers, the last one outwardly perfect—good job, nondrinker—but vicious and physically abusive when challenged. That's about when Godwin began to drift away from the rest of house. He spent his time in his room. He'd built a computer from a kit and used to rack up massive phone bills chatting on bulletin boards. He became increasingly isolated—not too unexpected, given all the time he was spending alone. Inside his head, there are dark shadows around all the memories. His mother and siblings would stop talking when he entered a room. He began to think they didn't like him. That they were plotting with his stepfather against him.

He read a lot of questionable self-improvement material he found on the Net and in cheap paperbacks. Ayn Rand. *Atlas Shrugged*. Changed his name then to "GOD of WIN" as his Internet handle. Because that's how he saw himself. Better. Smarter. Able to move ones and zeros around and shape the world. Typing long messages late into the night to people who didn't care about his high IQ, his natural superiority.

He had the skills, though. Like Stack, he's a self-taught coder. He learned everything he knows by doing it. He began hacking for fun and profit. He downloaded porn and sold it to his classmates. Got into school records, changed his grades. Got into bank accounts. Emptied them.

And left home just ahead of an arrest warrant from the local PD.

He was seventeen then. Same age as me when I left home. He knew he'd been sloppy. He left his digital fingerprints all over his first bank heist. Was determined never to make that mistake again.

The next years are a jumbled patchwork of images and impressions. He landed in South Africa, spent a few years there, bounced up to the Czech Republic, then Hungary, and then over to the United States. There might have been a wife in there, or a girlfriend. His memories of her are as insubstantial and fleeting as a ghost.

But he always managed to find work. People would see what he could do with computers, and they overlooked the strangeness, the blank spots on the résumé. Eventually, he found employers who saw those things as positive attributes.

Godwin—that was the name on his passport now—found his way to Romania and hooked up with the Boian clan when he reprogrammed a bunch of blank phone cards for them. He made lasting connections. Showed them where the real money was lurking in the dark corners of the Net. And pretty soon they were working for him. He started in identity theft, churning thousands of stolen credit-card numbers before moving into faked prescriptions, then from there into money laundering, which is where the real cash was.

Godwin was careful never to get too big, to become a priority for any of the international law enforcement agencies. They are all busy with the narcoterrorists, the drug lords, the various crime families and their corporate partners. Or they make cosmetic busts of the small players, the incompetents who try to sell a crate of heroin and weapons off the back of a truck to a group of Interpol agents.

Godwin lives in the middle. He services everybody. Accumulates very little. Keeps most of his own money in digital form, in well-secured offshore accounts.

He's never given up playing with computers. He still visits the message boards, still tinkers with software. He saw the code that Stack posted for encrypted transactions and instantly recognized the potential for his own business. Then he found Stack on the boards, and the two of them began talking about what would become Downvote.

Then he had his grand plan. His big idea. The final score, like they talk about in heist movies. A plan that no one else would see coming, with enough wealth to walk away forever as a reward. For him, it's not about the money. He has millions. He's already doing what he wants.

But the plan will prove just how much smarter he is than everyone else. All the governments, the cops and agents who have tried to track him down. Stack. And even me.

I can almost see it. Abruptly, his consciousness shifts.

"Did you get a nice long look inside my head?" he asks.

He's aware that I'm awake. He doesn't look up from his cards. He's not too scared of me, even though I could hurt him in a dozen ways without moving from this table.

I admit: I am impressed, despite everything. Imagine a bar catching fire and a nearly perfect stained-glass window forming out of the melted liquor bottles and wreckage. That's Godwin. He is, in his own way, a work of art. Battered and tossed around in chaos, yet somehow still complete. He could have collapsed into addiction or escaped into a stable job somewhere in a suburb. Instead, he became a pirate.

Godwin flips the cards over, one after another. He learned to play during his three-month stretch in that Philippine jail all those years ago.

When I don't answer, he speaks to me again. "You can't say you weren't warned. I told you I would get you if you kept coming after me. And I did. I know you better than anyone else."

"Well, I was unconscious for a while. But I trust you were a gentleman."

He smiles. "That's funny." Now that I can hear him, I see why he's used the voice-masking software over the phone. His accent is odd and distinctive, a collection of vowel sounds and consonants from every place he's lived. Australian burr with some Slavic tinge to the vowels, plus a hint of southern drawl in there too. It sticks in the ear. For someone like him, who wants to be anonymous at all cost, it has to be a liability.

"You know what I mean," he says. "I told you I would be able to handle you. From the very start. Take another look in my mind. See what you can see."

I do. And I realize why he's not afraid of me.

He's taken two precautions. The first is around his wrist. It's a knockoff fitness tracker that measures Godwin's pulse and movement. He's tinkered with the software a little himself. It's now linked via Bluetooth to a vest he's wearing under his shirt, which is why he looks a little bulky sitting there.

He's hooked himself up to a suicide vest. There are twelve small bricks of plastic explosive wrapped around his chest. The detonator is keyed to his pulse and respiration. If his heart stops, the vest explodes—and it's got enough power to kill everything inside a ten-yard radius.

That's a pretty good incentive for anyone close to Godwin, like me, to keep him breathing. But he's got another one too.

I can read his thoughts clearly. He's got Sara.

The memory is bright and distinct. She is cuffed and gagged, her injured arm pulled painfully behind her while a man holds a gun on her. The man—a hulking thug with a thick beard, one of Godwin's Romanians—marches her into the building that is across the way from us, disappearing into the dark entrance.

No chance of that now. Godwin got both of us. I don't sense her thoughts anywhere nearby, but that doesn't mean much.

"Where is she?" I ask, but Godwin shrugs. I scan deeper, but he honestly doesn't know. It's the only way to keep a secret from me: stay ignorant.

"I only know the phone number," he says, holding up a cell phone. "I gave my friends strict instructions. I suppose you already know what happens if I feel like I have to make that call."

I do my best to avoid the images and ideas running through his head now. He's told his men holding Sara to make the same threats to her about me. We're both being held hostage to guarantee the good behavior of the other.

"How do I know she's still alive? If you've already hurt her, why shouldn't I just stop your heart and trigger that bomb right now—"

Sighing, Godwin lifts a remote control from the furred surface of the table and clicks a screen on the wall to life.

There is a webcam image of Sara. Like me, she's tied down with packing straps, pined to a mattress instead of a table. Helpless.

But alive. Or at least she was when the video was taken. He knows that it will be enough to keep me quiet and polite.

The small hope of rescue I didn't even realize I had dies inside me. In the back of my mind, I thought that Sara might still come in, guns blazing, and spare us both a lot of trouble and anguish. For once, I thought, there might be an easy way out.

All right. I admit it. He really is pretty smart.

"She came looking for you, you know," he says conversationally, as if we were discussing the weather. "That's why she's here. She tracked your credit cards. Found out you flew to Laos. I had a man following her. I arranged for her to be picked up when she arrived. Cost me about fifty bucks, American."

I don't respond to this. He looks up from his cards. "Does that bother you? Knowing that her loyalty to you is what's going to get her killed?"

I think about that for a moment. "You were so certain that I'm not really human," I say. "What do you think?"

He shrugs and goes back to his game. "I think that you'd like to believe you care for her. She'll serve her purpose. So will you. That's enough for me."

He doesn't look up from the cards as he says this. He and Stack are like distorted mirror images of each other. Stack has internalized all of his pain, used it to lash himself into a contorted position where he cannot eat half of a protein bar without feeling guilt.

Godwin, on the other hand, wears his misery like spikes, and lets other people impale themselves when they bump up against him.

I've been threatened by a lot of people. It comes with the job. But as uncomfortable as it is to admit, Godwin creeps me the hell out. He moves with the deliberate pace of a spider on a web. I know he'd kill me without a second thought if he could.

But he can't. Not yet anyway.

"Why don't you just get it over with?" I ask.

He doesn't answer, but he can't stop the response that bubbles up in his brain.

<they want to see you> <want to know how much you know> <need the server software back too> It all spills from his head before he can derail his train of thought. He tries to focus only on the cards, only on the game, so I won't be able to get too much detail.

But it's tough, even for someone with his kind of mental discipline.

Zhang is coming. He's going to finalize the purchase of the code for Downvote. And Zhang's bosses, in whatever Chinese ministry or spy agency, want to make sure I don't have too much of it inside my head.

"They need to make sure they're getting an exclusive," I say, getting it now. "They don't want me walking away with the software they just paid you for."

He points a finger gun at me and puts his thumb down, like he's just shot me. "Exactly," he says. "They want to ask you a few questions."

"And if I can't answer?"

"I'm sure they can motivate you to be open and honest with them."

So I've got torture and death in my immediate future. Today is just getting better every minute.

"Then we're just waiting for Zhang."

"Are you really in such a rush for him to get here?"

"No," I say, meaning it. "I can wait. Where are we?"

He waves his hand at the open space outside the door. He doesn't have to speak out loud to answer, and he knows it. <*Golden Boten City*> pops up between his ears, and I get glimpses of a dilapidated small town, all new concrete construction, already being reclaimed by the jungle that surrounds it on all sides.

"What the hell is that?" I ask.

Godwin makes a noise. "This was a resort. Gambling is illegal in China. We're right on the border. So the Chinese allowed a casino to be built here. Thousands of Chinese poured over here every day, spent their money. Hundreds of millions changing hands. It began to get bigger and bigger. They called it 'Laos Vegas.' Grew like a tumor. And then, one day—"

"The Chinese shut it down," I say, seeing it. The power and telecom lines, which snaked from the China side, were suddenly shut off. The border stations were closed. No explanation. The money stopped flowing, almost overnight.

Almost nobody local was hired. The farmers who used to work the area were moved twenty kilometers south, and thousands of Chinese workers were brought in to run and clean the hotels and cook the food and wait the tables in the restaurants. They went back over the border, along with the prostitutes who staffed the brothels. The tables were run by contractors from Ukraine and the Philippines. They vanished as well. The cooked-food vendors, the beggars, the souvenir sellers, the small-time crooks who'd begun to steal money from the drunken gamblers—they all cleared out. Ten thousand people a day used to swamp Golden Boten City. It became a ghost town in less than a week.

"Why?" I ask Godwin.

He shrugs again. "Who cares? Maybe they opened it as a pressure valve. Let off a little steam. Maybe they let off too much. Whole place is scheduled for demolition now anyway. Let the farmers have the land back."

The building across the way was called the Kings Roman Casino. The sign is long gone but I pull the name from Godwin's memory. I recognize the front entrance. It's where they took Sara.

I think about that for a long moment. Then I turn to Godwin again.

"You know, Godwin, you were kind enough to offer me the chance to walk away, when all this started. Remember that?"

He smirks. *<bullshit artist>* *<never stops talking>* "So, you going to offer me the same chance now?"

"No," I say flatly. "I wanted you to know that no matter what happens, you are not walking away. You're going to die here."

That utterly fails to wipe the smirk off his face. He doesn't even bother to reply out loud to me. *<pathetic>* *<really expected better>*

"You don't have to believe me," I tell him.

"Generous of you—" he snorts.

I talk right past him. "But you keep saying how you've studied me like nobody else. How you know me so much better than anyone ever could. Maybe you should think about this, if you know me so well: Do I seem at all nervous to you?"

That gives him pause.

Because no, I don't look nervous. Or scared.

I know something Godwin doesn't. Yes, there will come a day when I do not walk away from one of these situations. There will be a time when my luck runs out. When I am not fast enough or smart enough or prepared. When even my talent won't give me an edge against the inevitable.

But it's not today.

Godwin's satphone buzzes to life less than an hour later. He picks it up and walks out of the open doors. He vanishes from my line of sight, and I can only barely hear him muttering quietly into the phone, but he's still close enough for me to read him.

<they're here> <approaching on the road now> <let them pass>

He ends the call and walks back into the small building, past me, and through a door in the back. I lose track of him. A moment later, a couple of his Romanians arrive. Their thoughts are neat and orderly, focused on a clear to-do list. They clear more space, put away Godin's deck of cards, set up chairs and a table, and then break open a fridge by the wall and set out plastic bottles of water. They're both carrying guns and knives, but they look positively domestic right now, making sure everything is just right for their guests.

I pick up Godwin's thoughts again, a low buzz of anxiety and tension. He reappears through the door in the back a second later. Now he's carrying a laptop. He brings it to the table and opens it and begins to boot it up.

He points, and one of the thugs goes through the door. I feel him wait there. Guarding the back.

More of the Romanians show up. The space is too small to fit them all comfortably—there are six of them, and they're all big guys—so they arrange themselves outside, in a loose kind of formation. Relaxed, but spread out in case of trouble.

None of them even look at me. I'm just another piece of furniture in the room.

Godwin's satphone buzzes again. He answers. "Yeah?"

<just passed us> <should be there any second>

Godwin hangs up and passes this along in Romanian. The thugs all turn their heads down the road, as if on a swivel.

I peek into one of their brains and take a look through his eyes. At the edge of Golden Boten City's main drag, where the road winds into the jungle again from between the abandoned buildings, a black Dongfeng Mengshi appears—the Chinese version of the Humvee. Same frame, same engine, a lot more armor. The name means "brave soldier."

It rolls along toward the men and Godwin's building. I snap out of the thug's brain just as it pulls up outside. I can see it myself now, framed in the open doors as it rolls quietly to a halt.

The Romanians part as the doors open. A group of six Chinese soldiers, wearing fatigues without names or insignia, emerge. None of them have their hands on their weapons, but they are all carrying. They look at the Romanians without expression. I read nothing but the mental equivalent of a blank stare from them. They're ready, but they're not eager. They're not about to start pulling triggers unless it's absolutely time to do so.

Then, from the backseat, Zhang steps out.

He doesn't look as happy to see me this time.

Zhang walks into the building and greets Godwin. They don't shake hands or bow or engage in any other fake pleasantries. Instead, they move as efficiently as a machine.

Godwin plugs a cable from his satphone into the laptop. Zhang opens a ballistic nylon black briefcase and takes out his own computer. They both sit down behind their machines and begin typing commands.

It's all highly anticlimactic. After all the chasing and shooting and people who have been killed and hurt, it's done in a few keystrokes. Zhang gives Godwin an IP address, and Godwin types it into his laptop. The satphone delivers the package of code.

Then they wait. Once the code is verified by Zhang's bosses at the other end of that connection, he will key in a payment. I can't see the amount in Zhang's mind, but it's blazing in ten-foot-high numbers in Godwin's: $1 billion.

"You got robbed, Godwin," I tell him. "You should have held out for two billion. You could have sold it to Facebook for at least that much."

He doesn't reply. Not out loud. *<I cannot wait for you to be dead>* He knows that's coming soon, and he feels a warmth that's almost like happiness.

Zhang frowns. He must sense it too. He doesn't look up from the screen, but he speaks to me.

"I want you to know I didn't want this. You should have gone with my men in Hong Kong. You'd be in prison, but you'd still be alive."

I almost laugh. "Well. As much as I appreciate that, you could save yourself the guilt and let me go."

He shakes his head. "I'm afraid that given your abilities and reputation, my current employers can't take the risk that you have the knowledge of Downvote inside your brain." Zhang looks up at me for the first time, staring directly into my eyes. "I am afraid it will not be pleasant for you. I am sorry for that."

That's about all Godwin can take. He snorts. *<oh for Christ's sake>* *<both of them>* *<what a load of crap>*

Zhang and I both look at him. Now I know Zhang is reading him too. He got the blast of contempt coming from Godwin.

"Is there a problem, Mr. Godwin?" he asks, in a perfectly polite tone.

Godwin does his best to throttle back his emotions. But the word <*freaks*> still slips from his mind.

"No problem," he says.

"He thinks we're inhuman," I tell Zhang helpfully.

"Shut up," Godwin snaps at me. "It's got nothing to do with our deal, does it? So let's get it over with."

"Yeah. About that," I say. "How do you know he's actually given you the code for Downvote? How can you be sure he hasn't just given you a bunch of old video games or something?"

"The code is being verified and decrypted as we speak. That's another reason we're waiting here. We could have easily done this meeting by a remote connection if we didn't have to retrieve you, Mr. Smith. But I find a personal meeting is good to remind people of their obligations. If Mr. Godwin has tried to cheat us, or planted a virus, then he will pay the consequences."

"You really trust him to come through for you?" I ask.

Godwin smiles at me. <*amateur*> <*looking for some angle*> <*won't work*> <*pathetic*> "We have something better than trust," he says. "Mutual benefit. We both get what we want. Zhang got the merchandise. I got the money. That's all I need."

He leans back, oozing confidence.

"That and the dead-man's switch on you," Zhang says.

Godwin's smile falters a bit. "Well. I believe in being prepared for all eventualities."

"You believe that as long as you're wired to that suicide vest, my sense of self-preservation will keep me from doing anything to you."

"Of course. You're a reasonable man," Godwin says.

"I don't suppose it's occurred to you how much pain I can inflict without stopping your heart?" Zhang asks.

Now Godwin isn't smiling at all. I feel a trickle of fear leak through his mind, like cold sweat.

"I don't think you'll do that," he says.

"Why not? I have what I want now. Why shouldn't I? Unlike Mr. Smith there"—Zhang nods at me—"you do not have anyone I care about as a hostage. Are you really prepared to die here, Mr. Godwin?"

Godwin's thoughts have turned dark. I see a bloodbath coming. The Romanians might not all speak English, but they definitely get the drift of the conversation. They've got their arms at their sides, loose and ready to grab their weapons. I'm sure Zhang must see this too. I don't know what he thinks he's going to gain by antagonizing Godwin like this.

"If I have to," Godwin says.

There's another long pause, and then Zhang breaks into the same brilliant smile I saw back in Hong Kong. "Fortunately for both of us, it won't come to that. It's not up to me whether this deal goes through. I am simply doing my job and ensuring delivery of a product. So it doesn't matter if I am inhuman or not."

There's an immediate sense of relief flooding into the room. <*Motherfucker*> Godwin thinks. <*kill both of you freaks if I could*>

He doesn't care that Zhang and I can both read him.

They look at their screens. <*It shouldn't be taking this long*> Godwin keeps thinking.

I look at Zhang. His face is placid. No way to know if Godwin is just impatient. Zhang seems prepared to wait all day.

The sun is high in the sky by now, and the heat has gone from intense to blinding.

And then a bad thought occurs to me. I've got a naturally suspicious mind, but this idea borders on paranoia.

Still. Paranoia has kept me alive this far. Something Godwin said earlier has been bouncing around in the back of my head: "The whole place is scheduled for demolition anyway."

If Zhang's bosses want to make sure that Godwin never sells Downvote to anyone else, why would they let him walk away?

And if they don't want to take the risk of me using my talent to suck the secrets of Downvote out of Godwin's head, why wouldn't they have that same fear about Zhang?

I speak up again. "You ever heard of the prisoner's dilemma, Zhang?"

He turns to me, looking slightly amused. Of course he has. He's probably twenty times as educated as I am. He was tutored from an early age by the best his society had to offer. I read whatever was available in underfunded public school libraries while the teachers ignored me.

But he answers me anyway. A real conversation is still such a novelty to both of us. "The prisoner's dilemma. Two men are held prisoner. If one betrays the other, he receives a reduced sentence. But if they both stay silent, then they both spend a shorter time in prison. The dilemma is whether they can trust each other."

"Right. I only mention it because it's relevant to our situation here."

"I only see one prisoner," Zhang says. "So really, it doesn't apply."

"You sure about that?"

He pauses. I can't say I really know Zhang. I've spent only a few minutes with him, and I cannot get inside his mind at all.

But I do know some of what he's done and how he's been trained. I know how he operates, and I can guess at the world he's been living in since childhood. I know because I have lived it. In some ways, I know him like I know myself.

And I know the only way I would walk into a trap is if I was arrogant enough to assume that I had already figured everything out.

"Let me ask you another question. How would you get rid of one of us? If you really wanted to be sure?"

He has to think for only a second. I'm sure he's spent time, as I have, lying awake at night thinking about how someone could kill or ambush him despite our talents. You can throw a mob at us, or a unit of highly trained soldiers, or put a sniper on a roof, but we've got ways to deal with all of that. That's what we were built to handle. You might get lucky, but there's a good chance we're walking away and leaving a lot of bodies behind.

If you're looking for a guarantee, you've got to remove the human element. Like a timed explosive. We can't read the mind of a clock. Or some other kind of booby trap, a doorway rigged with C-4 or a land mine under a step. But those methods still require some kind of verification after the fact. You have to send someone around to ID the body, or at least scrape up some DNA.

The best method would be a real-time camera focused on us as a target, followed by a threat we can't fight or outrun.

"Drone strike," Zhang says.

"I'm surprised they haven't done it already," I tell him.

He can't read my mind. I can't read his. But I can tell he's annoyed. He leans over in his chair so that we're almost face-to-face.

"What are you trying to say?"

"I'm saying we're all going to be dead pretty soon if we don't get the hell out of here."

"What?" Godwin says. "He's full of shit. He's trying to save his own ass."

"Think about it," I say to both of them. "Why should they let any of us leave? Why would they allow anyone else to know what they've just bought?"

Zhang frowns. "You think they would kill us all?"

"You don't?"

"You? Definitely," he says. "But they need me. I'm still an asset."

"I hate to deliver a crushing blow to your ego, but are you more valuable than a program that can steer entire masses of people? More importantly, are you more valuable than the need to keep that program secret?"

Zhang's frown only deepens. I can read the thoughts of some of his men, the ones who speak English. *<are we in danger here?>* *<would they really do that?>* *<they've done worse, I know it>*

"Are you worth more than a billion dollars, Zhang?"

There's a spike of anger and frustration. I feel murder headed my way.

"I've had enough of this," Godwin says, and takes a pistol from one of his Romanians. He walks over to me, jacking a round into the chamber as he does.

Zhang looks torn. He's really got no reason to defend me, and there's still the matter of the suicide vest Godwin is wearing.

"Wait," he says.

"For what?" Godwin snaps. "You want to be sure he doesn't tell anyone about Downvote? You want to empty his brain? Let's do it right here."

He puts the gun to my eye.

Fortunately, that's when the first missile hits.

/// 25

The Prisoner's Dilemma

The Chinese-made AR-1 has about the same range and firepower as the American Hellfire missile. Like the Hellfire, it weighs about a hundred pounds and finds its targets by laser guidance or satellite navigation.

And like the Hellfire, it can pierce forty inches of tank armor before it unleashes an explosion that's lethal to everything in a fifty-foot radius.

So the one that hits Zhang's Dongfeng out front blows it to pieces, and also removes the nearest wall, most of the roof, and half of Zhang's soldiers and Godwin's Romanians.

For a second, I don't see anything or hear anything. The table where I'm tied down flips up through the air, and I feel weightless.

Then gravity reasserts itself, and I land heavily on the floor, with what feels like a few hundred pounds of rubble to keep me company.

I'm pinned under the table, which is on top of me now. That seems to be all that's keeping a half ton of cinder blocks and scrap off me, however, so I'm not complaining.

I scan around in every direction. I don't sense Godwin, which is bad. If he's dead, then we've got another explosion coming soon, from much closer.

Nothing happens.

Godwin's alive. Definitely one of those good news/bad news things.

There is a shifting in the rubble near me. I crane my head to look. I can't see him, but the absence in the mental landscape tells me who it is.

Zhang appears a moment later. He does not look good. He's bloodied, and half his body is porcupined with wooden splinters from a beam that exploded. His rifle is still slung over his shoulder, however, and he's able to stand. He limps to my side.

"You might have been right," he says. He reaches into one pocket of his fatigues and pulls out a knife. "You know the solution to the prisoner's dilemma?" he asks.

For a second, there's every chance he's going to slit my throat. I don't speak.

Instead, he slices the straps, freeing me.

"Trust," I say as I sit up. "If the prisoners choose to act against their own interests, they both win. It makes no sense, but it produces better results."

He shoves the table aside and the rubble slides off, crumbling into a new pile among all the other wreckage. He drags me free before helping me to my feet.

"Let's find out if that's true," he says.

As fast as we can, we check the other men still in the room. Anyone who was standing by the door is ground meat. They went so quickly I didn't even feel them slip out of their lives.

There are a couple of Zhang's soldiers left, both carrying more shrapnel than he is, and one Romanian. The other gangsters—the ones who aren't dead—must have gone out the back with Godwin. The Romanian has a piece of rebar jutting through his leg, keeping him in place as effectively as a bear trap. His thoughts are a long, sustained note of pain and obscenity. I can feel the thing scraping around inside him, near bone. Ordinarily, I'd never try to move him. But the next drone strike could come at any second.

There are definitely going to be more. They took out the Dongfeng first because it was an easy target, and because it was transportation. They don't want anyone getting away.

So I put my hands under the Romanian's leg and yank as hard as I can. And feel his agony go from blinding to unbearable.

He screams as the meat around the rebar squelches and moves a few inches. Not enough to pull free, however.

I sense the punch coming before he throws it, and duck. He's screaming at me now. I don't speak Romanian, but my talent translates. *<take your fucking hands off me>* *<Jesus Christ that hurts>* *<kill you if you do that again>*

I'd like to tell him it's not much fun for me either, but I doubt he'd understand.

I take a deep breath and reach for his leg again and he finds his gun from someplace and points it at me.

The meaning of that would probably be pretty clear even if I couldn't read his mind.

"Leave him," Zhang says, hauling one of his men up in a shoulder carry.

"We can use him," I say. "He knows where Godwin is, where he's going."

And he might know where Sara is.

Zhang looks at what's left of the ceiling, which is open to the blue sky now. It would almost be comical if we weren't currently targets. The Chinese CH-4 drone can cruise at five thousand meters, which is almost twice as far as the unaided human eye can see. Even if we could spot it, as far as I know neither of us has heat vision to knock it out of the sky. The drones usually carry at least two AR-1 missiles, which travel at a top speed of 950 miles per hour to their targets. They can obliterate tanks, buildings, and every living thing within fifteen meters.

But I know what he means. We're visible. The drone's next pass could come any second. And if we're still in here, we might as well hold up umbrellas to protect ourselves.

"Look, you fucking moron," I scream at the Romanian. "You can't stay here. Another big boom, coming fast. You understand?"

I boost the words right into his mind and point at the sky, just in case that might help.

The gun wavers a little, but he still looks suspicious.

Zhang is struggling to get his soldier out the back. The other Chinese soldier is on what's left of the floor, groaning.

Screw it.

"I'll be back," I tell the Romanian, and hoist the Chinese soldier up. He feels like a sack of broken glass in my arms. I hobble across the ruins to get out the back door, just behind Zhang.

We rush into the jungle. It's not far from the backs of the buildings that line Golden Boten City's main street. The thick canopy should give us some cover from the drone's cameras or any satellite coverage.

We run as far and as fast as we can, trying to get outside the blast radius. I have a brief, stupid fear of snakes or picking up some kind of disease from some unknown species of frog, but that's probably curable. Being turned into a red mist by an AR-1 is not.

We're a hundred yards into the jungle when Zhang finally collapses and drops his soldier. They both gasp for breath on the ground. I deposit my soldier next to Zhang. He lands harder than I intend, and I feel all the damage he's sustained inside, the pain sloshing around my chest and gut as well as his.

I turn back toward the building.

Zhang says, "Don't be an—"

That's as much as he gets out before the next AR-1 hits, and the little gambling room is reduced to dust and slag.

The temperature rises to five thousand degrees at the center of the blast, and the shock wave throws me back a good six feet. I collide with Zhang and we're driven down into the soft undergrowth. What's left of my hearing blanks out completely, and my head feels as if it's been hit with a sledgehammer.

For a long time, nobody moves. We're simply not capable of it. The fires from the blast begin to catch and ignite the closest buildings. When I feel like I can turn my head without it falling off, I look over at Zhang. Talking is pointless; we're both still deaf from the strike.

He's still, his face composed. He looks up at the small bits of sky and sunlight that make it through the trees and leaves overhead.

They're not done yet. They can't be. It's just a matter of how many drones they've got, and how many missiles they're carrying. They've got to be searching for us, ready to drop another payload the second they see movement.

But Sara is still in there.

I heave myself to my feet and begin walking toward the main drag again.

My hearing is gone, so it's a surprise when Zhang grabs me from behind and yanks me backward.

I try to pull away. Shouting is pointless, so I try to make my point with gestures.

Whatever message I manage to convey, his answer is the same. He shakes his head. *No.*

I shove him back and head for the edge of the jungle again.

Zhang doesn't stop me this time. He goes to tend to his men.

I make my way carefully. Godwin and at least some of his people are still around. I don't sense them, but my head's a little scrambled, and they could still be close enough to fire a shot.

I'm almost at the place where the dirt gives way to pavement again.

There are vines and runners and roots cracking the surface already—the jungle anxious to take the whole city back.

I circle around the location of the last drone strikes, trying my best to stay under cover. The trees reach almost to the side of what used to be a convenience store, which is decorated with huge movie posters. George Clooney, his head the size of a satellite dish, watches me with a look of firm resolve on his features.

Through the gaps in the buildings, I can see the Kings Roman Casino, the building where Godwin's men dragged Sara.

I'm wondering if I can sprint across the road fast enough to outrun a missile when I feel the change in the air. I don't hear anything, because I am still deaf. But there is something like a high gust of wind that cuts through the stillness and humidity.

This time I have enough sense to dive for the ground.

The strike takes out the convenience store, and Clooney disappears in a fireball, his piercing eyes looking at me until the wall vanishes.

I scurry back into the jungle as far as I can, until the canopy above is thick again.

But it doesn't matter much. Whoever is operating the drones has decided against surgical strikes. Suddenly missiles begin to rain down on Golden Boten City, one after another. The buildings are hit almost in sequence, like a kid working through a line of alien invaders in a video game.

By the time they reach the Kings Roman, Zhang has found me. A missile hits the east side of the building first, which seems to dissolve like a sugar cube in hot tea. The center collapses, and it's pounded again by another strike, and even the bricks seem to be on fire now.

Then they go back and hit every place again.

Zhang sits beside me, and we watch, in awe and horror, as the entire town vanishes before our eyes in clouds of flame and debris, struck down by thunderbolts from some unseen and angry god.

I don't know how long it takes. Probably only a few minutes. It was not a very big place, after all.

It seems to last for hours.

When it is over, my skin feels cooked from the heat of the flames and my body feels pulped from the blast waves. There are pools of melted glass, and burning lumber, and places in the rubble where walls are still standing.

But nothing alive.

There is nothing left alive at all.

I am not even sure how to begin mourning Sara. We were too far away for me to feel her go, and I am almost sorry about that. Touching her mind would have been torture in the last moments. Feeling her fear, her desperation, as the missiles hit.

But it would have been contact. It would have been more than this.

As it is, I feel empty. I don't even have my old familiar cushion of rage to fall back on. I came here to kill Godwin for what he unleashed.

And now I'm looking at burning rubble, and wondering how much responsibility I bear myself.

At moments like this, I am actually glad when the shooting starts, because it keeps me from thinking anymore.

The first bullet goes high, snipping a branch off a tree right above me and Zhang. We both snap to attention and flatten ourselves to the ground at the same time.

I scan outward. I assume Zhang does the same, and finds what I do. Two of Godwin's Romanians. Moving toward us through the trees, about twenty meters out. We were so busy watching Golden Boten burn that we didn't even notice their thoughts.

They're not particularly quiet. They're pumped on adrenaline and anger. Teeth clenched, hands tight on their guns.

<double-cross us> <make you pay> <try to kill us from above, we send you to hell>

Somehow they've decided that this was all Zhang's idea, despite the fact that he was almost killed in the strikes too. It doesn't make sense, but you don't get a lot of rational thinking from men who have just endured a rain of hellfire from the sky.

There's another burst of gunfire overhead and to the left. I dip into their heads and see that they've lost sight of us. One stretch of jungle looks pretty much like another. It's easy to get confused.

Then I realize something. I heard the shots. My hearing is coming back. Everything still sounds muffled, but the noise of the outside world is beginning to leak back into my brain.

So I try to talk to Zhang.

"You going to do something about this?" I ask.

He looks at me like I'm an idiot. Another burst of gunfire over our heads, but closer. Homing in on my voice. I must be yelling.

Another burst.

Zhang scowls and pops up, gun in hand. He aims and fires just like I would, using not his eyes but his talent. He barely looks awake, he seems so bored.

But then, behind a plant I can't name, two men die. Their bodies drop, and I feel their thoughts end, cut off like a light switch being flicked. I pull away from them. I don't need to get sucked into their deaths on top of everything else.

Zhang lies back for a moment and seems to rest. I realize something: I can no longer sense the minds of the two remaining Chinese soldiers. They're gone. Their bodies are right where we left them, but they're gone.

I know what he must be feeling. The black hole of loss, amplified by whatever connection he had to the two men. Maybe they were friends.

Maybe they were just soldiers. But there was a string connecting them to Zhang, and I know it takes everything inside to resist its pull as another mind dies.

I wait for him to recover. At this point, it is a decision. He has to make it himself.

"This really has become a legendarily bad day," Zhang says after a long moment. It's almost a joke. I figure he's convinced himself to keep breathing. Keep surviving.

"What now?" I ask.

"They're not going to let us just walk out of here. Are you armed?"

"No. You have a spare?"

Despite what he said about trust, Zhang still hesitates before he hands over one of the dead men's sidearms. It's a QSZ-92, the Chinese version of the 9mm. I check it, then put a round in the chamber.

"Did you see how many Godwin had with him?"

"At least a dozen. He had men all around, waiting for you."

"Probably not many left. If there were, they would group up, try for a mass assault. Confuse us with numbers. One by one, they're only going to get picked off—"

Then we both sense it. A stray thought, at the edge of our range. There. About a hundred yards away. The outer limit of my reach. One of Godwin's thugs. I recognize the particular tang of Romanian on the surface of his consciousness before my talent automatically turns his words into something I can understand.

<see you how like this> <bastarzi>

And then *<grenade>*.

I see it come flying through the air a second later, and I'm already moving. So is Zhang.

The blast seems almost quiet compared to the missile strikes. Still blows an appreciable hole in the ground, though.

But we're not there anymore. I am moving back around behind Godwin's remaining thugs, using my talent like radar bouncing off them, stepping between the trees, keeping them at a distance.

I emerge from the foliage and see the thug about to pitch another fastball at the place where he thinks we are. I can feel the windup in his muscles, hear the countdown in his mind. He pulls the pin.

<five> <four> <three>

Which is when I break in and cramp his hand.

It feels like white-hot fire shooting up his arm as the muscles seize up. He's barely able to drop the grenade from his fingers. It bounces and rolls only a couple of feet away from the toes of his boots.

I feel the spike of panic shoot through him as he turns and runs as fast as he can.

It's not fast enough.

The explosion picks him up and hurls him a dozen yards, and his body becomes a pincushion full of metal fragments.

I feel it all. The pain takes me to the ground and blots out everything for a moment.

The jerk doesn't even have the good grace to die quickly. He lands hard after his body bounces off a tree, still bleeding and suffering. I'm stuck with every second of it.

I try to pull my mind away from his agony but it's like being rolled in barbed wire; it's going to take time to disentangle myself, even as he drops into the hole at the end of his life.

I am so busy with that I don't notice the other thug moving from the bushes behind, circling around toward me with his gun drawn. I sense him only when he is right on top of me, looking over the sights of an assault rifle.

He aims carefully. No expression on his face. His mind is equally blank. He's a professional, doing a job.

I raise my gun and try desperately to think of something that will stop him or slow him down, but I'm snarled in the mind of the man dying out a few yards away.

Then blood fountains from the thug's throat as it bursts open. I remember that I'm still pretty much deaf, and realize I didn't hear the gunshot that tore through the back of his neck and out the other side.

He collapses to the jungle floor, and I see Zhang behind him.

He's saying something, but I'm still too deaf to hear clearly. And anyway, I'm busy.

I line up the shot. Point the gun in his direction.

He looks surprised.

I fire several times, and he looks even more surprised when he doesn't drop dead.

But the Romanian thug behind Zhang does. He was bringing his rifle up to his shoulder when I shot him in the head and chest.

This one goes mercifully quickly. There is the usual hole in the world that opens when someone drops out of it. But I am ready for it this time. I pull away from the darkness there, and focus on Zhang, who is still staring.

I move closer to him. I try to speak, but my voice still sounds like it's being muffled by cotton. So I have to shout.

"What was that?" I ask.

He shakes his head. Gives me that amused look again. "Trust," he yells.

"Makes no sense," I yell back at him. "But it works."

"Godwin," he says.

He must still be out there, but I can't pick up his thoughts anywhere. Neither can Zhang, apparently.

"We can't shoot him," I remind Zhang. "The vest."

He rolls his eyes, a gesture I associate more with teenage girls than badass Chinese psychic soldiers. "Tell me something I don't know."

Then we cover each other as we move deeper into the jungle and begin to hunt.

We don't get very far before I start dragging. I have been shot and stabbed and drugged and beaten and blown up in the past week. I haven't eaten since Hong Kong, and I am shaky from too much adrenaline. I also haven't had my pills, and that always puts a crimp in my sense of humor.

Zhang is hiding his pain better than I am, I think, but he's still walking around with fragments of the building in him. He cannot lift one leg as high as the other when he walks, and he's holding on to his rifle with both hands like he's afraid he will drop it.

We are still more than a match for what remains of Godwin's thugs.

Their thoughts are lights and sirens against the backdrop of the jungle. We point and shoot like we're in a video game.

I pick up a man hiding, preparing to ambush us once we get about ten feet closer to his position.

"Over there—"

Zhang has already lifted his rifle. "I know," he says. He fires half a clip through the trees, and I feel the bullets stitch into a man who drops to the ground. He lives only a few seconds after that.

I pull myself away from the abyss of his thoughts as he dies, and I notice Zhang making a face, almost wincing.

"You feel that too?" I ask. I'm genuinely curious. This is the first chance I've ever had to talk to someone whose talent matches my own so closely. I wonder if he's got a trick that I don't know, or if he has some way of handling the pain and nightmares that I haven't learned yet.

Zhang doesn't seem in a mood to swap secrets, however. He wipes the sweat off his face with one hand and keeps walking. "How do we get out of here?" he asks. "Godwin had to have some way out."

I search my memory. I was in Godwin's head for a good long while.

Even if I wasn't looking specifically for this, it's possible it's still there. It's like picking apart a snarled ball of yarn, with one association leading to the next, all knotted together. Childhood memories leading to old songs leading to locker combinations leading to the names of lovers leading to favorite snacks.

I think I have something. A feeling of queasiness. Checking a pocket for Dramamine. Godwin is fine with flying in most cases. But he always gets airsick when he has to ride in a—

"Helicopter," I tell Zhang. "He came in by chopper, that's how he's going out. We need to find a clearing."

We circle carefully around the smoking crater that was Golden Boten City, in case the drones are still monitoring. There is a visible break in the trees just south of the main stretch of road. It's as good a place as any to start.

We don't come across any more of Godwin's men. But we both know that they're dead or gone. I can tell from the way Zhang moves—too fast, not checking around him. I can feel it too. There are no other minds in this building.

Still, I try to slow down, to be more careful. It's possible they're too far away. Or deeply unconscious. Or that Zhang and I are missing them completely as our reserves run lower.

But at the edge of the clearing, neither of us needs our talents to hear the sounds of a struggle.

And I pick up the familiar thoughts.

Godwin.

And Sara.

I don't know how and I don't care. I'm off and running, past Zhang, out into the open, and I see them both.

Godwin is pulling Sara along, a knife at her throat and his gun jammed into her side. Her hands are cuffed by zip ties behind her, keeping her off balance. Her arm still hurts with every step. If she struggles or resists, he can slice her carotid or disembowel her with barely more than a twitch.

I glance inside her short-term memory. Godwin's men pulled her out of the hotel and stashed her behind the place just after the software transfer. Godwin wanted her nearby, in case he needed to use her as leverage—against Stack, or possibly against anyone from the U.S. government, or me, in case I managed to somehow escape from Zhang.

Godwin grabbed her and hid with her in the jungle until the missile strikes stopped. He sent his men after us and called for his helicopter ride.

Now she's shell-shocked, like the rest of us, and she's tired and dehydrated and suffering a few cuts and bruises, and her arm hurts like hell from where she was strapped to a mattress for twelve hours.

But she's alive. Because Godwin was paranoid enough to know he'd need a hostage in case everything went south.

God bless him for being such an unmitigated bastard.

Neither of them has seen me yet. Godwin is trying to get her to move out into the open, using both the knife and gun to prod her. Sara is not making it any easier. She's moving like a sack of flour—heavy and slow.

His frustration is loud and clear to me all the way across the clearing. *<goddammit> <move, bitch> <have to get out of here> <before those things come back> <dammit>*

Sara, on the other hand, is just waiting. Quiet. Keen. Looking for the opening.

Within a second, she finds it.

He gets one step ahead and pulls at her with the knife, keeping its edge against her neck.

But he's extended his arm and opened a space between them. And that gives her enough room to move in close and check her shoulder right into his throat.

Even though it's her bad shoulder and brings tears to her eyes, she knocks him back with all her weight.

He gags and reflexively reaches for his neck with one hand. The one holding the gun.

Sara whips around and takes his legs out from under him with a hard sweep. He goes down on his back. He drops his weapons.

Sara kicks him hard in the ribs. And then the head. She stomps his fingers as he reaches for the knife on the ground. I can hear the crack of bone all the way across the clearing.

I start moving to help her, but she doesn't really need it. She is a professional, after all. I could watch her beat the shit out of Godwin all day.

But then I see what she's planning next.

And I've got to stop her.

I start running and shouting, "NO!"

I realize Zhang is a few steps behind, limping as fast as he can. He can see the plan in her head as well.

She doesn't know it's going to be fatal for her.

Sara doesn't quite hear me—she's been partially deafened by the explosions too. And most of her just doesn't care about the outside world. For her, at this moment, there's only one thing that matters—and that's making sure Godwin does not get up again.

She falls to the ground and rolls. I know what she's doing. So does Godwin. He tries to grab her, to tackle her.

He misses. She gets her fingers, behind her back, on the gun.

Years of practice flip it around, put the butt in her hand and her finger on the trigger.

Even behind her back, she can aim. She levers herself up into a half-sitting position and points the barrel at him.

She doesn't know. She's got no idea about Godwin's suicide vest.

Godwin doesn't care anymore. He is filled with nothing but rage. The inside of his mind is like the mobs that he's created. There is no tomorrow, no consequence, nothing beyond the need to hurt, to make someone else pay.

He launches himself at her.

Sara fires.

She's in a bad position. Most people wouldn't have been able to make the shot at all. But she's had a lot of practice. The bullet hits him low, in the upper thigh just below the hip.

I feel his femur shatter, and nearly collapse myself.

Godwin's weight goes sideways, and he goes down like a mudslide.

His blood pressure drops and his life begins to spurt out of him in warm, red jets.

The bullet hit the femoral artery. About half his blood just left his body.

Godwin is about to die. Which means so is Sara, if I can't save her.

I use the last of my breath to run to her side. She's doing her best to tie a tourniquet around his leg with his own belt, but the blood is still coming in great spurts. The exit wound is bigger than my fist.

I try to find some words to explain, but all I can come up with is "*run.*"

I pull at her. She doesn't understand. She thinks we can still salvage this.

<NO> <we need him> <Aaric needs him> <have to bring him back> <got to get him there alive>

I'm too weak to pull her away now. I pull open his shirt, show her the vest, but she doesn't quite realize what it means. She's too busy trying to keep Godwin alive.

Zhang lands heavily next to us. He looks too wrecked to run another step.

I lock myself into Godwin's brain, shoving past his higher consciousness and voluntary functions, and dive down deep to the place where I can monitor his heartbeat.

It's not looking good. His pulse is already weak and skipping. I pull at Sara again, words like "bomb" tumbling from my mouth.

That's a mistake. Her hands are already slippery from all the blood, and when I pull, I yank the tourniquet open again.

Godwin loses another liter of blood. It seems like it's drenching the ground under him.

"Can you defuse it?" I shout at Zhang.

He looks at me, and then at Godwin. His eyes widen in shock. He shakes it off and begins pulling at the suicide vest, tearing open the nylon, looking for the wires.

Sara looks at me, bewildered. *<what the hell are you doing?>*

"Sara, run," I say again.

And then it's too late.

Godwin's heart skips a beat. I can feel it.

His body has been through too much over too many years to endure this latest insult. His heart cannot take it.

I know, because I am tied right into his autonomic nervous system. I can feel it, teetering on the brink. His body is about to shut down.

I place my hands on his chest and prepare to start CPR. I don't know if that will be enough to fool the tracker, but I have to do something. As hurt and slow as we all are, we won't be able to get clear of the blast. Not in time.

As soon as I put my hands on Godwin, however, Zhang slaps them away hard. He looks at me like I'm an idiot. "Please don't move the vest," he snaps, with the kind of icy boredom that you hear only in combat or before something explodes.

Godwin's pulse dips again. Sara is cranking on the tourniquet, Zhang is doing his best, but his heart simply does not have that many beats left in it.

So I do something I've never tried before.

I reach in as deep as I can go, going below the brain, all the way down, right into the nerves. It's like swimming in arctic waters. He's almost gone.

I find the nerve endings, and I send a jolt into them. I force another heartbeat.

His pulse flutters against the tracker on his wrist. It's enough to keep the signal going.

I force another contraction of his heart. His blood moves like mud, but it moves. Another beat, and the tracker registers it.

Godwin barely has a mind left at all. I get only the faintest impressions of his life and memories now. He is cold. He cannot feel anything but the cold. He knows with sudden and sharp clarity that when he is gone, he will not be missed. Not a single person will mourn his loss. He thought he was superior, and now he is dying like everyone else.

"Almost there," Zhang says. I feel like I'm down at the bottom of a dark well, looking up at him. I can see his fingers, slick with blood, working on a wire and a battery pack.

I clench my fists and find the nerve endings again and push as hard as I can. His heart gives one more beat. His pulse bounces against the tracker on his wrist one last time, and the radio signal keeps beaming to the receiver on the vest.

But that's it. I am done. I cannot squeeze any more blood from this stone.

I reach for Sara's hand. She takes mine. And I wait.

The signal ends.

And Zhang holds up the receiver, disconnected cleanly from the vest. He's defused the bomb.

For a moment, we just sit in the clearing. The sun beats down on us. Insects begin to crawl in Godwin's blood.

What feels like hours later, I hear the sound of a helicopter.

/// 26

The Next Internet Outrage

Sara meets me outside the courthouse. Stack's first appearance in front of a judge is today, and she is here to help the legal team in whatever way she can. She has brought him a suit and tie from the *Nautilus*, which is docked in Oakland, where it was parked by the Coast Guard.

Stack has been held down here at the federal facility in Los Angeles, ostensibly because that's where the case was filed, but also because it's a lot less comfortable than the holding cells they have up in San Francisco. The prosecutors think this will make him more amenable to cooperation.

They haven't been inside his head. He's tougher than he looks. And he believes he's doing the right thing. That helps a lot of people bear what seems unbearable.

Or so I've been told. Personally, I'd take whatever deal they're offering and be sleeping in my own bed again.

Sara waits for me on the steps. Her bruises have faded to a dull yellow. They are only noticeable under her makeup if you know where to look.

"You look better," she says.

I don't, at least not in her eyes. I went to my usual suite of doctors once we got back from Laos, and they all marveled at the damage I'd managed to do in such a short amount of time. I've lost weight, I'm on a new course of antibiotics for the germs that wormed their way into my wounds, and I still get a ringing noise in one ear every now and then.

But I got a bunch of new prescriptions for painkillers out of it, so it's not all bad.

Downvote, at least, has fallen apart. The site went dark suddenly, and people moved on to the next Internet outrage. There have been three mass shootings and a couple of celebrity stalkings in the past month, but nobody can blame them on a website anymore.

Sara is ready to talk to me about the money. I'd like to cut her off before she begins, but I know she hates that. So she steels herself like she's about to rip off a Band-Aid and tells me what I already know.

"Look. It's probably going to be some time before Aaric is able to pay you for your work. I wanted you to know that. But you will be paid. I promise you that. Once this ridiculous case is thrown out—"

"I don't need to be paid. I started this with another client, remember?"

And, I don't add out loud, it's going to be a long time before the case is resolved. The government wants to make an example of Stack. Without Godwin, he's got nothing to trade with them.

"Aaric will pay you," Sara insists. "I will see to it."

There it is again. That faith. The world is going to be a better place. Or at least it will if Sara has anything to say about it.

"I told you, I'm fine. What about you?" I ask. "How are you going to pay the bills with your boss in jail?"

"I've got savings," she says. But in her head, I see that she is a little nervous. Her entire professional life is up in the air.

"You could find something else to do."

"He needs me," she says.

"What if I said I needed you?" I ask.

I have to give her credit. She laughs at me only inside her head.

"I think we both know how that would end," she says. "But it doesn't matter, does it? Because you're not going to say it."

I might argue the point. But then I pick up some familiar thoughts behind me, and I am determined never to let this guy sneak up on me twice.

I turn and face Agent Gregory Vincent, who is walking toward us and looking at me with something between a grin and a grimace.

"John Smith," he says. "You planning on interfering with a federal witness again?"

"Sara, this is Agent Greg Vincent," I tell her.

Sara just looks at him, but her mind goes cold. *<the guy who won't believe us about Godwin>*

"Right," she says. "I know who you are."

"You must be Sara Fitch," Vincent says to her. "Look, I'm sorry, but this story about some mystery hacker in Cambodia—"

"Laos," Sara interrupts.

She's angry because we did our best to get Vincent on our side. We tried to tell him what had happened to Downvote. We tried to tell him about Godwin.

The problem was, we couldn't prove a single thing. And Vincent already had what he wanted. He got a lot of credit for being ahead of the curve on Downvote, even if he didn't get to do much with his task force before the website imploded. There was just no incentive for him to go chasing down our ghost story. I could hardly blame him, even if I have the scars to prove it was all real.

"Right, Laos," Vincent says. "If you've managed to come up with some new evidence—"

"Do your job for you, in other words—"

"—we'll be happy to look at it. In the meantime—"

"In the meantime, Aaric stays a federal prisoner," she says.

"Witness," Vincent corrects her. "He's not a prisoner. He's a protected federal witness."

"Yeah, right," Sara scoffs. <*such bullshit*> "Protected from everyone but you."

"I'm sorry you feel that way," Vincent says, but he is far too pleased with himself today to let it bother him much. <*pretty*> <*hot*> <*clearly hates my guts*> <*too bad*> Next week, he's being summoned to Washington to testify in front of Congress about social media as a domestic terror threat. He's well on his way to another promotion.

"So why are you here?" I ask, mainly for Sara's benefit, because I already know.

"We still think that Mr. Stack can help us out with Downvote as well as Bankster. Tying up the loose ends."

Sara makes a little exasperated noise rather than calling Vincent all the names going through her head.

Vincent, meanwhile, has no doubt he's doing the right thing.

Two true believers, facing off.

"Well. I'd better get in there before the hearing starts. And if you do come up with anything solid, I'm always happy to hear it." He smiles at both of us again, giving me a particularly sharp look. <*eat it, Smith*> <*didn't need you after all*>

I bite down on any replies, mainly because I want him to leave before Sara decides to punch him.

He turns and walks up the steps, leaving a trail of satisfaction in his wake. It's a good day to be Greg Vincent. Not so much the case for Aaric Stack. I resist the urge to give Vincent some intestinal problems for the hearing.

Sara takes a deep breath and shakes off her anger. "I should go too. Aaric will be waiting."

She is due inside the federal building to hand over Stack's courtroom suit. Then she'll sit behind him and provide whatever moral support she can. Once they take him back to his cell, her plans are a little fuzzy.

But she does not have a moment's doubt that she's doing the right thing too. She believes in him. She knows he will win this, and that he will, eventually, go back to writing his software that will make us all better people.

We say good-bye, and she walks away without looking back, or even thinking about me, all the way to the doors.

///27

I've Got My Reasons

I walk into The Standard. The desk clerk notices me at once and smiles. The model, in her glass case behind him, does not look up from her book. Her mind is filled with details about embedded cultures and Tibetan rituals. She's got an anthropology exam coming up.

The clerk waves me over. I know what he has to say, but you have to follow the social graces, even when you don't feel like it. There is a man waiting for me on the pool deck, he tells me. I thank him and pass him a ten, even though I know he's already been tipped to deliver the message. Common courtesy. If there's a moral to this story, that's probably it.

I walk out onto the deck, with its bright blue Astroturf and pure white furniture. It is a textbook example of an L.A. day: there is just enough wind to whip the smog out of the sky, and the sunlight reflects off the pool like a chrome bumper. There is no one in the water, just an array of perfect bodies in bikinis lined up on lounge chairs.

Cantrell stands out like a boil on all that perfect flesh, sitting at one of the tables with a small bucket of iced beers in front of him. He's wearing a Hawaiian shirt that hurts my eyes even more than the sun and a bright red MAKE AMERICA GREAT AGAIN cap.

All of his attention is on the copy of *People* in his hands. He either doesn't notice or doesn't mind the glares he's getting from the crowd. That's Cantrell. The original Ugly American.

I sit down across the table from him. Cantrell reaches into the bucket and pulls out a Pacífico. "Beer?" he asks.

"It's ten thirty in the morning."

He snorts at that and passes me the bottle. "You're not working."

Good point. I take the bottle and drink.

He cracks open a beer of his own, takes a sip, and nods. As usual, he is the most Zen bastard I've ever met when he's guarding his thoughts. All I get from him at this moment is the taste of the beer on his tongue and the feel of the sun on his back. No surprise. He's had years of practice.

Then he breaks out of his meditative state. "How's your friend Zhang?" he asks. He knew all about Zhang, of course. He was the guy who told me about the Chinese EHF kids, after all.

"Never writes, never calls," I say. Zhang parted ways with us when the chopper landed back at the airport in Luang Prabang. The pilot was happy to take us. Our money was as good as Godwin's. But we didn't have a lot of time to talk. The Chinese government could easily pressure the Laotians to close the borders to any of us as soon as they realized we'd walked away from Golden Boten City. And Zhang had a much harder road ahead of him. All Sara and I had to do was get on a plane, and within a couple of hours, we'd be in Thailand, then on our way back to the States.

Zhang was still wounded, officially cut off from every support system he'd ever had, and alone. I'd given him all the money I had on me, and everything I could scavenge from Godwin's corpse. That, and his talent, would take him a long way.

Still, it wasn't going to be easy. The people he'd given his life and loyalty to had just betrayed him for what they thought were the best of reasons. I'd been there. It's not something you can just walk off.

"What are you going to do?" I asked him.

He shrugged.

"Maybe it's time for me to join the private sector as well," he said. He hesitated a moment, then asked, "What would you have done if you'd been wrong about that drone strike? If we'd taken you away, like we planned?"

"Does it matter?"

"I'm curious."

"I would have killed all your men, and probably you. And then I would have made my way back to Godwin and killed him too."

He gave me that amused look again. "You would have tried."

"I guess we'll never know."

Zhang bowed slightly. "Interesting meeting you, Mr. Smith," he said.

Then he turned away and vanished inside the terminal without looking back.

"What do you think's going to happen to him?" Cantrell asks.

"Why, you want to offer him a job?"

Cantrell laughs. "Shit, with his talents, on the open market? That boy's probably going to be a billionaire within a year."

"Speaking of money . . ." I remind him.

"Right," he says. "Well, then, let's get it over with."

We both fish in our pockets for a moment. I hold up a thumb drive. He holds up a phone.

"Five million for the code behind Downvote, as agreed," he says. "Just put the phone up to your eye, it will scan your retina, and the money will go straight into your account."

I never gave Sara her laptop back. It only took me a moment to retrieve it from the locker at the Luang Prabang Airport. She never even asked about it.

It still contained all the files we downloaded from Godwin's Romanian server. Including the Downvote source code. It took me about half an hour to download everything into the high-capacity thumb drive.

I don't know what the Chinese buyers are doing with their version of Godwin's program. Maybe nothing. Maybe they're waiting for the next round of protests before they try it out.

But Cantrell was very happy to arrange for the Agency to purchase it, especially when he heard that the Chinese had a copy.

I'm about to finalize the transaction. Then I hesitate for a moment. I look at the thumb drive in my hand.

"You don't want to verify the package?"

Cantrell smirks. "I trust you," he lies.

I still don't take the phone.

"What if I want a different payment?"

<*uh-oh*> <*what the hell is this now?*> "John. We had a deal." <*do not screw with me, son*>

"Yeah," I say, holding the drive just an arm's length away from him. Cantrell would not be above snatching it from my hand and trying to run. "But what's it really worth to you?"

"If you want more money—" <*sometimes, kid, you try my fucking patience, you do*>

"Not money. In fact, you can forget the original payment altogether. This is more concrete."

<*what the hell is this now?*> "What do you want, John?" Cantrell asks. The accent vanishes. This was always how I knew I'd pushed him almost too far, without even reading his thoughts. His words become as flat and monotone as a midwestern TV anchorman's.

But I know he'll have no real problem with this. It's even going to save him money.

"Get the feds to drop the case against Aaric Stack," I tell him. "Completely. He walks away. Total immunity from all prosecution going forward."

<what?> "And why would I do that?"

"Because the Chinese have this," I say. "And that's the price now."

He grins. *<son of a bitch>* "More importantly, John, why would *you* do that?"

"I've got my reasons."

"You really must like that little bodyguard." The accent is back. He is hugely amused by me again.

"Just make the call."

He takes his phone back and wanders away, one more guy on his cell in LA. Only his call connects with an encrypted line somewhere back in Virginia.

After ten minutes, he comes back to his seat and cracks opens a fresh beer. He doesn't say anything. I know the answer already.

I hand him the thumb drive. "Now, you know what happens if your guys don't come through on this?"

<tough little bastard> *<as usual>* "Yeah, yeah. We're all well aware of the damage you can do, John." He drinks. "She ever going to know that you're the reason she won't have to visit her boss in jail?"

"I don't think it would make a difference," I say. "She's a true believer. An idealist. Hard to change their minds."

"Yeah, I seem to recall having that problem with a couple of my recruits."

I actually feel a small surge of pride from him. He must have been drinking before I got out here.

But it doesn't matter.

Aaric Stack will not face any liability for his part in creating the code behind Bankster, or, for that matter, Downvote. And he will get to go on writing his software that will hopefully nudge us in the direction of our better angels.

Sara will help him do it. Maybe it will even do some good.

A young woman stands up from her lounge chair, passes in front of us, and jumps into the pool. We both watch her for a moment.

"She's young enough to be your daughter," I say. "Granddaughter."

"You know, I keep hearing how old I am," Cantrell says. "Brave new world out there. Software and algorithms are the new arms race. Data that steers people around. Automated crowd control."

"Guys like you and me, we're supposed to be obsolete."

He laughs, and it goes down deep and genuine. "I hear that every couple years or so. First it was satellites. Then spooky bastards like you. Then drones. And now this"—he holds up the thumb drive—"is supposed to put me out of business. And yet, somehow, I seem to keep cashing my paycheck."

"There's something to be said for the human factor."

"Damn right," he says, and clinks my bottle with his. Then he passes me the copy of *People* he was reading before I walked up.

There's a picture of Kira, still in her hospital bed, but with a bridal veil on her head. She's pale and thin, but smiling. Her fiancé holds her hand. The headline says KIRA COULDN'T WAIT ANOTHER DAY!

There's a quote pulled from the story below that, in big, bold letters: *Things like this really teach you to seize life's moments while you can.*

Armin told me about it when I called to tell him the man behind Downvote was dead. He said Kira decided to get married in the hospital, almost as soon as she was out of her coma. I wasn't invited to this one. Probably for the best.

"Well," Cantrell says, "at least somebody got a happy ending out of it." He swallows the rest of his beer and then belches. "Speaking of which. I got an appointment for a massage. Always good to see you, John. Let's do it again sometime."

He stands up and we shake hands. He's got his trademark shit-eating grin on his face, making me think that despite the fact that I should know everything, Cantrell has somehow gotten the best of this deal.

We both head back into the lobby. Cantrell walks out the front door.

I watch him go. I'm about to head to my room when I stop and think for a moment. Someone once said the definition of insanity is doing the same thing over and over and expecting different results.

So I detour in the direction of the front desk.

The clerk smiles at me again. "Something else I can help you with, Mr. Smith?" he asks.

"I need my bill," I say. That catches him off guard. He knows my deal here. So I make it even clearer.

"I'm checking out," I tell him. "It's time for something new."

Acknowledgments

As usual, this was not a solo effort. First and foremost, as usual, many thanks to my brilliant agent, Alexandra Machinist, and my peerless editor, Rachel Kahan.

I also interviewed several people who were kind enough to share their expertise with me.

Kent Moyer, CEO of the World Protection Group, told me what it takes to keep celebrities and executives safe from threats. Jessica Ansley, a personal protection specialist with the Executive Protection Institute, expanded my knowledge further and answered my questions about what it's like to be a woman working in that world. They were both extremely generous with their time and I appreciate it.

Thanks to the real Jezebel Todd, who is definitely not an assassin. (Honest.) Thanks as well to everyone at ICM and William Morrow and HarperCollins who worked hard to get this book published.

Dr. Jonathan Hayes, an outstanding author in his own right, helped me with a question about leg injuries. Brian Laing and Engin Kirda of Lastline, an Internet security firm, talked me through the shadowy corners of the Dark Web and explained it in terms I could understand. Andrew Komarov of Infoarmor was my guide through the world of high-stakes cybercrime and online theft. And thanks as well to Dan Chmielewski, who arranged my interviews with them and who continues to be my go-to guy for all questions related to high-tech security. The legendary Beau Smith remains my personal armaments consultant.

The "sheep, wolves, and sheepdogs" analogy comes from Lieutenant Colonel David Grossman's book *On Combat*. The response about treating people like sheep comes from David Graeber's *Debt: The First 5,000 Years*.

The use of "emotional contagion" techniques by Facebook is real, and was covered by Vindu Goel in the *New York Times* and by Micah L. Sifry for *Mother Jones*.

I also relied on the work of other authors and journalists for some of the real-world details in this book, including *How the Mind Works* by Steven Pinker; *So You've Been Publicly Shamed* by Jon Ronson; *Boomerang: Travels in the New Third World* by Michael Lewis; "All Governments Seem to Be Winging It Except for China" from Douglas Coupland's collection *Shopping in Jail: Ideas, Essays, and Stories for the Increasingly Real Twenty-First Century*; *No City for Slow Men* by Jason Ng; *The Dark Net* by Jamie Bartlett; *Who Owns the Future?* by Jaron Lanier; *How to Speak Money* by John Lanchester; *Pay Any Price* by James Risen; Andy Greenberg's fascinating and compelling coverage of the Dread Pirate Roberts and the Silk Road case in *Wired* (with reporting by Nick Bilton) as well as Sarah Jeong's pieces on the trial for *Forbes*; Ron Gluckman's story about Golden Boten City in *Forbes*; and dozens of stories and articles about online harassment, trolling, and Internet mobs from many sources, including Gawker, the *Guardian, Bloomberg Businessweek,* Buzzfeed, the *Economist,* Vox, the Verge, re/code, and others. My apologies to anyone I have forgotten or failed to mention.

Finally, I am once again grateful to my family, who give me everything and wait patiently while I spend my time typing words onto a screen. Any mistakes or inventions are entirely my own.

About the Author

A former journalist and screenwriter, Christopher Farnsworth is the author of the Nathaniel Cade/President's Vampire series of novels, which was optioned for film and TV and has been published in nine languages. Born and raised in Idaho, he now lives in Los Angeles with his family.

ALSO BY

CHRISTOPHER FARNSWORTH

KILLFILE

A Novel

"Fast, fun, and frenetic. A whip-smart edge-of-your-seat thriller."
— Ernest Cline,
author of *Armada* and *Ready Player One*

The author of *The Eternal World* seamlessly combines history, biotechnology, action, and adventure in this high-concept thriller in the spirit of James Rollins, Brad Thor, and Douglas Preston. Hunted by shadowy enemies with deep resources and unknown motives, John and Kelsey must go off the grid. John knows their only hope for survival is using his powers to their fullest—even if means putting his own sanity at risk.

THE ETERNAL WORLD

A Novel

"Excellent fantasy thriller."
— *Publishers Weekly* (starred review)

Five hundred years ago, a group of Spanish conquistadors, led by a young commander named Simon De Oliveras, landed in what is now called Florida, searching for gold. Instead, they found the legendary Fountain of Youth. When the source of the fountain is destroyed in our own time, the loss threatens Simon and his men. For help, they turn to David Robinton, a scientific prodigy who believes he is on the verge of the greatest medical breakthrough of all time. Now, the scientist must decide: is he a pawn in a game of immortals. . . or will he be its only winner?

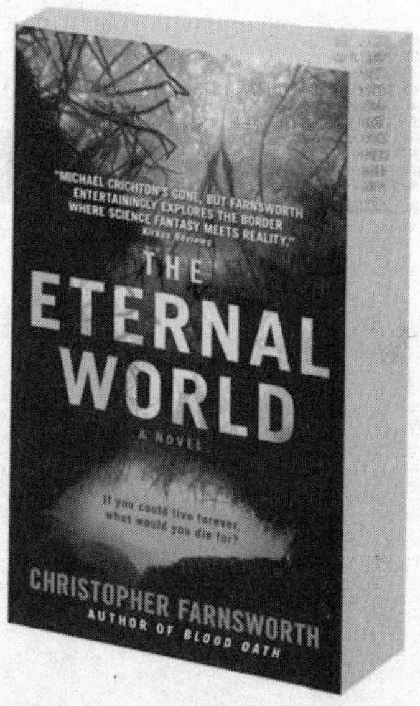